The Hanson Trilogy

Book One

The Hanson Legacy

Vincent M. Messbarger

The Hanson Legacy

Cocheta Publishing
A DIVISION OF COCHETA ENTERPRISES

Cover and layout design by Vince Messbarger

First edition (paperback) published 2012.

Library of Congress Control Number: 2008900461

ISBN: 978-0-9814984-0-9 (paperback)

SAN: 855-7276

Dedicated To:

My lovely wife, Stacia, who patiently and graciously bore the brunt of my first foray into the literary world.

My wonderful kids, Chrissy, Pookie, Lowell, Patrick, Red and Joseph, who like whatever daddy does, no matter how bad it stinks.

My sweet grandchildren, Celeste, Dawson, Leslie, Amber and Anthony, who are incapable of wrongdoing and to whom a portion of the proceeds of this book will be spent on spoiling them rotten...

...and to Benjamin Harris Hanson, PhD.

The man inside struggling to be free.

Acknowledgments

"Acknowledgment" sections in works of fiction are not customary, but so many fine people have contributed their time, ears, encouragement and expertise, that failing to have one in *The Hanson Legacy* would be nothing short of a crime. Without these wonderful gifts, this literary work would have suffered immensely and quite probably, never attempted or completed.

Of course, there is my family. My wife, Stacia, read each chapter as they were completed, giving me much needed support and plenty of quiet time when the creative juices were flowing. The Marines in my family: father, Jack; brother, Tony; son, Lowell and daughter, Jessica, gave me valuable insight into the Corps. My Aunt and Uncle, Jo and Benny Lewis, provided wonderful details of life in Northeast Oklahoma in the 1950s and 1960s. There are more than a few characters in *The Hanson Legacy* that were inspired by people whom I have personally known or admired from near and afar, past and present. I credit them with more than just providing inspiration, they helped make my fifty-plus years on this Earth rich and rewarding.

Colleagues also took time out of their busy lives to read *The Hanson Legacy* and provide valuable feedback. Doris Thorpe, RN read the rough draft as it was being written, as did Nathaniel Apatov, PhD., a man known to be a particularly tough critic. Both offered honest opinions, encouragement and helped me gauge how well the project was progressing.

Countless hours were spent researching subjects and checking facts. Oftentimes, it would take days just to make a single paragraph as descriptive and accurate as possible. Much of the subject matter involved ultra-secret "Black Projects," defense-related research programs (e.g. Stealth Technology) cunningly hidden from public view. With hard facts in extremely short supply, speculation about these projects are oftentimes nonsensical. There is, however, a cadre of dedicated souls, some of whom are experts in exotic defense technologies, that scour through journals, request Freedom of Information Act documents and hike up rugged trails to high desert mountaintops, laden with provisions and gear, for the rare chance that conditions will be just right to snap a picture of a secret base over 25 miles away. They share their findings on a most informative internet site. I speak of Joerg H. Arnu, webmaster of Dreamland Resort (www.dreamlandresort.com), and all the fine contributors who make it the definitive web resource on Black Projects, in general, and "Area 51" in particular. I cannot possibly name all the many standouts at Dreamland Resort who directly or indirectly assisted me with my questions. There is one, however, that deserves a very special hat tip: Andrew McLaughlin, Deputy Editor of Australian Aviation Magazine, who read and evaluated the rough draft. Chapters 50 through 52 are a direct result of his critique.

To everyone mentioned and as much to those who were not, your influence is evident on every page and I sincerely thank you with all my being!

Vince Messbarger, 2012

Prologue

For Dr. Benjamin Harris Hanson, the news of his impending death was as liberating as it was frightening.

"Looks like bronchogenic carcinoma, probably squamous cell." Dr. Sedgewyk announced without the slightest hint of emotion. "Judging by the CT scans of your chest, abdomen and head, I'd say it's pretty advanced. You have a significant mass impinging on your left main stem bronchus, some lymph node enlargement in your mediastinum and a very small lesion in your brain that probably represents metastasis of the primary tumor."

Even though the brilliant, 63 year-old Aerospace Engineer already deduced his diagnosis through careful research of medical texts and reputable on-line resources, hearing confirmation of it through Sedgewyk's overly blunt words felt like a powerful fist to the middle of his gut. He claimed no expertise in any field of medicine, but after studying a sizable amount of information about his worrisome symptoms he managed to learn a little something about lung cancer in the process. Sedgewyk merely confirmed what he already knew: his days were numbered. Even if he chose to undergo the best available treatments, death would likely overtake him before year's end.

Necessity forced Dr. Hanson to seek confirmation of his diagnosis from a physician outside of his employers' own medical staff, using an assumed identity and paying for everything in cash. It was crucial that "The Foreman" remain completely unaware of his illness because the bastard would instantly retire him from the project if he knew of it. Under Louis Hastings, "Retirement" had taken on a frighteningly different meaning than one would normally assume.

After decades of sacrifice in serving the needs of the project, every one of his retiring colleagues succumbed to one of a number of unfortunate "accidents" or "suicides." One-car rollovers, falling down stairs, drug overdoses, self-inflicted gunshot wounds to the head... those were the least creative of the project's retirement options. Hanson... no, the entire world couldn't afford whatever chilling form of "retirement" Hasting's had in mind for him when the time came. He had to stay alive long enough to complete a critical task he should have had the guts to engage long before.

The last 19 years had been a living hell for Ben Hanson. Louis Hastings viciously stripped his world of everything he held dear to his heart, sentencing him to a bleak existence where his body and mind were the only things of value he had left. Now, even those were tumbling in value with the onslaught of this latest blow to his health. The lingering concerns he had about personal safety during the execution of his long overdue mission completely vanished with the words "terminal cancer."

What brought Benjamin Hanson, PhD to the trenchant Internist was a cough associated with a deep and persistent pain to the left of his breastbone that started about three months earlier. The discomfort was mild at first, easily shrugged off as a pulled muscle. An occasional ibuprofen tablet worked well for a while, but as time went on, the pain demanded around-the-clock dosing for control. When the nagging cough started, Hanson instinctively knew something far worse was going on inside of his chest. Coughing was nothing new to Hanson. He was a heavy smoker and accustomed to the hack-fest that greeted him most every morning. This cough was different. It occurred in frequent spells throughout the day, it hurt and he sometimes coughed-up small amounts of blood.

"We'll need to get a biopsy of the tumor to be certain of what we're looking at, but this is a fairly classic presentation. Stage four, my guess." Sedgewyk went on, "Caused by smoking, you know. It's the one lung cancer we're most certain of the link to smoking. I'll set you up for a bronchoscopy and arrange a visit to see a radiation oncologist. Might need to surgically de-bulk the tumor if it blocks off a portion of your lung and breathing becomes difficult for you."

"That won't be necessary right now." Dr. Hanson said in a wavering voice. "I'll let you know when I'm ready to begin treatment."

"I must say Mr. Stanley, you are taking this news a lot better than most. What kind of delay are we talking about?" Sedgewyk asked while jotting illegibly on a medical consultation request form. "Squamous Cell can be quite aggressive. Without treatment you will die much faster. It won't be pleasant, either."

"Right now, it is much more important for me to get my affairs in order than to spend time in the hospital." He replied, trying to maintain his composure. "I am more concerned about the lesion you found in my brain."

In his usual unemotional and methodical way, the Internist spelled it all out. It was April and there was an outside chance he might make it through another Christmas, assuming he began treatment right away. Survival much beyond that was highly problematic.

Radiation therapy could slow the progression of the disease, perhaps even shrink the tumor somewhat, but not likely to be curative. Pain may become a serious issue affecting his quality of life, but he knew a good pain specialist who was not afraid to treat cancer patients. For Ben, the fear of radiation therapy, breathing difficulties, surgery and excruciating pain paled in comparison to the fear of losing his mental faculties. He needed to be unerringly sharp for the tasks that lay ahead.

"Right now, the lesion in your brain is fairly small and asymptomatic, but it does have an area of swollen tissue surrounding it." Sedgewyk explained. "The tumor mass will undoubtedly grow larger, as will the area of brain swelling. You might develop symptoms."

"Like what?"

"It could start as a seizure out of the clear blue sky. The lesion is located near your right motor cortex so you might experience weakness in your left arm or leg. It's hard to know exactly what symptoms will occur until they do. An oral steroid should help with the swelling. All that being said, the primary tumor will probably kill you long before the tumor in your head gives you any trouble."

"Your stark candor is very comforting, Dr. Sedgewyk." Hanson said with irritation unmistakably evident in his voice.

"I am what I am, Mr. Stanley." Sedgewyk replied, unaffected by the comment. "You are not the first person to negatively critique my bedside manner. You pay me to find out precisely what's wrong with you, inform you of your prognosis and list the treatment options available to you. Sugar-coating is not in my nature."

Hanson did not reply. He knew of Sedgewyk's reputation for ice-cold bluntness before booking his first appointment so there was no point in chiding him any further for it. He asked a few more general questions about treatment side-effects, then excused himself, taking with him a prescription for prednisone and promising to make a follow-up appointment he instinctively knew would never take place.

While taking the elevator down to the first floor of Medical Plaza One he remembered something a colleague once said about the death of his mother after losing a prolonged and futile battle with Progressive Supranuclear Palsy, the same horrifying disease that claimed the life of actor Dudley Moore.

"Dying is just the end-result of being born." He said. "I mean, we all go through it, Ben. The lucky ones? Well, they just blink out. You know, maybe it's a car crash, massive heart attack... whatever. No choices about what to do next. No time to think about your own mortality, just wham! Here one moment, gone the next. My mom... she was one of the unlucky ones. She got to think about it for a long, long time."

Ben Hanson was decidedly in the ranks of the unlucky, but he was not going to fade away unnoticed. Hearing Sedgewyk's medical equivalent of a death sentence, without even a remote chance for parole or stay of execution, finally freed him to complete a task he had, ashamedly, been too timid to start... even if doing so substantially shortened the little time he had left.

There was work to do. Important work well worth taking the extra precautions to insure his doctor visits, and other carefully choreographed movements around town, remain hidden from his watchful employer. He had no training in covert tactics but he was extraordinarily intelligent and highly adaptive. Dr. Hanson knew he would need to mobilize his considerable array of cerebral talents to successfully reveal the terrible secrets stored in a faraway mountain. For over six decades, those entrusted to govern and protect kept the whole of mankind oblivious to a startling new reality facing them. If Hanson's take on the meaning of this "new reality" was correct, the survival of the human race might very well depend upon his success or failure in the coming weeks.

Chapter 1

Dr. Hanson shook-off most of the bad news by the time he picked-up his medication and taken a circuitous route to his home in North Las Vegas... via two city busses and a taxi ride. His mind was beginning to focus on the task before him. With years already invested in assembling the critical components and carefully plotting every detail of his intricate plan, his own looming mortality determined it was finally time to execute.

By any definition, the plan was absolutely brilliant. If successful, Hanson would introduce the world to a new and potentially frightening reality while neutralizing a murderous nemesis hell bent on thwarting his every move. Like any highly complex endeavor, Hanson knew that hidden variables and less than precise execution could lead to a disastrous outcome. The plan required some physical exertion on his part and he wondered how years of chain-smoking and rapidly declining health would affect his ability to perform. It was yet another compelling reason in a growing list of reasons to begin initiating his operation at the earliest possible date.

There was still much to accomplish before he could begin. A professionally prepared, written summary encompassing over six decades of research needed to be polished. There were important names, dates and places, all required supporting documentation and cross-referencing. Lastly, there was the "package" of physical evidence, accumulated into his private collection without The Foreman's knowledge. Hanson obsessed about presenting a quality review of his work, primarily because the first critical step in his plan was to convince a well respected, high profile scientist to place his own reputation and career behind it. He had but a single shot at recruiting the scientist in mind. The mission would be over before it started if he were unable to solidly persuade his colleague with the assembled data. Though certain the nature of the physical evidence alone was enough to galvanize the most ardent skeptic into fervent belief, it wasn't in Dr. Hanson's nature to indulge in sloppiness.

Early in the planning stages, Hanson knew he had to bypass traditional methods of disseminating ground breaking scientific research and discoveries. Peer-reviewed publication and conferences were simply out of the question. His employer would see him in the grave long before he could submit anything to a scientific journal. Besides, Hanson was a scientific outsider, spending his entire career in a field of research few could scarcely imagine... or likely believe. He presented his meticulously prepared research results to a small number of highly selected peers and occasionally to a few others outside of the scientific community who were "in-the-know." In that extremely limited community of fellow scientists, engineers, investigators and insiders, Dr. Benjamin Hanson's reputation was that of a genius of staggering dimensions. To the outside world, only his impressive record as a student was available for public scrutiny. Without a visible reputation and the backing of a prominent academic or professional research facility, publication was all but impossible.

For the mission to be successful, Hanson determined this scientific revelation required presentation to millions of people at the same time. It was the only way he could insure that the information would take its' rightful place in the forefront of the world's mind. Cable and satellite communications, along with the Internet and global news networks made disseminating real-time information to the far corners of the earth quite easy. It could be made even easier by recruiting someone with a trusted, well-recognized face... and a popular forum.

Only two souls on earth had the cerebral octane, credentials, intellectual honesty and public forum to properly transfer Hanson's sobering reality to the peoples of the world. Although he mulled over the two choices at least a hundred times, Dr. Hanson instinctively knew who he would eventually entrust his legacy to: Timothy Alexander, PhD., Professor of Theoretical Physics at UCLA.

Chapter 2

Benjamin Harris Hanson was born on January 22nd, 1947 to Paul and Alicia Hanson of Quapaw, Oklahoma. Paul Hanson worked in mid-level management at a local industrial firm and Alicia worked at home raising her two sons, Ben and Paul Junior. Paul Sr. was a veteran of World War II, one of the thousands upon thousands of men and women who joined the armed services the day after warplanes of the Imperial Japanese Navy savaged Pearl Harbor. Paul chose the Marine Corps and proudly endured four rugged years with the 1st Marine Division in the Pacific, hopping from one bloody island to the next. From Guadalcanal to Okinawa, Paul Hanson was one of the fortunate Marines who survived the vicious battles on each of the seemingly endless stretch of Japanese-held, tropical hellholes the United States Marine Corps conquered.

After the war, Paul Sr. returned to Oklahoma and quickly married Alicia, his high school sweetheart, who nervously waited nearly four years for his return. The war changed her man. Paul was no longer the impish youngster whose harmless impetuosity made her belly laugh. He was more reserved and far less prone to engage in mindless frivolity. He was a solid man now, with unbendable convictions and a depth of maturity forged by experiencing the horrors of desperate warfare and years of wondering which sunrise would be his last. He was far more capable of handling a family than the boy she knew in high school. He was still her beloved Paul Hanson, only better. She, too, matured considerably since saying her goodbyes to Paul that chilly December morning in 1941. They were different people, yet in spite of time and distance, the love they shared matured with them.

Paul quickly found a decent paying job with the Picher Lead Company, the largest employer in northeast Oklahoma. A lucky break landed him a management position when his employment interview happened to be with a former senior NCO he served with in the 1st Marine Division. They had never met, at least not that either of them could recall, but Marine Corps blood flowed through their veins creating an instant bond between them.

His income was sufficient enough to afford a small but cozy two-bedroom home on the 500 block of South Cherry Street in Quapaw and a well-kept 1940 Dodge sedan he bought from "Blackie," a old friend of his Dads' who owned a garage on South Main in Commerce, a small town a few miles to the west. Paul and Alicia Hanson were far from rich, but they had what they needed. Most importantly, they had each other.

Scarcely four months after the couple's wedding, Alicia was pregnant with Paul Junior. Before that rambunctious bundle of joy was 9 months old she found herself pregnant with Benjamin. When the younger sibling was born, Paul Jr. was a rowdy 18 month-old and quite a handful for Alicia. Not yet toilet trained, adventurous and very jealous of his little brother, Paul Jr. demanded as much attention as the new baby did. More often than not, Alicia Hanson was exhausted at the end of each hectic day, but never complained about it. Like her mother and grandmother before her, Alicia Hanson embraced motherhood as if it were a religion. She believed her family was all the inspiration she needed, her toil an investment in the future. Paul took parenting just as seriously and both were whole-heartedly committed to passing the moral values of 1950s, small-town America to Paul Jr. and Benjamin. Their generation, the "Greatest Generation," endured and conquered economic disasters and bloodthirsty tyrants. Passing down the virtues of good citizenship, charity, honesty, hard work and self-reliance to their children was only natural.

While their ages were not that far apart, Paul Jr. and Benjamin could not have been any more different from each other than if born to different mothers on different planets. Paul Jr. was the bigger, more athletic and active of the two. By contrast, Ben was shy and introverted. What Benjamin Harris Hanson lacked in athletic ability he more than made up for in genius.

Throughout his childhood, Paul Jr. could usually be found seeking adventure, running around Ottawa County as if the world were going to end tomorrow. To him, his home was a magical place of mid-western creeks and rivers that held legendary, boat-sized catfish and spoonbills in their murky waters. There were towering, light gray mountains to climb, comprised of waste rock from the numerous lead and tin mines in the area. Like all of the locals in the area, Paul Jr. knew the monstrous, man-made mountains as "chat piles," and they were a lot of fun to play on. When he was not engaged in exploration, he liked to hang around dad when he tinkered on the family's basic blue, '46 Chevrolet. Benjamin, in contrast, was noticeably smaller than Paul Jr. and much frailer in appearance. Ben was never interested in climbing chat piles or pulling monster catfish from the Neosho River. No... his adventures waited for him in the pages of books.

The 1950s heralded the beginning of a profound public interest in science and technology. It was a time where imaginations turned to the sky. Jets were getting bigger and faster, rockets were soaring ever closer to space, and "B" movies featuring atomic mutants or brain-eating aliens from planet "X" were churning out of Hollywood at a dizzying pace. It was a superb time for a child genius to grow up in and Ben was the ultimate expression of the era. His brain absorbed anything and everything that involved science and technology. His nose was always buried deep inside a book about science, jet fighters, or his all-time-favorite subject: spaceships. Even when the family piled into the car for the usual weekend road trip into nearby Joplin to eat at their favorite restaurant, Ben would have one or two books in his hands. It was clear that from a very early age that Ben was no ordinary child. Fortunately his parents, though lacking any education beyond high school, did a remarkably good job of nurturing Ben's gifts.

Once he learned to read, Ben's appetite for reading material was insatiable. The family made frequent "book runs" to all the local public libraries in the tri-state area where they were on a first name basis with every librarian. Elsie Burke, the Chief Librarian at the Miami Public Library on North Main Street, took a special interest in Ben. She hand picked books and periodicals that she knew Ben would enjoy. Mostly, they were books about airplanes, modern technology and science fiction. She placed them on a special cart she reserved just for him, even adorning the cart with a flowery sign that read "Benjamin's Books." She frequently borrowed books from much larger public libraries in Tulsa and Oklahoma City because Ben's appetite for a rather narrow band of reading material always outstripped her small library's capacity to feed it. These simple and selfless efforts by his parents, educators and others in the community would greatly contribute to the development of one of the finest minds in modern history.

In spite of the huge differences between Paul Jr. and Benjamin, the elder took the big brother role quite seriously and was very protective of his younger brother. Because of his diminutive size and monstrous intellect, Little Ben often suffered the taunts of bullies. That is, only when big brother wasn't around. In his day, Paul Jr. liberally dispensed industrial grade "ass-whoopins" upon several local bullies to protect his younger sibling, and it proved to be a highly effective deterrent. As Paul Jr. and Ben grew older, they became best of pals, even though the only thing they really had in common were their parents and their parents' values. Paul Jr. eventually became a local high school baseball star, following in the footsteps of the legendary Mickey Mantle who grew up in Commerce. Ben became the academic star of Ottawa County, leapfrogging through the public schools and graduating from high school a full four years early.

"Little Ben," Paul Jr. would boast, "You and I, we're headin' places! I'm going to be Ottawa County's next Mickey Mantle and you're going to be the county's first Einstein!"

Paul Jr. would call Ben "Bert" in fun, and Ben would call Paul Jr. "Mr. Mantle." More often than not, however, Paul Jr. would call Ben a "shrimp" and Ben would call his brother a "Dumbass Jock," but only if mom and dad weren't around.

It was difficult for Ben to leave his big brother and parents behind when the time came for him to attend college at the University of Oklahoma. He was only 14 years old when he left home, but already had a full academic scholarship to the College of Mechanical

Engineering and a very promising future.

Paul Jr. never made it to the big leagues. He never even made it to college.

Late in Ben's junior year at the University of Oklahoma, on the night of April 11th, 1964, his mother called him with horrific news. Her sobbing was so profuse, it took Ben over 15 minutes to calm her down enough to hear what she was trying to say.

Paul Junior, his beloved big brother, was dead.

Chapter 3

Tim Alexander considered it great sport to trip-up his senior undergraduate students even though it was, admittedly, terribly unfair. Much like the proverbial "shooting fish in a bucket." They were all so eager to please. Even though it was just a few weeks before the spring-semester finals, he could see that most of them still couldn't believe they were actually studying under the "Great Theoretical Physicist and Television Star, Dr. Timothy David Alexander." The twinkling adoration in their eyes was the dead giveaway. It was now time for the traditional, year-end reality check to impart some last-minute humility into the outgoing students.

"Mr. Tillotson," he bellowed without a microphone. "Do you think mankind will ever travel at or beyond the speed of light?"

A thin young man near the center of the lecture hall stood up.

"Professor Alexander, any significant mass, say the size of a small spaceship, traveling at relativistic speeds, would require more energy output than the entire visible universe to propel it." He said nervously.

"Continue." Alexander urged, leaning a little forward.

"Yes sir," He replied, "and even if you could, there are problems peculiar to Special Relativity, as well."

"Go on."

"Sir, time dilation would create a situation where time on earth, relative to the space craft, would accelerate. A twin on earth would age much faster than his counterpart sibling traveling at relativistic speeds, yet time would appear to be completely normal in their respective frames of reference. We can prove time dilation exists by measuring the longer decay times that occur when subatomic particles, like muons, are accelerated to near relativistic speeds."

"How do fairly new concepts of "warp bubbles" and "wormholes" affect your answer to my original question to you?"

"Sir, those theories are very exotic and not everybody agrees they are even remotely feasible."

"Got ya!" Alexander thought to himself. It was all too easy. Even he brightest minds in his class consistently fell into his traps. "Keep going." He said.

"Warp bubbles and wormholes are a theoretical way to manipulate flat space-time to achieve Effective Supraluminal Travel. A spacecraft creates a warp bubble where space-time contracts in the direction of travel and expands behind it. Wormholes are shortcuts between two points in folded space-time. In both theories, the spacecraft would seem to travel at speeds vastly faster than the speed of light. The fact is we cannot bend flat space-time. Even if we could, the energy requirements to perform such a feat, even on the most microscopic scale, are on the solar system-size level. Thus, a spaceship achieving anything near relativistic speeds is physically impossible."

"Thank you, Mr. Tillotson. You did a phenomenal, well-learned job of not answering my question. You may be seated." Alexander paused for a moment. "How many people here think Mr. Tillotson was factually correct. Raise your hand." All but one raised a hand.

"You! The one who didn't raise your hand! Ms. Cullen? Tell us why you think Mr. Tillotson is wrong."

"To be honest, Professor Alexander, I really don't think he's wrong, but I've been in your class long enough to know when you have an ace up your sleeve!"

The entire class burst out in laughter. "Ms. Cullen, you know me all too well!" He grinned. "Mr. Tillotson was, indeed, factually correct. That is, given today's understanding of physics.

"At this level of your education, I would expect every single one of you to be able to intelligently explain the meat and potatoes of Newtonian Physics, Einstein's Special Theory of Relativity, and Quantum Mechanics. I would also expect you to be able to cover several huge chalkboards with pertinent equations."

Most of the class laughed at the remark. The few who did not, the more anal-retentive students, were nervously wondering if he were about to pick somebody to do just that.

"Mr. Tillotson, however, did not answer my original question. Does anybody remember what the original question was?"

"Professor Alexander?" A female student asked as she was standing up.

"Yes, Ms. Taylor."

"I believe you asked if he thought mankind would ever travel at or faster than the speed of light."

"Indeed, that is what I asked. What I got for an answer was a lecture on why relativistic speeds for spaceships were impossible. What I really wanted was his opinion. Now, my guess is that the learned Mr. Tillotson's opinion mirrors his answer. He has... as the rest of you have, and as many great minds in the history of science have, fallen into the trap of proclaiming the impossible based on an egocentric view of the current level of scientific understanding. I can assure you, our understanding of the universe around us is nowhere near complete. To proclaim that something is impossible, without having all the facts, well... that's taking quite a risk of being discovered a fool, perhaps even in your own lifetime... and we all know how hard it is to get tenure when your peers think you are a fool!"

Laughter erupted from the group of very bright undergrads.

"Hold on..." he added with a little theatrical pause. "What... what if I told you that each of you could easily make the earth's moon travel faster than light?"

The students began looking at each other as the predictable mumbling erupted and quickly gained in volume.

"The moon is almost 390,000 kilometers away and orbiting around the earth. If you position yourself so that the long axis of your body is perpendicular to the moons' orbit around the earth, then rotate yourself 360 degrees in one second, the moon will have orbited your body at 2.4 million kilometers per second. Mr. Tillotson, what is the speed of light in kilometers per second?" He asked with a grin.

"300,000 kilometers per second, professor."

"So, the moon traveled around your head at 8 times the speed of light."

"But professor, the moon really didn't travel that fast!" Tillotson objected.

"Why not? According to General Relativity, all coordinate systems are valid, are they not?"

It was easy to see that Tillotson was drawing a nervous blank.

"Relax, Mr. Tillotson. You shouldn't compare the velocity of the moon to something revolving on earth, even though General Relativity suggested you can. The moon was not overtaking the light reflecting off its' own surface in its' own inertial frame. Therefore, it was traveling at its' usual, lumbering sub-light speed. So now you need to add a caveat to General Relativity: You can only compare velocities within a single inertial frame. A caveat here, a caveat there... well, doesn't that make it a lot harder to completely trust the laws of physics we hold so dear?"

"How many of you believe in the scientific consensus on human-induced global warming?" He asked, setting up his next reality-check trap. To a soul, each student raised a hand.

"Really?" He asked with almost theatrical incredulity. "You believe there is a 'consensus?' Should I assume you also believe that there is no room for further debate?"

"Further debate is pointless and dangerous, Dr. Alexander!" A young Asian woman near the back of auditorium stood up and announced. "We are at a critical point where if we don't take measures to reduce our carbon emissions, our planet is going to die!"

"Ms. Tanaka, I am not a climatologist so I'm not going to claim that I have any special expertise in the subject. What I can tell you, as a scientist, is that there are far too many dissenting climatologists to claim a 'consensus' exists on global warming. More importantly... and I have to say I'm quite disappointed that I apparently failed to adequately teach this vital concept... debate is never, EVER closed in science! Every theory, no matter how old, cherished or hyped, is open to review, refinement, testing and if necessary, destruction. You should be highly suspicious of anybody who claims otherwise, especially if it is coming from someone or some institution outside of peer-reviewed science. Remember, politics, money and secondary gain are the ingredients of junk science. Objectivity and personal integrity are the fertilizers of sound science."

"I can think of many great statements of scientific 'fact' that have been proven wrong over the last several hundred years. Remember the 'Flat World' concept and the egotistical scientific "certainty" that the earth was at the very center of the universe? With all heavenly bodies orbiting around it? Scientific "facts" just a couple hundred years ago. More recently, at the beginning of the 19th Century, scientists soundly dismissed the theory that meteorites were extraterrestrial in origin. Rocks simply did not exist in outer space. At the turn of the 20th Century, many very smart people believed that the human body could not withstand speeds greater than 60 mph, and that 'man-lifting flying machines' were impossible because a 'scientist' had actually proven it so. Some claimed the sound barrier could never be broken. Other bright minds doubted the feasibility of manned space flight. The fact is, today's impossible often turns into tomorrow's commonplace."

"So, by now, I should have added a nice little element of doubt about how sound our currently held scientific beliefs are. If so... good! We have come quite a way, to be sure, but on the very long road to total scientific understanding we have barely reached the end of the driveway."

He reflected for a moment, looking at the youth who would, soon enough, take over the reigns of science.

"What I want each of you to glean from this lecture is this: Always keep your minds open and stay intellectually honest. Closed minds are stagnant minds, resistant to new concepts even when they make terribly good sense. Use the word 'impossible' sparingly. Instead, say 'not possible given our current level of technology and/or understanding.' By saying so, you acknowledge that something may be impossible now, but might be possible in the future, if our understanding of the universe changes and we develop technology to exploit it. Remember, just because you are a highly educated scientist, dare I say by virtue of taking this course, a scientist heads above other scientists," pausing a moment for the laughter to diminish, "that doesn't insure you are right all the time, especially when it comes to predicting the future."

It was starting to get late in the hour. Time to wrap things up.

"Socrates once said 'If I am the wisest man, it is because I alone know that I know nothing.' Learn to be humble, people. Don't let your ego overwhelm those Spock-like brains of yours! Dismissed..."

Chuckles broke out, mixed with the sounds of students standing and shuffling towards the lecture hall exits. A handful of students surrounded Dr. Alexander within seconds of the end of the lecture. A few needed to talk about various academic issues. Others wanted to punt around ideas they had. Of course, there was the usual small entourage of "butt-kissers" who hung around after class to shower the professor with praise for his 'awesome' lecture. If they thought that pelting Dr. Alexander's backside with kisses would help them academically, they seriously underestimated the man. In fact, Dr. Alexander loathed syco-phancy, but honest enough not to punish students who did it. He just tried to avoid it or prevent it from happening whenever possible. After 10 minutes, the group dissipated and Dr. Alexander made his way from Knudsen Hall to his cluttered office in the Physics and Astronomy building. As he was entering the building, his pager chirped.

Some people viewed pagers as some sort of status symbol or must-have accessory. Dr. Alexander saw them as wicked creations spawned in the depths of Hell by Satan himself. How many times had he plotted the violent murder of his electronic leash? The traditional methods of destroying pagers, flushing them down toilets or tossing them against walls, were not creative enough for a theoretical physicist. No... bombarding them with high-energy, subatomic particles at Michigan State's superconducting cyclotron was more his speed! "Burn baby, burn!" He thought with a smile as he read the number from the pager's LCD screen. The page was from the Department Secretary. Since he was only a minute ride up an elevator away, he didn't feel pressed to engage Satan's other sinister creation: the cell phone. A moment later, he was walking into the secretary's office.

"Hey, Sally. What's the page all about?" Alexander asked.

"There is a man on the phone who says he needs to speak with you." She replied. "He's very insistent."

"He wouldn't leave a number?"

"No, he wouldn't. In fact, he said he would stay on hold until you returned from your lecture."

"That's odd. Did he sound like one of those kooks that want me to endorse their cockamamie inventions on my show?"

"No. He was very polite... insistent, but polite. He really stressed how important the phone call was."

All the kooks thought their phone calls were important. "I know I'm going to regret this... Go ahead and forward it into my office."

Alexander walked into his office about the same time his phone began to ring.

"Dr. Alexander speaking."

"Thank you for taking my call, Dr. Alexander." The phone-distorted voice began. "I know you are a very busy man."

"What can I help you with today?" He reluctantly replied, certain that the next sentence would be a request for him to endorse a do-it-yourself nuclear reactor kit.

"Dr. Alexander, I have been watching your career for quite some time. You possess impressive credentials in your field and well known for your intellectual integrity. Most importantly, Dr. Alexander, you possess an open mind."

Polite, erudite... a nice bit of schmoozing... certainly a step above the usual kook. Now... here it comes... the sales pitch! Dr. Alexander cringed in anticipation.

"You also have a popular public forum. A television show called 'Science for the Rest of Us' on the Science and Technology Channel. I've watched it many times. Very highly rated, I understand."

There it was! A direct lead-in to the coming sales pitch. Will they ever learn that there is no viable market for a Heathkit nuclear reactor?

"Yes sir, it is," Alexander said quickly, "but I cannot promote your product on the show, or anybody else's for that matter."

"I'm afraid you have a pre-conceived notion about what this phone call is all about. Do you have a Fed-Ex package on your desk right now?"

"Why yes... I do." The disturbing thought of a detonating letter bomb crossed his mind. Since the Ted Kaczynski "Uni-bomber," anti-technology rampage of a few years back, high-profile academicians had been keeping a watchful eye on packages.

"Dr. Alexander, inside that box is the tip of an iceberg. It contains a summary of the research work I have been involved with for forty years. This information, when I give it to you in its' entirety, and in turn, presented to the public by you, will change mankind forever."

"Sir... no offense, but do you know how many claims like this I hear every month from the wacko fringe?" Alexander said with obvious exasperation. "I've got a letter from Jesus Christ himself right here in my desk!"

"At this point in time, I do not expect you to believe that I am any different from the 'wacko fringe' you speak of. The documents contained in the box before you will be more than enough to convince you to seek the rest. I must warn you, however, not to share these documents or their content with anybody. Every page contains highly classified information. Successfully disseminating this information to the public will depend upon keeping it between you and I, for the time being."

"OK, I'm a little intrigued. Who are you, anyway?"

"My name is not important. I will give it to you when we meet in person. For right now, examine the material I have sent to you. One week from this moment, I will call again. If you think the material is unworthy of your time, I will not bother you any further. If you find that the material is everything I claimed it to be, we'll arrange a meeting where I can show you the rest of the iceberg and answer all of your questions."

"Fair enough. One question... why are you doing this?"

"I am not a well man, Dr. Alexander. The information I am giving to you will help reverse a tremendous injustice and, hopefully, bring the nations of the world together to prepare for a common challenge. On a more selfish level, it will insure that when I die, Americans will know that my colleagues and I were dedicated scientists working in their behalf. Until next week, Dr. Alexander."

The phone clicked silent before he could say anything. Alexander set the phone in its' cradle and looked at the FedEx package. He could see right away it was from Las Vegas, a discovery that did not portent well. He picked the package up and gave it a shake. It was not heavy, no ticking and it didn't explode. "That's good!" He thought to himself with more than a little relief. He broke out an envelope cutter and began hacking the tape on one end of the box. A few seconds later, the tip of the iceberg was visible.

Thirty minutes later, he could barely stand up.

Chapter 4

Paul Hanson Jr. was having the time of his life camping with a couple of his baseball buddies at the base of a chat pile near an abandoned lead mine outside of Cardin. Littered with dozens of large concrete piers, the impromptu campground was what remained of long since demolished buildings that supported local mining. A bottle of cheap Kentucky bourbon found its' way into the tent and before it was empty, the three teens were seriously inebriated. After a period of loud banter, farting contests and empty boasts, Paul Jr. developed an uncomfortably full bladder. With some initial trouble standing up, he excused himself to take an urgent whiz. Grabbing the flashlight he stumbled out of the tent and towards a promising area of brush about 50 feet away. In spite of the alcohol coursing through his blood, everything around him seemed crystal clear on the cool, windless Friday night in April. Even the sound of the chat crunching beneath his canvas tennis shoes seemed unusually loud to him. Maybe it was because Paul Jr. was happy. Life was really going his way. Graduation was next month, he snagged the best-looking girl at Picher High for his prom date, he was heading to Arizona State University next semester on a full athletic scholarship and he was tying on a serious buzz with his best high school pals. If only all of life could be like a senior year in high school...

Paul Jr. reached the tufts of brush and began to step into an area between piers that appeared to offer a bit more privacy. As he leaned into the next step, something at the edge of the flashlight beam caught his eye. If his mind had been clear of the effects of alcohol, or perhaps if the flashlight had illuminated the object a fraction of a second earlier, he might have been able to avoid the extreme danger that was mere inches beneath his left foot. As it was, his momentum, plus a center of gravity that had already shifted forward for his next step placed him well past the point of no return. What he saw in the outer edge of the flashlight were partially uncovered boards lying side by side, boards that were undoubtedly covering one of the hundreds of abandoned mine shafts that littered the landscape in Ottawa County. They were much too thin and deteriorated to support Paul's weight, and quickly gave way with sickening crunch when his foot bore weight on them. Before he could manage a scream, the hapless teenager quickly descended into a very deep and very black hole. Even with the sudden adrenaline surge in his system the alcohol in his brain made him feel strangely relaxed, as if he were in slow-motion and this is somehow what he was supposed to be doing. After dropping 25 feet, his head struck something hard protruding from the mineshaft wall, mercifully rendering him unconscious. No pain, no fear, just pitch black.

By 1964, eighty years of lead and tin mining was declining in the tri-state area of Northeast Oklahoma, Southeast Kansas, and Southwest Missouri. What remained was an incredible labyrinth of man-made tunnels and caves reaching the size of football fields. The mining complex was so vast that large vehicles, lowered into the mine in pieces, reassembled and fitted with exhaust scrubbers, could literally drive underground from state to state!

After the big name companies all but ceased operations, the majority of the people left working the mines were the independent "gougers," who stripped the mines of any remaining ore and everything else of value left in them. This stripping included removing the rock pillars used to brace the ceilings. This practice led to some spectacular collapses over the years that created sink holes, or "subsidences" as they were called by those wishing to paint the frightening phenomenon with a more pleasing brush. One such "subsidence" in Picher took out a rather large portion of area located right behind the high school!

When the last of the gougers abandoned the mines in the late '60s, they shut off the water pumps that kept the water table from flooding the mines. The tangled matrix of tunnels and man-made caverns eventually filled with countless billions of gallons of water that became highly acidic by picking up hydrogen ions from exposure to oxidized iron disulfide. The water also acquired toxins from leeching lead, zinc and a handful of other assorted minerals from the waste tailings left behind. When the mines finally filled with this poisonous cocktail, it poured out of the old mineshafts and boreholes onto the land and surrounding waterways.

In the 19th century, people referred to Northeast Oklahoma as America's "Hay Capitol." By the late 20th century, the area had become one of the largest and most notorious EPA superfund sites in the United States. All totaled, massive subterranean mining encompassed over 700 square miles of the tri-state region. Of the thousands of mineshafts and boreholes drilled while the mines were producing ore, many hundreds were uncovered or poorly sealed hazards. Hazards that people sometimes fell into.

Paul's friends, David Russell and Shaun Erikson, never noticed him missing. They fell asleep in the tent shortly after he left and when they awakened the next morning, Paul was gone. Even though his sleeping bag was still there, they assumed he had risen early and returned home without them. They packed everything up, buried the empty liquor bottle in a pile of chat, then started the hike into Picher where one of the boys lived. Both wondered why Paul saddled them with the job of hauling all of his crap back. It wasn't like him to do something like that to his buddies.

"Teresa! That asshole snuck away to be with Teresa!" David suddenly deduced aloud. Well, that made sense. Teresa Chandler's house was not all that far away from where they were camping, she was impossibly beautiful and probably a lot more fun to be with than a couple of smelly guys. Their annoyance with Paul quickly melted away as they both wondered what Paul and Teresa did last night. "Lucky jerk!" Shaun added with a jealous grin. Like every other red-blooded teenage male who had seen Teresa Chandler, he had a long list things he would like to do with her!

It wasn't until Saturday afternoon that Mrs. Hanson became worried about Paul Jr. It was getting late in the day and he had yet to come home or check in from his overnight campout. She made phone calls to David and Shaun's parents and learned that the two teenagers had returned that morning, but that Paul wasn't with them. Her anxiety increasing, she began calling the parents of other friends with whom Paul frequently spent time. Nobody had seen her son since yesterday.

"This is not like Paul Jr. to disappear without telling us where he was going," she told her husband as her uneasiness was steadily growing.

She called back to Shaun's house and asked his mother if she could speak with him. After a few minutes of polite grilling, Shaun told her that they thought Paul had gone to Teresa Chandler's house but they didn't really know for sure that he did. Mrs. Hanson then called Teresa's house and quickly learned that Teresa was spending the weekend with her grandparents in Tulsa. Alicia Hanson was nearing panic. Nobody in Ottawa County knew where her son was.

Shaun Erikson was getting worried, too. If anything, Paul Jr. was reliable and now it seemed he had vanished. At first, Shaun tried to dodge Mrs. Hanson's questions about where he thought Paul had gone to, but concern for his friend was overriding his ability to maintain a flimsy cover-up. He called David and the two teenagers went back to the campsite. After 20 minutes of searching the area they found Paul's flashlight next to an open mineshaft. The switch was on and the batteries were dead. Fear swept over them as they both suddenly realized their friend must have fallen into the mine. They both fought back tears and screams as they rushed to the nearest house to call the police.

It was late afternoon by the time authorities were notified of the accident. By 6:00 PM, the Ottawa County Sheriff's Office was on the scene, followed by Engine Companies from Miami and Baxter Springs along with volunteer firefighters from Picher, Quapaw and Commerce. Dozens of others were also converging on the scene as word of what happened, and who the victim was, spread quickly through the community. Because the accident occurred on their property and involved the son of one of their employees, several representatives of the Picher Lead Company also showed up. A visibly shaken Paul and Alicia Hanson arrived just as the Miami engine company lowered a Commerce volunteer firefighter into the mineshaft. All present, except for Mrs. Hanson, knew this was not a rescue mission. Most of these mineshafts were between 200 and 400 feet deep and surviving a fall down one was virtually impossible.

Motherhood does not allow acknowledgment that there is no hope for a child until the fact is completely irrefutable. "Paul Jr. had to be alive!" She bargained. "They're not going to find him in that dreadful hole. He just went fishing and forgot to call home. He might be home now!" Nobody knew what to say to her, so nobody said anything. Paul Sr. did his best to soothe her, but the incomprehensible swirl of emotions that enveloped her, and his own overwhelming grief, made it terribly difficult for him to know what to do for her. For the first time in his adult life he felt utterly powerless. Even when he was crawling amongst his dead and wounded buddies on Okinawa, he never felt powerless. He was fighting a tangible, mortal enemy made of flesh and blood. He could shoot and kill the enemy with his thumb-busting M1 Garand. The enemy he faced now was formless and unbeatable. It did have a name: "Despair." He knew in his heart that Paul was gone forever and he couldn't protect his beloved wife from having motherhood's most vicious nightmare turn into cold reality.

Firefighter Jonathan Bruce was being lowered into the abandoned mine shaft that likely held the body of Paul Hanson. He was bringing with him a lantern, a duffle full of medical supplies, a long wooden backboard and a Stokes Basket; a rigid, wire-mesh cradle designed to secure and extricate the wounded out of rugged terrain. Jonathan volunteered to enter the mineshaft, even though there were paid firefighters at the scene, because he felt he knew these structures better than most and he had done this sort of thing once before, retrieving the body of a murder victim tossed into a mine shaft some 2 years earlier. "No doubt about it," he thought to himself, "this shit is spookier than hell!" It was one thing to be lowered into a working mine shaft where there were people waiting for you in lighted, man-made tunnels and caves, it was quite another to be lowered by rope into a hole with God knows what was waiting below you.

People dumped all manner of trash down the abandoned mineshafts of Ottawa County, including the corpse of a woman beaten to death by her husband during one of his all-too-frequent drunken rages. On that rather memorable trip into the unknown, Firefighter Bruce found the battered, partially decomposed body of an obese woman impaled on lumber discarded down the shaft. The stench in the close quarters of the mineshaft was unbelievable. There were other things in the darkness, too. Illuminated by his lantern, he could see trash, decayed bodies of small animals that had fallen into the shaft, a multitude of insects... and water, onyx-black water. Acidic enough to corrode away the nails that held miners boots together. Jonathan deduced that his particular mine shaft had been cut off from the pumps that kept the network of mines dry. He had no idea how deep the trash/water mixture was, and he didn't care to find out. His most vivid memory of that unpleasant trip was the rat perched on a board next to the corpse. Somehow, it had miraculously survived the 200 foot fall down the mineshaft. Even in the relatively dim light provided by his lantern, it was easy to see that the rat had been feeding on the ripening corpse. The sight was one he would relive repeatedly in his dreams. Hopefully, the Hanson boy's body had not yet become a rodent's delicacy.

After the Commerce firefighter had been lowered only a couple of dozen feet, he came across a broken four-by-four protruding from the wall of the mineshaft. As he maneuvered past it, he noticed that the board had what appeared to be a fair amount of dried blood on the jagged end, with what looked like a small piece of scalp hanging on it. With that bit of gruesome evidence, it seemed likely he would find the Hanson boy's body at the bottom of the shaft. He elected not to report this finding to the surface crews lowering him into the abyss. He saw the boys' parents arrive at the scene just as he entered into mineshaft and there was no point in starting the horror any sooner than necessary.

Ten minutes later he uneventfully passed the 200 foot mark. Throughout the ordeal, he kept praying that he wouldn't run into water. He was a natural swimmer, but he had no desire to float with a corpse in the unholy ooze that he would likely encounter. He kept a watchful eye out below him so that he could yell to the surface and stop his descent at a moment's notice. At 250 feet he could make out debris at the bottom.

"Slow it down!" He yelled at the top of his lungs, "I'm almost there!"

He felt the winch begin to slow his descent into the darkness. As he neared the bottom the lantern light slowly revealed a scene that was both terrible and a relief to the firefighter. The boy's badly broken, lifeless body was lying on a surprisingly small clump of discarded wood, trash and mining debris on a mineshaft floor coated only with blood, not flooded with the toxic water Bruce had feared. The young Paul Hanson's body was terribly mutilated. The nearly 300 foot fall and probable bouncing between walls on the way down resulted in multiple angulated and open long bone fractures, an obviously disrupted spine in several locations, grotesque facial swelling and a grotesquely open skull fracture. The firefighter reached the bottom and allowed several feet of rope to descend before yelling to the surface to stop the winch.

"I've reached the bottom!" He yelled. "I'll let you know when I'm ready to come up!"

He unzipped the medical duffel and spent over 30 ghastly minutes dressing and splinting the dead boy's injuries, including a thick dressing applied to his gaping head wound and placing a soft cervical collar on his horribly broken neck. Some would call his efforts a waste of time, but the boy's family was on the scene for God's sake! He couldn't bring him to the surface all busted up! Once finished, he wrapped the lifeless body in a blanket and secured it to the long backboard. With some difficulty he managed to muscle the body-laden backboard into the Stokes Basket then securely lashed the body/board combination into it. Since this was a body recovery instead of a rescue, vertical extraction of the Stokes Basket was acceptable. Jonathan attached the basket to the bottom of the line and himself to the line above the basket. This would allow him to be in a position to guide the basket through any obstacle above them, namely the four-by-four he encountered on the way down.

"Bring us up SLOWLY!" Jonathan yelled. Less than thirty minutes later, the shattered body of Paul Hanson Jr. and an exhausted firefighter emerged from the mineshaft. No cheers... no congratulatory pats on the back. Just the heartbreaking sobs of a bereaved mother and the promise of a sleepless night for Jonathan Bruce.

Chapter 5

Benjamin rushed back to his hometown as soon as his mother finished breaking the tragic news to him. Ben was accustomed to being lonely, but he never felt it as badly as he did on his trek back to Quapaw. Paul Jr. was as much a good friend as he was a brother and now he was gone. Not quite seventeen years of age, and late in his junior year of college, Ben was so much younger than his peers that he had very few friends. Even the ultra egghead-types in his advanced math, science and engineering courses wouldn't hang out with him, probably because they felt threatened by the combination of his age and formidable intellect. The double loss of brother and friend would hurt for a very long time.

As he drove through the cool, moonless spring night in the used 1960 Ford Falcon Ranchero pick-up his dad bought him for travel to and from college, he agonized over how something stupid like this could have happened to his brother. Paul Jr. often bragged that he knew the location of every working and abandoned mineshaft in the tri-state area. Realistically, how could he? There were so damn many of them! Some thought the total number of mineshafts in Oklahoma and Kansas alone was close to 4500, with hundreds of thousands of much smaller boreholes on top of that. An estimated one-fourth of the area mineshafts were unsealed hazards. Still, Ben knew his brother to be careful. Falling down a mineshaft was the last thing he ever thought would happen to him and he was sure the answers to his questions awaited him at home.

There were quite a few drawbacks to being a child genius. Ben was about two when his parents recognized his intellectual potential, a suspicion later confirmed by child development experts in Oklahoma City. He could read by age three and was solving complex trigonometry problems by age six. It was soon evident that Ben needed to be placed into higher grade-levels than his peers so that he could continue to be challenged. The drawback to this was that Bens' social development would fail to keep pace with his intellectual development. The more grades he skipped the greater the difference. In all, Ben would bypass four grades. Since most kids want acceptance by their peers and Bens' were becoming increasingly older than he was, he struggled with trying to grow-up sooner. His youthful appearance combined with a sincere desire to fit-in socially came across as bizarre to most children and a source of ridicule for Ben. Though easily capable of doing so, once he was in high school his parents refused to allow him to leap any further ahead. Socially, he never caught-up to his academic peers but he did develop a little more maturity than most kids his own age. The one thing he never developed was a quirky, egocentric personality that is all too common amongst intellectual giants. Ben's parents would have none of that.

Ben pulled into the familiar chat driveway on North Cherry Street a little after 4AM on Sunday. His dad was still awake but his exhausted mother was in a deep sleep induced by a sedative administered by the local General Practitioner, Dr. Stanton Buckley. Ben was sure his father had aged 10 years since he last saw him a few weeks earlier.

"Are you OK, Dad?" Ben asked quietly.

"No, Son... I'm not." He replied in a weak and cracking voice. "You and your brother have been my whole life... and I have always been so proud of you both. Why did this have to happen? Why? Why has God taken away one of my boys? I want him back! I want my little boy back..." The last trace of his stoicism had evaporated. Paul Sr. began to cry for the first time since the ordeal began.

Ben had never seen his father cry. Even when Granny Hanson died a few years back, Dad didn't cry... at least not around him. The sight of his father's tears and broken heart overwhelmed him. In spite of his powerful intellect, his mastery of mathematics and physics. In spite of his natural talent for solving problems, Benjamin Harris Hanson had no words that were adequate for the moment, nor did he have a clever solution to ease his father's suffering. He lost a brother and friend and his father was crumbling right before his eyes. He sat next to his dear old man, put an arm around him... and cried with him.

After a while, Ben stepped out onto the porch and sat on the bench swing. His dad had fallen asleep from sheer exhaustion and grief. Ben, however, was well beyond the ability to sleep. Directly in front of him the sun was beginning to cast a glow on the eastern horizon. There was just a smattering of clouds silhouetted against the deep oranges and purples of a new day's birth. In spite of tragedy's oppression, it would be a beautiful spring day in Quapaw.

The visitors would start coming after morning church services. These wonderful souls would arrive in droves to comfort his grieving family. A variety of home baked foods would soon cover the table and countertops and tears would flow like rivers. There would be decisions for his parents to make today, terrible decisions that no parent should have to make. Funeral arrangements, burial place, casket... each decision heaping insult upon injury. In the solitude of the still morning air Ben began to cry again, wishing he could remove these burdens from his parents.

"Big brother," he said, looking up at the lightening sky. "You always said we were going places. I guess I thought that meant we would go there together. God must have something more important planned for you. You were always there for me, Paul. I'm going to miss you so much..."

He paused for a moment, tears streaming down his cheeks, and began listening to the cheerful chirps of the first birds announcing the official start of morning.

"If I have to go it alone, you dumbass jock, I'll just have to become as good an engineer as you would have become a baseball player. I promise, Big Brother... I'll make you proud!"

He cried until the sun finally peeked over the horizon. He quietly went inside and began preparing breakfast. It was going to be one very long and difficult day.

Chapter 6

After his brother's funeral, Ben returned to Norman to finish his junior year at OU, promising to spend the summer with his parents in Quapaw after finals were over. He was sailing through the Honors Program in Aerospace and Mechanical Engineering and appeared to be poised to graduate at the top of his class next year. Ben had a keen analytical mind that could identify, dissect and solve a problem before most others could copy it down on paper. It was as natural for him as breathing, but then, school had always been like that for him.

Ben occupied the "top-of-his-class" position at every school and grade he attended, from kindergarten through undergraduate school. What kept him from becoming the classic underachiever, the bright student who made poor grades because he was bored, was due to grade skipping, the work ethic instilled by his parents and his passion to learn how to design and fly jets and spaceships. When he wasn't doing chores and acing tests he kept himself busy with reading everything he could about aeronautics and rockets. He was a 10 year old 8th-grader when the unexpected launch of Sputnik I rocked the American public. For Ben, the excitement of the dawning space race between America and the Soviet Union was just the catalyst he needed to keep him focused and propel him through years of formal education.

Even before he entered the University of Oklahoma his budding genius attracted attention outside of his home state. In his high school sophomore year, a Tulsa Daily World newspaper reporter heard about "Quapaw's Child Genius" and convinced her editor to authorize a feature story on him. She spent two days taking pictures of Ben's home and school; then interviewed Ben, his friends, family and teachers. It was published in the Sunday Edition the week following. At best the article ended up being mediocre piece of journalism, sporting a hodge podge of facts about Ben's education and his life with a few follow-up questions and answers about what he wanted to do when he grew up. It was evident that the reporter seemed quite impressed with the 12 year olds' matter-of-fact reply that he was going to become an aerospace engineer so he can design and build jet planes and rocket powered spaceships. The article was the talk of Ottawa County, but never picked up by the major news services for national distribution. Even so, a clipping service that scanned nearly every paper in the country for keywords that were of interest to an individual called "The Foreman" flagged the article. When it came across his desk, he scanned over it and placed it into a file folder named "Rising Stars."

"This one is worth keeping an eye on," he thought, then scratched a note to his secretary, directing her to establish a formal file on the Hanson kid. From that point on The Foreman personally reviewed the discretely updated details of Ben's academic progress twice yearly.

Chapter 7

"The young Ben Hanson will be the Valedictorian at Picher High, I see." The Foreman said aloud, even though nobody else was in his well-appointed office. "No surprise there. University of Oklahoma Scholarship, College of Engineering... good boy, coming along nicely!" As he read further into the academic information summary for the 6 months prior, he came across a story about his senior year science project that almost made him fall out of his chair laughing.

It seems that Ben decided to build a static, liquid-fueled rocket engine for his science fair exhibit. Lacking access to traditional and quite dangerous rocket fuels, Ben decided that he would use oxygen from a compressed gas cylinder and gasoline. He fashioned a combustion chamber and exhaust nozzle out of copper pipe and fittings, soldering them together as required. He took copper tubing and fabricated fuel and oxygen lines then attached them to the combustion chamber using carburetor jets. Since Ben was worried that the engine might melt from the heat, he assembled a water jacket around the entire engine that would connect to a running garden hose, acting much like the radiator in a car. When he ignited the small engine for the judges the oxygen pressure was apparently set too high, as a six-foot long, white-hot flame roared from the nozzle, igniting the project adjacent to his. If that were not enough, the noise from the engine was so loud that people began screaming and fleeing the auditorium. Ben quickly lowered the oxygen pressure and reduced the flame length, but the deafening noise continued to be almost as frightening as it was before. Ben finally cut off the oxygen and the engine promptly stopped, but not before one project was scorched and the bulk of the spectators present needing an underwear change. In spite of the chaos he caused, and much to his surprise, Ben still took first place at the fair.

Smiling, The Foreman set Ben Hanson's growing folder on his beautiful, richly hued, mahogany desk. In four years, perhaps sooner, Quapaw's child prodigy would likely be

Valedictorian of his class yet again and headed for graduate school. He began to write a summary and an assessment of Ben's performance on a form not unlike a physician's running progress note, and unceremoniously added it to his other notes written over the last two years.

"He'll want to go to Michigan post-grad," he thought almost aloud. "The University of Oklahoma has a fine post-grad program in aeronautical engineering and they'll recruit him hard, but Michigan Engineering has the high-powered Alumni. This Hanson Kid will pick Michigan and if they have a problem with his age... Well, I'll make a little call in the kid's behalf."

The Foreman finished his note, placed it in Ben's folder and set it onto a pile of other paperwork he would hand to his secretary for processing. Ben Hanson was starting the formal training of his already impressive mind. Undergraduate engineering school will make his mind even more powerful and graduate school will hone its' edge to the razor-sharpness The Foreman could use. The more he thought about it the more convinced he was that young Ben would be meeting him in the not too distant future.

Chapter 8

Ben Hanson's senior year in college had its share of difficulties, but academically he stayed right on course, mastering each subject with an ease that other students came to regard as "spooky." Always shadowing him, however, was the death of his older brother and how it was affecting his parents. He spent the previous summer in Quapaw helping-out around the house and doing his best to cheer-up his parents. His best guess was that he wasn't doing a very good job. They seemed so distant and older... much older. His mother was prone to spontaneous crying spells and his father didn't seem interested in the hobbies that once gave him so much pleasure. When he left for Norman to begin his senior year his mother could not contain her tears and his father looked like a man bearing more weight than he could handle. It was at that point Ben Hanson decided to do his post-graduate work at the University of Oklahoma so that he could study closer to home. When he announced his decision to the professors who had been vigorously recruiting him in his junior year, they didn't seem interested anymore. In fact, they suggested that he apply to the prestigious program at the University of Michigan!

Ben was more than perplexed. All along he wanted to go to the University of Michigan post-graduate program in Aerospace Engineering. They had everything: solid faculty and curriculum, reputation and very distinguished alumni. Obtaining Masters and Doctorate degrees from Michigan was his ticket into the thick of the field. Maybe even a shot at his wildest dream: The Lockheed-Martin Skunk Works. The faculty at the University of Oklahoma Engineering Department knew this was Ben's plan but they wanted him too. At least that was the impression they gave him. Now that he decided to stay in Oklahoma they seemed to be shunning him. Even more perplexing were the unsolicited and quite frequent phone calls that started to come from the faculty of the University of Michigan Department of Aerospace Engineering! If he didn't know any better, he would have thought somebody was trying to manipulate his academic choices. "But, why would somebody want to do that?" He thought. He quickly regarded the idea as utterly ludicrous and dismissed the possibility altogether.

Other interesting things began happening to Ben in his senior year. He experienced his first taste of romance, briefly dating a freshman named Tania Ashmore. She was a General Studies major trying to choose between medicine and several other completely unrelated careers. She was a full 2 inches taller than Ben with brown hair, brown eyes and slightly better than average looks. They had very little in common but the two things they did share a love for was Dairy Queen and movie theaters. She was good company with an infectious, little girl giggle and matching smile. For Ben, she was a welcome break from the loneliness that plagued him. Nothing serious developed between them and after a few months, more unsure of her direction than ever before, Tania dropped-out and returned to Enid. Her absence saddened Ben for a while and eating at the Dairy Queen would likely never be quite the same.

At the suggestion of one of his professors who's brother managed a Piggly Wiggly market in Edmond, Ben landed his first real job, working a couple of nights every week sacking groceries and stocking shelves. The name of the market chain always made Ben laugh, along with the smiling pig caricature. "Maybe Mr. Pig was smiling because he is completely oblivious to the plight of his relatives in the meat section." Ben mused to himself. The work wasn't all that hard and the extra cash meant he could step out on the town a little more, if he chose to, and buy gifts for his Mom and Dad come Christmas.

In February of 1965, Ben Hanson accepted the post-graduate school scholarship offer from the University of Michigan Department of Aerospace Engineering. He had to. The only other application he submitted was to the University of Oklahoma and they declined to offer him a position. Confused as he was, he accepted the inevitable. It seemed his future studies would take place much farther from home than he would have liked. Not that he wasn't excited about going to the premier campus for his chosen field of study, he very much was. It's what he originally desired, but his priorities changed and he wanted to stay closer to his parents who were still grieving from his brother's death. Everything had become so strange the last several months and Ben just couldn't shake the feeling that something was not quite right.

As predicted four years earlier by a total stranger he was destined to meet, Benjamin Harris Hanson graduated Valedictorian from the University of Oklahoma, Class of 1965, with a Bachelor of Science degree in Mechanical Engineering. He was one of the youngest students to graduate from the University and its' youngest ever Valedictorian. His parents were present at the ceremony and the pride they had in their son was self-evident. Because of his youth, Ben was a standout in the sea of red caps and gowns. He looked decidedly out of place, like an obviously underage teenager trying to sneak into a bar. In spite of how he looked, he earned his degree, his place behind the podium and the right to address his class as their top student. His speech was relatively brief, touching on the usual topics covered in such addresses, adding short comments on the civil rights movement and the "dark clouds gathering in Southeast Asia," referring to the March deployment of Marines to South Vietnam. He mentioned his father's proud military service in World War II and encouraged his classmates to be ready to serve their country when called upon. He reminded them of what John F. Kennedy had said about public service during his 1961 Inaugural Address. While not a seasoned public orator, Ben performed well enough to earn a healthy standing ovation and dozens of pats on the back.

"He looks real happy." Alicia Hanson said to her husband.

"Yes. Yes he does." Paul Sr, replied. "He's a good, hard-working kid. If there was anybody who deserves all of this attention, it's Ben."

"I wish he wasn't going to Michigan." She said, sadly.

"I'd like to keep him close to home, too, but his future is in Michigan. Ben is destined for great things, Honey. We can't be selfish."

"My head knows that, but my heart doesn't."

"It'll be alright. We have him for the summer again and we'll make it count." He promised.

"I know." She sighed, her mind drifting off to a time when she had both of her boys around the house. Tears began streaming down her face as she buried her head in her husbands shoulder and began to cry. Life had not been the same since Paul Junior's death and she was now losing her other son to a great big world. In her despair, she wondered if she would ever know happiness again.

Chapter 9

To say that The Foreman took his job seriously would be a gross understatement. He took most everything seriously. Born Arthur Wayne Marston, The Foreman learned the meaning of "serious" as a bomber pilot and Japanese-held P.O.W. during World War II. After completing 25 harrowing B-17 missions over Nazi-occupied Europe, Major Marston volunteered to train for the new B-29 Superfortress, a heavy bomber designed to fly very long-range missions. It was the kind of bomber necessary to traverse the great distances from American-held Pacific island airfields to the Japanese homeland. He completed his B-29 training at Clovis Army Airfield, New Mexico in December 1944 and joined the 497th Bomb Group based on the island of Saipan, Marianas.

After 10 successful bombing raids on Japanese-held territory, Major Marston's B-29 Superfortress "Betty Brimstone" was one of 279 B-29s tasked to drop their load of 37 M-69 incendiary cluster bombs on a sleeping, pre-dawn Tokyo. The huge but loose formation of enormous, four engine bombers launched from the Marianas airfield in the late night hours of March 9th, 1945. Pathfinder aircraft started the first fires of the raid to serve as a visual guide for the three waves of B-29s that were to follow. They flew only 7000 feet above the ground when passing over the city, waking thousands of citizens' only moments before unleashing living hell. Each cluster munition carried 38 individual incendiary bombs weighing a mere 6 pounds each. The M-69 was designed to rupture a mile above the target, allowing a wide dispersal of the individual bomblets. They exploded on contact, spraying the area with a flaming, jellified fuel similar to napalm. The effect of the massive raid was devastating. Within moments, huge fires were blossoming all over Tokyo. As the night went on, the leaping flames of the newly established fires combined with the flashes of bomblets exploding to create a vision that was both mesmerizing and horrific. Larger fires merged with even larger fires to become unstoppable infernos fueled by wooden buildings and gale-force winds created by the massive uplift of heated air. The resulting fire storm literally consumed all of the oxygen near it causing a surprising number of deaths by asphyxiation.

When the last burning ember in Tokyo died out, over 100,000 Japanese would be dead, 100,000 injured and 16 square miles of city charred beyond recognition.

Shortly after releasing his incendiary bombs, Major Marston throttled-up the four, 2,200 horsepower Wright R-3350 Double Cyclone engines on his Superfortress and began a slow climbing bank to the left. Just as he leveled out to a southerly heading, the B-29 felt as if being thumped by a large hammer followed by violent shuddering. In the light of the approaching dawn the crew did not see the single Mitsubishi J2M "Jack" fighter come in from the 5 o'clock high position. The brass at the 21st Bomber Command Headquarters were not expecting any Japanese resistance so they ordered the removal of all defensive weaponry on the B-29s in order to increase the bomb load. This left Betty Brimstone completely defenseless when the lone Jack fighter sent several 20mm canon rounds through the two starboard engines. The outboard engine, number four, exploded into flames almost instantly, throwing savaged parts of the massive 18 cylinder engine into the leading edge of the bright silver wing. A few moments later, the inboard engine, number three, burst into flames, having taken hits that ruptured the fuel supply lines and punched a hole into the engine crankcase. The aircraft immediately yawed and banked to the right. Marston worked frantically to restore level flight as his copilot, Captain Harry Westfall, radioed for assistance from the P-61 Black Widow night fighters that were flying cover for his wing of B-29s. Marston quickly shut off the fuel flow to the starboard engines in an attempt to starve the growing fires then feathered the propellers to reduce drag. Severely damaged during the first strafing, the control surfaces and hydraulics on the starboard wing were failing fast. A second round of strafing crippled the outboard, number one engine on the left wing. Thankfully, there was no third strafing. The Japanese fighter disengaged from the attack, presumably to shoot down other B-29s.

It was very clear what fate lie in store for Betty. With three engines on fire and tenuous control of his aircraft, Marston ordered his crew to abandon the Superfortress. He held the plane as steady as he could while his crew quickly bailed out at 9000 feet over the northern part of Sagami Bay. Marston and Westfall took turns preparing for their jump, and trimmed the disabled aircraft to fly as straight as possible... which wasn't very. The dying B-29 descended to 3000 feet by the time Marston and Westfall opened the emergency exit and bailed out. Betty made a slow rollover to the right and began a short corkscrew that ended unceremoniously in the middle of Sagami Bay. Several minutes later, Marston and Westfall were swimming in cold, hostile waters.

Not thirty minutes after landing in Sagami Bay, a shivering Marston and Westfall were picked-up by a Japanese coastal patrol boat and taken prisoner. It did not take long for the savage beatings to begin.

Incensed by the massive incendiary raid on Tokyo, the Japanese sailors were more than happy to return the favor. The kicks and punches were so vicious that Marston suffered several broken ribs, facial fractures and a broken right forearm by the time they reached an

Imperial Navy installation in Yokohama. Westfall fared no better with a list of cuts, bruises and fractures that rivaled Marston's. Throughout the beatings, Marston caught glimpses of the towering columns of smoke to the North. "Beat me senseless if you want, you bastards." He thought to himself. "I just bombed the ever lovin' shit out of your precious motherland and you can't beat that out of me!" A small but perceptible smile erupted on Marston's bloody face.

That cost him three teeth.

Of the ten men in Marston's crew, only four made it to shore alive. He learned later that two of his men were pulled from the cold water and beaten to death by the crew of the patrol boat that picked them up, their broken bodies dumped into the bay like common jetsam. The other four undoubtedly drowned or succumbed to hypothermia. The Japanese soldiers quickly separated Marston from Westfall and after a few days of interrogations and physical abuse, transferred him to the Omori Prisoner of War camp near Tokyo for endless days of solitary confinement, severe beatings and even more totally meaningless interrogations. He never saw his copilot or any other member of his crew again.

The Omori POW Camp was actually a man-made island reclaimed from the sea on the backs and blood of POWs from the Shinagawa Camp. There were several B-29 pilots and crewmen at Omori and Marston befriended them all, or at least to the extent his captors allowed. Marston would eventually endure 6 months of mental and physical cruelty at the hands of his captors. The closer American Forces came to invading the Japanese homeland the worse the abuse. The odds of dying during imprisonment at a Japanese POW camp approached 40% and a successful escape from captivity was virtually impossible. That is, unless you were Asian or Polynesian. By comparison, an American POW in Germany had a 98% chance of survival and many successful escapes to freedom occurred. Every serviceman and woman in the Pacific Theater knew of the wartime atrocities committed by the Japanese Imperial Forces, from the Nanjing Massacre to the Bataan Death March. The horror at the thought of becoming a POW in Japanese hands lead to many suicides of American servicemen facing imminent capture. Marston knew the odds and they sure as hell were not worth betting the farm on. Being alive at the end of each day was nothing short of a miracle. During his entire period of detention he made it a point to see every sunset he possibly could, never knowing if death would overtake him before the next day's end. Fortunately, Marston had no wife or kids to concern him and could only imagine the torture that the families of his fellow prisoners were enduring.

The Omuri POW camp was liberated on August 29th, 1945. Marston lost nearly 60 pounds and suffered from several broken bones that were in various stages of healing. In spite of his condition, Major Arthur Wayne Marston insisted on walking out of Omuri and into the loving arms of freedom. That moment of utter clarity solidified his already dynamic character. Having lost his freedom to a culture that embraced brutality and totalitarianism, then have it fully restored by the blood of his fellow countrymen, Marston vowed that he would never take his liberty for granted. He would spend the rest of his life making sure Americans never suffered that kind of horror again.

After the war, Marston was quickly promoted to Lieutenant Colonel and given a string of fairly high profile assignments in the Army Air Forces, including Deputy Commander of the 7th Bombardment Group at Fort Worth Army Airfield under the newly formed Strategic Air Command. His military record was exemplary, as was his devotion to duty. He had keen command and managerial skills and was relentless in his pursuit to conquer whatever mission objective tasked to him. Another quick promotion to Colonel occurred when he was absorbed into the brand new United States Air Force in September of 1947. By the end of 1947, Marston was in command of his own B-29 Bombardment Group in Arizona and under the thin roof of America's newest military service. Most considered him a shoe-in for Brigadier General. He was tough as nails and somebody who could make an impossible job look easy. In other words, he was Lieutenant General Brandon Slate's kind of Air Force officer.

General Slate, Marston's former deputy commander in the Pacific Theater and currently on special assignment for the Secretary of the Air Force, had a wartime reputation for driving his men hard and demanding perfection. In peacetime, he fought tirelessly against the shortsighted thinking in Washington that led to the overly massive disarmament of the Armed Forces in general, and the Army Air Force in particular. The World War resulted in ungodly, but wholly necessary, deficit spending. President Truman, along with many others in the legislative branch of government, wanted a balanced Federal budget posthaste. They assumed that since the United States had the atom bomb there was no need for a large military, so it was fiscally hacked to pieces. General Slate, however, believed the dire warnings of the Manhattan Project scientists. Nations other than the America already possessed various parts of the fission puzzle, most notably Stalin's Soviet Union. Given funding and the will to obtain the technology to manufacture enriched uranium 235 and plutonium 239, the scientists expected the US would not be the sole nuclear power for long. In fact, it only took a little over four years for that very thing to happen.

Considered one of the most valued assets in the Army Air Force, General Slate was a natural leader with a brilliant intellect and remarkably well connected in Washington, even though having spent relatively little time there. In July of 1947 he was assisting with the organizational planning and development of the soon-to-be separate Air Force when the Truman Administration tasked the Chief of Staff to the Commander in Chief and the Commander of the Army Air Forces with establishing a peculiar, quasi-military scientific research project of "vital" national importance. Slate was the first and only choice of the Army Air Force Commander. He took the reigns of the highly secret project in October of 1947, answering only to the new Secretary of the Air Force and certain members of the Truman Administration.

When the Soviet Union detonated its' first nuclear device in August of 1949, Slate's job acquired an air of urgency it hadn't had before. The Soviets, under the genocidal maniac Josef Stalin, now possessed the ultimate destructive power on earth. Did they have a project similar to the one General Slate commanded? If so, the country that made the first technological breakthrough in that arena might just destroy the other. During the manic period of non-stop Pentagon meetings that followed the Soviet Union's entry into the exclusive club of nuclear powers, General Slate suffered a non-fatal but crippling heart attack that would leave him with only 30% of the cardiac function he had previously.

At the time of General Slate's heart attack, Colonel Marston was working for the legendary Curtis LeMay at SAC Headquarters. LeMay quickly promoted him to Brigadier General to reward him for his work in helping to develop a "first strike" nuclear capability to deter the growing Soviet threat. The first plan called for delivering the entire 1949 inventory of just over 130 atomic bombs to 70 Soviet cities in 30 days. LeMay and Marston shared very similar views when it came to fighting wars.

"If you are going to use military force, then you ought to use overwhelming military force. Use too much and deliberately use too much... you'll save lives, not only your own, but the enemy's too." LeMay once said. His was a time-honored philosophy of warfare that Marston wholeheartedly agreed with. Crush the enemy soundly then dictate terms the vanquished must abide by. Works every time it's tried.

Marston became quite valuable to LeMay, but much like the rapidly changing fortunes of war, an urgent meeting with an ailing Lieutenant General Slate and the Air Force Chief of Staff drastically altered LeMay's plans for Marston.

"Art," LeMay started. "You remember General Slate, don't you?"

"Yes sir," he said. "We served together in the Pacific." Marston replied.

"He's got a job for you. An important one."

"Yes Sir." Marston replied.

"I need you to head-up a very unique and highly classified project, a project with immense importance to the security of the United States." General Slate said on cue.

"I'm honored, Sir."

"You should be. I can think of none better for the job."

"Thank you, Sir."

"There are some sacrifices you must make in order to accept this position." Slate looked him squarely in the eyes. "You'll have to retire from the Air Force."

"Sir?" Marston replied, trying to hide the shock.

"You will receive a second star, General Marston, and you'll get it just before your retirement in 30 days. I have been assured your Senate confirmation will be forthcoming by the end of next week." He paused, leaning back in his chair. "I am currently the commanding officer of this project, but I just spent the last 2 months recovering from a coronary. I can get around, but not without tiring easily. Truman has decided that this project must transition completely out of the military realm. The reasons for this will become quite clear during your initial briefing. You'll leave the Air Force with Major General retirement pay plus a handsome salary for heading-up the project."

Whatever this assignment was, Marston knew he had to accept it. Nobody in his right mind said "No" to Slate OR LeMay. If they thought you were the right man for an assignment, you were. It sounded interesting and Slate used the words "...immense importance to the security of the United States." It was a challenge in the making and a big one at that. Before LeMay or Slate uttered another word, Marston was ready to pounce on their little "project."

One month later, Major General Arthur Wayne Marston, USAF (Ret.) became the Director, "The Foreman," of Project Cocheta.

Chapter 10

It was time to update Ben Hanson's "Rising Star" dossier again and there was much to write. Project Director Marston was reclining in his almost overly comfortable leather office chair, sipping on a hot cup of Blue Mountain coffee and contemplating on Ben Hanson's future. A lot happened in his life in the previous 13 months. Marston learned of the death of Hanson's brother within 24 hours of it happening. Such a family tragedy can dramatically change the dynamics of how a potential recruit orders their priorities. Marston was convinced that Ben Hanson would become a valued part of his team, maybe even his successor, and was willing to pull all the strings necessary to make it happen. He knew Ben would decide to attend graduate school closer to home so he could spend more time with his parents. Hell, he would have done the same thing, but Marston couldn't allow Ben Hanson lose focus.

The fix was relatively easy, if somewhat expensive.

"Dr. Curtis McClelland?" A male voice asked over the phone.

"Yes, this is Dr. McClelland." Answered the Department Chair of the University of Oklahoma School of Mechanical Engineering.

"Chancellor Elkins, referred me to you. I need to speak with you about a student of yours, a Mr. Benjamin Hanson."

"Hanson? He's a good kid. Very smart, hard working... Has a natural instinct for solving complex problems. Without a doubt, he is the brightest and most intuitive student we have ever seen. The last few months of his junior year were tough for him, but you wouldn't know it by the quality of his work."

"I totally agree with you Dr. McClelland." The voice said. "He is a young man of enormous potential. I understand you are putting forth a considerable effort to recruit him into

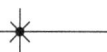

your graduate program in Aerospace Engineering."

" We think we have a good chance at keeping him here. We'll know more when he returns in the fall for his senior year."

"Dr. McClelland, I'll be blunt. I must insist that you cease all further recruiting efforts towards Benjamin Hanson. For reasons that I am not at liberty to say, he cannot attend your graduate program. I have arranged for him to attend the graduate program in Aerospace Engineering at the University of Michigan."

McClelland paused for a moment while the meaning of the unexpected words filtered to the rage center of his brain.

"How dare you tell me who I can or cannot recruit!" McClelland growled. "Who in Hell do you think you are?"

"Dr. McClelland," the voice calmly said. "I understand your disappointment, but I assure you this is the way things must be. Obviously, there will be just compensation for you and your department's loss."

"Compensation?" McClelland asked incredulously.

"In return for your complete cooperation in this matter, I have arranged for a generous endowment to fund a Chair in your department. With the knowledge and cooperation of Chancellor Elkins, I wired the sum of $250,000 to the University. My only stipulation is that Ben Hanson be kept unaware of our conversation and to the real reasons he will not be offered a graduate position at your University."

Dr. McClelland took another moment to take everything in. Chancellor Elkins had already agreed to this arrangement and left him completely out of the decision making process... in his own damned department! But what choice did he have? This character on the phone must have serious political clout and a wallet to match.

"Who are you?" McClelland asked, hoping to find some tiny shred of information he could use.

"I trust I can count on your complete cooperation." The voice said coolly, ignoring his question.

"What other choice do I have?" McClelland replied in an almost pleading voice.

"None, I'm afraid. I suggest you contact Chancellor Elkins at your earliest convenience. Good day." The phone line clicked dead.

Dr. McClelland slumped back in his office chair. "Ben Hanson is just a boy!" He thought. "A pretty damn bright one, but still a boy. Why in the world was this character so interested in where he goes to graduate school?" None of it made any sense to him. He pulled his Rolodex close and began looking for Chancellor Elkins phone number. He removed the target card and began to dial the number typed on it.

"Chancellor Elkins' office." The cheery female voice announced.

"Dennis Elkins please." McClelland said.

"Who may I say is calling?"

"Dr. McClelland."

"I'll put you through right away, Dr. McClelland. The Chancellor has been waiting for your call."

"Thank you."

"Curt!" A rather jolly voice answered with an unmistakable Texan drawl. "I see you've heard from our secretive benefactor!"

"What is going on, Dennis?" McClelland replied sternly. "Why has my authority over the Department of Engineering been bypassed?"

"Hold on there, nobody is trying to short-circuit your authority! This Hanson kid has attracted some powerful folks with no shortage of connections... or money, for that matter. I know this character you spoke to. I've done business with him before. Just as sure as hell he's one of those folks that gets what he wants. I suggest you let this go and start working on that new endowed Chair of yours."

"But..." McClelland started to say, but was quickly cut off.

"Give it up!" Elkins said with a lot more force and a lot less drawl. "This man is well out of our league. Be thankful your department was compensated for a loss that might of happened anyway, even without his help."

"I see."

"Look, I'm already late for a meeting. Give me a call tomorrow and let's set up a tee time."

"Sure."

With that, the call ended. Dr. McClelland didn't know all that much more than he did before. One thing he was certain of, Ben Hanson had a very powerful "friend" controlling his destiny.

Chapter 11

Paul Sr. and his son were spending a hot July afternoon in 1965 at Blackie's Garage in Commerce, drinking sodas and tinkering with old cars. Paul had no earthly idea why this friendly old mechanic was nicknamed "Blackie." After all, he was just as white as every other caucasian in the area was. As it so happened, his nickname was a mystery to everyone else, too. If asked, he would just smile and say "You wouldn't believe me if I told you," and that was that. Some speculated it had something to do with his military service with the "Rock-of-the-Marne" 3rd Infantry Division during World War I, but no plausible theories were ever produced. He was getting up there in years, but never seemed to slow down. He enjoyed teaching young Ben about cars and how to keep them running. "Boy, you might know how to build a space ship," he would tease Ben, "but you don't know shit about cars!"

That would quickly change.

As with everything else Ben Hanson set his mind on, he would master automotive diagnostics in short order. Before the end of the summer, Blackie would be asking Ben what he thought was wrong with a challenging mechanical problem. Paul Sr. could not have been prouder of his son and felt richly blessed to have him home for the summer. It might be the last chance for him to spend any significant time with his only son. Life was cruel that way. Fathers raise sons, teaching them everything they know about handling life, then forced to let them go. The melancholy Paul Sr. felt at times, still grieving over Junior's death and knowing Ben would be striking out on his own soon, was oppressive to the point of being almost unbearable.

When Ben returned home after graduation, his father began noticing the subtle and not so subtle changes that were shaping his son. He had to have grown 2 inches in the last year and his voice was deeper. He seemed more intense, more mature and becoming quite a handsome man judging by the "looks" the local girls were giving him. The "looks," however, were lost on Ben. While he longed for female companionship, he never considered himself much of a catch. Ben always thought that his brother received the bulk of the family's available "lady's man" genes, so he naturally felt uneasy around the opposite sex. Tania Ashmore wasn't really a "girlfriend," was she? Ben always regarded her more as a friend, but maybe it could have been more than that if he possessed more confidence. Maybe she would have stayed in school. Life is full of perplexing "what ifs." "What if," he had acted more romantically with Tania? "What if," his brother hadn't left him alone? The "what ifs" seem to be intimately associated with the twin brothers of "Guilt" and "Regret."

One Friday night late in July, Ben decided to drive into Commerce and enjoy a cheeseburger and fries at the Dairy Queen. Located on the west side of North Main Street at the Commerce Street intersection, the Dairy Queen was the local teenager's center of the known universe. On Friday and Saturday nights they would repeatedly cruise their cars up and down the 10 blocks that comprised the entire length of Commerce Street, from North Main to Route 66, then park in the Dairy Queen parking lot. Some of the boys would venture into Miami to taunt their High School football rivals; others would take their new girlfriends to see the famous Joplin Spook Lights in the hopes of scaring them into a state of extreme clinginess, a completely natural start to making out.

The mysterious Joplin Spook Lights, also called the Hornet or Seneca Spook Lights, had been a local legend since the old west days. The harmless lights that patrolled the area just over the Missouri state line at the extreme northeast corner of Oklahoma were a local tourist attraction of sorts. In the 1950s, a little store in the town of Hornet Missouri was the unofficial headquarters for "Spooklighters" who ventured out to the dirt road where the phenomenon was most often reported. Explained away in more enlightened times as a refraction phenomenon created by the headlights of cars traveling between Commerce and Quapaw on Route 66, thousands of people had seen them. Some reported encounters as close as within arms' reach... a remarkable feat for a "refraction" illusion. Nonetheless, they were far more likely to be a natural phenomenon rather than the ghost of a long dead miner eternally seeking his missing wife and children believed kidnapped by Indians.

Ben was about to leave when he noticed a strikingly beautiful young woman looking at him from another table. It was Teresa Chandler, his brother's girlfriend at the time of his death. When their eyes met she immediately stood up and walked over to his table. She was wearing a light blue, knee-length skirt with a white blouse. Her shimmering dark brown, waist-long hair was pulled back into a ponytail that seemed to sway almost magically behind her. She was obviously glad to see him.

"Ben? Ben Hanson? Is that really you?" She said with genuine glee.

"Hi, Teresa." Ben replied a little nervously. He was notoriously self-conscious when speaking to women, even one he had known for many years. He hadn't seen Teresa since his brother's funeral well over a year earlier and was fairly certain Miss Chandler was even

more beautiful now than she was before. "It's nice to see you again." He added, feeling like the world's worst conversation-starter.

"It's been a long time, Ben. I've heard a lot of great things about you." She smiled, sitting down across from Ben. "Youngest Valedictorian ever at OU! Wow, you and I are the same age, and you're already a college graduate! Smart man!" She said tapping an index finger to her head. "I understand you're heading to graduate school in Michigan."

Ben felt his heart begin to pick up speed. "Yeah, I really wanted to stay closer to home, but I guess the University of Michigan is where I'm supposed to be. Where are you going to college?" He asked clumsily, quickly trying to make her the center of the conversation instead of him.

"I'm going to hang around here for a while." She said, pleased that Ben seemed interested in wanting to know what she was up to. So many boys spent entire conversations talking about themselves, the "interesting" lives they were leading and what great things they were going to accomplish. Even Paul Jr. had been a little guilty of that sort of behavior. Ben was obviously different. He was somebody who had already achieved wonderful accomplishments, yet he didn't start a conversation by bragging on them. "I've always wanted to be a nurse, so I'm going to take nursing courses at Northeast Oklahoma."

"You would make a very good nurse, Teresa." Ben said in all honesty. "You were very kind and generous to my family after my brother died, even though you must have been very sad yourself. I don't know a whole lot about what it takes to be a nurse, but I would bet that caring about people would be the most important quality to have."

"What a sweet thing to say, Ben!" She said, taken back somewhat by the compliment. She had always considered Ben as Paul's quiet little genius kid brother. Even though Ben and her were the same age, Ben just seemed to always have an air of "kid" about him. Maybe it wasn't because Ben was really a "kid," but because he was harder to notice in the sheen of Paul's undeniable charisma. Paul Jr. was the handsome and popular jock that always commanded the limelight. Ben was more like Paul's shadow trying to exist in a sea of stadium lights. Whatever the case may be, it was easy to see that he had certainly done a lot of growing up in the last 15 months. He was noticeably taller, and something else she had never considered until now: Ben was kind of cute. No, Ben WAS cute! Handsome, not in the same sort of way his brother was, but in his own distinct way. She was feeling the start of an attraction to Ben. Was that an OK thing to feel? Now it was Teresa's turn to be nervous.

"I really miss your brother, Ben."

"I do, too." Ben said sadly. "My mom and dad have not been the same since he died. I try to cheer them up, but I don't think I'm doing a very good job. Going to school in Michigan isn't helping matters, either."

"I can't imagine what it must be like to lose one of your own children, Ben. I can't imagine losing my little bother or sister, either. It must be horrible." She said, her eyes glistening with the first sign of a tear. "The only thing I know for sure is that, when I lost Paul, I didn't think the hurt would ever go away, but after a while, I learned to accept what happened and I moved on. Your mom and dad just need more time. You need more time." She added in a soft and reassuring voice.

Ben's held his head low, trying to fight off the sadness and tears. Then he felt her hand touch his and begin to lightly squeeze it in a way that immediately soothed his aching heart. Her other hand followed shortly afterward, and mimicked the healing touch of the first. The caresses to his hands were so much like the ones his mother used to give him when he was young and suffering from the sadness that resulted from never fitting in. He looked up at her and smiled. There was so much more to her beauty than met the eye. Maybe it was a kind soul that lay beneath her skin that made her so beautiful. There was a strange feeling overcoming him, a pleasant one. All seemed right with the world, at least for now. The tender moment they shared would pass. She would go her way and he would go home and bury his nose in a technical journal... but the moment didn't pass.

"I think I know why my brother was so crazy about you." He finally said, looking back down at the table. "You're as nice a person as you are pretty."

She squeezed his hands. "Ben, look at me."

Ben almost froze solid, his heart racing. He'd said something stupid and ruined the whole conversation. Damn! He looked up slowly. She had a gentle smile on her face.

"Ben, I think that is the nicest thing anybody has ever said to me!" She said, her face almost glowing. "Your brother was a very special boy and I really liked him a lot. He was fun to be around and I can't think of anybody who didn't like him. Even kids who were jealous of him still wanted to be his friend!"

She paused, watching a reluctant calm overtake Ben's face. "Ben, I think you are every bit as special as your brother, maybe even a lot more special. You're not like other boys and I mean that in a very good way. You worry about others more than you worry about your-self... like your parents. You were more concerned about their suffering than your own. You also made me feel that what was going on in my life really was important and interesting to you. Not many boys do that!" She leaned closer. "And not once did I catch you staring at my blouse." She said in a serious whisper.

Ben froze again, his eyes as big as a pair of dish plates. Teresa began giggling and only after several unsure moments did Ben finally relax.

"You should have seen the look in your eyes when I said that, Ben Hanson!" She laughed.

"I didn't know what to say!" He smiled. "You sounded so serious!"

"Your brother never told you what a kidder I was?"

"No, he didn't." Ben looked right at her with the straightest face he could muster. "All he ever talked about was your blouse."

It was Ben's turn to laugh as Teresa began crossing both index fingers in the classic "naughty" gesture. They both were giggling now.

"Ben, do you like to go to the movies?" She asked, reaching back to his hands and squeezing them again.

"Sure." He replied, fully sensing that Teresa was starting to feel the same sorts of indescribable emotions that he was.

"If you ask me, I might say 'yes.' " She whispered.

"Teresa, I would love to go see a movie with you, but... I mean... Is it proper?" He stammered, hoping that there was a way to make it work. He was riding a sinusoidal pattern of wanting very much to see if something might develop between him and Teresa, alternating with feeling guilty about even having such thoughts in the first place. "You know how bad the gossip can get around here. I don't want somebody to say bad things about you."

"He's always thinking about others, first." She thought to herself. Ben was certainly a shining standout amongst the high school boors she had been dating. Teresa was accustomed to having men look at her. Perhaps "stare at her" was a better way of putting it. It was both the blessing and the curse of being beautiful. She first noticed these "attentions" at the age of twelve, about 2 years after her father had noticed the unwanted looks his daughter was getting from men who should know better. Mr. Chandler, who could be quite an imposing figure when angered, verbally threatened a number of men, ranging in age from 16 to 72, with the beating of their lives if they ever looked at his ten year-old daughter again. Of course, the looks continued, only better concealed. The threats did accomplish one thing, not once did any man ever come close to molesting her.

Teresa only became more beautiful as she grew into womanhood and as a result, she never had a shortage of boys wanting to be her boyfriend. The common behavior that each of them seemed to possess were giving her looks that gave away the thinly veiled sexual desires they harbored. Teresa never saw a hint of that in Ben's eyes. He made her feel, well, at ease. The conversation was comfortable because it was real and without any hidden sexual agenda.

"Ben, if there is one thing I do know about your brother is that he loved you very much. When your name came up in conversation, he would start bragging about all the things you were up to. He was proud to be your big brother. If Paul were here, right now, he would encourage you and your parents to press on and be happy. I know that in my heart. I know that he would encourage me to do the same."

"I know, I just don't want..." Teresa put an index finger to his lips.

"You are unlike any boy I've ever met. I don't feel uncomfortable around you at all." She winked and Ben began to smile. "Your brother would not have a problem with this and the gossipers are going to gossip anyway. I would like to go to Miami and see a movie tomorrow and I do not want to see it with anybody but you. We can call it a date, or we can go as friends. Your choice." She winked at him again and started to giggle.

"You are forcing me to choose between two very nice things." Ben replied with feigned fatalism and a touch of inner confidence that wasn't there a few moments earlier. "Might I be greedy and go to the movie with you as a friend and as a date?"

"Deal!" She said with a smile. "And if you're real lucky, I'll let you buy me popcorn!"

"I'll make sure I have enough money to cover any such good fortune I might have!'

"That would be very, very wise." She squeezed his hands for the last time, leaned forward, and kissed him on the forehead. "I've got to go. I told my dad I'd be home 15 minutes ago. If I push my luck with him, you might end up going to the movie without me! Pick me up at six. The 'Sound of Music' is playing at the drive-in. I hear it's pretty good. Bye!" She waved as she slipped-out the screen door that led to the parking lot.

With that, Teresa Chandler had entered Ben's world, quite by accident or perhaps by divine intervention. Whatever force was behind it all, Ben could scarcely believe what had just occurred. He even briefly entertained the idea that it was all just a dream. Later, when he arrived home his mother commented about the faint but unmistakable pattern of lipstick on his forehead. If there had been any lingering doubts about the reality of what happened at the Dairy Queen, his mother's discovery of irrefutable evidence on his forehead dispelled it.

Ben told his mother what had happened, wondering how she would react to the news that he was about to start dating the girl his brother was dating at the time of his death. When he finished, he noticed that his mom looked as if she were very pleased.

"Miss Chandler is a fine young woman. She comes from a very nice Christian family and her friends are the right kind of company to keep. I'm not surprised she's attracted to you. You're a nice-looking man with a big heart and you have the same kind of greatness in you that your brother had."

"Thanks, Mom." Ben said, as a great feeling of relief came over him. "I was so worried that this might look bad and I didn't want Teresa to get hurt or anything."

"From what I know of Teresa, she can handle gossipers. There are a lot of people who think that beautiful women are naturally shallow and brainless. Miss Chandler is not shy at all when it comes to setting people straight about that. I think you two will make a wonderful couple."

Moms always had just the right words to say.

Ben and Teresa's first date was predictably nerve wracking at first, but they quickly found an almost unnatural comfort developing between them. They watched the movie from the cramped comfort of Ben's aging Falcon truck, which fortunately, had a bench seat and a transmission shift lever on the steering column. Teresa sat close to him, eventually holding his right arm and resting her head on his right shoulder. It all seemed so natural to the both of them. That wasn't to say that Ben's mind, in moments of practiced self-doubt, wondered if Teresa was really attracted to him because of her relationship with his brother. She hadn't given him any reason to believe that were true and would be pretty weak behavior for someone who had a reputation for being emotionally strong. So... Ben decided to enjoy his new and welcomed friend instead of dwelling on vaporous insecurities.

After the movie there was the obligatory ice cream cone at the Dairy Queen followed by the reluctant drive to Teresa's home on South Vantage Street in Picher. By this time they had found each other's hands. Ben didn't want the evening to end, but there they were, standing on the front porch of her parent's small wood frame house so typical of the small mining communities in Northeast Oklahoma.

"I had a wonderful time." Teresa said quietly.

"I did too! You are a lot of fun to be with." He replied, matching her level of whisper.

"So are you."

"When can I see you again?"

"How about tomorrow? You can come eat Sunday dinner with us."

"Sounds great!" He replied with an excited whisper, "I promised my dad I'd spend some time with him and Blackie at the garage after morning services so dinner would be perfect!"

Then came the awkward moment of silence, when a couple at the end of their first date wonders what comes next. In the mid-1960s, a proper mid-western couple had only three options. The first option, and the one most disappointing to all men, was verbal only. It probably had the worst prognosis, as well. A simple "Good night" and a closed door were tantamount to declaring that another date was unlikely. The second option, the hug, was a bit more promising. A hug could effectively transmit how someone felt about another. Some girls simply did not kiss on the first date so they might use a lingering hug to send the message that a second date was his for the asking. The third option, the "Holy Grail" of first dates, was the kiss. That was a clear message that even a dull-witted man could understand. The eternal questions for men were "What are the signs she might be receptive to a kiss?" and "When is the right moment to try?" These questions plagued men in the closing moments of a date with a woman they wanted to see again. Ben wanted to kiss Teresa, but fear of rejection had a death-grip on his mind.

Teresa sensed the turmoil within Ben. She had seen it before, but in this case, she really did want Ben to kiss her. She knew that Ben had little experience with women, an innocent quality about him that made him that much more attractive to her.

"Ben..." She said quietly. "Aren't you going to kiss me?"

Ben blinked hard and in an instant, the doubts about what to do next dissolved into thin air. He smiled at her in understanding, took a small step towards her to bring them close then he kissed her... his first real kiss, and she was kissing him back! His heart was racing wildly. It all seemed so surreal, yet another dream he was going to awaken from... but it WAS real, and she was a real woman who desired his closeness. He wanted the kiss... the moment, to last forever. Reluctantly, the warm and beautiful first kiss they shared had to end, but at that very moment, a love that would span a lifetime was born.

Ben and Teresa would be inseparable for the remainder of the glorious summer of 1965.

Chapter 12

Kevin Loeffler, the new Chief of Operational Security for Project Cocheta, was busy, carefully reviewing the records of every "employee" in his charge. Recruited from the highest levels of FBI Counterintelligence, Loeffler was one of the world's leading experts in the art of catching people who try to remove classified information from other people who wish to keep it secret. Loeffler had been quite content at the FBI where his efforts to combat all manner of espionage was both recognized and appreciated. When the FBI director himself, along with a gentleman he would eventually know as "The Foreman," paid him a visit in his Washington office a few short weeks before, he was very reluctant to accept the quite generous offer proposed to him. They asked him to resign from the FBI and head-up a security operation, the details of which they would not discuss with him until he agreed to the terms. The money was unbelievable, but the devil is in the details and he would have to accept the position having not even met so much as a mischievous demonic imp trainee. In the end, he trusted the FBI Director's recommendation that he take the job. Something about "Huge importance to national security" helped sway his decision, too.

The core of the Project Cocheta staff was, to a soul, certifiable geniuses... and geniuses were squirrels until proven otherwise. Loeffler dealt with a number of them at the FBI and almost every one had some sort of annoying quirk or a self-absorbed pompous ass. According to The Foreman, each member of the core scientific staff met strict behavioral and intellectual criteria. The dumbest one in the group had an IQ estimated at 175, but in spite of the briefing, Loeffler was sure they all scored high on the squirrel-o-meter. If there was one thing he learned in the better part of two decades at the FBI, "reports" and "assessments" were not nearly as reliable as personally sniffing out the details. He would interview and get to know every one of the core staff. If any one of them were a security risk, he was certain he would have no problem spotting it.

To be successful at the FBI, or in any other enormous Federal bureaucracy, one needed to know what a bureaucracy was in the first place, then learn how to navigate through it to get things done. Loeffler could play the various Federal bureaucracies he had to deal with as well as Eric Clapton could wail on a guitar, yet he hated bureaucracies more than anything. They met almost every scientific criteria for being a living organism. They consumed nutrients, but instead of food, it was money. They grew, not out of any biologic need, but to dominate their sphere of influence, or "niche." They defended themselves vigorously, yet conserved "energy" by only responding to situations that threatened the integrity of the bureaucracy. They procreated by expanding their sphere of influence to include real or contrived objectives outside of their original charter. Loeffler could only laugh at people who honestly believed that any given bureaucracy served anybody other than the bureaucracy. Like every other living creature on earth, it served itself, first and foremost.

Now, if you were clever and wanted to get a bureaucracy off its' self-serving fat ass, you had to find a way to publicly humiliate it. That constituted a direct threat to its' relevance, therefore a threat to its' funding... its' "food." Project Cocheta had no bureaucracy and it answered to no bureaucracy. It had a well-delineated objective, nearly limitless funding and nobody screwed with it. Nobody. There were no soundbite-seeking, superfluous politicians snooping around the place with cameras in tow; no reporters looking for ludicrous angles to discredit the mission; no self-proclaimed "experts" passing judgment on the project armed with only the most superficial information and understanding. Just a handful of insiders who secured whatever the project needed, from glow discharge mass spectrometers and scanning electron microscopes, to the cash needed to fund the enormous payroll. Project Cocheta was well beyond mundane, off-the-budget "Black" projects. It was the "Black Hole" of black projects and like the celestial phenomenon, nothing visible ever escaped from it.

Loeffler was an admitted cynic and quite proud of it. After 20 years or so of law enforcement experience, 4 as a military policeman in the Army, and 16 with the FBI, Loeffler learned to trust nobody, except perhaps the cops around him. Even then, they had to first prove they were worthy of his trust. Loeffler, like many others who start careers in law enforcement, was going to help make the world a better place by putting the "bad guys" behind bars. It didn't take long before his naïve idealism would shatter before a hard pounding by the reality hammer. The "bad guys," he soon found out, didn't always look like hardened sociopaths. Some of the most damaging criminals in history were the ones who posed as servants of the people! There were Criminal Court Judges more interested in making social statements than meting out justice, and "activists" who considered anybody in uniform, military or otherwise, to be enemies of the state. There was the press, who rarely got anything right, except of course when it synchronized with their political ideology. There were politicians who leaked sensitive information for political gain and corporate executives who sold advanced technology to America's enemies. Most disturbingly, there were average citizens, everyday Joe Six-packs, who willingly gave sensitive information to foreign intelligence services in return for pitiful sums of cash. The sad fact was that, due in large part to espionage carried out by her own citizens, America's enemies were already developing countermeasures to 75% of all secret military hardware by the time they are introduced to the battlefield. Within three years of these deployments, operational countermeasures were fielded 50% of the time! One need only look at the design of the Russian Buran space shuttle to see that America's ability to maintain state secrets was much like a colanders' ability to hold water. If that were not frustrating enough, for some inexplicable reason, when these traitors are exposed or arrested, they have more rights than their victims, the diligent citizens who exposed them or the cops that arrested them! Loeffler felt he had every reason to be cynical. Yet, it was this honed cynicism and rabid mistrust that helped him catch the deadliest enemies stalking his country.

To Loeffler, the "geniuses" he was tasked to keep an eye on were all potentially dangerous. They had access to information so important, so classified that any attempt to label its' relevance to national security would fall far short. All it would take is one idealist or one greedy little bastard to expose Project Cocheta. "Well," he thought to himself, "that sure as hell wasn't going to happen while he was in charge of security!" Like his predecessor, who died of a massive stroke in the very office he was moving into, Loeffler was given wide latitude to do whatever was necessary to keep Project Cocheta and its' secrets well beyond public scrutiny. That degree of latitude even included the use of deadly force. Loeffler hoped he would never have to exercise that option, but he was also certain that if it ever became necessary he would do so without hesitation.

Kevin Loeffler looked in each dossier for signs of a potential security risk. Every "asset" had to undergo a yearly security review that, in theory, left no stones unturned. Debt loads and spending habits, associations, both public and private, telephone records, girlfriends, boyfriends, wives, husbands, friends, paperboys... all were scrutinized carefully. Each asset had his or her very own dedicated security "specialist" assigned to them. Most of these specialists represented the best field agents Langley had to offer. The rest came from Quantico or were high-end, military special-ops types. Each had two equally vital jobs: to protect the asset and to observe their movements for signs of unusual behavior that might indicate they could be leaking information. Yet, with these impressive measures already in place for decades and a near perfect track record for keeping information sequestered in the remote Canadian compound, Loeffler felt there was no better way to judge where a person's head was at than to find out personally and he intended to start with this character: Dr. Benjamin H. Hanson.

Hanson's dossier stood out for a number of reasons, the most important of which was a document that detailed the "1992 Incident." During that period, an undesirable level of idealism surfaced, but Dr. Hanson wisely backed down after heavy leverage was applied. In Loeffler's eyes, that incident, and what he felt was The Foreman's overly harsh way of dealing with it, made Dr. Hanson a man that might have enough motive to compromise the project. He might do it because of the idealism that landed him in hot water to begin with, or perhaps revenge for the loss of his family's companionship. Other, more recent behaviors were beginning to surface that may or may not be worrisome. His specialist was periodically loosing track of him in Vegas and Hanson wasn't using his credit cards or cell phone as much as he usually did. Was there something to it? Probably not, but "no stone left unturned" meant just that. Loeffler didn't become one of America's best "Spookbusters" because he was sloppy. He finished his preliminary review of the project member dossiers and placed them into the "out box" on his desk, all of them except for one.

Benjamin Harris Hanson, PhD. would be Kevin Loeffler's first investigative project at his new job.

Chapter 13

Dr. Alexander had trouble taking it all in. Spread out across his desk were the most amazing documents and photographs he had ever seen. "Amazing" was simply not the right word. "Life-changing" was the right phrase. They couldn't be fakes, could they? He analyzed each one carefully, noting that the technical language used was far too complicated and incredibly accurate to be the result of some hoaxster, unless of course the hoaxster was a freakin' brilliant physicist or engineer! The pictures were detailed and of the highest quality. Visual references were included in each frame for size comparisons. Some photographs had captions with arrows pointing towards items of interest. Other photographs were quite self-explanatory. There were analysis reports, test results and all manner of highly technical data. But of all the documents included in this "care" package, the most disturbing was the one dated May 2nd, 1952.

The document was a report written by a very prominent anthropologist named Wilhelm Heischler, who passed away nearly 30 years earlier. Alexander knew a little something about Heischler, only because his story was so strange. As he recalled, Heischler was considered one of the most brilliant men of his day and authored several well-rounded books that explored the complex interactions between different civilizations that abruptly meet for the first time. There were countless examples of such interactions throughout history, and such collisions were rarely graceful. Most, in fact, were quite deadly. Over fifty years later, most still consider Heischler's books definitive works on the subject. Heischler, however, did not have the staying power of his texts. He disappeared from public view in the early 1950s, essentially becoming a hermit of sorts and only ventured out of his home in rural Oregon to buy provisions. Nobody knew why Heischler decompensated the way he did. Most chalked it off to schizophrenia, but Dr. Alexander knew why. The impact of the report he wrote was too much for him to handle.

Heischler's report sent chills down Alexander's back. The stranger would get his meeting when he called and make sure his program would be the vehicle to distribute this important data to the world. He would, of course, compare the writing styles between the report and one of Heischler's books, maybe see if he can find a signature to compare to the one on the document. Dr. Alexander knew that if he were to go on National Television and make these documents public and later find them to be an elaborate hoax, his career would plop into the toilet. He was no fool and prudence demanded that he approach everything cautiously. He picked up his phone and dialed a number in Silver Spring, Maryland.

"Science and Technology Channel, Darrell Aceveda's office." An unexpected male voice announced.

"Mr. Aceveda, please"

"Who may I say is calling, please?"

"Dr. Alexander"

"Oh... Hi, Dr. Alexander, this is Beverly's son, Anthony. I'm covering the phones for mom while she takes a short break. It's good to hear from you."

"I didn't know the Science and Technology Channel had a 'Take your kid to work' day."

"Dr. Alexander, you're always making jokes! You know I'm almost 17!" The young man replied with a touch of contrived embarrassment. "Mr. Aceveda is showing me the TV business."

"Very good, Anthony. Maybe someday you can help me with my show."

"Oh! I'd like that a lot! Here, let me ring you into Mr. Aceveda office. See ya!"

The phone clicked and the familiar, intermittent warble of the ring began.

"Tim! How are you doing?" Aceveda asked sounding every bit as bright and cheery as you could always expect him to be. "Are you ready to start shooting again next month?"

"I'm fine, and yes I'm pumped about next season. We have a great series of topics to cover." Alexander replied with somewhat less enthusiasm than Aceveda had anticipated.

"What's wrong?" Aceveda said, turning the voice brightness level down by several notches.

"Nothing. I just had a question to ask you. Just a preliminary inquiry, mind you."

"Ask away, my friend. I'm your producer, if you can't ask me something, then it ain't worth askin'!"

Alexander laughed. "How hard would it be to do a live show?"

"A what?"

"A live show. How hard would it be to make something like that happen?"

"What kind of live show are we talking about, here? What kind of topics?"

"The surprise announcement of an important scientific discovery, but I couldn't say what that discovery was until the cameras go live."

"Difficult, very difficult... but not impossible. Technology is not the problem, my friend. Marketing will throw a fit if they don't have a topic they can advertise twenty times an hour for a month prior to the show. And getting the big shots to sign off on something as risky as a live broadcast? Now, THOSE are problems!" Aceveda paused, beginning to see things more positively. "One thing you have going in your favor on this is that people like you. When you talk to your audience, you don't talk down to them, you talk TO them. It is obvious to everyone who watches your show that you love to teach. It is no wonder that your show is one of the highest rated on cable. Everybody knows and loves Dr. Alexander! This is real firepower to wield when we approach the anointed ones with your proposal."

"It's not a proposal, yet." Alexander cautioned. "I'll know more in a week."

"Can you tell me what it is?"

"Sorry, I can't tell you that, but if this information turns out to be true, the announcement will likely become the most memorable moment in television history."

"Holy shit, man! What the hell are you saying?"

"It will be big. Really big."

"If it's that big, why don't you just hold a press conference?"

"The supplier of the information chose me and my forum to disseminate the information. He was very clear. Perhaps he doesn't trust the coverage I would get from the mainstream media."

"So, this isn't one of your discoveries."

"No, I'm afraid not."

"So, what would you like me to do?"

"Just hold tight, for now. I'll get back to you in a week or so. Oh... and don't mention the details of this conversation to anybody."

"You got it, buddy. Anything else I can do for you?"

"Not that I can think of. Give my regards to Beverly."

"Sure will."

The phone disconnected. Tim Alexander paused for a moment, wondering if he had done the right thing. Well, he had to know if it was feasible to organize such a feat so that he could inform the stranger when he called... if he called. Tim had the uneasy feeling that he was starting to plod down a road so richly gilded with great intentions that the increasing heat from it's destination was not likely to be noticed. "Jitters," he thought, "the 'great' Tim Alexander had the jitters." He laughed a somewhat nervous laugh at himself, then after locking the world-altering documents in his desk, left his office for a short trek to the staff lounge where a strong cup of coffee awaited. No doubt the strong coffee would eliminate his jitters...

Chapter 14

Marston was looking over young Ben Hanson's "Rising Star" file for the first time since he started graduate school. "Hmmmm... This is interesting... a steady girlfriend! Teresa Rose Chandler..." Marston observed, pondering the brief before him. "Eighteen, enrolled in Nursing School at Northeast Oklahoma A&M, above average intelligence, and dating our young Mr. Hanson's brother at the time of his death. Interesting dynamics there." He began looking over a grainy photograph of Teresa and Ben holding hands, sitting on a park bench at 5th Ave. NW and A St. NW in Miami, Oklahoma. "Stunning young woman! Ben, you are doing OK for yourself... just stay focused."

The brief on Teresa Chandler was just that: brief. Her grades were above average, no trouble with the law, Homecoming Queen, works part-time at the local drug store. Parents pay their fair share of taxes and then some. "She's a nice, stable kid." He thought, "Probably a real good thing for Ben right now, so long as he remains on track. If he didn't, the girlfriend would have to go." Marston did not savor busting up relationships, but he did what was necessary to make sure he got the talent he needed... and keep it once procured.

It was nearly impossible to overestimate Marston's power to manipulate lives. Project Cocheta was top priority and the Heischler Doctrine was the justification for carte blanche control over anybody who stood in the way of, or otherwise hindered the mission. It was acceptable for the core staff to have wives, husbands and children, so long as they did not compromise the project. Marston wasn't running a Convent or Monastery for crying out loud, but let a family member get flaky enough to shake-up the performance of one of his assets and he would straighten it out quickly. This unsavory task, accomplished in an unforgettable way, insured that the unwanted party never traveled within a thousand miles of Las Vegas. Divorces and monetary settlements with the former spouse were quick and more than generous... considering the alternatives. Rarely, a real troublemaker would find it difficult take a hint and more drastic, long-term solutions, including incarceration, became necessary. Children of assets posed a much greater headache for Marston. He could make children leave Las Vegas in a heartbeat but preferred to fix problems in a way that kept the asset with his or her kids. A man or woman could readily get over losing a troublesome spouse, but separate them from their kids and you have all kinds of long-term problems. Fortunately, Marston only rarely dealt with that sort of crap.

The summary report from the University of Michigan was encouraging. Ben hit the ground running, chewing up his graduate school classes with the same gusto he had always exhibited towards his studies. There was one noticeable difference, however. The report had words in it never before used to describe Ben. "Outgoing," "gregarious," "cheerful..." Marston smiled. Ben Hanson was in love with this Chandler girl... good for him! Marston closed the thickening dossier on Ben. "Hope it works out for you..."

Chapter 15

Ben Hanson always enjoyed school, but graduate school was a dream come true. His every course and research was directly related to aerospace engineering, with nary a hint of the "knowledge integration" courses a university forced upon the undergraduate student as a prerequisite for a Bachelor's Degree. Rounding out a formal education was lofty justification for such courses, but suffering through "Early Modern and Contemporary British Literature" only rounded out one's ability to sleep bolt upright during a lecture. Wind tunnels, airfoil design, propulsion systems... That was Ben's cup of tea and he was swimming in a very large and happy cup of it!

Life now had a completely different meaning for Ben. Before Teresa, subdued brush strokes of various grays and white adorned the canvas of his life. She was the missing, utterly perfect brush stroke that finally brought the vibrant colors of joy and deeper meaning to his once sad and lonely painting. Education had a purpose beyond learning all one could about a particularly interesting field of study; it was a way to insure that his future family would always have everything they needed. Ben and Teresa's love for each other continued to grow unabated over the three years Ben spent pursuing his PhD at the University of Michigan. Each reunion with Teresa was more wonderful than the one before and Ben traveled to Oklahoma as often as possible to rejuvenate his soul with her love. Even strangers who saw them together instinctively knew that they were a couple meant for each other.

As he had every year he was away from home, Ben returned to Quapaw for the 1967 Christmas holidays. He was in his last year of Graduate School and preparing a dissertation entitled "Advanced Control of Radical Airfoils for More Highly Maneuverable Aircraft" for his Doctorate. As usual, he was ahead of schedule and permitted himself the luxury of leaving campus a few days early. Teresa squealed with glee when he showed up early at her parent's house, presenting her with a bundle of fat, red roses. They held each other for what seemed like hours, kissing frequently and as passionately as possible, considering they were not entirely alone.

"Teresa, my one and only-est love," Ben said with a grand bow and gush of blatant overacting, "would you and your parents like to come over to my parents house for Christmas Eve?"

Teresa giggled at the sight of Ben bowed so low his head was at his knees. "Ben, my one and only-est love, you had better stick to designing airplanes 'cause you'll starve as an actor!" She giggled at him some more. "I don't see any reason why we couldn't. We were waiting on you to get home so we could make Christmas plans."

"Well, plan no more, my sweet, because I have some great news to announce and I want everybody together when I make it!"

"And I suppose you are not going to tell me what it is until Christmas Eve?"

"That would be a big 'yes' my love."

"Benjamin Harris Hanson! I cannot believe you would torture me like this! You know how I am!"

Ben sneered at her playfully and laughed. He did indeed know how Teresa Rose Chandler was: a woman who could not stand having a secret kept from her. She had been known to vigorously shake wrapped gifts in an attempt to discover what the present or surprise was, then beg relentlessly to be told what it was if the shaking yielded no clues. At first, Ben would easily bend and tell her what her gift was. Later, he learned he could have great fun teasing her with it. More often than not, the teasing led to tickling and laughing, then to hugs and holding each other. Ben considered it a pure "win-win" situation. He still kept the secret and get in a little extra "close-time."

"Teresa?" Ben asked.

"What, you sneaky little butt hole?" She replied with an ornery grin.

"You know how to drive a Chandler girl crazy?"

"How?"

"Tell her you have a secret!" Ben began laughing.

"You ARE a little butt hole!" She announced with faux indignation. "Mom! Ben is being mean to me and he said he knew how to drive you crazy!"

"Why you..." Ben started chasing her around the living room. Teresa was giggling uncontrollably, when after one lap around the coffee table, she let him catch her. They were both laughing and giggling and as Ben had predicted, she began to tickle him and he returned the favor.

"Children, children, children!" Teresa's mother, Rose Chandler, exclaimed with a broad smile as she walked into the living room from the kitchen where she was preparing dinner. "Do I have to send you two outside?"

"Hi, Mrs. Chandler." Ben said while holding Teresa from behind as she tried to wiggle around for a better angle to tickle him.

"Ben was being mean to me! See? He won't let me go!

"Young lady, did I not hear you call Mr. Hanson a 'butt hole?'"

Teresa turned around to look at Ben, then snorted a laugh. "Well, he is!"

Ben pulled his arms back so that his hands had a firm grip on her waist, then playfully dug his fingers into what he learned long ago was Teresa's bull's eye for tickling. The sweet spot was just below her rib cage on both flanks. Her knees buckled as she began shrieking a combination of laughter and begging Ben to stop.

"Tell me you love me." Ben said while sticking his fingers into her soft and ticklish flanks.

"No, you butt hole!" She said, gasping for breaths between fits of laughter. Now rolled into a ball on the living room floor, she was trying to outmaneuver Ben.

"Go on, admit it. You know you do!" He saw that she was running out of breath and slowed the tickling down.

She rolled on her back, keeping herself at arms reach from Ben, laughing at the same time she was trying to catch her breath. She was wearing a bright red, knit sweater and blue jeans that fit her lovely figure just perfectly. Ben could never get enough of looking at her, constantly amazed at how beautiful she truly was, but it wasn't her beauty that captured his heart. It was her sweet soul, her boundless charm and wit, and her ability to bless Ben's heart with a gentle touch or the smile that betrayed her love for him.

"Ben Hanson, of course I love you! Somebody has to!" She stuck her tongue out at him.

"Mrs. Chandler?" Ben asked?

"Yes, Ben."

"Didn't you teach Teresa her manners?"

"Yes Ben, I did, but Teresa has a tendency to do things her own way. Ask her about her wild romp in the grocery store when she was three years old."

"No, mom! Don't tell Ben that story!" Teresa halfheartedly pleaded. She actually thought it was a charming story, but it was customary to act as if she didn't want it to be told.

"I'm all ears, Mrs. Chandler." Ben said while smiling at Teresa.

"My Teresa has always had a bit of a free spirit about her. One day, she couldn't have been more than three, we were in Miami at the grocers when I turned away from her for a moment to pick out some produce. When I turned back around, all I saw was her clothes on the floor next to the cart and her little bare rear end four aisles away running as fast as she could! To this day, I do not know how on earth she undressed that fast!"

Ben was howling.

"Thank you mother!" She said, continuing the facade of embarrassment. "Ben! Stop laughing! Don't encourage her!"

Ben leaned over and kissed her on the forehead. "You've always been adorable, haven't you?" He said softly.

She wrapped her arms around his neck and gave him a warm, lingering kiss. "I'm so glad you're home, Ben. I've missed you so much."

"I missed you, too, sweetheart."

Chapter 16

Christmas Eve in Northeast Oklahoma was a truly magical experience in 1967. The day before, a deeply penetrating arctic cold front collided with moisture-laden air from the Gulf of Mexico and the Pacific to produce a layer of freezing rain that coated everything with a thin but beautiful layer of shimmering ice. Eventually, the freezing rain gave way to snow and a solid 14 inches of it fell in less than 24 hours, turning the woods and farmland of the surrounding countryside into a scene worthy of display on any Yuletide greeting card. Even the monstrous chat piles took on the appearance of alpine peaks, giving the area somewhat of an Old World ambiance, if you were inclined to stretch an imagination or two. The small towns of Ottawa County sported festive holiday decorations and the townspeople were every bit as festive on the inside as their towns were on the outside. It was going to be a beautiful, if somewhat chilly, "White Christmas" this year!

Towards the end of the 1960s, crass commercialism had not quite buried its' fangs into the Holiday Season, but even after it did, "Small Town America" was still the place to go if you wanted to enjoy an intimate Christmas celebration. Lacking the hurried lifestyle that defined "metropolitan," small towns afforded the time and atmosphere necessary to allow neighbors to meet and enjoy one and another. Ben and Teresa were products of small town values and traditions. Both shared a genuine love for the Christmas season and the rejuvenation of family bonds that came with it.

When Ben awoke to the sight of a world turned beautifully white, his heart soared. What a wonderful backdrop for the "Special Announcement" he was going to make that evening! Ben had no trouble keeping his secret from his pathologically curious girlfriend, much to her chagrin. In fact, Ben told no one about what the subject of his announcement would be. After all, the only perfect secret is one you keep only to yourself. He busied himself with straightening the house for his mom and shoveling snow for his dad. He found a box in the garage filled with assorted holiday baubles, some dating back to well before he was born and even a couple that once adorned the beloved Christmas Trees of his parent's youth. He used them to finish decorating the house and the beautiful Douglas Fir that he and his father purchased three days earlier. Ben wanted everything to be perfect and he spent the bulk of Christmas Eve fretting over the smallest details, that is, when he wasn't opening the oven to savor the aromas of his mother's holiday cooking.

Teresa and her parents arrived at five in the evening and treated to a sumptuous turkey dinner with mashed potatoes, green bean casserole, thick homemade egg noodles, cranberry sauce and pumpkin pie. They ate until each felt as though exploding had become a tangible possibility.

"You know, Mr. and Mrs. Hanson," Teresa said as she was taking her plate to the kitchen. "Your son has been torturing me with this 'special announcement' secret of his since he got here. I bet he's going to say he's decided to wait until New Years to tell us. I think he likes being mean to me!"

"Ben," Paul Sr. asked with a grin. "Have you been mean to Teresa?"

"Yes, sir. I have." Ben replied from the living room.

"Thank you for being honest, Son."

"You're welcome, Dad."

"Mr. Hanson, you are not helping at all!" Teresa said, smiling and shaking her head. Teresa loved Mr. and Mrs. Hanson as much as she loved Ben. When she really missed Ben, she could always pop in on the Hanson's for comfort and a reassuring talk. In essence, they treated her like a daughter and she loved and respected them as she did her own parents.

"Bill, do you have any idea what this special announcement is?" Paul Sr. said, addressing Mr. Chandler in almost a whisper. The last thing he wanted was Teresa mercilessly teasing him about being as bad about secrets as she was.

"Not a clue, Paul. My guess it has to do with a job offer." He replied.

"That's my take on it, too."

"Attention, everyone!" Ben grandly announced from the living room. "Bring your eggnog into the living room, it's time to stop torturing Teresa!"

Teresa plopped on the couch in front of Ben. "This 'announcement' of yours had better be good for all of the mental suffering you have put me through the last several days!"

Ben warmly smiled at her while ushering the parents into the living room. What WAS he up to?

Both sets of parents seated themselves and without hesitation, Ben began his announcement.

"Merry Christmas!" He said cheerfully.

His audience heartily returned the greeting.

"Teresa Rose Chandler," Teresa froze at the words. She thought Ben's announcement was going to be something about him. Something he accomplished, or maybe he had already found a job. She should have known better.

"Two and a half years ago, my life changed forever. Where there had been sadness, there was joy. Where there had been loneliness, there was wonderful companionship. Where there had been terrible loss, there was a beautiful love to replace it with." Tears were beginning to well up in his eyes and his voice struggling to keep from breaking.

"You had to be a gift from God, Teresa, because no man could ever be worthy enough to be blessed as richly as I have been since you came into my life." Ben paused. "Into your gentle hands I present to you my heart, which has become completely and eternally yours. I shall never take a breath that doesn't belong to you. I will spend my days loving you and my sleep at night filled with dreams of you. All that I am and ever will be, is yours."

He knelt down in front of her and held her hands with his left hand while reaching into his shirt pocket with his right hand to retrieve the engagement ring he was hiding in his shirt pocket. Teresa, all but paralyzed, had tears streaming down her satin cheeks. She dreamed of this moment all her life, when her true love would ask her to marry him, but she didn't think it would happen until after Ben graduated.

"Miss Chandler, I cannot possibly describe how much I love you, but I would like to spend the rest of my life with you trying to find just the right words. Teresa, my only-est, will you marry me?"

Teresa was openly crying, as was her mother and Ben's mother. The men were, as the felt they had to be, stoic, with only a hint of excess saline in their eyes.

"Yes Ben," she sobbed "Yes I will!"

Ben slipped the diamond engagement ring, that he sacked groceries the past year to earn, over her left ring finger. "I love you, sweetheart!"

"Oh, Ben! You make me so happy! I love you, too!"

They fell into each other's arms and began soaking the left shoulders of their shirts in tears. It was the happiest moment of Ben and Teresa's life and it happened on a magical Christmas Eve, with fresh snowflakes falling from a dark gray evening sky... and love seemed to fill and overflow from a small wood frame home in the tiny mining town of Quapaw, Oklahoma.

Chapter 17

By the time Ben Hanson was in his last year of Post-Graduate Education, he had attracted quite a lot of attention from the aerospace community. His reputation as a problem solver of savant proportions made him a desirable rarity that every major and minor company in the industry coveted. Northrop, Boeing, Douglas Aircraft Company, General Dynamics, Lockheed-Martin, NASA... All were interested in the young genius and in the spring of 1968, each sent a high-profile representative to the University of Michigan in hopes of landing him. Inundated with requests for an audience, Ben graciously took the time to hear them all. The phone in his dormitory never seemed to stop ringing.

Marston, however, was biding his time.

At some point, Ben would narrow his choice to two or three companies, but in the end, Marston knew he would choose Lockheed-Martin. That is, if they offered him the Skunk Works. Marston had no doubt in his mind that is what they intended to do. Ben's talents would be completely wasted anywhere else. He would almost certainly bore with mundane projects that failed to challenge his impressive intellect. Any company lucky enough to land the soon-to-be Dr. Hanson would be foolish beyond belief if they plugged him into some entry-level cubical to design balsa wood gliders. Indeed, the Lockheed-Martin Skunk Works had the track record that would genuinely excite Hanson and Marston was certain that he would accept no challenge less than the absolute cutting edge.

The Lockheed-Martin "Skunk Works" was born in 1943 when the legendary engineer, Clarence "Kelly" Johnson, hand-picked engineers to design a super-secret jet fighter, the XP-80 or "Shooting Star," for the Army Air Forces. The German Luftwaffe was far ahead of the allies in jet and rocket-propelled aircraft and America needed to catch up quickly. Tasked to design a competing fighter built around the British "Goblin" jet engine, Johnson's crew was given 150 days to submit a prototype. Working nearly non-stop, they managed to complete the prototype one week early. Johnson's success, credited to his "no nonsense" and highly non-conformist organizational strategies, bypassed much of the ludicrous red tape that entangled bureaucracies and strangled efficiency to death.

The Skunk Works went on to achieve many revolutionary aeronautical engineering successes during the 1950s and 60s, such as the U-2A "Angel," the exotic SR-71 "Blackbird" and the utilitarian XC-130 "Hercules." These aviation marvels and their variants, engineered long before the invention of computer-aided design, would remain in service into the 21st Century. In spite of the impressive reputation and achievements of the legendary Skunk Works, what Marston was going to offer Ben Hanson was far more challenging than they, or anybody else could offer. If he were correct, Ben would instantly jump on the chance. He had always been right about Ben in the past, he would be right about him again. Still, it never hurt to stack the odds.

"Lockheed-Martin. How may I direct your call?" The all-business feminine voice announced.

"Lance Rylander, please."

"One moment while I connect you to his office."

"Lance Rylander."

"Lance, this is Art Marston."

"Dammit! I knew you were going to call! Dammit all to hell! The best talent available in the last 25 years and you're going to snatch him up for yourself!"

"I need him. He meets all the stability criteria, he's a certifiable genius and he may be the best natural problem-solver to ever surface."

"Well, I could use him, too. The stealth projects are starting to flesh out and he would be a hell of an asset. Have you seen his Doctoral Thesis? What in God's name am I saying? Of course, you have seen it! You probably know his mother's underwear size! Art, this kid could help us solve all kinds of aerodynamic and stability problems that are going to crop up in these stealth aircraft."

"I know you're disappointed, but my little project takes precedence over everything else."

"Yes, I know. I was just hoping you would keep your greedy little fingers off of him."

"Look, I am certain that Hanson would have jumped at a spot in the Skunk Works. So much so that I'll make sure something sizable rolls your way... as compensation for Lockheed's loss. If Hanson doesn't take the bait I toss at him, he's yours, and I'll see to that personally."

"You're just a regular Santa Claus, Art."

"Santa Claus could do wonders with just half our budget. It helps to have unlimited access to Uncle Sam's wallet."

"No amount of begging will change your mind, will it?"

"Not likely. I'm counting on this boy to bring a new perspective into the project. If he is the brilliant problem solver I think he is, maybe he'll shake things loose."

"Fair enough." Rylander replied with resignation, "Oh, by the way, any serious breakthroughs recently? It's been a while since anything has come off the top of your mountain."

"You know I can't talk about our work over the phone."

"Do you ever lighten up?" Rylander asked.

"Sure I do, son, but most of the time I don't have that kind of luxury."

Marston hung up the phone, then immediately dialed another number, a local one.

"Hello?"

"Mr. Hanson?"

"This is Ben Hanson."

"My name is Arthur Marston and I am a Special Project Manager for the United States Government. Your outstanding academic achievements have come to my attention and I would like to schedule a meeting with you in order to discuss employment opportunities within my project."

"That is very kind of you, Mr. Marston, but I have pretty much made up my mind as to where I'm going once I finish graduate school."

"Then congratulations are in order!" Marston replied without missing a beat. "You will enjoy working for the Skunk Works. They are a proud and distinguished group of professionals. You will do very well there."

"How did you know I chose the Skunk Works, Mr. Marston?" Ben asked, more than slightly shocked that a total stranger knew something that he had not told to a single soul.

"Just an educated guess, really. It is no secret amongst those who are trying to recruit you that Lockheed had the inside track all along."

Ben felt relieved. Mr. Marston just repeated the scuttlebutt on him and it happened to be correct. For a moment, Ben thought there might have been something kind of sinister about Marston.

"Might I ask a favor of you, Mr. Hanson?" Marston continued. "Before you officially commit to Lockheed, would you allow me the privilege to discuss with you, in person, the advantages and unique challenges of working in my department? You will find that our generous salary and family benefit package far exceeds that of our competitors. The research you will be involved in is much more challenging than anything our rivals can possibly offer you. Of that fact, you can be absolutely certain. Lastly, you will be serving your country and her vital interests in ways that you can scarcely imagine."

"More challenging than working at the Skunk Works?" Ben scoffed.

"As I said, Mr. Hanson, you can be absolutely certain."

"That is a very tall order, Sir." Ben scoffed again, only with measurably less conviction.

"Yes it is."

Ben hesitated. There were only two possibilities: This character was the biggest con artist to ever walk the planet, or he wasn't. If he wasn't, then what in the world was he working on? There was a solid confidence in Marston's voice that left him wanting to believe every word he said. A sociopath, Ben remembered from an Abnormal Psychology elective, can be just as convincing, but something inside told Ben that Marston was on the up and up. Even if he wasn't, Ben could always say "No."

"When would you like to meet, Mr. Marston?"

"I am already here in Ann Arbor. I can meet with you at your convenience."

"Can you be here in 30 minutes?"

"Less than that, if you require."

"Thirty minutes will do. Do you know where the Northwood One Single Graduate Student Housing complex is?"

"North Campus... Bishop Street at Beal Avenue, I believe."

"Apartment 1075."

"I will see you in 30 minutes and thank you, Mr. Hanson, for allowing me to discuss this opportunity with you."

"You're welcome, Mr. Marston."

Marston hung up the phone, then stood up from his hotel room desk and retrieved his heavy trench coat from the bed. It was a cold and windy March day in Ann Arbor and there was snow on the ground. Still, it was a lot warmer here than at the Cocheta Research Facility.

Chapter 18

Almost one week to the minute after the mysterious gentleman first contacted him, Dr. Alexander's phone began to ring. At this point, he couldn't be entirely sure of what he might be getting himself into, but what he had seen in the FedEx box was intriguing enough to warrant further investigation.

"Dr. Alexander speaking."

"Greetings, Dr. Alexander." The voice began. "Before we get started, I would remind you that the material you were given is highly classified. For your protection it would be best if we did not speak in specifics over the phone."

"Agreed." Dr. Alexander replied, experiencing ever-increasing doubts as to the wisdom of what he was doing. "Highly classified?" "For your protection?" This is going to get out of control! Yet, Alexander felt as if he were a moth mesmerized by a bright flame. Alexander's instincts told him that it might be professional suicide to proceed, but the hard-core scientist in him wanted, no... needed to learn more.

"I trust that the material I sent to you was satisfactory."

"It was."

"Would you care to see more?"

"I would."

"Have you spoken to anybody about this?"

"Only to inquire about the feasibility of setting up a live television broadcast of my show, otherwise I have not."

"Good... Listen to these directions carefully. You need to drive your personal vehicle to Las Vegas Saturday next. Travel with nothing other than your driver's license, sufficient cash to pay for 2 days worth of expenses to include gas, food and cab fare... and bring a change of clothes. Under no circumstances will you have a pager, portable GPS, or cellular phone on your person, or in your car, outside of the Los Angeles area. Do not bring a debit or credit card. Since you will be traveling through the desert, I recommend servicing your car accordingly and that you carry 2 or 3 gallons of water. Wear dark sunglasses and a hat at all times to obscure your identity. Park your car at the MGM Grand and at 9:00 P.M. catch a cab to Harrah's Casino. Stand outside the Casino in the shopping mall area with your hat and sunglasses on. I will contact you there."

"Noted." Alexander replied.

"Any questions?"

"No."

"Then I will see you on Saturday next."

"Very good."

"Dr. Alexander?"

"Yes."

"This will be well worth your trouble."

"I'm certain it will be."

The phone went dead. "He was worried about me being followed!" Alexander thought, a new wave of dread coursing through his body. If he's worried about me being followed, the caller was almost certainly being followed.... but he has to know that! This is not a stupid, careless man. He must have devised some way to evade the people following him, or they would have shut him down after the first call and thrown me into the pokey. The situation was starting to seriously encroach on his better judgment and Alexander began to toy with the idea of not showing up to this surreptitious Las Vegas appointment. He began to sort through all the endless reasons why he should run like hell from it, but none could hold a candle to the reason why he shouldn't. If what he had seen and read was not an elaborate hoax, then he was obligated as a scientist, and a human being, to bring these discoveries to the forefront of the collective consciousness of mankind. To do anything less would be to betray his profession and more importantly, his species.

Chapter 19

Ben was pondering the meaning of the brief phone call from Arthur Marston while he tidied up his small apartment. What could be more challenging than working to develop cutting-edge aircraft technologies? Space? He had already talked to a representative from NASA. The Apollo moon missions were just around the corner, a space station in the works and a reusable shuttle in the planning stages. It was certainly a good time to be an engineer involved in America's Space Program, but Ben would be only one of countless NASA engineers working on dozens of ongoing projects. The Skunk Works offered a more intimate working environment where Ben felt he would have a far better chance to contribute in a meaningful way. Besides, he would be working elbow-to-elbow with some of the most brilliant minds in his field! Ben felt greatly honored when Lockheed's Chief Engineer took the time to fly to Ann Arbor and personally offer him his dream spot in the Skunk Works. The only reason he didn't accept the position right away was because he promised to himself, to Teresa and their future children, "mini-Hansons," as Teresa once referred to them, that he would listen to all comers. After all, he was going to be a family man soon.

So, Mr. Marston was a government official recruiting a soon-to-be PhD in Aerospace Engineering... and the job he had available was "much more challenging" than working on the most advanced technology developed by America. The only thing he could think of was that Marston might have Soviet technology that he wanted him to pick apart. That would hardly be a challenge. The Soviets had smart scientists, to be sure, but during World War II, they only stayed in the ballpark of aviation technology by stealing three American B-29s, then copying them to create the Tupolev Tu-4. They became an early nuclear superpower by acquiring America's weapons secrets from treasonous scientists of the likes of Klaus Fuchs. They may have become America's greatest rival, but they are certainly not our technologic superiors, or even our equals. No... Assessing Soviet technology is not likely to be what Marston was talking about.

Then it hit him.

"If the technology is more challenging than ours and the Soviets... No, that can't possibly be it!" His mind was beginning to shift into high gear. There MUST be another explanation, but as hard as he tried, he couldn't come up with any other possibility. "I'm missing something, because this just can't be possible!"

A knock on his apartment door interrupted Ben's frantic thinking. It was Marston. He walked over to door and hesitated. He needed some kind of strategy, but none was forthcoming. Maybe he should just let Marston recite his sales pitch. Perhaps he'll say something that would confirm or dispel his disturbing new hypothesis. Ben, somewhat reluctantly, opened the door.

"Ben Hanson?" The man asked. Ben saw that he was an older gentleman; perhaps early 60s, about Ben's height of six foot, with a medium-heavy build, but that was hard to judge underneath the heavy trench coat. He was wearing a conservative, and mildly out of style, charcoal gray felt suit hat that likely experienced 10 or more winters. He reached out his right hand to shake Ben's; in his left, he sported a medium sized leather briefcase.

"Mr. Marston." Ben replied, reaching out to shake the man's hand. "Nice to meet you and please come in. Can I get you something warm to drink?"

"I'm fine, thank you." Marston said, removing his trench coat and hat. Ben took his outerwear and stored them in a small closet near the door's entrance.

"Please have a seat and make yourself comfortable."

Marston sat down on Ben's small sleeper-sofa that comprised the bulk of seating places in his small living room. Ben pulled a wooden chair from his dining room table and sat down in front of Marston.

"Mr. Hanson, I want to thank you again for allowing me to discuss the open position in my department that you are so well qualified for."

"I have to say, Mr. Marston, I am very intrigued by your claim that the position you would like me to fill is more challenging than working at the Skunk Works."

"It is not an empty boast, Mr. Hanson. To be sure, your research will not only be immensely challenging, it will be vital to the National Security of the United States."

"What, exactly, would I be doing?"

"The precise details are highly classified, Mr. Hanson. In order to brief you more completely on the project, you must formally commit to working for us."

"That is a lot to ask for, Mr. Marston. I'm going to have a family soon and I need to be able to make an informed decision concerning something that sounds like it will have a great impact on family life."

"Mr. Hanson, I am going to be very blunt with you. I have been following your academic career since you were in high school. I was right about you then and I am right about you now. You possess the most valuable mind to emerge in this country for at least the last quarter century, not because you have the highest IQ in the land, but because of your amazing ability to solve complex problems. Somehow, your mind is hard-wired to be far more flexible than the rest of us linear thinkers. You seem to use altogether unique approaches to problem solving. All of your academic evaluations comment on this ability and it is this great analytical gift you possess, along with your emotional stability and belief systems, that make you the perfect candidate to work on our team."

Floored by what Marston had just said, Ben took a few moments to respond. "Mr. Marston, you seem to know quite a bit about me."

"For National Security reasons, you, your fiancé and your immediate family have been thoroughly checked by the appropriate federal law enforcement agencies. It was critical to do this before I could offer you a position."

Marston could see that Hanson was somewhat angered by the invasion of privacy he and his family were blissfully ignorant of, so he decided to change tack.

"Mr. Hanson, I have already taken the liberty of securing a new home for you and your fiancé in a very nice neighborhood of young families. I have also arranged for your wife to finish her Bachelor of Science Degree in Nursing at a respected University in the town that you will live in. Your salary will be roughly $125,000 per year, with full medical and dental benefits and 4 weeks paid vacation per year. A generous pension plan is also part of the package. You will work for two weeks at the research facility then you will be off for two weeks. You will have your own furnished office and access to a comprehensive library of relevant books and current journals. You will have free reign to perform any tests and conduct research as you see fit. If the facility does not have a piece of equipment you desire, I will personally obtain it for you as quickly as possible. Our annual budget is more than sufficient to cover your research expenses. You will be able to stay current in your field by periodically attending professional conferences. On occasion, at a moment's notice and at any time of the day or night, I will send you on what we call a "field trip," where you will conduct highly important data gathering. Recreational facilities at the research facility are first rate, as is the apartment that you will live in when you are on a 2 week rotation."

The change in tack had the intended effect. Ben could hardly believe his ears! The salary was astronomical for an entry-level aerospace engineer in the late 1960s. The benefit package, home, college for Teresa, unlimited research budget... He never dreamed such a windfall was even remotely possible! His new family would have more than enough to start out on. The work schedule had its' positives and negatives, but certainly nothing close to a "deal-killer."

"Mr. Marston, your offer is more than generous." Ben stated, trying to hide his shock. "What about security measures for me and my family? My research would seem to involve highly classified national defense projects. Naturally, I would want assurances that my family is under protection at all times. Also, I'm still uneasy about not knowing anything about the research I will be doing."

"Clever boy, got me into a little corner! He's fishing for a piece of the puzzle and trying to get me to admit that his family will require protection." Marston thought to himself.

"Security for you and your family will begin from the moment you agree to become part of the team." He said aloud, "It will be ever present, but for all intents and purposes, invisible." There wasn't much he could do about that one. Lie to him, and he accepts the position, he never trusts project management again.

"As far as precise details of your job description, I cannot divulge that information without a commitment. If you accept my offer today, I am prepared to fly you to the project site immediately to begin your briefing. You would be back in Ann Arbor by Sunday evening."

Ben took a moment to rethink. It is defense-related, but really can't be the Soviets. That still left him with his "disturbing" hypothesis as the only possibility. The protection would be needed to prevent an enemy from kidnapping a project scientist to extract information, or a family member to use as leverage. Ben decided to test the hypothesis. Perhaps Mr. Marston's reaction might prove useful in solving the mystery.

"Mr. Marston, will I be involved in the reverse engineering of extraterrestrial technology?"

"Mr. Hanson, I'm am not in a position to answer that question." Marston said without pause, his facial expression betraying nothing. "The conditions pertaining to obtaining any further information prior to employment are not negotiable."

"Oh my God!" Ben thought, feeling a mix of triumph over figuring out Mr. Marston's little "secret," and horror that an obviously advanced alien species was visiting the earth. Marston could have said "no" if that were not the case, without compromising what the project was really all about. Instead, he avoided any kind of answer. Now he had to make a decision, but really, what options did he have? There is no way he could turn Marston down! To work on extraterrestrial technology was beyond fantastic! Almost as amazing was the fact this Marston character was going to pay him handsomely for something he might otherwise do for free just to be part of an elite team unlocking the most incredible secrets in all of human history.

"Mr. Marston."

"Yes."

"Take me to see this 'project' I'm going to be working on."

Chapter 20

Kevin Loeffler thumbed through the project shift schedules for the last ten years, noting that Dr. Hanson had not taken any time off during that period, that is, until the last month. Hanson's reputation as a tireless worker was legendary, but even Loeffler, another avowed workaholic, could not fathom going that many years without a real vacation. So, why is he taking a vacation now? Hanson requested, and was granted, two blocks of leave, giving him ten consecutive weeks off. That certainly was not suspicious. Many project staff members had done that over the years, but it did represent a distinct change in Hanson's usual patterns. Humans, like most animals, have predictable patterns of behavior. Changes in habits, schedules, or lifestyles, especially abrupt ones, might be a sign that malfeasance is brewing. Hanson was well into his third week of his ten weeks off, yet he had not left Las Vegas at all. Not only that, his tail lost him a total of three times now, two of which were at the same time, on the same weekday, one week apart. Coincidence? Loeffler didn't believe in coincidence. Only fools chose to ignore patterns early on and Loeffler was no fool. In times past, Loeffler's predecessors might have summarily dismissed Hanson's subtle changes in behavior. After all, Hanson was a likable, well-respected sort of guy. He was the last one anybody would ever suspect of espionage. Loeffler laughed inside at the notion. The one holding the handle of the knife sticking in your back was ALWAYS the last person you suspected.

To get a better feel for his behavior, Loeffler needed to chat with the "Specialist" assigned to Hanson. It might even be necessary to assign more personnel to cover Hanson's movements. If he was up to something, Loeffler would get to the bottom of it, then stomp on him like a cockroach. Traitors were, in fact, lower than cockroaches in Loeffler's mind. He spent too many years serving the people of his country, watched too many colleagues die in the line of duty and suffered through two divorces from wives who could not endure the domestic fallout of his job, to tolerate treason. Anybody who would compromise the security of the United States and her citizens for money, or some flaky political belief… any reason for that matter, deserved less compassion than he would dispense to a cockroach.

Since Hanson was on leave, the only security action Loeffler could take was to increase the level of surveillance on him. Their little "get-to-know-you" chat would just have to wait. In the meantime, he would scour Hanson's personnel record, phone and cellular logs and his bank account statements for any clues that might shed light on these variances in a usually well-ordered, predictable life.

Chapter 21

The plain white G-1159 Gulfstream II executive jet was parked in the General Aviation area of the Ann Arbor Municipal Airport. Other than the registration number N528MH, there were no other markings on the aircraft. At the base of the jets' staircase were two large men, both dressed in black and very warm looking trench coats. They were utterly expressionless as Ben Hanson and Arthur Marston walked up the stairs and entered the cabin of the small jet. Ben had never been in an executive jet and the butterflies in his stomach were beginning to feel more like a stampeding herd of buffalo. They each hung their heavy coats in a compartment behind the cabin entrance and took seats facing each other at the front of the aircraft on the port side. There was a hardwood, fold-a-way table between them and across the aisle lining the starboard side of the cabin, a relatively narrow bench seat. Behind them were two sets of facing seats identical to theirs. The seats were wide and luxurious, made of the softest shale-colored leather. Ben was certain they would wrestle consciousness away from him if he let his guard down. The two men Ben figured to be a security detail entered the aircraft, closed and secured the cabin door, then took seats at the very back of the Gulfstream. Within moments, Ben heard the twin turbofan engines whine to life, causing a noticeable increase in buffalo activity in his gut.

"Are you OK, Mr. Hanson?" Marston asked, sensing the tension building in Ben.

"I'll be OK, Mr. Marston." Ben replied with as much stoicism as he could muster. "It's just that I've never been in a jet before."

Marston laughed. "Mr. Hanson, you have enough education to design aircraft that can fly circles around this one! You'll be just fine. To be honest, I know how you feel. I had a plane shot out from under me during World War II. Hadn't been all that crazy about getting back into them since. By the time we get back here on Sunday, you'll be a seasoned veteran."

"Can you tell me where we are going?" Ben asked, fully expecting a refusal to his request.

"Project Cocheta Research Facility in British Columbia. That's where you'll be working. 'Cocheta' is an American Indian word that means 'That you cannot imagine.' Not sure who originally came up with that name for the Project. Very fitting, though."

Ben thought for a moment. Mr. Marston didn't hesitate to answer his question. Perhaps he could find out a little more. He had said little since Ben had agreed to join the team, only explaining the highly classified nature of the research and had him sign a document that swore him to secrecy. Lastly, he signed a document that informed him of the terrible duration of imprisonment, even the possibility of capitol punishment, if his mouth came loose at the hinges.

"Mr. Marston, I was right, wasn't I? I will be working on extraterrestrial technology."

"Son, I have prepared a complete briefing for you at Cocheta. All of your questions will be answered, I assure you." Marston paused to look straight into Ben's eyes. "You are a member of the team now, Mr. Hanson. You are entitled to know most everything there is to know about the project. As of an hour and a half ago, you are even on the payroll. In fact, we have already deposited a paycheck into your checking account. It is an advance on your salary through July 1st, 1968, less taxes. The sum was, I believe, $16,250. You should have more than enough to treat your fiancé to a very nice wedding, honeymoon, and obtain new, reliable transportation for the both of you. The short answer to your question, however, is 'yes,' you will be working on extraterrestrial technology."

To think something is one thing, to hear it is quite another. Hearing Marston confirm his "disturbing" theory was unsettling. The increased whine of the turbofans signaling the beginning of the takeoff roll made the uneasiness even worse. Several seconds passed before the Gulfstream rotated and made what Ben's stomach could have sworn was a perfectly vertical climb. A few minutes later the sleek business jet leveled out to a northwest cruising altitude of 28,000 feet. It wasn't until then that the blanching of Ben's knuckles and fingertips began to subside.

"You'll get use to it. Trust me!" Marston said with a knowing smile.

Ben just shook his head.

"Tell me Mr. Hanson, what do you know about 'flying saucers?'"

Ben looked at Marston for a moment, wondering why he chose to use the words "flying saucer." That term in the scientific community was one you only used in jokes, usually to belittle the subject or anybody who believed in them. The term "Unidentified Flying Object" of "UFO" was somewhat more acceptable, scientifically. It was unbiased in the sense that it simply labeled an aerial phenomenon not readily identifiable as just that: unidentified. It was also a superior term because it did not refer to commonplace dinner-ware. While the American military was the first user of the acronym in 1952, it would take nearly 20 years before the term "UFO" gained a wider public acceptance. Some believed that the "U" in "UFO" should stand for "Unexplained," others thought "Unconventional" was more appropriate. There were even those who came up with very elaborate definitions of what constituted a UFO. An astronomer and UFO investigator by the name of J. Allen Hynek once wrote that:

"A UFO is the reported perception of an object or light seen in the sky, or upon the land, the appearance, trajectory and general dynamic and luminescent behavior of which do not suggest a logical, conventional explanation, and which is not only mystifying to the original percipients, but remains unidentified after close scrutiny of all available evidence by persons who are technically capable of making a common sense identification... if one is possible."

Because the definition was very difficult to memorize, let alone pronounce, "Flying Saucer" would suffice for most people to encompass anything weird in the sky. Since Ben was a science child of the 1950s, when the flying saucer hysteria was at its' wildest, it was perfectly natural for him to believe in them. What fledgling young scientist didn't believe? He spent many a night wondering if, or when, little green men were going to climb through his window and haul him off. Sometimes he would sit in his backyard and watch the night sky in hopes of seeing one.

One of his all-time favorite movies was the 1953 release of H. G. Wells' War of the Worlds. It both fascinated, and frightened him... terribly. Soon after seeing it for the first time, he retrieved the novel from the Miami Library and literally read it non-stop. Ben found the previous Century's style of writing somewhat difficult to follow, which made the non-stop read even more of an impressive accomplishment. The book was quite different from the film, the former set in the late 19th Century England, the latter set in 1950s Los Angeles. The Wells novel painted an eerie mental picture of invincible Martian war machines perched upon a tripod of mechanical legs, with "articulate ropes of steel dangling from it," decimating the English town and countryside with their "heat-ray."

"Forthwith flashes of actual flame, a bright glare leaping from one to another, sprang from the scattered group of men. It was as if some invisible jet impinged upon them and flashed into white flame. It was as if each man were suddenly and momentarily turned to fire."

The movie, however, depicted the war machines as more or less disc-shaped objects that moved around on barely noticeable tripod beams. They blasted the popular landmarks of Southern California with a deadly combination of spark-emitting "heat-rays" that sprayed from the altogether creepy, three-eyed periscope and the green "skeleton ray" that flashed from their wing tips, turning hapless humans into skeletons before becoming a handful of ash on charred ground. In the end, both book and film ended with mankind pummeled to the very brink of extinction, saved at the last moment by the pathogenic microbes that literally coat everything on the planet. Hanson later came to realize that the microbe most likely responsible for killing off the Martians was a strain of Salmonella served routinely in the dormitory cafeteria at the University of Oklahoma. In any case, H.G. Wells was certainly well ahead of his time. Ben began to wonder if Wells would prove to be a far better prophet than he was a novelist.

"Well, Mr. Marston, I really don't know that much about them because, up until about two hours ago, I didn't believe in them. You know, Special Theory of Relativity and such. Seemed like such an insurmountable problem. I guess Einstein was wrong and all the weirdos were right."

"Trust me, Ben... Is it OK to call you Ben?" Ben nodded. "The weirdos are still wrong and Einstein is still mostly right. The highbrow physics stuff is way out of my league, I'm afraid. I am a people and systems manager by trade. My job is to make sure things get done and sometimes to make sure things don't get done. I also recruit the best of America's best intellectual talent so that we can analyze every aspect of the data we receive. Essentially, I oversee the entire project. That's why you may hear some refer to me as 'The Foreman.'"

"How did we come across alien technology in the first place?"

"Apparent mishaps, catastrophic system failures... a few were simply abandoned." Marston said matter-of-factly. "They didn't leave any blueprints or instruction manuals, however. That's where you come in."

It was all starting to sink in, now. "This is unbelievable! Alien technology! Do you know where they come from? What do they look like..."

"Whoa, Ben." Marston interrupted. "By the end of he day, you'll have a clear idea of what we are up against. For now, enjoy the ride. I need to call ahead and make some arrangements."

Marston unbuckled his safety belt and made his way to the fore section of the Gulfstream. Ben's mind was running rampant. He had a million questions he wanted to ask but didn't know which ones to start with. He leaned his head against the window and stared at the sea of white, cottony nimbostratus and stratocumulus clouds below him and the wispy cirrus clouds above. The blue sky between was the most vivid he had ever seen. In the span of a few hours his life had radically changed. The world, no... the universe had become much smaller. An alien civilization, or perhaps civilizations, were paying visits to earth and learning that fact was akin to having a profound religious experience. In one brief moment of disclosure, the way he looked at the daily business of human beings was forever changed.

Ben naturally began to wonder what the aliens were up to. Marston said, "...what we are up against." That had a very ominous tone to it. Were we at war with them, or preparing for a war with them? What do we know about their capabilities? If we went to war with them, would we stand a chance? The questions bubbled to the surface of his consciousness at a frenzied rate. This job he so impulsively accepted… Impulsivity was not something that Hanson gave in to very often, but what do you do when someone offers you a position that you simply cannot decline? He decided to give himself a pass on that one. To turn down such an offer would have been sheer lunacy.

More questions quickly arose, questions about the all-too-possible and quite disturbing consequences of his recent actions. What would Teresa think? Other than his parents, she was the most supporting soul he had ever met, but was he making assumptions he probably should not? We'll have to relocate to whatever town Marston wants us to move to. Will she be OK with that? The secrecy issues… will Teresa be comfortable with not knowing anything about what her husband did for a living? "Damn!" He thought, "I should have talked to her first." Even if he had, what would he have been able to say? Ben closed his eyes and tried to clear his head. What was done was done. If he had screwed up, he had only himself to blame. He longed for Teresa's gentle touch and counsel at that moment, wishing she could help him make the transition to this new and perhaps terrible reality. He was certain of only one thing, that a lot more of his questions would have answers before the end of the day.

Before long Ben succumbed to the power of the soft, otherworldly comfort of his leather seat and aided by the sedative effects of lower oxygen tension in the cabin. He was sound asleep by the time Marston returned from the fore section of the cabin with a ham sandwich and a bottle of Pepsi for him. "The boy's had a big day so far." Marston thought to himself, "If he only knew how much bigger it was going to get."

Chapter 22

Ben awoke to the whining sound of flaps lowering to the 10 degree position on the Gulfstream's wings. Looking outside the cabin window, he immediately noticed that the jet was considerably lower than it had been. Underneath an almost cloudless blue sky was a vast expanse of deep forest wilderness and small, glacier-carved mountains in every field of view. Numerous streams and small rivers passed beneath the jet, marking the valley bottoms between crops of mountains. He could make out the location of smaller streams by the discontinuity of the forest canopy. Small to medium-sized lakes were plentiful in the area, peppering the landscape with deep blue liquid jewels. There were also irregular patches of snow-covered land that broke the monotony of trees at the lower elevations. The sight was breathtaking and quite unlike anything he had ever seen before.

"We're well into northern British Columbia, traveling northwest." Marston said.

Ben was startled, momentarily. He had not realized that Marston was watching him. "I'm sorry I fell asleep, Mr. Marston."

"Nothing to worry about. These jets have a way of lulling people to sleep. Do you see that ridge of small mountains just to the left of our direction of travel?"

"Uh huh."

"Cocheta is in the valley, about halfway through. It's fairly high up, almost 4000 feet above sea level... and it's cold. We should be on the ground in about 3 minutes."

"It's beautiful out here."

"Yes it is."

The jet banked slightly to the left and followed a valley between two mountainous ridges. The tops of the trees were very distinct now, causing Ben to increase his grip the armrests. A few moments later, the Gulfstream banked to the right, making an almost 70 degree turn to the north. With a short-duration whine and a noise that sounded like a car running over a couple of large rocks, the landing gear deployed and the flaps extended to 20 degrees. Though well versed on every control surface on the aircraft and the smallest nuance of the physics that allowed it to fly, Ben's grip on the armrests tightened even further. Off to his left was a mountain peak towering about 1500 feet above their current altitude. Pressing his head against the window, Ben could barely make out the southern tip of the runway. The jet was traveling much slower now and Ben could see most every detail of the snow-covered ground below him... and it was rising fast. Not surprisingly, so was his heart rate. The jet made small adjustments to line-up with the runway and a few moments later, a tall, razor wire fence raced underneath the aircraft followed by the dark gray runway threshold in bold contrast to the cotton white ground. The nimble jet angled its' nose slightly upwards then seemed to float over the runway. "Ground effect," Ben thought, his heart banging away inside of his chest wall. Then, with a pronounced "thump," the two main landing gear touched down followed a few seconds later by the front landing gear. As the pilot engaged reverse thrust, Ben watched the passing of the black runway distance markers. Each sported a contrasting white, single-digit number that indicated how many thousands of feet remain before the end of the runway. (6)000... (5)000... (4)000 (3)000 feet... the plane slowed to a pace, turning left onto a short, perpendicular taxiway, then turned left again onto the main taxiway that paralleled the runway. At the midpoint of the main taxiway, the jet turned right on a much wider and shorter taxiway led to a large tarmac with only one building on it. Ben noticed something else as the aircraft taxied: Marines. There were United States Marines guarding the research facility!

As soon as the jet slowed to a stop, Ben anxiously started to unbuckle his restraint, but Marston motioned him to remain seated. The two large men in the rear stood up and walked to the cabin door. The lead man unsecured the cabin hatch, pushing it downward and deploying the integrated staircase with apparent ease. By that time a brand new, plain white International Harvester Travelall approached the jet, along with a squad of very serious-looking Marines on foot, each carrying an M-14 rifle. A well-insulated fellow exited the Travelall and made his way to the aircraft. Marston stood up and motioned Ben to do the same. The two silent passengers exited the aircraft, followed by Marston and Ben, both donning their heavy coats as they walked down the stairs.

It was definitely cold outside, Ben thought, realizing that he would have been a bit more comfortable if he had put his coat on while still inside the jet. Ben decided that he needed to seriously rethink his wardrobe now that he was going to be working in a place where brass monkeys routinely lost the equipment to procreate. The scenery, however, was awe-inspiring enough to temporarily distract him from the chill in the air. From where Ben stood there were mountains at every compass heading. If one looked to the south, you could readily make out the short valley the jet had just traversed on final approach. To the north the valley continued, gently sloping upwards between two mountain ridges that curved to the northwest. What Ben saw to the west of the airfield, however, was nothing short of astonishing. The mountain to the west was more like a long, somewhat tortuous ridge with a steep eastern face. Not more than 500 yards from the center of the airfield, recessed into the solid rock of the mountain, was a building of monstrous proportions. At first, the building reminded Ben of a large aircraft hanger, with what appeared to be an immense door, offset to the left of center, that moved laterally to expose what was inside. The door was three-quarters of the height of the building and at least a fourth of the width. Unlike a conventional hanger, the construction appeared to be entirely made of concrete, with the exception of the huge steel door. There were no windows to be seen anywhere on the building, but there was a long, gray-steel balcony, perhaps it was an observation deck, connected to a door two or three stories above the ground just to the right of center. Ben quickly estimated the width of the building to be at least 1000 feet, based on visual clues provided by vehicles parked near the building. The building was rectangular, with a length-to-height ratio of about four or five to one, making the estimated height to be about 200 to 250 feet. Large, long horizontal beams protruded at regular intervals from the solid rock overhanging the building. The beams supported a heavy wire mesh that, Ben surmised, was for catching boulders that might fall from the mountain. No doubt, there were regular inspections and preventative "grooming" of the mountain face to identify and remove loose boulders that might pose a hazard to the project members below. There were two smaller, but structurally similar buildings in the mountain wall further to the northwest, roughly 100 feet from the large building, and 100 feet apart from each other. A small number of standard-sized doors were visible, and each building had what appeared to be a cargo bay. The paint on all three buildings matched the moss green that was naturally abundant in the area, with no visible markings of any sort observable from Ben's vantage point. Dozens of Marines scurried about airfield and tarmac with purpose, as if preparing for something.

The man from the Travelall walked up to Marston and began shaking his hand.

"Art, glad you're back in one piece." The man said. "Oh, and congratulations on your successful recruiting trip."

"Ben," Marston said, stepping back to allow Ben to come face to face with his colleague, "This is Charlie Brogan. He is the Deputy Chief of the Cocheta Research Facility.

"Pleasure to meet you, Mr. Brogan." Ben said, reaching out to shake the man's hand.

"Mr. Hanson," Brogan said, grasping Ben's hand, "the pleasure is all mine, I assure you! We have been anxiously looking forward to you joining our team for quite some time now."

"Thank you, sir. I am very honored to be here."

Brogan turned to Marston. "Art, the busy little Rooskies at Plesetsk boosted another

Zenit-4. Flyby is about 90 minutes from now. We're going to roll the Gulfstream into the hanger."

"Mr. Hanson, my good friend here, Mr. Brogan, has just informed me that a Soviet spy satellite will be passing more or less overhead in about an hour-and-a-half. We like to tidy-up a bit by making all of the people, cars and airplanes disappear before it gets here. I doubt it fools them, but keeping the size of our force hidden from the enemy is sound military doctrine. Now, let us get on to the reason that you are here. We have a complete briefing arranged for you, but rather than make a bad first impression by burying you in paper, I would like to show you something that will put everything that follows into perspective. Please come with us." Marston motioned Ben to get into the Travelall.

A few minutes later the Travelall pulled into a marked parking area in front of the largest of the three buildings. When Ben stepped out of the vehicle the full scope of the massive building became apparent. The doorway was just 10 yards or so to the right of the mammoth door that Ben suspected would be opening soon to provide shelter for all who sought refuge from the nosey reconnaissance satellite soon to pass overhead. Ben noticed that the opening of the huge structure was thirty feet inside the gargantuan, man-made cave, probably to decrease the chance that a spy satellite might get a good view of it. The building itself was so tall that Ben wondered how effective that tactic really was. A satellite crossing northwest to southeast, at angle of 45 degrees or so, should get a nice shot of the lower half of the door. Some cover is better than none at all, Ben guessed. He had no way of knowing that the first military spy satellites were launched well after the completion of the structure he was analyzing. The designers were actually concerned about high altitude reconnaissance aircraft discovering what was inside the mountain.

Ben looked around him and noticed that there were only a handful of exposed buildings on the installation, and with the exception of the small concrete airfield building, the others were essentially wooden sheds. There was, however, a sizable number of low profile, camouflaged concrete structures with long, narrow openings on all four sides. They appeared to be bunkers... or pillboxes. Ben wasn't sure of the military terminology, but it seemed clear to him that they were fortified, defensive positions placed in an arc in front of the building complex and staggered in such a way to make a frontal assault on the facility an act of suicide. Just in front of these structures were the two lakes, adding another huge hurdle to overcome if one were insane enough to attempt a raid. The runway was located approximately 100 yards from the outer edges of the lakes. A thick, razor wire hedgerow ran along its' entire outer length making an arc at each end of the runway to join the mountain roughly 400 yards from the edge of the outermost buildings. An inner razor wire hedgerow paralleled the outer, separated by 250 yards of completely barren land. This was almost certainly a "kill zone" Ben guessed and it probably contained thousands of land mines, too. Only an overly wide taxiway from the airfield allowed unimpeded access to the complex, assuming of course, that all the Marines in the bunkers covering the taxiway were doing needlepoint during an attack. To top off the facility's defenses was a battery of MIM-23 Hawk surface-to-air missiles located at each end of the runway. Several Marines were hurriedly camouflaging the tracked vehicles that carried three, sixteen-foot pure white missiles each. The radar vehicle, located towards the middle of the airfield, had Marines camouflaging it, as well. It was more than evident to Ben that Project Cocheta was well prepared to keep unwanted guests away from the front porch.

The door into the main building had no Marines guarding it. In fact, it didn't even have a lock on it. Brogan opened the door for Marston and Ben and followed them inside.

"Mr. Hanson," Brogan said, "this is our hangar and receiving area. It is large enough to accommodate a Boeing 707 with plenty of room to spare. In fact, the brand new Boeing 747s they're starting to build in Everett will easily fit in here, too."

Ben was awestruck by the enormity of the chamber. "You could FLY a 707 in here!" Ben thought to himself. The horizontal depth of the building was at least 500 feet, perhaps even 600 feet. Enormous steel support frames arched to the distant, heavily braced, corrugated metal ceiling above. Attached to this huge framework was a colossal hoist system of movable girders that could easily lift heavy objects and move them to any point within the large chamber. Square pods of high-wattage mercury vapor lamps mounted on the ceiling evenly illuminated the hangar. Ben couldn't remember seeing any power transmission lines coming into the facility so he made a mental note to ask about that. Aviation support equipment was everywhere, along with a multitude of small carts, a forklift here and there, and palates of building materials and supplies neatly positioned next to the north wall. At the rear of the hangar was literally a building within a building, spanning from the south wall to perhaps halfway across the artificial cavern. It was about four stories tall and without windows. It also had an unusually large door in front that appeared, at least from a distance, to open and close much like a conventional aircraft hanger does. In contrast to the unguarded door they just passed through, the small door next to the very large one had two M14 toting Marines standing guard and that was the direction they seemed to be heading.

"I thought you might like to take a look at what we have in this building first." Marston said. "Oh, Charlie, do you have a pass for Ben?"

"Of course." Brogan replied reaching into his coat pocket to retrieve a royal blue, clip-on ID card with "VIP" written in bold white letters. "Here you go, Ben. Clip that on to your coat just below your left collar bone."

"Thanks." Ben said while reading the fine print on the card. "Project Cocheta Research Facility V.I.P. Pass, Unauthorized use of this pass is punishable under Title 50, Chapter 23, Subchapter 1 of the US Code and can result in a fine up to $5000 and/or imprisonment up to one year." Ben clipped the card onto his coat, the meaning of the word "Cocheta" hitting home. This truly was a place one could not possibly imagine.

"The first name proposed for the Project was the 'Foreign Aerospace Technology Evaluation and Reverse Engineering Project,' or 'FATEREP.'" Marston began, "The acronym was very accurate in its' description, but not very catchy. Military types really like clever acronyms and this one was neither clever nor did it roll off the tongue with ease. None of the other proposed acronyms were any better. Someone came up with 'Project Cocheta' and it was eventually deemed a clever enough name with its' vague, mysterious meaning. We even have a nice, unofficial logo." He said, pointing a finger at a large, circular wooden plaque hanging on the north wall to their right. In the center was the cartoon character who would eventually be known as Marvin the Martian, wearing his usual attire of green tights with a thick, gold plank tutu, matching Roman Centurion-esque gold helmet topped with a stiff bristle floor brush, white tennis shoes and holding a pair of smoking silver ray guns. His furrowed white eyes were glaring out of a featureless, black marble of a head. "PROJECT COCHETA" was centered above the famous cartoon Martian and "Tu Vis Mihi Valde Furio" centered below.

"That is hilarious!" Ben laughed at the logo. "I'm afraid I didn't take much Latin in school... What does it mean?"

Brogan looked at Ben with a smile and said "You make me very angry!"

They all laughed. The sign always brought a smile to Marston's face and it looked as if the kid appreciated the humor, at least the cartoon and quotation part of it. In fact, the logo had a much darker side to its' humor. "No sense in pointing it out to him now." Marston thought, "He'll get the rest of the 'joke' when he reads the Heischler Report."

A few minutes later, they reached the building, and the two Senior NCO Marines guarding it.

"Gunny Sergeant Hoyer and Staff Sergeant Wickert, how are you doing today?" Marston asked.

"Very well, sir!" Hoyer replied with standard issue Marine Corps enthusiasm.

"Same here, sir!" Wickert said just as smartly.

"May I see your IDs please?" Hoyer asked.

Brogan and Marston unclipped their badges and handed them to the formidable Gunnery Sergeant. Ben was fumbling with his, finding his fingers were nervously clumsy.

"This is our new Aerospace Engineer, Ben Hanson." Marston said. "He'll start work in July."

Ben handed his visitor pass to Hoyer.

"I see... Can I please see a picture ID?"

"Yes sir." Ben said, reaching for his wallet.

"Do NOT call me sir! You may call me 'Gunnery Sergeant Hoyer' or 'Gunny Sergeant Hoyer' or 'Gunny.' I am NOT a 'sir!'"

Ben looked as if caught shoplifting. "I'm sorry sir... I mean Gunnery Sergeant Hoyer." All the color had left Ben's face. He managed to get a hold of his wallet, but was having trouble with the fine motor dexterity needed to negotiate the recess that contained his driver's license. Then came the loud metallic bang that signified the opening of the massive outer door of the complex. The noise startled Ben and he dropped his wallet on the floor, several cards and IDs spilling out of it. Ben came about as close to urinating on himself as one can without actually doing so.

"I'm sorry, sir, really! I mean Gunny. Damn!" Ben bent over to pick up the mess he had created. Hoyer looked at Marston and Brogan with a stern face; then gave them a wink. They both fought off laughs as they shook their heads.

"Here's my ID." Ben said sheepishly. The groan of the opening door was becoming loud enough to be obnoxious.

Hoyer looked at his badge and ID for a few moments. "Everything seems to be in order." He handed the cards back to Ben and opened the door. Marston entered first, followed by Ben.

"Don't touch anything, son!" Hoyer said to Ben as he walked in.

"I won't, sir." Ben replied, not catching himself fast enough.

"Do you have trouble understanding the English language, boy? Do NOT call me "Sir" again!" Hoyer barked loudly.

"I won't sir, I mean Gunny!" By that point, Ben was totally whipped. Brogan grabbed his shoulders and ushered him into the building, smiling at Hoyer and shaking his head. When the door closed behind them, Hoyer and Wickert had themselves a grand laugh.

"Gunny, that boy almost shit himself!"

"It was too easy. Like hunting deer at a petting zoo!" Hoyer said. Undoubtedly, Hoyer and Wickert would repeat the story at the chow hall and all would have a great laugh. Each Marine who heard the details would be reminded of their first hours of basic training at Parris Island or San Diego and how a drill instructor with impossibly bulging neck veins, screaming at the top of his lungs a mere 2 inches from your face, could make you feel like you were about to soil your underwear.

The three stopped a few feet into the spacious building. Ben was still fumbling with his wallet when Brogan let go of his shoulders. He looked up as he was attempting to place the wallet back into his pants. The wallet hit the floor, spilling its' contents once again.

What Ben Hanson saw at that moment rendered him utterly and completely speechless.

Chapter 23

Dr. Alexander thoroughly enjoyed the drive to Vegas. The weather was nothing short of perfect for a 300 mile, top-down desert drive in his 2004 Corvette convertible. He left early enough to take his time, stopping in Barstow for lunch, then easing his way through the Mojave Desert at only the speed limit. Seventy miles-per-hour in a car capable of speeds approaching 180 would seem exceedingly boring to a sports car enthusiast, but Alexander was in no hurry and he did not want any entanglements with the law before he had a chance to commit what was likely to be some sort of felony that evening. If this "mystery man" he was going to meet in Vegas that night was under surveillance, it might be impossible to avoid "entanglements." Whatever fate awaited him in Las Vegas, while driving there, he was going to clear his mind and enjoy the freedom of a loose schedule and not having a cell phone ringing constantly.

As he was standing in front of Harrah's Casino, wearing a ridiculous black cowboy hat and dark sunglasses, waiting for his meeting with a man who would likely hand him irrefutable proof of the existence of extraterrestrial visitation, Alexander marveled on how life had so dramatically changed for him in the last 2 weeks. Alexander was a scientist in the classical sense, demanding overwhelming proof before he would sign his name to any theory trying to become or replace a scientific "fact." That was not to say that he had a closed mind. Quite the contrary, as he had tried to impart to his undergrad students not quite two weeks before, Tim Alexander was famous for his open-mindedness. However, just because a scientist is very careful about proclaiming something impossible, does not mean that he necessarily believes that "something" is possible at all. Indeed, what could more illustrative of that than the question of alien visitation? Alexander never said he did not believe in extraterrestrial life. After all, life on other worlds was a mathematical certainty. Privately, he did not believe that aliens were visiting the earth now, or ever likely would. The distances were too great and the physics required to effectively "shorten" those distances too improbable. For years, he had used the "Faster-than-Light" and other similar lectures to try to instill scientific open-mindedness in his students. Yet, at any moment, a man would arrive to shatter his own private narrow-mindedness. As excited as he was about learning more of this amazing truth, Alexander couldn't help but feel like a bit of a hypocrite.

"Dr. Alexander." A voice behind him said, startling Alexander from his thoughts.

"Yes." He replied, turning around to view the source of the voice. The man was about 5 feet 10 inches tall, maybe 145 pounds. He was older, perhaps early 60s, wearing an Arizona Cardinals ball cap, dark sunglasses, blue jeans and a red T-shirt that had a "mule playing a slot machine" caricature on it with the caption "I Lost My Ass at Harrah's!" below. Alexander guessed that the man purchased the shirt within the last few minutes to aid in slipping his tail, that is, if he had one. Alexander hoped like hell that he did not.

"Please come with me." The man motioned to Alexander to follow him towards a cab waiting on Las Vegas Boulevard. There was plenty of Saturday night sightseers, gamblers, street people, hucksters, porn peddlers and drunks to negotiate before they reached the waiting cab. Undoubtedly, the crowd was part of the mysterious stranger's plan. The man opened the cab door for Alexander, then walked around the cab to enter in the opposite side.

"The Orleans please. Take a long route, if you don't mind." The stranger said to the cabbie.

"Sure thing, buddy." The cab driver replied. "Couple of fruits I got here." He thought in bigoted disgust. The older one was quite the gentleman, though. A real "lady's man!" The cab driver laughed inwardly at the thought. He had been a cab driver in Vegas for 12 years and picked up all kinds of weird twosomes. He could not recall ever seeing a fruit open a cab door for another fruit. "Who said chivalry was dead!" He thought with another hidden laugh. He'll have to tell his brother-in-law about this one.

The cab made quite a circuitous route to the Orleans Hotel and Casino on West Tropicana, taking 45 minutes to arrive at a destination that was only a 15 minute drive in the worst of traffic. The stranger did not attempt to start a conversation. The only sounds he did make were occasional salvos of a hacking cough, which he tried in vain to suppress. Alexander followed the cue and remained silent throughout the after-hours cab tour, as if Las Vegas actually had an "after hours."

They arrived at the Orleans a shade past 10:30PM. The stranger paid the cab fare, plus a very healthy tip that pleased the cabbie immensely.

"Hey, you two can ride in my cab anytime! Just call the number here and tell the dispatcher you want Stan to pick you up!" The cab driver yelled to them, pounding at the telephone number painted on the side of his cab as they began walking away. The stranger just nodded without turning around. For fruits, they weren't very lovie-dovie. Fruits or not, business was business and he'd haul those two to the Wedding Chapel of their choice AND be the Best Man if there was a big fat tip in it.

They entered the casino, making their way through the banks of one-armed bandits to the main tower elevators. After showing his hotel pass to the security guard at the elevator entrances, the silent man and Alexander boarded an elevator destined to the upper half of the hotel. Once inside the elevator, alone, the stranger broke the silence.

"Sorry for the silly, clandestine spy routine, Dr. Alexander. An unfortunate necessity, I'm afraid. My name is Benjamin Harris Hanson. You can call me 'Ben.'"

"I've been looking forward to meeting you, Ben. I recognize your name from one of the reports you sent to me. If I remember, I believe you had a 'PhD' after your name. You can call me 'Tim' by the way."

"Thanks for coming, Tim, and thanks for stepping way out on a limb like this. Oh, here we are." The elevator reached the 10th floor without stopping, the door slid open and Hanson exited left with Alexander close behind. "Room 1004." Hanson announced as he inserted the card key into the lock. After two failed attempts at unlocking the electronic dead bolt, a third attempt, done almost precisely the same way as the first two, resulted in the welcome, flashing green LED. They entered the thankfully empty room and took off the silly hats and sunglasses they were wearing.

The room was spacious enough, having a standard compliment of hotel furniture consisting of two queen-size beds, television, chest-of-drawers, a table, and a small sofa with matching chair. The bathroom was not shabby, either. The only thing not obviously part of the décor was a plain 12x12x24 inch cardboard box on top of the far bed. Since the hotel was huge, yet not located on the famous "strip," Alexander surmised that the rates were probably more than reasonable. In Vegas, they practically gave rooms away, counting on the guests to shower their casinos and shops with the bulk of their life savings. Like everything else that could be bad for you, Las Vegas was harmless... if taken in moderation.

"Tim, please, have a seat." Hanson said, starting the coffee machine. Coffee and cigarettes had become the chemical alpha and omega of his very existence. Up until 1992, Hanson was essentially vice-free, except for over-indulging in hard candy, much to the pleasure of his pirate-of-a-dentist. Hanson swore Dr. Arkov would have made a much more realistic sadist in the Little Shop of Horrors than the fictional Drs. Orin Scrivello or Phoebus Farb. That particular year, 1992, was the most difficult of Hanson's life. He lost the bulk of his soul and his zest for life that year, replacing it with the familiar loneliness of his youth and a pair of chemical vices, one of which would end up killing him in the not to distant future. The ever-increasing pain in his chest and the searing discomfort of every cough was a constant reminder of how much he had lost. If all went well, eight days from that night he will have made good on an old promise and, perhaps, changed the course of human history. Then, and only then, would he allow himself to die with some measure of peace.

Alexander took a seat on the small sofa, and Hanson to the chair across from him. Alexander noticed that Ben Hanson looked almost gray in appearance and would have been surprised to know that his new acquaintance was 15 years younger than he looked. When he coughed, the grimaces on his face spoke volumes. He had said that he was "not a well man" and Alexander was guessing that Hanson understated his condition by a fair amount.

"The coffee will be ready in a few minutes, if you want some." Hanson said, then he leaned forward, a much more serious look came over his face. "Tim, I have been working for the government since 1968, the year I obtained my doctorate in Aerospace Engineering from the University of Michigan. The program is highly classified, even higher than the Manhattan Project and it has been in existence since 1947. Unlike the Manhattan Project, which involved many different contractors, laboratories and Universities, Project Cocheta utilizes a hand picked think-tank of sorts to discover the secrets of extraterrestrial technology. The project is located in the northern British Columbian wilderness at a joint US and Canadian site called the Cocheta Research Facility, or CRF."

For the next three hours and an equal number of coffee pots, Dr. Alexander listened in stunned silence as the ill man before him explained, in marvelous detail, what he had been doing for the last 40 years. He also described the contents of the box, which both electrified and horrified Alexander. Hanson answered all of his questions and elaborated on his grand plan to release the information to the world, both the good and the bad. Alexander listened carefully to the details. His show was to play a vital part in the dissemination of this world-changing knowledge and Hanson made it very clear that secrecy was paramount. If anybody learned of this plan, the wrong sort might catch wind of it, shut it down and toss everyone in prison. Alexander was none too keen about the prospect of going to prison, but he already made up his mind to press forward many days before. The future of civilization might very well hang in the balance. What is one Theoretical Physicist compared to that? Who knows, maybe he could still do his science show from behind bars.

"Tim, do you have any questions?" Hanson asked.

"No, I know exactly what I'm supposed to do." Alexander replied. "One week from tomorrow night. It's a tall order, but I've been told I have the clout to pull a live broadcast out of the Science and Technology Channel's ass."

Hanson laughed. "I have always admired your show, Tim. It is obvious that you enjoy teaching and your reputation for fairness and open-mindedness is legendary. I couldn't think of anyone better to entrust this project to. When this is all over, you will become a very controversial man. Some may even accuse you of treason. You up to it?" Hanson smiled.

"Sure, I suppose the truth is worth it. Besides, controversy can only be good for ratings."

Hanson laughed again. "Take care of yourself. Oh, don't forget these, Tex." Hanson handed him his cowboy hat and shades.

Alexander donned his "disguise" and started for the door, the still sealed box cradled in his left arm. "You do the same."

Tim Alexander stepped out of Hanson's hotel room and made his way back through the glaring lights of the casino and to the hotel entrance where a cab was already waiting for him. Ten minutes later, he was placing the precious box into the trunk of his Corvette at the MGM Grand. A Corvette convertible trunk is barely big enough to squeeze in a small narrow suitcase and Alexander was worried that the box might not fit. He really did not want to put it into the passenger seat in case he was pulled-over by the police. In many a patrolman's eyes, Corvettes and other high-end sports cars were breaking the speed limit even when they were waiting at a traffic signal. His fears about the trunks' suitability were unfounded, but not by much, as the rear deck lid closed without any substantial pressure on the valuable cargo.

It was definitely not a "top-down" drive back to Los Angeles. Deserts were freezing cold at night; then add a 70 mph wind to it... No thanks! Top up, heater on, and maybe listen to the AM band, where he could entertain himself through the wee hours of the morning listening to pseudo-scientists, new-age spiritualists, abductees and other assorted nut cases talk as though they really believed what was coming out of their mouths.

Alexander's mind frequently drifted back to his conversation with Dr. Benjamin Harris Hanson. He was certain he would never see Hanson again. At least not alive. The man was sick and he wasn't taking very good care of himself. Alexander had nothing but the utmost respect for him. He was a very gifted man. His entire life was devoted to quietly serving America and advancing scientific knowledge in an area of research extremely important to all of mankind. Yet, only a handful of people on earth knew of his contributions. What was his reward? Losing everything that was dear to him! If Tim Alexander had anything to say about it, the legacy of Dr. Benjamin Hanson would be boldly chiseled into the masonry of the human race.

Chapter 24

Loeffler had no doubts, now. Hanson was up to something and his gut feeling told him it was big. A week earlier, he assigned a second "specialist" to assist the primary and placed additional listening devices in his home and BMW. The bugs picked up nothing except the usual household sounds of the television, garbage disposal, toilet flushing, benign phone conversations and a lot of coughing. "Got a bad case of bronchitis from all that chain smoking." Loeffler thought, never considering the hacking might represent something far worse. He made a few trips to the supermarket, ate dinner at The Tillerman one evening, then made a single stop at Blockbusters. Not a hint of anything out of place, even on Friday, the day Loeffler fully expected Hanson to do something out of the ordinary. He had done so the previous two Fridays, which alerted Loeffler to a potential pattern change. By Saturday morning, Loeffler dismissed the second specialist, allowing him to be with his laboring wife.

That turned out to be a huge mistake.

Not more than three hours later, Hanson opened the garage door and went for a drive into town. That, in and of itself, was not a huge concern. What became troubling was when Hanson went into the upper-level, Sears entrance to Meadows Mall... with a medium sized box that he retrieved from the trunk of his BMW. His specialist had no trouble tailing him in the mall where Hanson milled about, only stopping once to make or answer a cell phone call and order a fat pretzel. He took the pretzel and stood next to the wall to the right of the bakery. He propped up the box next to him on the white tile wall near the Mall exit and leisurely nibbled on the pretzel. Suddenly, Hanson grabbed the box and headed out the exit door, depositing the half-eaten pretzel into a wastebasket. Outside, a cab was waiting to spirit him off. The specialist ran to the door in time to see what kind of cab it was and jotted down its' number. He scrambled across to the opposite side of the mall and into the parking lot in front of Sears where he and Hanson parked. There was an outside chance that Hanson would take the cab back to his car, so he waited in his for several minutes while placing a cell phone call to his boss.

Loeffler was furious. He ordered the agent to hold his position while he contacted the cab company to find out where the cab had taken Hanson. With any luck, the cab would still have Hanson in it. There was, however, a huge problem. The cab company would not give Loeffler the information he sought, at least not at first. A phone call to the Las Vegas Metropolitan Police Department was required and several precious minutes evaporated while the information request, made by Loeffler's LVMPD contact, worked its' way to the Vegas Adventure Cab Company. A full 20 minutes passed from the time Hanson ducked out of the mall to the moment Loeffler learned that the cab dropped-off Hanson at the Citizen's Area Transit Route 211 Bus Stop near Michael Way and Smoke Ranch Road. Loeffler relayed the information to the waiting agent while he pulled up a map of the Citizen's Area Transit Bus routes on the Internet. "Damn!" Loeffler said out-loud. The 103 Route on Decatur Boulevard is very near the Michael Way bus stop and it runs right back to the Mall! This posed another serious problem for Loeffler. Hanson could be doubling back to pick up his car, or he could be catching a bus along any of the four other routes that were within a short walk. He was too far away to be of any help, so he had to make a decision on where to deploy his only asset. For someone with absolutely no training in this sort of thing, Hanson was very good at ditching a tail.

Loeffler elected to send his asset to the bus stop. Hanson probably guessed his car was trackable, so doubling back to the mall didn't make much sense. No, Hanson was catching a bus somewhere. The question was: which bus to follow? That area of Vegas was a small tangle of bus routes and stops. The permutations were endless and Hanson was very, very smart. Smart enough to use the one permutation Loeffler was not likely to think of.

The "specialist," a former FBI agent named Dawson Wingate, raced to the bus stop, hoping that Hanson would still be there when he arrived. Of course, he was not. Entirely too much time passed since Hanson gave him the slip. Time to park and see if he could find somebody who might have seen him. Basic crime scene investigation one-oh-one, locate a witness who saw the suspect, ascertain the suspects' direction and mode of travel, then attempt to stay on his tail by locating other witnesses along his direction of travel. Much easier said than done, considering Hanson "...could be halfway to Palm Springs by now!" Loeffler yelled at him in frustration when he barked at him to start tracking Hanson at the bus stop. Of course, unless Scotty beamed him to Palm Springs, Hanson had, at the most, barely enough time to reach the city limits of Las Vegas. He parked his car at a vacant lot on the corner of Smoke Ranch Road and Apricot Lane and started his investigation by asking three elderly women at the west-bound Route 211 bus stop if they saw an older gentleman carrying a box get into a bus. None had, as they just arrived there, so he ran across the street to the east-bound bus stop. There was a young man dressed in the inexplicable "Gangsta" fashion of the day, holding a skateboard in his lap and apparently waiting

for the next bus.

"Excuse me," Wingate said, "did you happen to see an older man here a little earlier carrying a box?"

"Yo, Dawg. I seen him 'cross da street 'bout 30 minutes ago walkin' dat way." He said pointing his finger west. "You Five-Oh?" The kid asked,

"No, just need to keep an eye on him. Thanks!" Wingate began jogging west on Smoke Ranch Road.

"No big, Five-Oh!" The kid laughed. Who was he kidding? He knew a cop when he saw one!

Wingate quickly reached the bus stop at Smoke Ranch Road and Winwood Street. One young Hispanic woman with a small child said she thought she saw a man carrying a box walk past a little while earlier, turning right at the next intersection to the west, North Jones Boulevard. Thanking her, he quickly ran to the intersection and looked to the right. Three or four hundred yards away, Wingate noticed a north-bound CAT bus stopped... and there was Hanson boarding it! Not that he could really make out Hanson's face from that distance, but the clothes matched what he was wearing earlier and he was carrying a box. Wingate knew he would never catch it on foot, so he began to sprint back to his car while speed-dialing Loeffler on his cell phone.

"Loeffler speaking."

"I got him!" Wingate said with an airy voice consistent with talking and running at the same time.

"Where?"

"He's on the 102 Route heading north on North Jones. I'm running back to my car so that I can catch up to the bus and watch where he gets off."

"Hold where you are, Wingate! The bus doubles back just a few miles up the road. Wait at the nearest south-bound bus stop on North Jones... Let's see... at Cartier Avenue and board it. If he's on it, stick with him. The 102 Route comes to within a mile-and-a-quarter of Meadows Mall. He may still be trying to double back to his car for some reason. If he's not on the bus, then get off at the next stop and head back to your car. I'm on my way to the area now. Keep me posted."

Wingate turned around and walked back to North Jones Boulevard to wait at the Cartier Avenue stop. It made sense to wait for Hanson's bus to return, but his gut feeling told him that he would not be on it. Hanson was much too clever to return to his car. No, he was getting off the bus somewhere north of here. If he were Hanson, he would catch a cab after getting off the bus. Carrying that box made him too easy to remember, but then, why was Hanson carrying around a large box, anyway? Surely, he was smart enough to figure out how visible that made him. Wingate's "cop sense" was tingling. Something was amiss, but he couldn't quite grasp what it was.

The bus returned to the area about 45 agonizing minutes after it left. If Ben wasn't in the bus, the chances of finding him would greatly diminish. Wingate entered the bus, paid his $1.25 fare, and made a quick scan of the passengers. There, all the way in the back, was Hanson! He was leaning against the window with his baseball cap on and his head tipped down, as if taking a nap. The box was under his left arm. Cap, tee shirt, box... It was Hanson, all right. Wingate quickly took a seat near the front of the bus and dialed Loeffler.

"Leoffler speaking."

"I'm on the bus with Hanson."

"Good job! Where are you at now?"

"Southbound on North Jones, coming up on Lake Mead."

"I'm about a half-mile behind you. Call me when he gets off the bus. We need to have a talk with Dr. Hanson about violating his security agreements."

"Yes sir." Wingate ended the cellular call.

The bus made its' way all the way down to the Tropicana Avenue bus stop before Hanson stirred to exit the rear door of the vehicle. Wingate speed-dialed Loeffler.

"He's getting out at Tropicana Avenue."

"Roger that. You get out too. I'm pulling into the filling station just behind you."

"He's off the bus... and heading your way." Wingate stood up to exit the front of the bus.

"Come in behind him and I'll step out in front of him."

"Roger." Wingate replied. "Ben Hanson was in for a big surprise!" Wingate thought to himself.

Loeffler made his move first, stepping out from a phone stall to block Hanson's path. This was going to be Kevin Loeffler's first face-to-face meeting with Dr. Hanson, that is, if the man in front of him had actually been Ben Hanson.

"Damn!" Loeffler yelled loudly, stopping in front of the man pretending to be Benjamin Harris Hanson. "Wingate!"

"What's wrong?" Wingate replied, jogging the last few steps to where his obviously furious boss was fuming.

"Hey!" The unidentified man said. "Are you the two dudes I'm supposed to be playing a joke on?"

"Wingate, does this look like Hanson to you?"

Wingate stared in disbelief. The man was wearing Ben's hat and tee shirt and in his arms was the same size box Ben was carrying in the mall. "No sir. All I saw was the cap, shirt and box and assumed he was Hanson."

"You guys don't look very happy." The man said. "Are you cops or something? Am I in trouble?"

"No, sir, you are not in trouble at all, and we're not cops." Loeffler said, changing the tone of voice. "Can you tell us where you met the character that pulled this joke on us. We'd like to play a little joke on him."

"Sure. I was standing near the bus stop at North Jones and North Rancho when the 102 bus pulls up and this older guy, kind of sickly lookin', coughin' and shit, gets out, comes up to me and asks me if I want to earn a quick 200 bucks, in cash! 'Damn straight I'd like to make 200 bucks!' I told him. Well, this town is full of nutballs, and some things just ain't worth $200, if you know what I mean." Wingate and Loeffler smiled and nodded in agreement, sending a subliminal signal for him to go on with his story. "He says 'No, it's not that sort of thing.' Then tells me he's playing a joke on someone and all I have to do is wear this tee shirt and cap that's just like his, and carry this empty box. He told me to get on the same bus he got off of when it comes back the other way, grab a seat as far back on the bus I can, then act like I'm asleep with my head down so people couldn't see my face. You know, like the bums do when they sleep on the bus sometimes. It sounded like a little fun, and I sure needed the 200 bucks. He told me I needed to get off here, too. He said you guys would laugh real hard when you found out it wasn't him. He also said you'd give me 50 bucks if I done a good job. You look pissed, not happy."

"He got us good, that's for sure." Loeffler said, looking at Wingate, who winced at the remark. "The box you have there, was that the only one he had?"

"Nope, he kept the box that was inside this one."

Loeffler and Wingate looked at each other. Hanson was good. No, Hanson was brilliant! Loeffler even felt a surge of... admiration? He had thoroughly embarrassed both of them. He knew he had a tail and he toyed with the security agents just as a cat plays with helpless mice. "Ben Hanson, we really need to have that heart-to-heart talk." Loeffler thought.

"Did you see where he went when he left the bus stop?"

"Yep. He walked down a block and right on Foxcroft."

"Mr. Wingate, would you say this gentleman did a good job fooling us?"

Wingate looked down. He would never live this one down, and put the odds of keeping his job at about 20%. "Yes sir. He did a very good job."

"Well then, pay the man!" Loeffler said with faux jocularity.

Wingate retrieved three of the four $20 bills from his wallet. It was all of the cash he had on hand. "Here's 60 bucks. I included a 10 dollar tip."

"Thanks!" The man replied gleefully. "You all are not going to be too hard on this guy, are you? He don't look too well."

"We won't. Thanks for the great sport!" Loeffler replied, motioning for Wingate to follow him.

They headed to Loeffler's black-project issued, Mercury Metallic Lexus LS 460. Wingate knew it was best to keep his mouth shut unless Loeffler asked him something, which he genuinely didn't want him to do right now. They both entered the vehicle in silence. Loeffler fired up the 380 horsepower V8 and gunned the nimble sedan into the traffic heading north on South Jones.

"He's long gone, you know." Loeffler said, breaking the uncomfortable silence.

"I know." Wingate replied.

At the very same moment, only one mile to the east of Loeffler and Wingate, the 104 CAT Bus was arriving at the stop located on Cameron Street at West Tropicana Avenue. Ben Hanson casually stepped out of the bus with his precious cargo and made his way into the south entrance of The Orleans Hotel and Casino.

Chapter 25

Ben looked in mute awe at the machine before him. It was a real, no-kidding, completely intact example of extraterrestrial aerospace technology! The craft was easily 40 feet in diameter and roughly 9 to 10 feet tall at its' thickest. It was more or less discoid in shape, with more mass above its' rim than below. The machine was gunmetal gray in color and had a most unusual satin sheen to it that made focusing on its' surface very difficult. At first glance, the color of the craft appeared to be solid. On closer examination, slightly lighter gray oval "spots," about ten inches in diameter, were visible and evenly spaced along the objects' rim. There were no windows, protruding antennas, intake or exhaust ports, vents, insignia, control surfaces, or much of anything else, for that matter. There were no rivets, seams, welds, joints, bolts, or other visible method of attaching one part to another. It did however, have landing gear and a hatch. The landing gear consisted of three, presumably retractable pads mounted on astonishingly small diameter rods that extended into the fuselage through slight recesses in the lower hull, allowing the pads to make a perfectly flush fit. The landing gear kept the object about five feet above the floor. The hatch reminded Ben of a wedge of cheese cut from a much larger discoid piece of cheese. It was about 3 feet wide at the edge, two feet at the upper hinge located ten feet towards the center of the disc. A four-foot deep portion of the lower hull was part of the upper hatch, allowing the lower half of the hatch to serve as a ramp. There were no struts, hinges, or hatch reinforcements seen.

"It's... it's incredible! Do you mind I get closer?" Ben asked almost sheepishly.

"You can play in it if you want!" Marston said, laughing.

Ben walked briskly to the craft instead of running. He didn't want to seem, well, giddy or childish. Yet, that was exactly how he felt. When he reached the rim of the object, he touched it with the palm of his hand. It was unusually cold, considering the warm ambient temperature of the building. It was also the smoothest surface he had ever encountered in his life. It felt as if the skin of his hand were numb, or maybe floating on a thin, impenetrable barrier of air that prevented the skin from actually making contact with the metal below. The effect was unsettling. As hard as he tried, Ben could not grip the surface of the hull.

"This is very strange." Ben said. "The surface is colder than the room and it's so smooth I can't get my fingers to stick on it! It must have some kind of ultra-smooth coating or it is flawlessly polished right down to the molecular level!"

"Nothing sticks to it." Brogan said. "Believe me, we've dumped everything on it. Molten sugar, epoxy, burning rubber, peanut butter... It all slides right off."

"Good technique for reducing drag." Ben said, gliding his hand over the rounded rim of the alien craft, attempting to decipher the secrets of this remarkable technology by feel. "It does have an airfoil, of sorts." He continued, "The upper hull is more dome-shaped and the lower hull is significantly flatter. Airflow creates lower pressure where air travels faster over the longer distance created by the dome. The pressure differential creates lift. Discs are notoriously unstable, though... No vertical stabilizer... No control surfaces..." He paused for a moment and looked under the craft. "No exhaust ports or thruster nozzles... Mr. Marston, I don't think this is a spaceship."

"We don't either, Ben." Marston confirmed. "We think these variants are brought here in something else and are specifically designed to fly in our atmosphere."

Ben stopped for a moment. "Variants?"

"There are a handful of confirmed variants."

"Here?"

"Yes, however, most are recovered wreckage. This craft is our showcase specimen. We acquired it 10 months ago in the Quebec wilderness."

"Bodies?"

"Not from this craft, but yes, we do have bodies. Most are in pretty bad shape."

Ben's blood chilled considerably and his skin felt as though thousands of tiny spiders were crawling to and fro just below the surface. He would see the bodies tonight, no doubt. This very first evening on the job was quickly shaping up to be the most bizarre of his entire life. Halloween was coming a little early this year.

Ben continued to slowly walk around the rim of the craft, saving the open hatch for last. "Thrust vectoring." Ben said. "No control surfaces or stabilizers, so it must use some kind of thrust vectoring for maneuvering and stability."

"Go on..." Marston said, encouragingly.

"It picks a direction, then draws air around it in such a way to create both lift and thrust. Hmmm... The desired leading edge would naturally tilt in the direction of the induced flow to reduce drag... Wait a minute, what kind of power source does this thing utilize?"

"We're not sure Ben." Marston said, shrugging his shoulders. "We know it must generate unbelievable amounts of power, but we have yet to figure out what the source of that power is. One other thing... and this little item has produced a great deal of controversy here... even if we did know what the power source was AND we knew how to light it up, should we? This craft was abandoned and as far as we can tell, it is completely intact. Some think it might be booby-trapped. If we turn it on and the power plant goes nuts, would we even know it? Worse, would we be able to stop it? The nuclear physicist on the team has proposed all manner of exotic power sources, from fusion to harnessing the power released from the annihilation reaction between matter and anti-matter. So, the question is: If the power plant detonates, will it vaporize this mountain, or a quarter of the planet?"

Ben shook his head. "Maybe neither. Didn't you say you had wreckage? What kind of damage occurred to the surrounding area in those circumstances?"

"Some just made impact craters, others detonated in the air, leaving debris fields on the ground, but no massive damage to the area. Some believe the Russian Tunguska detonation of 1908 was due to a catastrophic power plant failure on one of these vehicles. Others say it was a comet. Whatever it was, it flattened a serious parcel of prime Siberian real estate. We thought about the possibility that we were seriously overestimating the destructive force of a power plant failure, but the other side of the coin is that the creatures that pilot these craft may have, perhaps by some automatic mechanism, neutralized the power source before impact or detonation. It sounds highly improbable, but who really knows what is possible and impossible any more. And the fact remains, we still don't know for sure whether or not the intact craft has been booby-trapped."

"I see your point." Ben replied. "There are no visible means of propulsion on this machine, so it must use some sort of external means. Thrust vectoring without thrusters... I remember hearing about some ongoing research by a Swedish Electrical Engineer... name starts with an 'A'... like 'Alvin' or something similar... Hannes Alfvén! That's his name! Anyway, he is working on something he calls 'magnetohydrodynamics.' Basically, you move charged particles with an electromagnet to create thrust. Seawater, plasma, and liquid metals could be used. Maybe this vehicle creates plasma around it by using enormous heat to strip oxygen and nitrogen of electrons, then it contains the plasma and vectors its' discharge in the opposite direction of travel with a highly powerful, dynamic and controllable magnetic field. It would require an enormous amount of energy to do that and I'm guessing it's probably louder than hell with all of the electrical crackling and popping...

unless they found a way to baffle it." Ben passed a hand over one of the faintly lighter gray oval areas on the smooth rim of the hull. "Bet this has something to do with it. These probably superheat the air to create the plasma. They would be white hot, maybe even look like a row of lights, or windows, after dark. Come to think of it, the plasma around the ship might make it appear to be glowing at night."

Marston and Brogan looked at each other in silence, each knowing exactly what the other was thinking. Ben Hanson, not quite 21 and not quite a PhD, just spent ten minutes looking at extraterrestrial technology for the first time and produced a plausible theory on how it worked. Marston felt a great deal of satisfaction at that moment. He had subtly and sometimes not so subtly manipulated Hanson's life to get him to come to Cocheta. He also invested a great deal of time, energy, and an unholy sum of taxpayer cash to make sure it happened. Watching Ben Hanson pick apart every detail of that machine made the whole effort worthwhile.

Ben took a closer look at the landing gear, amazed at how small in diameter a single strut was. "The metallurgy on this craft must be phenomenal. That strut is no bigger around than my little finger, yet it supports... Do you know how much this thing weighs?"

"Eleven thousand, nine hundred sixty one pounds... with a full tank of gas." Brogan said with a grin.

Ben smiled and shook his head. He was going to have fun working here. "I thought it would weigh a lot more. Still, these tiny struts are supporting a tremendous amount of weight and they are straight as an arrow. What kind of metal is this?"

"The hull and most of the other parts of the ship are made of a strange alloy of titanium mixed with a handful of other known metals." Marston said. "The individual metals are not unusual. After all, the Periodic Table of Elements should be universal no matter what planet you're from. It was the method in which they were combined that makes the alloy so strange. We simply can't duplicate it and we've tried every conceivable way except, of course, the correct one. It is lightweight, unbelievably strong, but not so strong that it can completely contain a power plant explosion or a high-speed impact."

"Incredible!" Ben said, continuing his inspection of the craft, taking his sweet time getting to the hatch, which he found himself mortified by the very thought of entering it. "The whole craft looks like it was sculpted from a single piece of metal."

"Ben, the construction of this vehicle is nothing short of fantastic. The tolerances on the fit of that hatch you are coming up on are astounding. When you close it, you cannot see it anymore! We had to use a diamond-tipped punch to mark the edge of the hatch so we could find it again! The fit is so precise, they use no gaskets to seal the door. We have pressurized the interior of the craft to 100 pounds per square inch and detected no leaks from the hatch! Another technology we cannot duplicate."

"What about contraction and expansion of the metal with heat and cold. That kind of tolerance would bind up the hatch in a heartbeat if there were even the slightest amount of temperature difference between it and the hull."

"The alloy neither expands or contracts at any extreme of temperature." Brogan said, waiting to see the look on Ben's face. He wasn't disappointed.

"Impossible!" Ben said, eyes betraying his utter disbelief. "That can't be right!"

"Somehow, they have figured out a way to do it. The alloy is quite remarkable, but a complete mystery to us." Brogan said matter-of-factly.

Ben would now have to rethink "possible" and "impossible" from now on. The whole damn machine was improbable, but... there it was and it was not "swamp gas," or a zigzagging "meteor," or a 7000 mph flock of "geese." It was real and it was undeniably not of this world.

"How do you open the hatch, anyway?" Ben said, worried that Marston and Brogan would figure out he was stalling.

"There are two, ever so slightly faded round spots underneath the lower hatch." Brogan said. "You put two fingers on them simultaneously, then voilà! The hatch glides open without a sound. There are two similar spots on the bulkhead at the internal threshold of the ramp that opens and closes the hatch from inside. Oh, by the way, there are no creatures lurking about in the disc. They're all outside, so it's safe to go in."

Ben furrowed his eyebrows at the remark, then laughed at himself. "The stalling was that obvious?"

"Yep..." Marston said, "but don't worry about it. Everybody stalls at the hatch."

Ben stepped up to the hatch entrance, mustered a bit more courage and began walking up the ramp.

Chapter 26

After Alexander left the hotel room, Dr. Hanson sat down on the small sofa, laid his head back and closed his eyes. It was done. The machinery had been set into motion and in 8 days, if all went as planned, the world would be set on its' ear. No less than a million things could go wrong in that period of time, but he had carefully chosen the right people to see the "project" to its' conclusion. Now the question was; what if his scheme actually succeeds... what of the consequences to the social fabric of the human race? Dr. Hanson had far more faith in the species than those who made policy affecting them.

Well over half of the American population believes in extraterrestrial life, undoubtedly primed by the increasingly fantastic images of the universe provided by a multitude of popular science fiction films released over the last fifty-plus years. Humans working side-by-side with "Wookies" and "Vulcans," fighting to protect the galaxy from evildoers, both human and alien, is common fare. Other motion pictures of the genre showed a much darker side of existence in a universe where earth was not alone. They depict the peoples of world fighting for their lives' against aggressive, exploitative extraterrestrial cultures. Like Hanson's favorite boyhood movie, more recent cinema releases and television series depicted desperate battles between human and alien forces. Famous landmarks of human achievement or political power explode before the viewers' eyes. In the end, the noble peoples of the earth invariably defeat the unwanted invaders, usually by some clever trick the aliens never expected. The most recent last ditch saves for the human race included a computer virus to destroy city-sized alien warships, and Hanson's all-time favorite: causing cerebral fragmentation by playing old recordings of Slim Whitman.

Hanson's thoughts deepened. He would not live long enough to see the truth played out. There was no galactic cavalry; no high-minded league of planets; just earth, with its' proper size and distance from its' star to support a teeming biosphere... Along with a huge supply of liquid water and other valuable natural resources. Everything indicated that the aliens likely regard Earth as a pretty little gold mine ripe for the picking. The people of the world needed to know that and they needed to prepare. Hanson was well aware that universal acceptance of this truth would be difficult to attain. The human race was currently preoccupied with the murderous rampages of radical religious groups who claim their God gave them license to kill the innocent en masse. Most disturbing was the specter that such vile groups might obtain nuclear weapons, bringing new meaning to the term "wanton slaughter." Was the world too busy trying to subdue its' own enemies of peace and stability to effectively prepare for a potential enemy from space? All Hanson could do was set the ball in motion. It would be up to the world to decide what to do with the new reality it was about to find itself in.

Hanson wasn't optimistic. Even in his own lifetime, he saw the human "ostrich maneuver" performed flawlessly on countless occasions, each time leading to the inevitable mass suffering that results when a clearly identified danger festered from lack of attention. Only time would tell if the information he passed along to the world would have enough impact to change the priorities of those who had the power to make things happen.

Of immediate concern to Hanson was what to do about the Projects' security personnel he undoubtedly pissed off. They would track him here. On previous occasions when he purposefully lost his security detail to surreptitiously attend physician appointments, he had no packages. His movements were designed to convince the tail he benignly lost him in a crowd. The sheer audacity of his latest disappearing act was not only quite satisfying; it was an exercise in bridge burning. He knew he could never return to the project. In all likelihood, he faced an arrest and confinement on suspicion of espionage. His home would be ransacked, his car stripped and his assets frozen. His cover story that he was "...meeting his girlfriend and that he wanted to keep her out of the Projects' scrutiny..." might give them pause, but they would likely assume it was a lie. Hanson prepared for these eventualities, making appropriate, last-minute financial arrangements, filling his pocket with dozens of $100 bills he had stashed in his small wall safe and destroying the few remaining incriminating documents he had at home. He wasn't afraid of what might be in store for him. With weeks, maybe a few months left to live, the shadow of approaching death was more disconcerting than the criminal justice system. Hanson resigned himself to serving some jail time. In fact, he was counting on it.

The only choice Hanson had to make right then was whether to go back to his car and placed into custody there, or wait until they show up at the Hotel. He had room service, TV, a comfortable bed and paid for two more days in advance. The choice seemed obvious, but Hanson had an overwhelming urge to stack the odds even more in his favor. He stood up from the sofa, gathered the few belongings he brought with him and placed them into a plastic laundry bag. He wiped clean every surface conceivably holding a fingerprint and left his room for the last time. He caught a cab outside of the east casino entrance and made his way to the ornate, Old World-style Venetian Hotel. He requested a deluxe suite and paid $2000 cash for four nights and incidentals.

It was nearly 4:00 AM by the time he settled into the luxurious bed. The coughing hadn't been all that bad today, he thought. He had some trouble with the walking part of his mission, but that was to be expected. Maybe the coughing just seemed better because he was concentrating on performing his last official "duty" as a Cocheta scientist. Hanson cherished the "good" days, when the pain and coughing were bearable. Unfortunately, those days were starting to become scarce.

Sleep overtook Ben Hanson within a half-hour, aided by a stiff dose of Nyquil from a bottle he brought with him from home. He probably bought himself a day or two extra by relocating to the Venetian and vowed to use those last days of freedom eating what he could in the fine restaurants on the premises and enjoying the solitude of an almost overly comfortable room.

His dreams that night took him back to far happier days when life had meant more to him than just surviving from day to day. Teresa and his children often visited him in his dreams and he welcomed the ethereal experience, for it was the only contact with them he would ever have. Sometimes, he would wake up in the morning to a soaking wet pillow, a sure sign that they had touched his heart that night. Ben Hanson became a shell of a man without his family, and now, in the twilight of his existence on earth, Ben actually welcomed his impending death. Dying emotionally for almost two decades... it was time to get it over with. He only wanted to hang on long enough to see his final "project" come to life.

Seven days to go.

Chapter 27

Loeffler and Wingate had no luck finding anyone who saw an older man carrying a plain cardboard box in the area of Hanson's last known location. They even went door-to-door on Foxcroft, Lorille and Maverick streets, but came up empty. The more they searched in vain, the angrier Loeffler became. It was time to change tactics.

"Wingate!" Loeffler barked angrily.

"Sir?"

"We're getting nowhere here. We need to pull up the bus service route map and see where each of the routes that pass near here, travel to. Maybe something will jump out at us. I'll drop you off at your car. You go to the Meadows and check on Hanson's car, then meet me back at the office."

"Roger that."

A few minutes later, the Lexus roared to life and both men were heading south on North Jones Street. Loeffler would find Hanson if he had to look under every stone in Southern Nevada. One nagging question kept coming up in his mind: Why was Hanson openly toying with them? It wasn't his style to do such things. Dr. Hanson was supposed to be the quiet, unassuming type. He kept to himself and except for his little problem in 1992 and a recent penchant for disappearance, he had no problems towing the company line. It occurred to Loeffler that Hanson might actually be doing something fairly benign, like getting a little "tail" or something of that nature. The man had not dated a woman for years, and if that was what he was up to, Loeffler could easily let it go. After all, the man was probably lonely and it was perfectly acceptable for project staff members to have a love life. Then another possibility popped into his head. Maybe this woman has become important to him. Maybe he wants to protect her from what happened to his wife and kids, but that still didn't explain the brazen way he decided to play his games today. He had to know that the Foreman would can his ass instantly for making his security chief look like a Keystone Cop. Genius or not, the Foreman didn't need that kind nonsense in his organization. Loeffler wondered if there was something else. "Making a statement, perhaps?" He thought. Undoubtedly, there were important missing pieces to this puzzle, but for now, he had to assume Hanson was involved in espionage. It was time to notify The Foreman and the FBI.

Loeffler dropped-off Wingate at his car and proceeded to the Alan Bible Federal Building at 600 Las Vegas Boulevard South. The Las Vegas office of Project Cocheta was located on the 5th floor next to the Defense Contract Administration Services. The sign on the door, however, read "Office of Technology Advancement, Las Vegas Division." It wasn't listed in the phone book, nor was it listed on any of the office directories. During federal business hours, there was a sweet, middle-aged female secretary at a reception desk that politely dispensed with the lost or the curious and handled phone calls from the Projects' personnel. As sweet as she was, former FBI agent Celeste Kremer could produce an H&K USP semi-automatic pistol from a concealed mount under her desk and put three .40 caliber slugs into your forehead before you could blink an eye. As a 5th Degree Black Belt in Tae Kwon Do, she could choose to toss you about like a cheap rag doll if she didn't feel like wasting bullets. Without a doubt, Kremer was one secretary you did not want to annoy.

Behind Kremer's desk was a wall that concealed the true nature of the office. The Foreman, Loeffler and the Las Vegas Personnel Director, Maryanne Plant, each had their own, well-appointed office. The duty officer, of which there was one present 24 hours a day, had a smaller office at the rear of the largest room, which was a command post of sorts. On the wall of this large room was a massive, low-tech magnetic status board that held the names and locations of all of the non-military personnel at Cocheta or Vegas. Each name, their job title, home and cellular number printed on a large magnetic card and placed in the category that fit their location and status. For each "principal" currently in Las Vegas, there was a security officer assigned to protect them and monitor their movements. While the same information was available nearly instantly on each of the computers in the office, the status board was much easier and quicker to read.

Several workstations were located around the large room where one might track the location of each principal's vehicle using a system not unlike that of the popular GPS and Cellular Phone-based roadside assistance company OnStar or Lojack, only far more sophisticated. The office communications capabilities included encryption and decryption of communications sent to, or received from, Cocheta and other agencies "in-the-know." A flashing red light above the status board, along with a pleasant but persistent doorbell-like tone would announce the arrival of a priority message. This usually meant that a UFOIOS or UFO "Incident of Significance" had occurred and that additional information and/or command directives would be forthcoming on a separate encrypted terminal.

There were five categories of UFOIOS alerts. The most common alert was UFOIOS

"Cat One," a UFO sighting on, or near a military installation, classified research facility, such as the Los Alamos National Laboratory, or classified testing center, such as the Air Force Flight Test Center - Detachment 3 at Groom Lake, or as it is more popularly known, "Area 51." A "Cat Two" alert was the confirmed crash of a UFO, or any site where physical evidence of UFOs existed. This was, naturally, quite a rare occurrence, but generated enormous excitement at the Project. "Cat Three" was a highly unusual CIRVIS (Canadian-United States Communications Instructions for Reporting Vital Intelligence Sightings) report of a UFO filed by a military, commercial, or private pilot. Project Cocheta was not one of the "official" recipients of CIRVIS reports, as specified in the Joint Army-Navy-Air Force Publication (JANAP) 146(E) directive that spells out the official civil and military pilot procedures for reporting unidentified aerial threats to the United States or Canada. Nevertheless, the Project received copies of these reports from U.S. Northern Command in Colorado Springs via CINCNORAD, the Commander-in-Chief North American Aerospace Defense Command at Cheyenne Mountain. "Cat Four" was a very compelling UFO report, supported by profound photographic or video evidence, submitted by a civilian. The last category, "Cat Five," was reserved for the unthinkable. It would be issued when military sources confirmed an aggressive, extraterrestrial move against military or civilian targets, or if there was credible evidence of an impending invasion. The Cocheta Research Facility in Canada also received copies of every report and alert.

Naturally, the Project Cocheta scientists were most interested in "Cat Two" reports, as this usually triggered a "Field Trip" to gather crash site data and retrieve the evidence or wreckage for in-house analysis at CRF. Reports falling under categories one, three and four, were reviewed and forwarded to the various work groups analyzing the data for clues that might shed light on the technology they were studying. A Cat Five alert would place all Project Cocheta employees on immediate call-back status and dramatically increase the defensive posture of the Marines at CRF.

Loeffler was traveling east on Alta Drive when he called ahead to the Duty Officer on an encrypted wireless connection, advising him that he would be returning to the office shortly. This was a customary security precaution during non-business hours. There were certain protocols that governed this type of communication, but a password was not one of them. Had Loeffler offered a "password," the Duty Officer would interpret that as a code that the security chief was a hostage, and heading to the office with his abductors. Breaching the reinforced steel and concrete outer walls, floor, and ceiling of the office would take a tremendous effort on the part of anybody who dared to try. The world, however, abounds with monuments to the arrogance of indestructibility.

The Project Cocheta office was more than prepared for an unwanted entry. There were junction boxes located all over the office, each no further away than ten feet from each other. Each box contained one large red button, and a second, much smaller red button underneath a protective cover that prevented accidental activation. The large red button initiated a controlled, 20 second shutdown of every computer and workstation in the office. Activating the smaller red button sends a powerful electric pulse into the motherboard and hard drives of the same. Since data mirroring between the Las Vegas office and the Cocheta facility was secure and automatic, no data was actually lost. If faced with the hostage scenario, the Duty Officer was to press the large red button, then call the building's security detail, the FBI, and the LVMPD to advise them of the situation. He would then secure the six-inch thick steel outer office door and reinforce it with four heavy steel braces inserted between notches on the door and steel plates anchored into the floor. The Duty Officer would then access a small armory and obtain a laser-sighted M8 Carbine loaded with a 100 round drum of 5.56 x 45mm NATO ammunition, fitted with an M26 12 gauge shotgun module, and an M320 40mm grenade launcher module to be kept within arms reach. If a determined force managed to gain entry into the Project Cocheta office, they faced a hail of hypersonic lead, buckshot, and perhaps a grenade or two. Some Project Cocheta personnel felt the security measures at the Las Vegas office were overkill, akin to hunting mice with an elephant gun. The Duty Officers disagreed, arguing that whether you use a mousetrap or an elephant gun, the end-result was always a dead mouse. The use of an elephant gun, however, was only overkill until you happen across the unexpected, 5000 pound mouse.

Loeffler unlocked the outer office door with his key, entered, and locked the door behind him. He walked to the left side of Ms. Kremer's desk and placed his index finger into a hidden tube underneath the left corner of her desktop. An eerie red glow emanated from beneath the desk while the finger print scanner verified Loeffler's identity. It also measured the oxygen saturation in his blood, the presence of pulsatile blood movement in his finger, and its' temperature. These measurements were necessary to prevent someone from using a disarticulated digit to gain access into the inner office. The Duty Officer, of course, was watching everything via images obtained by a small, essentially imperceptible, fiber optic lens and filament protruding from the upper left-hand corner of the office, routed through a small hole in the reinforced wall, and connected to a video camera located in the inner office. Three other fiber optic monitoring set-ups covered the outer office, and one covered the 5th floor hallway leading to the outer office door. The inner office door, which looked quite unremarkable considering it had 6 inches of steel reinforcing it, unlatched with a sustained buzzing noise. Loeffler opened the door easily, aided by a hydraulic system that all but negated it's weight.

After greeting the Duty Officer, Loeffler entered his office and took out a cold diet soda from a small refrigerator he kept there. He sat at his desk and logged into his computer. Almost immediately, a status window appeared on his 23 inch LCD monitor. This screen alerted Loeffler to emails that were waiting for him to address and a visual representation of the operational status of every security element under his authority in both Las Vegas and CRF, including the sizable Marine detachment. Loeffler noted that here was nothing other than Hanson that required immediate attention. Tabs at the top of the window allowed access to various functions vital to keeping track of Project Cocheta staff and the security personnel responsible for keeping them safe. Loeffler clicked on the tab labeled "RT Tracking." The screen changed to a scalable map of Las Vegas. A pull-down window labeled "Personnel" was located on the right of the map. Loeffler clicked on the menu and scrolled down the names until he highlighted "Hanson, Benjamin." Almost immediately, a flashing red arrow appeared on the screen. Zooming in on the map revealed that the arrow point was precisely where he thought it would be, Meadows Mall. He clicked on another tab labeled "WWW." Internet Explorer was already running, and on the last web page he visited, the map of all the CAT Bus routes in Las Vegas. He zoomed to the area where Hanson had hired his decoy. Within a half-mile to a mile of his last known location, there was six bus routes: 101, 102, 103, 104, 106, and 219. He carefully studied how the routes converged on the area. He eliminated the 102 Route because that was the one Hanson used for his embarrassing rouse. The 103 Route was the farthest away and a healthy walk for a long-time chain smoker. It also went around the parking lot of Meadows Mall. Since there was no way for Hanson to know exactly how close they were to his backsides, taking the 103 might increase his chance of being seen as the bus passed by. He decided that Hanson would not take the risk and dismissed the route entirely. That left four routes to analyze. The 219 stayed in the northern most quarter of the metropolitan area, from North Las Vegas to the Centennial Parkway/Highway 95 area in the far northwest corner of the city. The route traversed mostly residential neighborhoods but did loop around the Cannery Hotel and Casino. Was that where Hanson had gone to meet his girlfriend or pass state secrets to one of America's enemies? He jotted down the hotel and looked at the next route, the 106. That route led directly to the main bus terminal across from city hall, about eight blocks from the Bible Federal Building. From there, Hanson could catch another bus and go most anywhere in Vegas, or he could walk a couple of blocks to the Main Street Station Hotel and Casino. Loeffler added the name of the Hotel to his list of possible locations. The next route he analyzed was the 104, a north-south route confined to the western part of Las Vegas. Loeffler noted that, similar to the 103, it passed along the east side of Meadows Mall on Valley View. Loeffler dismissed that route for the very same reason he dismissed the 103: too risky. The 101 Route was the last to consider. The 101 was another, north-south route on the west side, that stayed almost entirely on Rainbow Boulevard. It was a long route, passing through residential neighborhoods, past several large shopping centers and strip malls, but nothing of interest except for a few small motels between Rainbow Boulevard and US 95 at Lake Mead Boulevard. Those would need checking for completeness. Loeffler took one last look at the area where Hanson vanished. He noted the Santa Fe Hotel was within a very short bus ride or perhaps a walk if Hanson was feeling his oats. That establishment required checking as well. Loeffler knew that Hanson might have taken a cab instead of a bus, or maybe he did both. If so, the search would be a ridiculous waste of time and manpower. However, to give up without a fight was, without a doubt, not in Loeffler's short list of options. Daylight would be fading away soon, so he quickly formulated a game plan to cover the hotels and motels he identified. Loeffler, himself, would cover the Main Street Station. He called the Duty Officer into his office and gave him a list of agents to call and what their assignments would be. If located, the order was to detain Hanson until Loeffler and the FBI could get there. Once the Duty officer left the room to carry out his assignment, Loeffler stared at the phone for a few moments. He had two phone calls to make. One to the FBI to alert them to the situation, impound Hanson's vehicle, and search his house; the other call would be to The Foreman.

The Boss was going to be thoroughly pissed.

Chapter 28

Ben had to bend over and duck his head somewhat to enter the alien flying machine. Walking crouched; he passed along a short corridor and through a black, and very much terrestrial curtain, obviously placed there by more familiar creatures. When he was fully inside the vehicle and could stand upright, the sight before him was the very definition of the word "surreal." It took his eyes a few moments to adjust to the lower light level within the craft, but like the external surface of the machine, he had trouble focusing on the surface of the various features within it. There was some sort of incredibly even internal illumination but Ben could not make out any obvious light sources. It seemed as if the light was coming from nowhere. Maybe everywhere... the entire interior surface of the craft could be the light bulb, fluorescing without being obvious about it. The Interior was a half-moon shape, with the only visible entrance or exit being the one he just entered, and it was located at the precise center of the flat side of the half-circle. The interior had a radius of approximately 15 feet, and surprisingly austere. The ceiling was mildly dome shaped with the highest point perhaps 80 inches above the deck at the spot that most likely represented the horizontal center of the craft. At the semi-circular bulkhead, the height dropped to roughly 70 inches, barely enough height for Ben to stand without striking the top of his head. Along the semi-circular bulkhead was a seamless shelf that extended out approximately 24 inches at a downward angle of about 10 degrees. The edge of the shelf was approximately 30 inches above the deck. The flat, presumably aft, bulkhead was remarkable for the doorway and a strange string of what appeared to be hieroglyphics etched into the top of the bulkhead. Arranged in groups of four, the first symbol at the top left and each of the following 3 symbols in the group placed 45 degrees down and to the right of the one before. The new set of four symbols began directly above the fourth symbol of the previous set and horizontally aligned with the first. This angled striping of symbols continued, uninterrupted, across the bulkhead. Most remarkable of all was the absence of chairs, tables, windows, switches, gauges, buttons, and CRTs. There was no labeling of anything on the shelf, deck, ceiling, or the forward, semicircular bulkhead. Like the hull, there were no external signs of rivets, seams or welding. Everything appeared as if molded as a single unit.

Ben's mind began to swim in his skull. He was actually standing inside of a... well hell! He was standing inside a flying saucer! The fantasy fodder for Ed Wood films and nightmares for pre-pubescent egg-heads was entirely real and right under his feet! When he thought about the alien floor beneath him, he thanked God it didn't have the same lack of traction the outer hull did or he'd be flat on his butt, sliding around inside a flying saucer and bouncing off the bulkheads like an ice-hockey puck! In spite of the almost barren interior, Ben was engrossed in taking in every detail of what must certainly be some sort of control room or what a seaman might call a "bridge." The gravity of what the presence of this machine meant to the human race was completely lost in the marvel of it all.

"So, what do you think?" Marston asked, fully aware he had walked up behind Ben without his knowledge.

Predictably, Ben jumped and turned around, weak-kneed. "Good God, Mr. Marston! Are you trying to give me a coronary?"

Marston laughed. "Sorry, Son! It's the cruel streak in me."

Ben quickly shook off the effects of adrenalin. "It's not what I expected."

"In what way?"

"There's not much in here. At least, there's not much in here you can see."

"It is puzzling, to say the least."

"How tall are the creatures who operate these machines?"

"They average between 48 and 54 inches tall."

"So this slanted shelf would be at chest level... They do have chests, don't they?"

"Not exactly like ours, but the anatomists call it a 'chest.'"

It was a banner day for subcutaneous spiders. Any talk of extraterrestrial beings was simply too spooky for Ben's taste.

"The shelf must be where the control panel is, but I can't see any markings on it at all. Very strange..." Ben paused. "What range of electromagnetic wavelengths do they see?"

"We don't know. Most just assume it's roughly equivalent to ours."

"It's possible they might be able to see well into the infrared and/or the ultraviolet spectrums." Ben said. "The control panel might be covered with instruments that we simply cannot see, or maybe they wear some sort of image intensifier tuned for the wavelength of the instruments. I wonder if the trouble I have focusing on the surfaces of this thing has anything to do with the band of electromagnetic spectrum they prefer."

"Seems possible, but you're starting to bump the ceiling of my physics knowledge. We'll put it to The Conclave on Monday."

"The Conclave?"

"Every Monday afternoon during the two week "on cycle," all of the investigators and administrators meet in the conference room to discuss new ideas, hash over old ones and learn the details of highly screened and pertinent UFO sightings. The Conclave determines the best way to approach a problem or research initiative. We also have small workgroups that gather after The Conclave meeting. These groups are comprised of specialists in related fields, like Aerospace Engineering and Physics. They discuss the research goals for the coming week and analyze any data forwarded to them from sources in the field, usually military. As far as UFO sightings go, to make it to the level of The Conclave a UFO sighting must involve a pilot, occur near a sensitive installation or result in high-quality photographic or motion picture evidence. If we took the time to review every sighting in our "catchment area," we would be wasting a lot of time with hoaxes, misidentified natural and man-made phenomenon, delusions and other pure nonsense."

"Impressive organization!" Ben said, starting to genuinely feel he had made a sound choice in gainful employment.

"We have always felt that a multidisciplinary approach was the best way to achieve results. One genius working alone can accomplish marvelous things, a couple of dozen geniuses working together... You get the picture."

Ben shook his head in agreement. He took another brief scan around the "bridge." "Mr. Marston, it doesn't appear the creatures that fly this craft are fond of sitting. They must have some sort of way to counterbalance inertia or they would fly off their feet and make a mess on the wall behind them."

"There are chairs in here, Ben."

"Where? I don't see anything but a floor that is suitable to sit on!"

"I want you to watch something. Look where I'm pointing." Marston pointed towards the curved bulkhead opposite of the doorway. He stepped back to the flat bulkhead and placed two fingers on a spot just to the right of the entrance. Instantaneously, four chairs, of sorts, appeared in front of the angled shelf, and four more, two on each side of the door, appeared in front of the flat bulkhead. They seemed to appear out of nowhere with a distinct "pop," followed by a very brief hiss. The chairs were very thin, connected seamlessly to the floor by a pedestal no more than two inches in diameter. They resembled a shallow ice cream scoop, made with a material having a more reflective quality than the rest of the interior.

"How did you do that?" Ben shouted in amazement.

"There is a spot here by the door that deploys or stows the chairs when you touch it with two fingers. The first guy who discovered this spot, quite by accident mind you, set a world's record for the hundred yard dash!"

"I can imagine!" Ben laughed nervously. "How does it work?"

"It took us a while to figure it out. We had to bring in a high-speed motion picture camera and some hellaciously hot flood lamps to slow the process down enough for us to see what was going on. It is a very clever invention! The chair material deploys from a seamless port on the deck. The material itself has astonishing memory, forming what amounts to be a balloon that is almost the same dimension as the finished chair. Then, millions of tiny metallic beads instantaneously fill the balloon followed by a powerful vacuum that removes the gas from the balloon without removing the beads. This causes the chair material to collapse on the beads, making it incredibly rigid. All of this occurs in about one one-hundredth of a second. Stowing the chair is somewhat slower; a snail's pace at one-fiftieth of a second. We think they stow the chairs this way to allow easier access to what we believe are service panels to the inner-workings of the craft. Since everything appears seamless, we haven't quite figured out exactly where the panels are, or how to remove them... yet. Well, short of indiscriminately blasting them off."

"Amazing!" Ben walked to the nearest chair and felt the seating surface. "Very soft! Too bad the chair is Munchkin-size. I don't think I could fit my human butt into that little thing."

"Ben, we had better get going. There are a few more things I want to show you before we grab some dinner."

"Sure, Mr. Marston."

Both men exited the craft and met Brogan at the doorway guarded by the two Marines who took great delight in flustering the young and nervous Aerospace Engineer student. Brogan managed to acquire a cup of coffee during Ben and Marston's tour of the alien contraption.

"Glad to see you were thoughtful enough to bring us a cup." Marston said sarcastically.

"Hey, this was the last cup. Besides, the Marines are brewing another pot." Brogan replied in a defensive tone. "It'll be ready by the time we finish showing Ben the 'Locker.'"

"What is the 'Locker?'" Ben asked.

"The Meat Locker." Brogan replied.

"It's where we keep the alien corpses, Ben." Marston added.

Ben's stomach began gyrating at the thought of viewing dead extraterrestrials. By the sound of the macabre nickname for the morgue, the aliens were likely to have died quite violently. The spiders under his skin began doubling in size and activity.

"Ben, before we head to the Locker, there is one other thing you should know about our little flying saucer over there." Marston said ominously.

"What's that?"

"They know we have it."

"Who's 'they,' the Russians?

"No, the aliens."

Ben's face went white... and the spiders began to riot.

Chapter 29

Loeffler started his search for Dr. Benjamin Harris Hanson at the Main Street Station Hotel lobby. He spent no less than three hours showing a picture of Hanson to the hotel and casino staff, cab drivers and perfect strangers, asking if they had seen him, or any older male carrying a 12x12x24 cardboard box. Not a soul had seen him, or anybody remotely resembling him. He kept in touch by cell phone with the other security personnel scouring their assigned targets, each coming up as empty as Loeffler. Hanson hid himself well and Loeffler was woefully short of the personnel needed to find this human needle in the very large and neon-illuminated haystack known as "Sin City."

It was starting to get late, so Loeffler advised each agent to grab some chow then patrol around the hotel lobbies and casinos until further notice. Loeffler decided to eat dinner at the Pullman Bar & Grille, ordering a ribeye and a house-brand microbrew. Loeffler experienced very little of the city since he took over as Project Cocheta security chief. Splitting his time between Vegas and CRF, Loeffler was trying to quickly familiarize himself with the responsibilities he accepted a few short weeks earlier. Strangely enough, with all of the traveling throughout his career, he was in Vegas only once, for a whole twenty minutes, sitting in the first class section of a MD-11 waiting for Chicago-bound passengers to board. Loeffler was not a creature of the night by any measure, so much of what Vegas had to offer was lost on him. Still, Loeffler thought the display of millions upon millions of bright, sequencing lights along the famous, casino-saturated "Strip" was nothing short of spectacular. Beyond the electrical kind of illumination, the city was a brilliant beacon in the middle of nowhere, luring human moths to the flames of unbridled nightlife and gambling. "What happens in Vegas, stays in Vegas" might be a catchy slogan, but maxed-out credit cards and friends with big mouths were likely to bring "what happened in Vegas" to the attention of an angry spouse.

The food was very good and the beer... Well, the "Black Cherry Stout" wasn't bad, it's just that Loeffler preferred a more traditional taste, like an ice-cold Coors fresh from the brewery, or one of the local pilsners in Germany you secretly iced down in the hotel so the locals wouldn't see you drinking it cold. It was difficult for Loeffler to distinguish a Saturday night in Las Vegas from any other night of the week. The hotels and their casinos, restaurants and bars were busy most every night and the Main Street Station was no exception. Loeffler didn't care for crowds. Nothing but bad things happened in crowds. It was entirely too easy to lose a suspect in an area packed with people. In weeks past, Ben Hanson, a rank amateur, used crowds quite effectively to part-company with his security shadow. In a sea of people, two agents could easily exchange an envelope or a flash drive without anybody suspecting a thing. Crowds were also vulnerable to terrorist attack and when frenzied, a crowd could become a human wave of stampeding death or criminal mayhem. Not surprisingly, if given the choice, Loeffler preferred working an open playing field where everybody's face was visible. The careful observer might learn a surprising amount of information about what his opponent was up to by analyzing facial expressions and body language. Crowds made these careful observations virtually impossible.

Loeffler paid his tab and slowly walked through the hotel lobby and casino, scanning as many faces as he could along the way. At about three in the morning, Loeffler called each of his men for an update. The agents at the Cannery and the smaller motels along US95 saw and heard nothing. Wingate, assigned to the Santa Fe, also struck out.

"Sir, I had a thought about Hanson I'd like to share with you, if I could." Wingate asked.

"I'm listening."

"Did you get the impression that the in-your-face way Hanson lost us was overkill? As if he was trying to make some kind of a statement, or something?"

"It crossed my mind."

"As smart as he is, he could have slipped out of town quietly, but instead, he made a big show out of it. He really has no place to go anymore. He knows we'll get the FBI and the locals involved and eventually we'll reel his sorry ass in. It's almost like catching him is part of his plan and the wild goose chase is for personal satisfaction. The question is: Is it possible he wasn't finished humiliating us?"

"I'm not sure I follow you."

"What if Hanson's final destination was designed to be one more slap to our face."

"I see... You think Hanson is someplace right under our noses."

"Yes sir. Maybe not right now, but at some point today I believe we must have been right on top of him."

"Sounds like you have an idea where."

"It's just a hunch, sir, but I think he was close by when we pinned his stand-in. I'm just basing that on how pissed I would be if I found out that Hanson was in the neighborhood when we were cornering his decoy."

Loeffler considered the theory that Wingate was proposing. Hanson had him chasing his own tail all day long, knowing damn good and well he would be getting angrier by the minute. What better way to cap off a sporting session of insult by adding injury to it! Wingate might be on to something!

"Wingate, if you're right about this, I'm going to personally reimburse you for that sixty bucks you shelled out earlier. Do you have a map of the CAT Bus Routes?"

"No sir, I don't."

"Hold right there. I'll call you back within the next half-hour or sooner."

Loeffler closed his cell phone and began jogging to the hotel lobby. He arrived at the front desk within a few minutes.

"Ma'am, do you have a phone book or a map of the city bus routes?" Loeffler asked the young Hispanic woman working the graveyard shift at the Hotel Lobby.

"Yes sir, I do. Since we are right next door to the Main Bus Station, we always keep a supply of the route maps available for our guests. Would you like one?"

"Yes Ma'am, I would!"

With a "Thanks!" Loeffler took the map and sat on a plush sofa located in the lobby foyer. He quickly found where he and Wingate "caught" the bogus Hanson, then he scanned the immediate area. It was so obvious that it jumped right out of the page at him! Hanson was there! Every neuron in his brain was screaming the proclamation. At the very end of two CAT Routes he had summarily dismissed, the 103 and the 104, was a large hotel and casino not a mile from where they bagged the wrong guy! "The unmitigated audacity of that bastard!" Loeffler raged to himself. He flipped-open his cell phone and dialed Wingate.

"Wingate here."

"Dawson, Hanson's at The Orleans! Call the other teams in and have everyone meet me at the registration desk."

"You got it, sir."

"Oh, and Dawson..."

"Yes sir?"

"Strong work!"

"Thank you, sir!"

Loeffler closed his phone and began walking quickly to the parking lot. The dogs were back on the scent.

Chapter 30

Dr. Alexander slept-in very late Sunday, dragging himself out of bed at the unheard of hour of four in the afternoon. The meeting with Hanson and the early morning drive back from Vegas was more tiresome than he had anticipated. Though he arrived home safely, the trip was far from uneventful. On Interstate 15, several miles south of the well-lit Nevada state line just northeast of Cima Road, Alexander passed a gruesome sight of highway slaughter. From what he could see, the shredded remains off a late model Mustang was in the median that separated the highway into north and south lanes. Several rescue and law enforcement vehicles were on the scene, and each had strobe or rotary lights running, illuminating the surrounding desert with a visual cacophony of red, blue, yellow and white lights. Several rescue personnel attended to the twisted remains of the sports car and the injured or deceased passengers within. Portable lights were shining on the wreckage, bathing the extrication effort in progress with harsh, halogen glare.

Alexander could make out two, sheet-covered bodies lying some distance away from the carnage, undoubtedly ejected from the vehicle while it was in a disintegrating roll. Even in the early morning hours when weekend traffic on this stretch of the Interstate was normally light to moderate, cars had backed up for several hundred yards in the southbound direction. Strangely, patrol cars completely blocked the northbound lane, even though the location of the accident entirely confined to the median. Behind the California Highway Patrol cars were glowing red flares in two lines across the road, perhaps 150 feet apart. It wasn't until Alexander heard the distant rhythmic popping of a helicopter did he realize why the northbound lane had been blocked. An Air Ambulance Bell 222 from Las Vegas was approaching from the northeast, its' nose-mounted searchlight scanning the ground below. As the helicopter neared its' makeshift landing zone on the north bound lane, the characteristic "chopping" sound became more distinct and increased in intensity. The pilot was increasing the pitch, or "angle of attack" of the constant speed rotor blades. This maneuver created additional lift and slowed the rate of descent to a hover just above the roadway. The rotor wash blew dust and dirt away from the landing zone, creating dust clouds strangely illuminated by the multitude of flashing beacons. Once the helicopter touched down, the pilot removed the rotor blade pitch, allowing gravity to firmly anchor the helicopter to the highway and drastically decreasing the amount of noise to the familiar, high frequency whine of a jet turbine. The side door slid backwards and two flight crew-members in Columbia blue jumpsuits exited the helicopter with large cloth medical packs and scurried to the wreckage.

The traffic in the south bound lane began to move just a little faster than a crawl and before long, the scene of death and suffering was but a faint light show in the Corvettes' rearview mirror. Alexander couldn't help but wonder what circumstances led to the deaths of at least two people he knew of. Did the driver fall asleep? Was alcohol involved? Excessive speed? He remembered hearing something about "Prom and Graduation Season," a time of year rescue workers dreaded because of the senseless highway maiming and death that occurs when high school seniors, already mesmerized by the illusion of youthful invincibility, overindulge in freedom and alcohol for the first time. Perhaps the grim scene behind him was such an occurrence. One night of reckless abandon followed by an eternity to pay the tab. To the family of the victims, the unfairness of it all defied logic, but then, life rarely adhered to any kind of "fairness" doctrine. It was not likely that Alexander would ever know what the cause of the accident was, unless he felt compelled to research the incident on his own. The Los Angeles press would not bother with such a story so far out of the metropolitan area, unless of course, the death toll was greater than four.

Alexander rolled over on the bed, now facing the small table on top of which rested the unopened box that Hanson had entrusted to him. He was too exhausted to open it when he arrived home, but the longer he looked at the box, the more his somnolence evaporated. He made a quick trip to the bathroom to silence his unruly bladder, then dressed in his usual Sunday attire, consisting of loose fitting cotton shorts and an "ugly" shirt, which was typically a cheap Hawaiian shirt with a near fluorescent pattern of tropical birds, flowers, surfboards and palm trees. He took the box from his bedroom and placed it on his dining room table. It was time to open it.

Hanson briefed Alexander on the contents of the box so there would be no nightmarish surprises awaiting him. Even so, the evidence that Hanson had placed into the cardboard container would undoubtedly cause a marked increase in his heart rate when he finally laid eyes and hands on it. He carefully cut the clear packing tape that sealed one of the long sides of box that Hanson marked as being the top. The uppermost layer was bubble wrap, and underneath were two large folders, one contained dozens of photographs, the other, a thick stack of reports, evidence analysis and a sealed 9x12 inch envelope. Alexander would look at those later. He removed the folders and found another layer of bubble wrap, but he could see through it enough to get excited about what was lying beneath. The moment was electrifying. He peeled the bubble wrap back, exposing several pieces of metal from extraterrestrial vehicles. Each piece had a manila-colored tag tied to it. One such tag marked "Corona, New Mexico, 1947 ("Famous Roswell Crash" - bhh)," identified a 1 inch by 2 inch by 20 inch long, twisted, and jagged bit of metallic scrap. He gently picked it up and discovered that it was impossibly light, much lighter than a similar piece of aluminum would be and darker in color, more like unpolished pewter.

Alexander considered the moment in which he found himself. In his hand was not only a piece of extraterrestrial technology, but of modern American folklore. Everybody knew about the supposed Roswell UFO Crash. It was standard reading fare for flying saucer buffs since the crash was re-introduced to the public in 1980, over 30 years after the US Army Air Force installation at Roswell announced to the world that they captured a flying saucer. On the orders from higher Army Air Force officials, the statement was later retracted and the "Weather Balloon" story substituted in its' place. The rest of America slowly learned of the crash from a motion picture and several television documentaries, including a rather spectacular, if highly dubious, "autopsy" film shown on a major television network. The Roswell incident became the granddaddy of all conspiracy theories, surviving solidly intact for decades. In spite of the growing number of "official" crash sights and shady claims made by equally shady locals attempting to capitalize on the subject and the tourism dollars surrounding it, the Roswell conspiracy theory seemed to be indestructible. Alexander was not only holding proof of alien existence, but of the extraordinary effort to keep the knowledge of alien visitation from the peoples of the world.

The Corona specimen felt as if it were something that he should be able to bend or break quite easily. The exact opposite was true. Alexander tried to bend it by simply grabbing both ends to bow the metal, but he failed to produce any deformation whatsoever. He put on his tennis shoes and tried to bend it by placing the bar of metal on the soles of both shoes, then pushing the piece away with his legs while holding onto its' ends. Once again, the metal retained its' original shape. He reached into a kitchen drawer and retrieved a small towel, wrapping it around one end of the metallic bar. Alexander walked out the front door of his small, three bedroom home and placed the protected end of the metal bar in a narrow space between his homes' brick wall and a thick, steel post that marked the beginning of a chain-link fence that enclosed his back yard. Standing next to the fence, he began to pull backwards on the unprotected end of the alien artifact, using the post as a fulcrum and the brick wall as immovable resistance to his lever. The metal remained completely rigid against his best efforts to alter its' shape. In spite of its' tremendous resistance to deformation, the condition of the odd metal clearly suggested that it was capable of being damaged.

Alexander abandoned any further efforts to bend the Corona specimen and returned indoors. He looked over the other artifacts, taking each out of the box and examining them. Each seemed to represent a different alloy, however, all except one were extremely lightweight. The metallic specimens, eight in all, came from an equal number of different locales around North America. Three each were from Canada and the western United States, one from Northern Mexico and one from the deep south. The dates ranged from 1942 through 2001. Alexander detached the tag from one of the smaller; ultra-lightweight pieces marked "Northern Nevada, 1960." He filled his kitchen sink with water and placed the misshapen metal into it. As he suspected, it floated, only proving two things, the ancient observation that an object will float if it weighs less than the liquid it displaces and that the metal didn't react violently with water, like pure potassium and sodium does. He dried the extraterrestrial scrap metal with a towel, replaced the tag, and set it on the table with the rest of the growing spread of documents and salvaged metal from flying saucer mishaps. It was time to uncover and remove the final layer of evidence hidden underneath yet another layer of bubble wrap. Alexander removed the protective layer and lifted out the long, three-inch thin cardboard box that had been uncovered.

He already knew what was inside the box, as Hanson warned him about it ahead of time. He also added a warning about opening the sealed containers within the box. Considering the contents of these sealed containers, Alexander was about as likely to do that as he was to go grocery shopping in the nude. He set the box gently on the last of the open areas on his table. He used a kitchen knife to carefully cut the packing tape along the lid of the box. Once free, he lifted the lid off and removed a second Styrofoam lid underneath. Pressed into another piece of Styrofoam were several, 24 to be precise, large glass test tubes containing an assortment of formalin preserved alien tissue samples. Alexander recognized a square box pressed into the Styrofoam next to the test tubes as the container that would protect fifty prepared microscopic slides of different tissues. The sight was gruesome and immensely fascinating at the same time. If the tissue samples were obtained from the equivalent of an alien cow, Alexander would have felt nothing but scientific curiosity. Change the animal from an extraterrestrial Holstein to a highly evolved, intelligent being and uneasiness joins curiosity.

Hanson labeled the two-dozen tubes by date and specimen type. Since Alexander was not an expert in anatomy or histology, the bulk of the specimens were more or less amorphous to him. One specimen, however, was quite obviously a traumatically amputated finger. Alexander took great care when removing each of the test tubes for inspection, especially the one containing the alien digit. The last thing he wanted was E.T.'s finger on his kitchen floor. If something like that did happen, the specimen would not have lasted long. Quark, his male Cavalier King Charles Spaniel, who was still at his neighbor's house for a weekend of dog-sitting, would have snatched such a rare delicacy before its' second bounce. He thought about the sight of his obese, food-centric dog rocketing across the kitchen to gobble-up a scientific specimen of incalculable value and how he would explain such a tragedy to his peers. The thought was worth a lingering grin. "Uh... My dog ate the finger." That was a career-killer for sure!

Alexander noted that the finger articulated much in the same way as human fingers do. He knew that grasping and manipulating small objects required opposing digits. In humans, the thumb opposed the other four fingers. Hanson mentioned that the extraterrestrials had four fingers, two pairs of opposing digits, on each hand. He believed this hand configuration, along with an extra finger joint and the resulting longer length of each digit, gave the aliens greater finger dexterity than humans possessed. The color of the digit was a light grayish cream color, undoubtedly altered from its' original color by the preservative solution of 37% formaldehyde, 13% methanol, and 50% water. Alexander could not make out any fingernail, hair or prints on the finger. He finished looking at the specimen tubes and fixed-mount slides then placed them carefully back in their designated place in the Styrofoam cradle. His whole table was covered with the box and its' contents.

"Bless Carla's soul," he thought to himself, "Earth-shattering revelation or not, if she were alive and saw me working on her dining room table, she would have kicked my sorry butt!"

Mrs. Carla Faith Alexander, Tim Alexander's wife of 4 years, died of ovarian cancer three years earlier. They met at UCLA, where Tim was a newly-appointed professor in the Physics Department and Carla, a graduate student on her way to a Masters Degree in Education. While there was a strong and mutual physical attraction between the two, the courtship floundered to a degree because of busy schedules. After Carla completed her Degree, she moved back to her hometown of Tacoma, Washington to accept a high school teaching position with the school district. Tim and Carla kept in touch with frequent phone calls and after six months of separation, both realized that they really needed each other. She finished out the academic year and moved back to Los Angeles to be with Tim. They married 3 weeks later in a brief civil ceremony and bought an overpriced house near the UCLA campus that was intentionally too big for them. Both Tim and Carla came from big families, so talk of children started before the ink was dry on their marriage certificate. They decided to hold off on having children for a few years so that they could establish careers and build up a savings account. By the time they were ready for their household to grow, some three years later, Carla began having chronic lower abdominal pain. Dismissing it as "female problems," the pain persisted month after month and Carla began losing weight. Tim insisted that she see a gynecologist for her symptoms, but her denial that anything serious was going on delayed her diagnosis well past the point of no return. She fought the cancer as best she could, undergoing chemotherapy followed by a total abdominal hysterectomy, excision of her ovaries and de-bulking the tumor load in her abdomen. Tim was by her side through the whole ordeal and was there at her bedside when she slipped out of her painful, earthly chains.

Tim was devastated by the loss, yet thankful that Carla was finally free of her suffering. He thought of her often and could never quite bring himself to date again, even after 3 years. He soothed the ache in his heart by immersing himself in his work and teaching his students about the mysteries of the Universe, a chore that never lost its' ability to cheer him up. As his reputation grew, so did the number of women who sought his company. After he started his show on the Science and Technology Channel, Tim Alexander became somewhat of a celebrated bachelor, earning a mention in a People Magazine article listing the most eligible bachelors in the world. Of course, Alexander thought it was all patently ridiculous. He would date again, it just wasn't time yet.

Dr. Alexander carefully repacked the box exactly as he found it, except for the pictures and reports. He would spend that evening and the next reading the reports and studying the photographs before returning them to the box. In keeping with Hanson's precise instructions, he would keep the sealed 9x12 inch manilla envelope out of the larger envelope it came in.

Hanson's plan was very clear. Instead of flying, Alexander was to drive a rental car to the East Coast on Tuesday to personally ramrod the live "Special Announcement" down the throats of the executives at the Science and Technology Channel. He would take the boxed evidence with him, since he was far less likely to have it searched in a car traveling cross-country than sending it through a post-9/11 airport baggage check. When the time came, the televised statement would be up-linked to the Science and Technology Production Group transponder on a geostationary telecommunication satellite 22,240 miles overhead, then broadcast back to earth so local cable companies and subscription satellite services could decrypt the signal and distribute it to their customers.

The first thing Alexander was instructed to do in the Washington D.C. area, however, was to make a stop inside the Beltway to hand deliver the sealed envelope to an influential friend of Dr. Benjamin Harris Hanson, someone Dr. Alexander was genuinely looking forward to meeting.

Chapter 31

Louis Hastings, Project Cocheta "Foreman" since 1985, slammed the phone down in his CRF apartment located in the underground civilian housing tunnels. His new security chief just notified and briefed him on the evolving Hanson situation. Loeffler was supposed to be the best, yet he let a damn amateur give him the slip AND make an ass out of him at the same time! He was seriously regretting the day he signed-off on the paperwork authorizing Loeffler's appointment. "Well, that was something that could be changed very easily." Hastings vented to himself.

He picked up the phone and dialed the Cocheta Command Center.

"Triple C, Master Sergeant Orlando speaking."

"This is Hastings. Put the Watch Officer on."

"Aye aye Sir!"

After a few short moments on hold, the phone clicked back to life. "Major Alleyne speaking. What can I do for you tonight, Mr. Hastings?"

The sound of a female introducing herself as a Marine, and in this case a Marine field-grade officer, was more than irritating to Louis Hastings, it was a crime. To him, women had little business being in the military, especially the Marines. He envisioned America's most vicious enemies howling in laughter at a nation who would entrust its' security to armed forces with little girls in it. It was a national embarrassment of immense proportions. Hastings considered himself lucky to have never served along side women soldiers, or worse, underneath women officers. Considering he never served a day in the Armed Forces of the United States, luck had little to do with it.

"Where is the Lear?"

"Plant 42, Sir."

"Get it back here. I need to return to Vegas."

"Aye aye, Mr. Hastings. I'll see to it immediately."

Hastings hung up the phone. It was going to be at least four hours before the plain white Lear 35 returned to CRF from Palmdale, California and the business jet would need to be fueled and serviced for a return trip to Vegas. Five hours minimum before he could get en route... He laid down on his bed and closed his eyes. "What was that sonofabitch up to?" Hastings asked himself. According to Loeffler, Hanson had become erratic over the last few weeks, putting the slip on his tails by deftly assimilating into crowds. Add the complete absence of cell phone usage along with no credit card purchases during those times when he was unwatched, one might get the impression that Ben Hanson did not want his whereabouts to be known. Now, in broad daylight, he thumbs his nose to his tail and vanishes in spectacular fashion... with a box that could contain just about anything or nothing at all. In Hasting's book, that kind of activity was espionage until proven not to be, and even if it wasn't, Hanson was out for good.

The appointment of Louis Hastings to head-up Project Cocheta revealed a fundamental change in the management philosophy of those shadowy figures that inherited the reigns of oversight. Hastings was a ruthless bureaucrat, obsessed with protocol and secrecy. Like Marston and Brogan before him, he had a real talent for getting things done. Unlike his predecessors, Hastings motivated his staff primarily through intimidation. He worked his way up the State Department ladder by utilizing a combination of natural talent, hard work and several well-placed knives in the backs of coworkers who made the mistake of trusting him. Hastings did get results, spectacular results in fact, but his ruthlessness, noticed at all levels of the State Department, made the top of the food chain especially nervous. Since it appeared that Hastings' sole loyalty was to his ambitions, the real power within the State Department didn't want him within striking distance, and they were the ones who held his future in their hands. Hastings rise to the top eventually ran into a ceiling of his very own creation. Even so, his devotion to doing whatever was necessary to get an important job done, even if the tactics were distasteful, aggressive, or downright unethical, garnered the attention of a powerful Project Cocheta "insider."

By the time Brogan reluctantly retired from the Project in 1985 due to deteriorating health, the makeup of the "oversight group" had also changed. The net result of these changes was by no means subtle. New members of the group had a much more negative view of the average citizen of the United States than the members they replaced. They viewed Americans as lazy and overly dependent upon the government to assist them in nearly every aspect of their lives. If it were revealed that alien visitation posed a genuine threat to the world, then add that their great benefactor, Uncle Sam, was completely impotent to stop them.... mass hysteria and impossible demands upon the government would surely ensue.

It was the middle of the Reagan Presidency, the first strong and overwhelmingly popular Commander-in-Chief since John F. Kennedy and the United States Government was not interested in appearing to be weak against any enemy. Besides, the extraterrestrials made no aggressive moves since the beginning of the "Modern Era" of UFO sightings in 1947. Perhaps they never would. Arguments reinforcing the decision to continue keeping the existence of intelligent extraterrestrial life a secret from the public were suggested by the Top Secret 1952 Heischler Report, then later strengthened by the 1960, NASA-commissioned Brookings Report that suggested societal disintegration might occur if such knowledge were made known. If these reasons were not sufficient to keep the lid on Project Cocheta, there was the fact that after nearly 40 years of hard work and vast billions of off-budget dollars later, the reverse engineering of alien technology had been agonizingly slow, producing very little in return for the huge investment. So why risk pandemonium and embarrassment on pure conjecture? Thus, the consensus amongst the oversight group was that the Cocheta Project, the most classified research project on earth, needed to remain secret, quite possibly forever.

In spite of the slow progress, there was little question that reverse engineering needed to be continued. Almost certainly, the Soviets had their own "Cocheta." Perhaps the Chinese had a similar program, but most intelligence sources didn't believe so. The Chinese tended to acquire advanced technology by stealing it. The cold war was still on and the balance of power would switch dramatically if the Soviets or the Chinese Communists were to gain access to the technology behind the outrageous performance of even the most mundane of flying saucers before the United States did. The need for extreme secrecy was self-evident. The United States could ill afford another Klaus Fuchs/Rosenberg spy scandal when it came to guarding the secrets of alien technology. It was not a matter of trimming a few years of research and development time, like when Soviet spies stole America's nuclear secrets in the '40s, or the Chinese spies in the '70s, '80s and '90s. It meant overnight world domination with technology that could deliver a nuclear warhead 6000 miles downrange in just a few minutes rather than the half hour required by ICBMs. There was no earthly defense for this nightmare scenario.

With Brogan retiring soon, the overseers needed to choose a project director that would take a hard line on security and secrecy, perhaps even get his hands dirty if need be. One well respected member of the informal, yet deadly serious council, put forth Hastings' name, along with a brief synopsis on why he was a perfect candidate for the job. A short but very vocal debate on managerial philosophies ensued, the few remaining dinosaurs objecting to Hastings' cutthroat track record. In the end, the overseers, not quite unanimously, agreed to offer Hastings the position. "Offer," of course, was not quite accurate. Hastings would take the job, or his State Department career would continue to flounder, perhaps ending abruptly with a bogus charge of sexual impropriety. Hastings, it seemed, did not hold the patent on ruthless behavior.

The Foreman allowed himself to sink further into his comfortable bed inside a bedroom located beneath several hundred feet of snow-capped solid rock. His mind drifted back to the last time he had a run-in with the brilliant Benjamin Hanson, PhD. Back in 1992, Hastings put his foot up Hanson's ass because he had gotten way out of line and almost succeeded in starting an insurrection amongst the principal players at Project Cocheta. Hastings crushed the fledgling rebellion by stepping on the back of its' leader's head. It had been all too easy. Hit a man hard at his most vulnerable spot and he crumbles. Hanson's soft underbelly was his family and Hastings exploited his weakness with the impact of a sledgehammer. It might be possible to use Hanson's family again, but Hastings wouldn't need to. He could have Hanson held on suspicion of espionage, treason, even aiding terrorists, though gathering enough evidence to eventually substantiate these charges before a Grand Jury might prove terribly difficult. Breaking his security agreement was only grounds for dismissal from Project Cocheta, and making Loeffler look like an inept idiot was certainly not a criminal offense. The key to what crime had been committed, if any, was in that box of his. If they could confiscate the box and it was full of State secrets, Hanson would rot in prison. If they couldn't retrieve the box, or if it was full of sex toys for a girlfriend, Dr. Hanson would likely go free, but not without a month or two stint as a prison bitch. Once he was free, Hastings would deal with him as he had dealt with every other potential information leak that left the program. Without a doubt, The Foreman was going to thoroughly enjoy crushing Dr. Benjamin Hanson one last time.

Chapter 32

"The aliens know what's in here?" Ben asked shakily. "How do you know that?

"They routinely keep an eye on us." Marston said without any detectable concern. "Since we impounded this jewel you see before us," Marston began pointing his finger at the alien flying disk, "we have been getting regular visits from our extraterrestrial friends."

"Regular visits?" The shakiness in Ben's voice was becoming quite noticeable.

"How many in the last 30 days?" Marston asked Brogan.

"I think 18... We average a confirmed sighting every other night. We track eighty percent or so on our surface-to-air missile radar. Most keep their distance, usually in the passes to the south and north, and on occasion, they land there. A few have flown directly overhead. No aggressive moves, though, just surveillance. About 75% of the sightings are at night. It's been four days since our last visit... We're overdue. You might get lucky tonight!"

Ben shuddered.

"When one is spotted," Marston added, "the Marines are alerted and take their positions out front. They pride themselves on trying to improve their deployment times, so when you hear a "Code Green" announced on the overhead paging system in your room or see it on your pager, stay out of their way because they WILL run over you! Everyone notified has the option to go outside and witness the event, except the photographers on duty. They are required to respond to an observation deck that has a battery of cameras ready to roll. We have acquired some very amazing photographs, I assure you."

"This is a lot to take in." Ben said, inwardly retracting the thought he had earlier that Cocheta was going to be a fun place to work.

"Too late for cold feet." Marston said almost too bluntly.

"I know, sir. I'll be fine."

"Good." Marston said, lightening the tone of his voice. "There is one other thing you need to learn before you actually see it. Sometimes our little friends follow the planes flying into and out of this facility. Most of the time they take the six o'clock position, making it impossible to see them. Occasionally, they fly in plain view to the left or right of the aircraft."

If these two were trying to shock the hell out of Ben Hanson, they were doing a damn good job! Ben didn't know what to say and the look on his face betrayed it.

After a few moments of uncomfortable silence, Brogan decided to break it. "We are now beginning our descent into the Cocheta Research Facility, the earthling-run chop shop for stolen flying saucers. Please fasten your safety belts. If you look out your left window, you will notice a fast-attack saucer called "The Martian Maggot," sizing-up our jet for destruction by an ACME Illudium PU-36 Explosive Space Modulator. Therefore, we may, or may not be landing shortly. In any case, we thank you for flying Air Cocheta!"

They all laughed at the joke and it did help Ben relax a little, but there was a tangible nervousness to the laughter. Ben guessed what it was without asking. If there were ever hostilities between the two worlds, CRF, and any aircraft flying into it, would cease to exist in a matter of seconds.

"C'mon, let's take a quick peek at the Meat Locker." Marston announced. "I'm getting hungry."

"Am I going to be able to eat after seeing this?" Ben asked.

"Better to see it on an empty stomach. The custodial staff hates it when we take people to The Locker right after they've eaten." Marston replied, puffing his cheeks and pointing to his stomach.

They walked out the exit and greeted the two Senior NCO Marines.

"You OK, boy? You don't look so well." Gunnery Sergeant Hoyer asked Ben.

"I'm fine, Gunny. Thanks for asking." Ben replied, remembering to use the right title.

"You learn quick, Mr. Hanson. You're going to fit in just fine here. By the way, I heard your Dad was a Marine."

"Yes, Gunny, he was. I know he still considers himself a Marine and he is very proud of his service. You can never get him to talk about it, though."

"Son, no man should endure what your father did in the Pacific. Maybe someday he'll talk about it, maybe he won't. Don't press him, though."

"You seem to know a lot about my Dad."

"Only what Chief Brogan filled me in on. Most of us Marines are Corps history nuts. I've read about the ferocious battles your Dad fought in. Just kind of pieced it all together. Get with me later and I'll let you borrow a couple of good books on the Marine Corps in the Pacific theater during World War Two. We'll turn you into a Marine, yet!"

"Thanks, Gunny!"

The trio walked towards the far corner of the hanger within a hanger, turning right towards the back of the huge, man-made cavern. The back wall was solid rock, except for square concrete recesses resembling pictures of bunker or tunnel entrances he had seen. Each entrance had two armed Marines guarding it, both probably senior NCOs. After a few moments, they reached the entrance marked "BUILDING 100, SECTION ALPHA" in bold, black letters. A large, double steel doorway, painted a chromate green, was located at the center of the concrete face. Each side of the doorway was tastefully decorated with an assortment of fake rubber meats, including steaks, hams, and the ubiquitous rubber chicken, no doubt in reference to what lay beyond the threshold.

"Greetings Mr. Marston, Mr. Brogan, Sir," The First Sergeant on the left said. "May I see your IDs, please?

"Sure." Marston said, handing over his badge. "Your wife have that baby yet, Di Bernado?"

"No sir. She just keeps getting bigger and bigger... and she's got another month to go! I swear, if she gets any bigger, I'm going to paint 'Goodyear' on her sides!"

"You don't tell her that to her face, do you?"

"No way, sir! She's crazy pregnant! I say something like that to her and next morning, I wake up dead!"

"Keep it civil, Di Bernado. We can't afford to lose one of our best Marines." Marston laughed.

"You know I will, Sir."

Hanson noticed a huge difference between the all-business, borderline cold Project Cocheta Chief he had met several hours earlier, and the Marston that was taking him on a tour of his facility. The man was clearly comfortable around servicemen and his colleagues, exhibiting a strong, confident aura and a friendly, if somewhat dark sense of humor. Ben heard of the phenomenon of "dark humor" before. People who work in fields that involve daily contact with disturbing circumstances, like death and dying, often turn to macabre jokes to lighten the serious atmosphere of their workplace. The rubber meats and Commander X were undoubtedly examples of people coping with the bizarre, otherworldly things underneath their mountain and the rightful owner of those things watching their every move on the outside.

The formalities of identification checks concluded, the trio entered the large, long hallway beyond the yellow-green doors. The well-lit hallway had doors located intermittently on both sides. Each door had signs that marked them as offices; others were clearly laboratories, sporting wider, double doors. Ben read each as they passed by; "Kelly M. Amerman, MD - Pathologist," "Histology Laboratory," "Matthew H. Littleton - Diener," "Autopsy/ Examination Room - Restricted Access," "X-Ray." They stopped at the large double-doorway labeled "Morgue - Restricted Access" located on the same side of the hallway and 30 feet or so beyond the Autopsy/Examination Room. Marston produced a key from his pocket and unlocked the door.

Being "after hours" and having no windows, the room was unlit and extraordinarily dark, the only hint of illumination coming from the open hallway door. Marston stepped inside and activated the overhead lights for the room. Ben stepped into the now brightly lit room. The first thing he noticed was the obvious decrease in temperature from the warm hallway. That was to be expected. Didn't want any "ripe" aliens, now did we? Ben couldn't imagine what a decomposing extraterrestrial must smell like and he wasn't interested in finding out, either. He half-expected to see alien bodies lying about the morgue, each in various stages of dissection, along with assorted body parts stored in large pickle jars. The morgue was not like that at all. It was very clean, smelling of disinfectant with white tiled floors and walls that gave the room an ambience not unlike that of a very large bathroom. There were two fixed mount stainless steel tables in the middle of the room with stainless steel buckets under each. To the left, there was an office desk with a phone on it next to a large bookcase full of what was presumably reference material. One long light box for reading x-rays adorned each wall to the left and right. To Bens' disappointment, there were no radiographs displayed. On the right was a swinging double door that connected to the adjacent Autopsy Room.

The wall at the back of the relatively large room was unlike the others in that it had only one feature: sixteen stainless steel plates, approximately 6 feet in height, each with two stainless steel doors, one above the other, that looked like thick, windowless oven doors. Ben instantly determined that they were refrigerated lockers for dead bodies. Dead, and quite likely mangled, alien bodies.

"Welcome to the Meat Locker, Ben." Brogan said. "This is where we temporarily house our guests while we examine them; determine a cause of death, which is usually quite obvious; then make a final disposition of their body."

"How many bodies do you have?" Ben asked.

"Total? Thirty one." Brogan said. "Nine bodies are in exceptional shape, with little external signs of trauma. Eighteen bodies are mutilated or decomposed to various degrees. Four are in pieces and we are only estimating that the tissue comes from four different individuals. When we finish with them here, they are either embalmed, or flash-frozen and stored, depending on their condition."

"Were any of them alive when they were found?"

"Two were, but both died before we could get there." Marston said. "One succumbed to its' injuries, the other was shot in the head by the Montana rancher who found it. Apparently, the creature jumped out from behind a piece of wreckage and scared the shit out of him. Can't say I blame the rancher, really. He called the authorities when he got back to his ranch house, but when we arrived at his home, he was so frightened of the creature and the fact that he had killed it... well it took several hours to talk him into showing us where the crash site was. Within a month, the guy sold his ranch and moved his family to Helena. That was four years ago, and it was the closest we have ever come to finding a live, viable alien at a crash site."

"How many do you have in here?"

"None that are fresh. The others are in storage... but we do have Locker 32." Brogan announced.

"Locker 32?"

"Our reference specimen." Brogan said. "It is an embalmed extraterrestrial that we keep in Locker 32, the one in the far, lower right-hand corner of the refrigerated lockers. It has undergone a unique dissection, allowing the viewer to get a good idea what the creature looks like on the outside and on the inside. Come with me."

Ben followed Brogan and Marston to the locker. His knees were feeling wobbly again, but he was becoming used to it. By the time they made it to "Locker 32," Ben's heart rate had doubled. Brogan grabbed the lockers' handle, rotating it downward to free the door from its' closed position. Almost immediately, Ben could smell the pungent embalming solution. Inside the locker was an extendable stainless steel tray that aided in transferring bodies to and from gurneys. On top of the tray was a large, lumpy and mostly opaque plastic body bag that betrayed only very indistinct shadows of what lie inside. Brogan unceremoniously pulled the tray out, which was roughly knee high to the three men. The shadows in the bag were much more distinct in the bright light of the room and it was quite clear that a smallish body lay within it. Brogan reached for the large zipper tab, partially obscured by a half-inch, black cloth zipper cover that ran the entire length of the body bag from the upper left hand corner, extending across the top then curving around to the right edge and

to the bottom of the bag before curving to the lower left-hand corner. From head to foot, Brogan revealed the alien creature inside.

Chapter 33

The Project Cocheta security agents converged on The Orleans Hotel within several minutes of each other. Loeffler met the teams as they arrived and assigned individual agents to watch for Hanson in specific areas around the Casino or Hotel. The agents were to query the staff as well and show them their picture of Hanson. Loeffler, himself, would take the east side of the Casino and registration desk and try to find a staff member who might have seen the wayward scientist. He needed to stay near the registration desk anyway because the Special Agent in Charge of the FBIs' Las Vegas Field Office was on her way to the Orleans to meet with Loeffler. All Loeffler requested from the FBI was a Federal Law Enforcement Officer with the authority to make an arrest in case they nabbed Hanson. Neither he, nor any of the Project Cocheta security personnel had that capability. He might also need the added clout of the three-letter acronym "FBI" in case additional investigative techniques had to be employed. When he called to fill her in on the embarrassing details of the search for Hanson and to request a Field Agent be present at The Orleans, she said she would handle it herself, adding that they found something in Hanson's BMW that Loeffler would be interested in.

Special Agent in Charge (SAC) Hannah Simpson arrived in the hotel lobby at about 04:30 AM. Loeffler had never met her before, but the navy blue jacket with "F.B.I." silk screened in huge yellow letters on the back was a dead giveaway. She was fairly tall, perhaps 5 foot 7 inches, very attractive, with shoulder length, curly red hair and a fit build. She had a very intense, business-only air about her; yet, strangely, that didn't seem to interfere with her femininity at all. Loeffler found himself somewhat attracted to her, but now was not the time or the place. He had an asshole to catch and that asshole might be holed-up in this hotel.

"Special Agent Simpson?" Loeffler asked.

"Yes?"

"Kevin Loeffler. I spoke with you earlier."

"Pleasure to meet you, Mr. Loeffler. I hope you don't mind, but after you requested us to impound and search the suspects' car, I checked with Washington to find out who the hell you people are. They never answered my question, but did tell me that you were former FBI and that if you needed us to bring in Jesus Christ for questioning, I was to see to it personally."

Loeffler laughed. "Thank you, Ms. Simpson. Your help is very much appreciated. I know you are very busy, so we'll try not to waste too much of your time."

"Washington said my time is your time, so it's definitely not being wasted, sir. Speaking of car searches, here is the item I spoke to you about. The car was absolutely spotless, except for an envelope we found in the trunk. Because of the way it is marked, I elected not to open it." She said handing Loeffler an envelope she produced from a jacket pocket.

Loeffler examined the envelope. It was a standard, number 10 white envelope addressed to "Mr. Kevin Loeffler, Chief of Security – For Your Eyes Only." He tore open one end of the envelope and retrieved the typewritten message that was dated yesterday.

> *Dear Mr. Loeffler,*
>
> *Please forgive me for my bad behavior today. It was quite ill mannered of me to treat someone I have never met so rudely. Your reputation as a relentless investigator precedes you, Mr. Loeffler, so I'm sure that you and I will have much to discuss when we finally do meet in the very near future.*
>
> *In the meantime, I have taken the liberty of transferring ownership of my car, home and all of my worldly belongings into your name. It seems that I will not be needing them anymore. I know that you would never be allowed to keep the property for yourself, so I thought you might assist me in converting these belongings to cash and distribute the funds to the widows, children, and grandchildren of the Project Cocheta scientists who have "retired" since 1985. Of course, you may reimburse yourself for any expenses entailed in executing these sales and I would not complain if you kept a few thousand dollars commission for yourself.*
>
> *One other request: My children and grandchildren are entitled to funds in my savings account. I have mailed them checks to cash that will effectively deplete the account to a zero balance. Please do not freeze this account. There is no need to. A detailed audit of this account will reveal that my salary has been the only source of funds deposited into it and a check with the IRS will reveal I have overpaid my taxes every year since 1968.*
>
> *Thank you for your time and patience. I am looking forward to meeting you in the next few hours or days.*

Sincerely,

Benjamin H. Hanson, PhD.

Chief Scientific Advisor

Project Cocheta (ret)

PS: You might want to consider taking Special Agent Simpson out to dinner. I under-stand she is single, has a nice sense of humor and quite attractive.

Loeffler stood there, staring at the letter in stunned silence. Hanson was full of sur-prises, but that one topped them all!

"Mr. Loeffler, is everything OK? What does the letter say?"

"Ms. Simpson, I'm going to need to go over this letter with a fine-toothed comb. Mr. Hanson seems to be trying to tell me something."

"Like what?"

"I'm not sure, but I will get to the bottom of it. For right now, let's keep the existence of this letter between you and I."

"You got it."

Chapter 34

"Tim, that is a very tall order in such a short time!" Darrell Aceveda said, hoping like hell Dr. Alexander was kidding.

"That is the way it has to be. I have no wiggle room on this, so you don't either." Alexander said firmly. "This goes down on Sunday night or I resign effective immediately."

"You can't do that! You're under contract!" Aceveda reminded him.

"Then sue me. Take everything I own! I won't even fight it!"

"Damn, Tim! Is it really that important?"

"I wouldn't kid you about something like this."

"OK, I'll go to bat for you, but only because you have never led me wrong before. I'll take it to the brass this afternoon."

"Thanks, my friend!"

"One other thing, is there a bone I can throw to marketing? They are going to eat me alive!"

"No bones, but tell them I'll be in the DC area by Friday morning to shoot whatever spots we can for the weekend. Until then, tell them to put a slide with my picture on it with a voice over saying that I have an important scientific announcement to make live during prime-time hours on Sunday. Tell them to make a big deal out of it, because it IS a big deal!"

"I'll do what I can."

"I know. If you hear anything, call me this evening, on the number I gave you. See you on Friday." Alexander said, and ended the call on his new, "throw-down" pre-paid cell phone, which he purchased using a part of the substantial sum of cash Dr. Hanson had given him to travel on. He planned to rent a car at LAX, arriving there by a rather circuitous route to shake anybody who might be following him. He was to pay for everything in cash, including a sizable deposit the rental car company would require. Like his trip to Vegas, he was not to use a credit card or personal cell phone, only the pre-paid phone, and that would be for emergencies and to keep in touch with Mr. Aceveda.

Dr. Alexander had no doubts that the Science and Technology Communications executives would give in to his demands. His shows' high ratings made them vast sums of money due to the higher-value advertising slots it created. They could easily afford one episode of eccentric behavior from their top star. The only risk to doing what he wanted is if Alexander said something completely ludicrous on live TV. Since Tim Alexander was not a man prone to that kind of behavior, the risk to them would be negligible.

The renowned physicist began packing for the trip while contemplating the next 6 days of his life and beyond. Hanson's plan seemed to have every contingency covered, except for the one where Alexander got himself caught, or died in a car crash. "Or... maybe Hanson has a back-up plan for that sort of thing, too?" Alexander wondered. Dr. Hanson was very careful and his clever plan was both simple in concept, yet terribly complex in its' proposed execution. Many people would need to behave exactly as he predicted in order for the plan to work. Hanson was an accomplished scientist, but was he just as brilliant in predicting the behavior of people, some of which he barely knew? Tim Alexander shuddered for a moment as the thought he just had saturated his consciousness. He was going to trust this man to predict the traditionally unpredictable!

He went over his three options once more. Quit now, turn Hanson in, and let his plan implode. Tempting when racked with fear, but screwing a colleague and keeping knowledge of vast importance from the public was not his style. Proceed and fail. Surely, they would give him probation and plenty of Junior Colleges and High Schools would fight each other to hire him. Proceed and succeed. The truth made known. What is at the core of every scientific endeavor: to unlock and share the truth with the citizens of the world.

Like there was any real choice at all...

Chapter 35

By human standards, the creature was hideous. Ben stared at it for several moments in a sort of trance, utterly frightened by its' appearance, yet completely fascinated by the notion that, before him, was the nude remains of an intelligent creature from a planet likely to be many light years away. The creature was definitely humanoid, about 56 inches tall and quite dysmorphic when compared to human anatomy. The skin color was a light bluish gray, but Ben speculated that the real skin color might be significantly different if saturated with oxygen instead of formaldehyde. The head was unusually large, reminding Ben of children born with hydrocephaly, or more commonly called "water on the brain." The anatomist carefully dissected away half the skull on the left side, exposing the left cerebral hemisphere of the brain. The most noticeable differences between the alien brain and the human brain was the rounder overall shape of the alien brain, a non-discernable temporal lobe, and a far greater degree of "folding" of the entire cortex. Thankfully, Ben had taken anatomy and physiology as a senior in high school and as with everything else, remembered it all. The "folding" of the cortex allowed more surface area. The more surface area, the more evolved the brain. The aliens had a comparatively larger cranial vault as well, allowing for even more folding of the cortex. It was clear to Ben that these creatures were likely to have intellects well beyond that of humans. The eyes were abnormally large as well, with huge pupils and very dark irises that gave the illusion of giant black eyes. In reality, the size of the alien eyes probably reflected the amount of ambient light on their home planet, or perhaps they were nocturnal. The very subdued light level Ben noticed in their aircraft might be very comfortable for them. Like most of the higher evolved predators on earth, the alien eyes were forward set, giving them binocular vision and much greater depth perception. The thought that these creatures were predators was disquieting to Ben. Maybe he would have felt better if the aliens had eyes on the sides of their heads, like sheep in petting zoos. The nose was an inverted chevron slit. The mouth was also a slit, with no features in common with humans. There was no filtrum under the nose, no lips or vermilion border, no chin dimple, and no hair of any kind. Teeth? There were none that he could see, and he was not about to stick his finger in its' mouth to find out. The ears, if you could call them that, were very low set, and appeared to be nothing more than forward set, semicircular ridges with a membrane located in the center. The neck muscles where boldly defined and somewhat bulky, probably due to the large head they had to support. The chest was decidedly bird-like, with the breastbone forming an outward ridge instead of being flat. Ben had a friend in elementary school that had a chest that looked very similar. If he remembered correctly, the medical term for it was "pectus carinatum."

Circling the entire torso was an obvious incision that reminded Ben of a full-sized human anatomy model he had once seen. The whole chest and abdominal wall was removable to reveal what was underneath. Was that what they had done to this alien corpse? The arms were remarkable for their length compared to their torso. The alien arm was noticeably longer, extending to mid-thigh. The hands only had four digits and what looked like two opposable thumbs. The legs seemed more proportionate in length than the arms and like the hands, the feet had four digits, differing only in that they were almost equal lengths and shape.

"Ben Hanson, meet Alice Kramden." Brogan said. "We named her that because her husband finally sent her to the moon. Or, at least into outer space."

"Alice? This is a female?" Ben asked.

"Hard to tell, isn't it? External morphology is identical between males and females and without what amounts to be a gynecological exam, it's impossible." Brogan said.

"Both males and females have a simple perineal slit. The males, however, have what resembles 'claspers' in sharks, only instead of folding flat against the skin like a sharks' do, both of the alien male 'claspers' retract into the slit when not in use." Marston added.

All were thinking the same thing: alien sex must be very, very creepy.

"One of the doctors told me something interesting about this." Marston continued. "We humans have a period early in our fetal development when you cannot tell the difference between male and female. It's only after testosterone is introduced do the male parts enlarge and close up. He also said that if the tissues do not respond to testosterone for some reason, the fetus develops as a female, only without a uterus and the testicles stay inside the abdomen. The child is genetically a male, but looks female. The truth comes out when the kid fails to have a menstrual cycle. I can't remember what the doctor called the syndrome. "Testicular something... feminization? Anyway, he said the alien males have a vestigial or maybe a dormant organ that resembles the uterus and ovaries of the females. It is located behind the 'blind pouch' that holds the 'claspers' when retracted. He theorized that, under extreme circumstances, the male might become hermaphroditic."

"This is all very strange." Ben said, trying to remember how normal life had been when he woke up that morning.

"You up to taking a peek inside?" Brogan asked.

"It can't get any stranger than alien genitals, can it?"

Brogan and Marston laughed. "Not likely!"

Brogan put a pair of latex gloves on and grasped the edge of the torso incision on the right hand side of the alien corpse. In a surreal instant, Brogan lifted the entire chest and abdominal wall, including rib cage and musculature, away from the corpse, revealing the viscera underneath.

"Most higher evolved animals on earth have what anatomists call a mid-sagittal plane, meaning that if you were cut along this plane, you would split the animal into mirrored halves. Humans are like that, except for the internal organs of the torso. The aliens are much more symmetric than we are." Brogan said. "Take a close look at the organ arrangement."

Ben wasn't going get any closer than he already was. The smell of formaldehyde was powerful and it was starting to burn his eyes and nostrils a bit. He could see that the overall division between chest and abdomen was similar, as was the placement of the lungs and heart. Everything else was quite different.

Brogan continued. "To start, they have a three-chambered main heart that lies in the center of the chest with two pulmonary veins, two atria and two aortic arches. Venous blood from the body is routed from two, vena cava directly to the lungs by way of two small, stand-alone hearts that function much the same way as our right atria do. The arrangement is completely symmetric. The creatures have two livers, no spleen-like organ that we have been able to identify, a single large horseshoe kidney, a centrally-located stomach, pancreas and bladder, with the only asymmetric organ being the bowel, which does not seem to have the same kind of distinct divisions our small bowel and colon does. We do think water absorption occurs in the last portion of the bowel, just to keep things moving along, so to speak, but there is only microscopic evidence of this, not a separate organ like our large intestine."

"They seem so radically different from us, yet I get the feeling we have quite a bit in common. DNA?" Ben asked.

"Charlie, you better field this one, too." Marston said. "As you have probably guessed, Mr. Brogan here is a lot better with biology than I am."

"Sure." Brogan replied. "Yes, the aliens have DNA, but we're not sure what the significance of this is. Theories abound, the most popular ones are 'DNA Seeding' of earth by aliens hundreds of millions of years ago, or by meteors originating from other planets that eventually collide with earth. Another theory suggests the aliens are actually highly advanced humans traveling back into time. One theory suggests that humans are nothing more than a high school science project for extraterrestrial biology students."

"The most popular and likely theory?" Brogan paused. "DNA is relatively common in the universe, given planets are likely to form and evolve in ways very similar to that of earth. The aliens have 52 chromosomes, with one pair in an XX or XY arrangement to determine male and female. The number of chromosomes doesn't necessarily mean they are physically more evolved than we are. Some plants have over 200 chromosomes. Someday, it may be possible to directly compare human DNA sequences with alien DNA. When or if that day comes, a lot of questions about how related we are will be answered beyond a shadow of a doubt."

"I don't know about you, but I'm starving!" Marston announced. "Ben, if you want, we can come back here tomorrow after the formal briefing. Seeing all this, do you think you can eat anything?"

"If I can get the formaldehyde smell out of my nose I can." Ben replied.

"Good! The Friday and Saturday Night Buffet are always the best meals of the week. Afterwards, I'll show you your new home away from home and give you some homework to complete before tomorrows' briefing."

"Homework?" Ben asked, the word suddenly reminding him how tired he was. It may be 7PM at Cocheta, but his body was on Michigan time, three hours ahead.

"Just some light reading that will lay some of the groundwork for the 10AM briefing. You can read it tonight or early tomorrow morning. It shouldn't take you more than twenty minutes or so."

"That sounds fine."

"OK then, lets get to the cafeteria!"

Marston led the group out into the hanger where the outer doors had already been secured to hide aircraft and equipment from the pesky Soviet spy satellite that was passing overhead. They entered an unguarded door near the middle of the north wall of the hangar. The featureless hallway beyond, or aptly put, "tunnel," was perhaps 16 feet tall and wide and 75 feet in length. It connected the hanger to a complex series of tunnels, rooms and dormitories that made up the non-military housing. Like a fine hotel, Cocheta boasted most every amenity, and all were located in this area. The trio passed by a Laundromat, gym, swimming pool, lounge and game room on the way to the dining facility. Marston commented that the facility also had a 10-lane bowling alley and sauna located elsewhere in the fantastic maze of living spaces chiseled out of solid rock. In addition, located between the non-military underground housing and the underground Marine complex was a common-use Exchange Store with a small Commissary. The Marine barracks sported many of the same amenities as the non-military complex, plus a small arms range, an outdoor track and a football field for physical fitness training and outdoor sports when weather permitted. Cocheta was essentially a small town, located deep inside of a mountain, smack in the middle of nowhere.

Ben chose the rib-eye steak, medium-well, with a baked potato and broccoli au gratin. Boston Cream Pie was on tap for dessert and like the beef and vegetables, it was marvelous. Afterwards, during the session of postprandial small talk that inevitably breaks out amongst friends and co-workers, Marston warned Ben about the hazards of eating in the cafeteria. "You've got to watch yourself. The food here is so good that you could end up weighing 500 pounds and we'd have to haul your fat ass back and forth from Vegas on a C-130 cargo plane!"

"Las Vegas?" Ben quickly replied. "Is that where Teresa and I are going to live?"

"That's the place." Marston said suppressing a yawn. "The city that never sleeps."

"Why Las Vegas?"

"Existing infrastructure." Marston said, trying to shake off the yawn that was trying to emerge. "No other reason. Las Vegas is the closest major city to classified and unclassified government testing facilities like the Tonopah Test Range, Nellis Air Force Base and Range, Nevada Test Site, where they conduct nuclear weapons tests, and Groom Lake. We already have transportation assets at Nellis Air Force Base to haul workers and scientists to and from Cocheta. Eventually, the plan is to build stand alone facilities at Las Vegas McCarran airport, but that is at least 4 to 5 years away."

"You'll like it there." Brogan added. "Lots of things to do in the city and in the area. Lake Mead is nice. There are more people in Vegas that own boats than you might think and they haul them back and forth to the lake. Seeing a trailered boat on a desert highway is quite a sight for the uninitiated. The neighborhood you will be living in is actually near Nellis Air Force Base. First rate, mostly affluent young couples with small children. Several of your colleagues live there already."

Of all the places Ben might imagine himself living in, the Las Vegas area was not one of them. "Sin City", at least by reputation, was a far cry from the quiet, Northeast Okla-homa lifestyle he grew up with. Living in Norman and Ann Arbor was more than a fast enough pace for Ben. Reality, however, was that Aerospace Engineers lived in big cities or taught on big campuses. Even if he had declined the Cocheta position, his post-doctoral lifestyle would likely never be as slow and relaxed as it was in Quapaw.

"Las Vegas was not what I had in mind, but Teresa and I will make do." Ben said. "You said Teresa could finish nursing school there?"

"University of Nevada, Las Vegas. She's essentially enrolled for the fall semester, just a matter of submitting some required paperwork and transcripts to complete the process. She can even get her Masters Degree there." Marston said.

"Mr. Marston, Mr. Brogan, you seem to have thought of everything!"

"We try hard to do just that." Marston replied. "Like I mentioned to you earlier, we've been watching you for quite some time and huge sums of money and favors have been invested to insure that we had the best shot at recruiting you. We knew all along that you were the most gifted and qualified individual to surface in this country in many decades and we wanted, no... needed you here to help us solve our little technology problems. I assure you, we go to great lengths to protect our investments and part of those measures are to insure that our people are well taken care of."

"Huge sums of money? Favors?" Ben wisely thought to himself. How could that be? He never took any money from anybody except his parents. Was he talking about bribes? Bribe who, and to what end? He had rightfully earned his scholarships, grades and degrees, but what about his choice of schools? Did Marston have anything to do with the University of Oklahoma's refusal to offer him a position in their graduate program? If so, why would Marston want him at Michigan? Ben was very pleased with the education that he received at Michigan, so it was difficult for him to believe he had suffered any harm. Well, except that he really wanted to live closer to his parents after Paul Junior's death. Of course, then there was the benefit of living closer to Teresa, as well. None of it made any sense, at least for the moment. Ben decided to pass on any questions he had about the "investments" Marston had made in his behalf and just be politely grateful. Maybe, someday, when he felt less like a junior apprentice and more like a member of the team, he would query Marston about those "investments."

"Thank you, sir. I appreciate everything that you have done for me, and for Teresa." Ben said, with all honesty, even as he was temporarily shelving dozens of questions that were popping into his head.

"We expect results in return for this extravagant, Air Force-style living we're providing you, young man!" Brogan laughed, his inside joke poking fun at Marston's Air Force past. It was common practice for servicemen in other branches of the Armed Services to make fun of the Air Force. Charlie Brogan, a retired Navy Captain, never passed-up the opportunity to take a jab at them.

One joke commonly told amongst servicemen was how the Air Force went about building its' bases. The first priority was the golf course, then "O" Club and housing. By the time these essential facilities were completed, the money appropriated for the base was completely spent, requiring additional funding from Congress to build the more mundane facilities normally associated with an Air Force Base... like runways and hangers. Ben sensed that the comment was an inside joke aimed at Marston, but lacked the insight to find humor in it beyond the obvious taunt.

"Ben," Marston said, "what Mr. Brogan really meant to say is that we expect you to work hard for your country in return for what it has, and will do for you and your family. We have unbelievable technology in our hands, technology that, if developed first by the wrong people, would not just tip the balance of power on this planet, it would knock it on its' ear. We don't expect miracles here. Reverse engineering technology this advanced is grueling and quite tricky. In twenty-one years of effort, we have produced surprisingly little."

"What have we duplicated, so far."

"Only the simpler alloys have been reproduced. We are successfully using some of them in Aerospace applications. The powerplant or reactor, propulsion system, avionics and the more exotic alloys continue to elude us."

"It's not difficult to understand why the project has produced so little over the years." Brogan added. "The technology we study is hundreds, perhaps even thousands of years ahead of the human 'state-of-the-art.' What hinders us the most is the lack of a technologic 'frame of reference.' In other words, if you don't know what something does, it is impossible to understand its' function or importance, let alone duplicate the technology in any sort of meaningful way. Take one of today's most advanced solid-state circuits and hand it to Leonardo da Vinci. Don't tell him anything about it other than it comes from a spaceship designed to go to the moon and back. How much luck do you think one of the greatest scientific minds of the Renaissance would have reverse engineering the circuit and putting it to the same use as it would be 500 years in the future?"

"I see what you mean. Sounds like I have my work cut out for me." Ben replied.

"That, my new friend, is an understatement." Marston said with a smile. "There are people here who have put in enough time on this project to retire, yet the net results of an entire careers' worth of work has essentially been zip. The one thing we do know a great deal about is the creatures' themselves. At least, we know how they're built and we know they are mortal."

"When we started Project Cocheta twenty years ago, we had no idea what was possible or impossible. We had possession of ultra-advanced technology; perhaps our enemies did, too. The cold war nuclear arms race had already begun and the alien hardware seemed to promise a lightning-fast delivery platform that was essentially indefensible. Maybe the extraterrestrial power source would prove more deadly than the thermonuclear bomb. None of the major players knew what could be reverse engineered, only that they needed to be the first to do it. We started a super-secret arms race that was invisible to the public and the vast majority of our own government. Then there was the equally important question of what in hell the aliens were up to. They buzzed around our military assets with impunity, much as they do here. Hell, they even made a radar-tracked fly-over of Washington D.C.! Truman was fit to be tied! In fact, that little incident single-handedly funded, in perpetuity, our little slice of Heaven here."

"What are the aliens up to?" Ben asked. "Do we have any idea?"

"Not anything concrete." Brogan said. "But we did hire a one Wilhelm Heischler to help us answer the question. Dr. Heischler was a renowned anthropologist who specialized in the study of cultural "clashes." In fact, his conclusion on what our little gray buddies might be up to is your homework assignment. Speaking of that, maybe we should all turn in for the evening. You have got to be tired by now."

"I am, a little." Ben replied, purposefully downplaying how tired the most bizarre day of his life had made him.

"Then I guess it is time for me to show you your new apartment." Marston said.

With that, the trio made their way to the main, "West" corridor of the underground system of tunnels. The complex was quite large, with two main north-south hallways called 'East Corridor" and 'West Corridor," and two main east-west hallways called 'North Corridor" and 'South Corridor". The complex thus divided into nine sections, much like a tic-tac-toe grid. Blocks "A" "B" and "C" were the closest to the northern face of the mountain. These blocks contained the support facilities and Cocheta amenities. The apartments were located deeper in the mountain in blocks "D" through "I." Smaller hallways interconnected with each other between clumps of apartments and each had what amounted to be a street name. Ben's apartment was located in the large apartment area of "H" block, all the way to the back of the complex. The hallways aptly bore the names of planets, moons, and stars. Ben's apartment, H-12, was located at the corner of Phobos and Deimos, the moons of Mars.

"Here's the key. It's all yours." Marston announced. "The Heischler Report is on your desk. We took the liberty of stocking your refrigerator if you get hungry. Why don't we meet in the cafeteria, say, 9AM for some breakfast. There is a phone directory on the desk, along with a map of the facility. I'm in the directory, so if you need me for anything, just call. We do have ways to make non-traceable outside calls, but you need to be briefed on that capability before you can use it." Marston paused for a second, as if trying to remember what he had left off the list of essentials to tell Ben. "Oh, and if you hear a 'Code Green' on the intercom, follow the green stripe on the hallway floor if you want to see one of our local flying saucers in action. The stripe leads you to the nearest exit. Just remember to bring a heavy jacket. You could freeze the family heirlooms off out there!"

"Thanks, Mr. Marston, Mr. Brogan."

"See you in the morning." Brogan replied.

The two project managers walked back in the direction they had just come on Deimos, then turned right on "East Corridor" a few small hallways away. Ben unlocked his apartment door and entered, turning on the lights as he went. The apartment was much larger than he had imagined, perhaps because he was accustomed to living in cramped dormitories. It was carpeted except for the small kitchen and dining area. It had an ample living room, a single bedroom with a bathroom and an office with a respectably sized hardwood desk and bookshelves full of engineering reference books and journals, all of which were current. The living room had a new sofa and love seat, coffee and end tables with lamps, along with a stereo cabinet and console television. The bedroom had a king-sized bed, chest of drawers, nightstand and a fair-sized closet with a heavy coat already on a hanger, his name stenciled on the back. The kitchen had an electric stove, a refrigerator stocked as Marston promised it would be, and a toaster. The cabinets were full of dishes, glasses, pots, and pans; the drawers were full of dinnerware and other assorted small kitchen utensils. The only odd thing Ben noticed was the complete lack of windows, but he was in the bowels of a large mountain, so an apartment with any kind of view was not likely to exist. The living quarters were more than acceptable to Ben, and it would become his Canadian home, two consecutive weeks out of four, for the next 40 years.

As curious as he was, Ben was too tired to read the Heischler Report that night. Within ten minutes of entering his apartment for the first time, he stripped to his underwear and fell into bed. He set the mechanical alarm clock for seven and turned out the lights. The room was almost pitch black and except for the almost inaudible compressor noise his refrigerator made, silent. A deep sleep overtook Ben Hanson within minutes. Thankfully, there were no dreams of embalmed aliens or tailgating flying saucers. Teresa was the only one waiting for him...

Chapter 36

Loeffler learned that The Foreman was due to arrive at The Orleans around 1:30 in the afternoon. He spent the entire morning with a fresh crew of Project Cocheta security agents, along with a small detail of Special Agents from the Las Vegas FBI, making tangible progress locating the elusive Benjamin Hanson. The security tapes from the registration desk, taken the afternoon before, showed a man checking into the hotel wearing a ball cap with dark sunglasses, carrying a plain cardboard box roughly the size Hanson was toting around when last seen. The man was coughing, too. The video image was not the best quality and it was obvious the man in question was keeping his face turned away from the camera, but he really couldn't be anybody else but Hanson. Too many coincidences and the time stamp on the video, within 15 minutes of their "apprehension" of Hanson's decoy, confirmed Wingate's theory that Hanson's choice of hotel was designed to be yet another public spanking.

According to the registry, a man by the name of "Hermann Jason Brainish" checked into the hotel, paid cash for 3 days, and left a cash deposit for incidentals. He checked into room 1004, with no record of him checking out. The name caught Loeffler's eye. Knowing Hanson, any alias would have to be an "in your face" gesture. The "Brainish" surname was too obvious and not very clever... way beneath Hanson.

"Special Agent Simpson, are you good with anagrams?" Loeffler asked.

"Fair... Why do you ask?"

"I've got a hunch that 'Hermann Jason Brainish' is an anagram for Benjamin Harris Hanson."

"Only one way to find out."

Hannah Simpson retrieved a note pad from her FBI jacket pocket and wrote both names down. She first counted the number of letters in each name, exactly twenty in both. The first test completed and passed, she began crossing out letters common to each name. If at any time she found a letter that belonged to one and not the other, the name was clearly not an anagram. Each letter, down to the last "h" in "Brainish," had a corresponding letter in Benjamin Harris Hanson.

"Yep, it's an anagram!" She announced.

"I swear I'm beginning to like this guy, in spite of the fact he has me chasing my own tail all over Vegas. Can you grab a couple of agents and come with me to his room. With any luck, Dr. Hanson will still be there."

Loeffler and Special Agent in Charge Simpson, along with two other FBI agents and an assistant manager of the hotel, made their way to the 10th floor. The hotel manager quietly cleared the rooms on the floor and then blocked one end of the hallway while an FBI agent blocked the other. Loeffler, Simpson and the remaining FBI agent approached the door to room 1004 quietly. As they reached the doorway, the law enforcement officers unholstered their Glock Model 23 pistols. There was no reason to suspect that Hanson was armed, or would put forth any kind of resistance whatsoever, but every law enforcement officer knows that sometimes even the meekest of individuals might decide to "check out" in a blaze of glory and a hail of bullets rather than go to prison.

"Room service!" Simpson called out.

No answer.

She repeated the phrase and knocked on the door at the same time, still no answer. Loeffler took the card key and positioned himself to the right side of the left opening door. Simpson and her back-up were positioned on the left side. Simpson lightly grabbed the door handle with her left hand, her right hand clutching the Glock, holding it in a ready position. Loeffler removed the "Do Not Disturb" sign, silently inserted the card key and withdrew it. A fraction of a second after the first green blink of the LED, Simpson pulled the door handle down and burst into the room with her back-up in tow, both screaming "Freeze!!! FBI! FBI!" a tactic designed to both startle and disorient the suspect into ineffective action or time-wasting indecisiveness. Loeffler followed closely behind. He carried no firearm, even though he had a license to carry one. Within a few seconds, it was evident that Hanson was no longer there. The beds had wrinkled comforters, but did not appear slept in from the night before. There were piles of ashes in the ashtray, a small amount of coffee in the carafe and a few meaningless pieces of trash in the wastebaskets. After a half-hour of searching the room for evidence, Simpson ordered it sealed and dusted for fingerprints. Maybe they could find out whom Hanson met with, if he met with anybody at all.

With Hanson gone, and Hastings arriving at any time, Loeffler and Simpson assigned assets to watch the endless hours of security tapes from the various video cameras about the Hotel and Casino. Hanson would undoubtedly show up on some of these tapes and perhaps the person, or persons he was meeting with would also show up. For the moment, that was all that he could do.

Loeffler was exhausted. He had been up for well over 24 hours, and he needed a nap, a shower and a shave. With Hastings on the way, those niceties would have to wait. The last thing Loeffler needed was for that asshole Hastings to catch him sleeping. He took Hanson's letter out of his pocket at re-read it. Loeffler's mind was somewhat dulled by sleep deprivation, but even so, a few things about the wording of Hanson's letter stood out. Without a doubt, Hanson anticipated his eventual apprehension, or perhaps he was going to allow Loeffler to catch him. Hanson had to know that Loeffler could not possibly accept his personal possessions, let alone auction them off on eBay and keep a commission. It was where he wanted the proceeds to go that bothered Loeffler: the widows and relatives of retired Project Cocheta scientists, and he used quotation marks to highlight the word "re-tired." The dramatics must have a point and Loeffler guessed that Hanson wanted him to look into the fate of the scientists that have retired since 1985. "But... why 1985?" He asked himself. What change occurred in Project Cocheta from 1985 onward?

"Loeffler!" A voice shouted at him from across the casino, jarring him from his thoughts. Damn... it was Hastings!

"Yes, Mr. Hastings." Loeffler replied, standing and quickly stuffing Hanson's letter back into his pocket at the same time.

"How in God's name did you allow Hanson get away? And how come you haven't caught his ass?"

"He's quite clever ..." Hastings cut him off.

"Clever? More clever than you?" Hastings yelled, loud enough for everyone in the lobby to hear. "So what in the hell did I hire you for? He's a rank amateur, you're the professional for Christ's sake! Hanson's a fucking scientist! Book-smart, maybe, but most of them can't find their ass with both hands!"

"Hanson is different."

"Bullshit, Loeffler! I know Hanson better than you do! You dropped the ball, pure and simple. Face it and take responsibility for it! Now, what have you done so far to clean up this mess you've made?"

Loeffler successfully fought off the urge to plow his fist into Hastings face. From what he knew of Hastings, and his previous personal encounters with him, his reputation as a bureaucratic prick of staggering proportions was not about to be refuted today.

"We have confirmed that he was a registered guest here in The Orleans as of yesterday afternoon. We have him on the lobby security tapes. He was in room 1004, which we raided a short while ago. He apparently abandoned the room sometime in the middle of the night. We are currently reviewing all of the security tapes from the hotel and casino to see if we can find out if he actually met with someone and what time he left the hotel."

"How many of our people are working this?"

"All that we can spare. The FBI has also provided valuable manpower and assistance."

"Fine." Hastings replied, looking Loeffler in the eyes. "You had better catch this asshole in short order, or you can kiss your overpaid position goodbye!"

Loeffler fought off the urge again, but this time it took Herculean strength to do so. Who in the hell did he think he was talking to, some first-year academy cadet? Kevin Loeffler was bagging the cleverest of foreign spies while Hastings was doing what? Twenty years of babysitting dead aliens and managing a bunch of docile scientists who he just acknowledged "can't find their own asses?" Then something struck him. Twenty years ago... That was 1985! Hastings took over Project Cocheta in 1985! Hanson WAS trying to get him to look into something and Hastings was a part of it somehow. Maybe whatever Hanson was pointing him towards could end up becoming a lot more satisfying than a simple, bone jarring punch to Hasting's face!

"I'll get Hanson, Mr. Hastings. You can be certain of that. After all, he is only a scientist."

Chapter 37

Ben's internal, circadian clock woke him up at 4AM and annoyingly, would not let him sleep any further after 30 minutes of trying. The Heischler Report was calling him and in spite of the feeling he needed more sleep, he turned on the bedside lamp and forced himself out of bed. After a trip to the bathroom and retrieving a cold glass of orange juice from the refrigerator, Ben sat down at his new desk to open the folder placed neatly on top of it. The first page was a cover letter written by Dr. Wilhelm Heischler. The words "TOP SECRET" were hand-stamped in bold red letters across the top right of the page. The first line of document also read "TOP SECRET RESTRICTED," only it was typed and under-lined. The date of the document was 02 May 1952.

MG Arthur Wayne Marston, USAF (Ret.), Project Director
Project Cocheta
Wright-Patterson Air Force Base, Ohio

Dear General Marston,

Submitted is my evaluation of the probable intent of the extra-terrestrial biological entities currently scouting our planet, and the eventual outcome of interaction between our cultures. I trust this assessment will fulfill that which your project scientists requested of me. Undoubtedly, you will find my conclusions quite disturbing and my equally disturbing recommendations are not likely to be accepted by those whom possess the power and influence to adopt them.

On a more personal note, I want to thank you for the thorough briefing and allowing me to examine the profound amount of physical and case evidence your project has acquired. It was instrumental in helping me understand the nature of our visitors and produce the most realistic conclusions. Unfortunately, for personal reasons I prefer not to disclose, I cannot engage in any further research into this area. Of course, I will keep my involvement with your project, as well as my findings, in strictest confidence.

Sincerely,

[Signed]

Wilhelm F. Heischler, PhD.
Professor and Chairman
Department of Anthropology
Harvard University
Cambridge, Massachusetts

A handwritten note to Ben followed.

Ben,

Dr. Heischler retired immediately after submitting this paper. He moved his family to Oregon and for all intents and purposes, disappeared from view. I've always felt guilty about this. I might have shown him too much, too quickly...

Marston

Ben pondered the cover letter and Marston's note. He clearly frightened Heischler with what was shown to him, or perhaps Heischler frightened himself with his own conclusions. It seemed as if Heischler believed there was a global apocalypse on the horizon and he elected to hide under the bed. His curiosity piqued, Ben read on.

TOP SECRET – RESTRICTED   TOP SECRET

An Analysis and Threat Assessment of the Behavior Exhibited by
Extra-terrestrial Biological Entities

Wilhelm F. Heischler, PhD.

(For the purposes of this assessment, it is assumed that the reader has been fully briefed on the presence of extra-terrestrial biological entities on this planet and the technology that appears to have brought them here.)

Part 1: Comparative Evolution of Extra-terrestrial Biological Entities and Humans

In order to effectively evaluate and reasonably predict the behavior of the entities that are currently visiting our planet, certain assumptions are made about the nature of the universe and the formation and development of planets in particular. The first assumption is that the physical laws of nature that are present in our region of space apply to all regions of "normal" space. Since there is no observable or mathematical reason to believe otherwise, we shall consider the first assumption to be valid. Therefore, given the vastness of outer space and the near infinite number of stars, the development of our solar system is highly unlikely to be a unique process in the universe. Planets the size of earth, located desirable distances from their star, might also develop, age and die in similar ways.

The second assumption is that the biochemical precursors of primitive life must also be present on planets that form and develop in the same way that earth did. Carbon is one of the most common elements found in the universe and it happens to be highly reactive with many other elements. Carbon forms the very backbone of life on earth, and it would likely do the same on similar, developing planets.

The third assumption is that when life emerges on these worlds, it would be subjected to evolutionary pressures similar to that found on earth. Creatures would naturally diversify in order to exploit environmental niches. Competition for limited resources in a dynamic, developing world would drive species that poorly adapt into extinction while rewarding survival to "the fittest." Since higher intelligence broadens the adaptability of an organism, therefore enhancing its' survivability, it follows that intelligent life in the universe may be far more common-place than previously imagined. The Extra-terrestrial Biological Entities navigating through the atmosphere of our planet appear to be a limited confirmation of this postulation.

The fourth assumption is that intelligent creatures capable of manipulating their environment with the use of tools will congregate to further enhance their survivability, thus becoming more evolutionarily competitive. Such creatures would require appendages that facilitate the creation and effective use of tools. Many intelligent species on earth lack such appendages, severely limiting or eliminating their ability to manipulate the environment they live in. For example, Porpoises are quite intelligent and very successful organisms, but lack appendages to manipulate their environment beyond cooperative hunting strategies.

The fifth assumption is that evolutionary pressures drive congregations of intelligent beings to do what is necessary to insure survival, including the use of warfare to acquire desirable land and resources in short supply. Likewise, threatened congregations will resort to warfare to protect themselves from aggressors. While the term "evolution" is most commonly used in the biological sense, I believe it also applies to congregations, or more aptly put, "cultures" of intelligent beings. The most successful cultures are those congregations of beings that exhibit a distinct evolutionary advantage over other cultures. The Roman Empire was an ancient example of such a highly successful culture. When the culture began to decay through neglect, corruption and declining military competence, they lost their evolutionary advantage and succumbed to the Germanic Barbarian onslaught.

The sixth assumption is that advanced technology further enhances survivability, therefore is evolutionarily advantageous. Technologically advanced cultures easily succeed over ones possessing obsolete or primitive technology and there are countless examples of technology mismatches that led to the extinction or assimilation of "lesser" cultures. The Romans, for instance, deployed advanced weaponry to the battlefield and eventually subdued a large portion of the known world. The Europeans brought advanced technology to the New World and had relatively little trouble conquering the technologically inferior native Indians. In the fight to survive, rocks and bones are inherently superior to clenched fists. Spears and arrows are superior to rocks and bones. Firearms are superior to spears and arrows. Atomic bombs are superior to everything else known. As resources on a planet dwindle, the survival stakes for all cultures become more pronounced. A technologically advanced culture is likely to use its' advantage to dominate the planet by controlling the remaining natural resources in order to preserve its' own future.

The seventh assumption is that evolutionary pressure, just as it applies to primitive life forms and the development of cultures on a single planet, must also exist between planets with intelligent life. Continuing depletion of resources on a species' home planet would naturally stimulate the search for resources on other worlds, asteroids and moons. If the species of one planet should encounter a desirable planet with intelligent life, the outcome of this interaction would likely depend upon the level of technologic advancement possessed on each side. If the mismatch is large, the more advanced culture is likely to conquer and assimilate the lesser. It is conceivable that such an evolutionarily successful culture may extend its' control over several planets through the same process.

In my previous published works, I have analyzed the complex interactions between differing civilizations, in particular, those meeting for the very first time. Generally speaking: the more difference between cultures, the more catastrophic the outcome for the weaker of the two. There have been notable exceptions to this generalization. For example, the all-too-common animosity that erupts between cultures that share a common ancestry, but differ enough in religious beliefs to war viciously amongst each other. Clearly, history suggests the most successful cultures have two advantages over their rivals: technological superiority and the willingness to aggressively use that technology to conquer their opponents and/or defend themselves from challengers.

Part 2: Dominant Culture

Should the seven postulations I have suggested prove correct, then we must assume that the alien culture visiting our planet represents the highest evolutionary product of their world, both physically and culturally. They have successfully met every evolutionary challenge their planet and competing cultures have given them. They are, at the very least, the "Dominant Culture" of their own species, and since they have achieved advanced space travel, may represent the dominant species over multiple planets. If this is true, it is impossible to overstate the implications to our planet and the human race.

For clarification, I purposefully avoid the use of the plural term "Dominant Cultures" because I firmly believe that the end-result of evolutionary pressures applied by the depletion of limited natural resources results in a single, highly competitive culture dominating a planet. It may be difficult to visualize this happening on earth because of the hundreds of different cultures that currently exist. I would remind the reader of the ultimate intent of Adolf Hitler not a decade before this writing. If the Nazis had developed the atomic bomb instead of America, Hitler's dream of establishing a German "Master Race" as the Dominant Culture on Earth might very well have been realized. There is no single, dominate human culture at this time because most natural resources remain abundant. As population density on the planet increases and strategic resources dwindle, aggression between cultures will undoubtedly occur and the most dominant one will eventually emerge.

The alien culture in question, having mastered their planet and possessing the most advanced technology developed, have the ability to extend their dominance to other planets, if they so desire. Of course, by doing so, they run the risk of encountering a culture more technologically advanced than their own. In this case, however, the alien culture has encountered Earth and the technology mismatch between our cultures is quite profound. Without doubt, the current level of human-developed technology is quite impressive. We have demonstrated controlled and uncontrolled nuclear fission and there are hints that hydrogen fusion may be within our grasp. Our rockets have skirted the boundaries of outer space and manned orbital space flights are likely to be only a few decades away. Technology is rapidly advancing along all fronts of human endeavor. In contrast, the most superficial physical examination of the alien technology, the performance characteristics of their vessels as reported by trained observers and the fact that they have quite possibly achieved interstellar space travel, proves that they are far more technologically advanced than any culture on Earth, perhaps by tens of thousands of years or more.

In summation, it is clear the alien culture in consideration possesses at least one of the two advantages characteristic of a "Dominant Culture" as compared to the most influential cultures on Earth, technologic superiority. Next, we must attempt to ascertain the willingness of the alien culture to use their clear advantage to conquer the cultures of earth. Comparing observed movements of the alien craft to long-proven, military strategies reveal clues to the presence of potentially aggressive behavior.

Part 3: Tactical Behavior

Since the first sightings of so-called "flying saucers" occurred some 5 years ago, significant amounts of sound data has been gathered concerning their tactical behavior. A considerable percentage of credible sightings have occurred in and around military installations and classified research facilities. The vehicles approach silently and quite often penetrate base perimeters. Power disruption is a common occurrence, but it is not known if this is purposeful or a side effect of an exotic propulsion system. Overall, this behavior is consistent with intelligence gathering, much the same as the time-honored military strategy of scouting an enemy without engaging him in combat. Traditionally, very small groups of lightly armed soldiers perform scouting by covertly gathering information in enemy territory. Stealth and speed are critical as capture alerts the enemy of the presence of intelligence-gathering and could provoke an "incident" if the opposing sides are not in a state of war. Since the aliens do not conceal their presence during "scouting" operations, a more ominous possibility exists: they are completely unconcerned about our offensive or defensive capabilities and whether or not their activity might spark a conflict between the two worlds. This seems to suggest that, militarily, the aliens consider us so technologically inferior that we pose no significant threat. An appropriate analogy would be a duck hunter fearing retaliation from his prey after shooting at them.

In keeping with the concept of forward scouting operations, the extraterrestrial entities have not aggressively engaged any United States civilian or military asset. This may also be a clue as to the size of the possible alien expedition to our planet. The current assessment of the craft used in these "scouting" missions is that they are short-range, unarmed vehicles, incapable of interplanetary or interstellar space travel due to a complete lack of identifiable provisions found at wreckage fields or inside partially intact craft. This suggests that so-called "mother ships," or hidden bases on this planet, or perhaps the moon, support local operations. Assuming the extraterrestrial entities do not originate within our solar system and given the vast distances between stars, it may take dozens of years to notify the home world of their findings and even more time beyond that to mount a military operation against us, if they choose to do so.

Of course, it is also possible that the extraterrestrials are merely studying our planet, perhaps with the similar detachment we give to amoebas under a microscope. It might even be possible that we are under evaluation for eventual contact. While these possibilities may be more comforting, I do not believe they are consistent with the probable existence of universal evolutionary constants for all planets supporting life. The universe, unfortunately, is likely to be a very violent place.

Part 4: Conclusions

1) The Earth is currently under investigation by a highly intelligent and technologically advanced extraterrestrial civilization.

2) The extraterrestrial biologic entities represent the most evolutionarily successful, intelligent species on their planet.

3) The culture they represent is the most dominant culture on their planet and likely achieved that status by force.

4) This alien culture may have attained dominant culture status over one or more planets in addition to their own, and if so, likely achieved that status by force.

5) The alien culture has taken an active interest in this planet, and observations of their actions strongly suggest a militaristic stratagem. Invasion is the likely objective and outcome.

6) Given the vast technologic mismatch between humans and the extraterrestrial biologic entities, negotiating favorable terms for coexistence is highly unlikely. Unannounced, massive invasion of this planet is far more likely to occur than the arrival of a diplomatic envoy.

Part 5: Recommendations

1) Duplicate the alien technology as quickly as possible. Time is of the essence. If the alien technology can be successfully reverse-engineered, we may achieve military equality, therefore increasing our chances of survival.

2) Continue the official policy of obfuscation. The public must remain unaware of the danger facing this planet until effective defensive measures are developed. It will serve no practical purpose to frighten the bulk of the human race

with a possible invasion scenario in which they are completely powerless to stop. The negative impact on society would be immeasurably catastrophic.

3) Do not provoke premature confrontation. The military must not fire upon the aliens unless attacked first. The militaries of the world must unite in this policy. We will need as much time as possible to develop effective weapons and strategies.

4) Institution of a complete global ban on wireless communications. Our planet is, essentially, a very noisy locator beacon. Even if the current alien culture visiting our planet proves to be non-aggressive, the overwhelming odds are that the next one will not be. This recommendation is quite radical and impractical, to be sure, considering our world's reliance on radio communications. Many will argue the damage is already irreparable, with over 50 years of radio transmissions already radiating into space. It seems prudent, however, to insure that future generations need not fear that their everyday communications may be drawing unwanted attention.

5) I strongly recommend that when the human race accomplishes interplanetary and interstellar travel, the use of extreme caution is in order to avoid drawing attention to our planet. Unmanned spacecraft must not exit our solar system and should not contain any information that would give away the origin of the probe.

6) In order to identify potentially aggressive extraterrestrial threats, I recommend extensive, passive monitoring of the sky for radio signals from space. In addition, I recommend that, under all conceivable circumstances, any extraterrestrial radio signal received go unanswered. Isolation tends to be an unpopular option for humans, but in this case, isolation is essential for our long-term survival as a species.

7) The world must somehow unite against the threat that faces us all. If the scientists of the world could work together in an effort to unravel the mysteries of the alien technology, we might stand a fighting chance as a species. If we remain divided, our extraterrestrial foe might very well exterminate us while we fight amongst ourselves.

8) Pray to the Almighty for deliverance.

Submitted this day, 02 May 1952,

[Signed]

Wilhelm F. Heischler, PhD.
Professor and Chairman
Department of Anthropology
Harvard University
Cambridge, Massachusetts

Attached to the document was another note from Marston. This one typed.

Ben,

The document that you just read was taken quite seriously at first. The UFO hysteria that gripped the world in the early 1950s created great consternation within the government. Then, about 6 weeks after this report was given to me, Washington DC was inundated by local UFO sightings that persisted for over 2 weeks. Many legislators saw them, as did a handful of the Pentagons' top echelon. I even saw three at Andrews Air Force Base on the 20th of July! The government's reaction to this quite pompous Alien air show was to etch Project Cocheta in stone.

Over the years, the influence of this report on national policy has waxed and waned. NASA, for instance, has all but abandoned the recommendations made by Heischler. They wish to be the center of attention and their recent successes in manned space flight (and sympathy generated by last year's catastrophic failure) have made them quite powerful. Not surprisingly, in 1960, NASA commissioned its' own version of the Heischler Report. It was titled "Proposed Studies on the Implications of Peaceful Space Activities for Human Affairs," also called the "Brookings Report." A copy of it is located in your bookcase. It is quite lengthy, discussing several aspects of space travel and its' impact on the human race. In spite of the fact that it is obvious that NASA did not bother to tell the authors about our little "collection," the report almost mirrored one of the essential recommendations of Heischler, suggesting that it might be prudent to keep secret some the information about the existence of alien life. It also repeated one of Heischlers' observations that a society who faces a new, superior culture might collapse as a result. In spite of this seemingly ominous concordance, many within NASA believe Heischler was wrong about the intentions of our extraterrestrial visitors and use one of the Brookings Report conclusions that states the discovery of extraterrestrial intelligence might actually bring humanity together as supporting "proof." They do concede that keeping their existence secret is a "reasonable course of action at this time."

Personally, and as a former military officer, I believe almost every word of Heischler's report, and if it were within my power to do so, I would institute all of the recommendations he made. I have learned that it really pays to prepare for the worst possible scenario. Unfortunately, every year that passes without any evidence of impending alien aggression weakens Heischler's arguments in the eyes of the powerful policy makers who are "in-the-know." In fact, NASA even plans to launch interstellar probes within the next 4 or 5 years, completely disregarding Heischler's warnings! NASA is good for one thing though: they are wonderfully adept at creating marvelous technology with their huge budget!

We can speak more about this report at breakfast. See you there! - Marston

Ben laid the report on his desk and took another drink of orange juice. The Heischler

Report was yet another massive jolt to his previously well-ordered universe. Strangely, he didn't feel nearly as shocked about this as he had been about everything else he had seen or learned the day before. He attributed the barely noticeable rise in his heart rate to being emotionally numbed. "I'm minding my own business, then WHAM! He thought to himself, "You fly me across the continent; tell me aliens are visiting the earth; show me their toys and expect me to figure out how they work; then toss in a dissected humanoid body for good measure. The very next day, you tell me these creepy little devils might be planning to invade our planet and we have about as much of a chance of repelling them as stopping tomorrows' sunrise. I mean, it can't get worse, can it? So, there is no compelling reason to get my underwear all twisted, is there?"

Ben's gut feeling was that Heischler was probably right on the money. He was a renowned expert on the clashes between human cultures, and he made basic assumptions about the probable universal, evolution-driven development of "dominant cultures" that were terribly hard to argue against. In the 16 years since Heischler submitted his report, science gathered a tremendous amount of data about the universe and evolution, but nothing that would change the validity of it. To Ben, the most disturbing aspect of reading the report was knowing that the human race needed to be rallying together to prepare for earths' defense and nobody was doing it! Surely, every major world leader knew about the aliens and the threat they posed... or did they? The world condition suggested that, even if they did know, our human squabbles were obviously more important to them. Vietnam was beginning to look like a major conflict, the Cold War was perpetuating the constant nuclear threat, Communist China was emerging as a major global player, and if that were not enough, western culture was being assaulted by groups of people who were anti-everything traditional, no matter how successful "traditional" had been! It was all madness! What will our petty differences amount to if we all become ducks in an alien shooting gallery? Heischler's eighth recommendation, even if overly dramatic, said it all: "Pray for deliverance." Well, Ben Hanson vowed to do his part and work like hell to uncover the countless mysteries of alien technology. Maybe, someday, the world will take a break from the usual madness and scientists everywhere will get a chance to contribute to the effort. Paraphrasing Arthur Marston, "the more minds working on a difficult problem, the better."

Ben made his way to the bathroom for a much needed shower and shave. He did his best thinking in the shower, but he had trouble focusing on any particular topic amongst the dozens of topics that flooded his mind. He decided to let go of the aliens and science for the moment and enjoy the warmth of the water cascading over his head and down his body. There would be plenty of time for thinking and calmly absorbing additional blows to his "ordered universe," later.

Chapter 38

It had taken Loeffler the better part of four days of meticulous investigation to narrow his search for Ben Hanson to one of two Las Vegas hotels, the Luxor or Venetian Hotel and Casino. It seemed increasingly obvious that Dr. Hanson was not interested in fleeing the city. In fact, capture, but not immediate capture, was his goal. Loefflers' security teams scoured hours of video from The Orleans, with Hastings breathing down their necks every minute. Loeffler never wanted to harm someone as much as he wanted to snuff the last breath out of Hastings. The Foreman contributed absolutely nothing to the effort, other that criticizing every move Loeffler made and down playing the importance of each critical move forward in the investigation. The only laugh Loeffler had during those three, sleep-deprived days was when Wingate suggested that Hastings had to wear a necktie to keep the foreskin from slipping over his head. The mental picture of that never failed to bring an inner smile and a chuckle to the exhausted security chief.

The first major break came when one of the security cameras tagged Hanson leaving the Hotel at about 8PM. A security camera located at the guarded Hotel elevators showed Hanson returning to his Hotel room at about two hours later with an unknown person wearing a western hat and dark sunglasses. In addition, Hanson had a different shirt on when he returned, no doubt a tactic to help him elude anyone who might be following him. The shirt, however, had an amazing clue on it: the name of the place where he had likely been, Harrah's Casino. Over the previous 24 hours, Hanson had more than proven he wasn't prone to making stupid mistakes. The shirt could be yet another clue designed to aid in his own capture, or maybe buy him more time by sending the posse on a wild goose chase. It was entirely too early in the chase to know for sure which tack Hanson was taking, so Loeffler made a mental note of the possibilities, then sent a pair of his men to Harrah's to check it out.

The two suspects on the Orleans video did not speak to each other before passing the elevator security check, but Loeffler wondered aloud what were the odds that two guys wearing hats and dark glasses at night would walk through a casino and into the same elevator together? "Well, this IS Vegas!" as FBI Special Agent in Charge Simpson reminded him. Still, Loeffler had a gut feeling that Hanson met with this man and was proven right when a security camera caught the same man leaving the Hotel well after midnight... carrying the same box Hanson walked into the hotel with! This new suspect had engaged in the transfer of a box that may or may not contain something of vital importance to national security. Loeffler had to assume the worst and the manhunt suddenly took on a new, more urgent feel. Time became critical and every minute that passed the more distance this new suspect would undoubtedly put between him and Loeffler's team. The security chief looked at his watch when he noted the time on the surveillance tape and sadly realized that enough time had elapsed for the suspect to be well on his way to any destination on earth.

The next big breakthrough came late on the second full day of the investigation when an FBI team managed to track the second suspect to the MGM Grand by painstakingly going through dispatch logs of the Taxi Companies who had cabs waiting at the Orleans during the time the suspect was observed leaving the Hotel. The FBI agents found the actual cabbie that transported him, but could not determine if the man entered the hotel or walked into the parking lot. Special Agent in Charge Simpson assigned an FBI team to monitor the MGM Grand and review their security tapes. Simpson also requested LVMPD to lend them any "spare" detectives they had, which brought an instant chuckle from Captain Eddie "Hound Dog" Spencer, who never had any detectives to spare. However, since he owed Simpson a favor or two... or several, he supplied a pair of veteran detectives who had stagnant cases from which they needed to take a break. Simpson also requested and given instant approval for assistance from the Phoenix and Los Angeles field offices. The investigation was beginning to turn up large hotels that required several investigators to adequately search and/or stake out.

Another giant step forward came on the fourth full day of the search for Ben Hanson when it was determined that he had taken one of two cabs from The Orleans at the time a casino security camera taped him leaving the east entrance. One cab went to The Luxor, the other to The Venetian. Unfortunately, the cabbies didn't remember much about the men they had given rides to, except the one going to the Venetian wanted to take the "long route so he could see the lights." Neither man recognized a picture of Hanson shown to them. Loeffler assigned himself and Special Agent Simpson to The Luxor, figuring the cab going to the Venetian was likely carrying a tourist. He was close to capturing Hanson. He could feel it in his gut, but even though he was sure Hanson was, or had been, at the Luxor, he was still smarting from earlier "assumptions" that bit him on the ass. Loeffler wanted every base covered and assigned one of his security agents to check the registration log at the Venetian, following-up as indicated.

Loeffler wasn't quite so sure of his chances in capturing the second suspect. By day three, there were no tangible clues about the man in possession of the all-important box. A security tape from a camera in the MGM parking lot showed a man carrying something out to a car in the early morning hours of Sunday, but the video was moderately out of focus, dark, optically noisy and the subject entirely too small. It was impossible to see what he was carrying and exactly what kind of car he was getting into, although it did seem to have the shape of a sports car. The videotape was FedEx-ed to Headquarters for enhancement, but the quality was so poor that nobody expected anything of use. The team assigned to the MGM remained at the hotel, watching for somebody they fully expected to be thousands of miles away from them.

Simpson and Loeffler drove to the Luxor Hotel and Casino to begin what Loeffler hoped would be the last chess move in his quest to capture the elusive Benjamin H. Hanson, PhD. The Luxor, located at the southern end of the famous Vegas "Strip," was a gambler's wonderland in an exotic, ornate blend of ancient Egyptian architecture and modern amenities. A huge, onyx pyramid, guarded by an impressive, imitation sandstone "Sphinx" overlooked the 9th busiest airport in the world, McCarran International.

The Luxor was a very familiar landmark to Loeffler and the Project Cocheta employees, as it was located directly across South Las Vegas Boulevard from the enigmatic JANET airline terminal on the northwest side of McCarran. This was the facility where well over a thousand Project Cocheta, Groom Lake, and other "Black Project" employees caught flights in unmarked 737-66N airliners to their respective destinations. "JANET" was a call sign used by the pilots identify the aircraft to air traffic control, the official meaning of the acronym was "Joint Air Network for Employee Transportation." The unofficial meaning, however, was "Just Another Non-Existent Terminal." In times past, the United States Government refused to confirm or deny the existence of the facilities that JANET serviced, therefore the consensus amongst those who board the jets on a regular basis was that they too, were not likely to exist, along with the terminal and it's collection of 737s, Beechcraft B200C King Airs, and Beechcraft 1900s. In spite of the overwhelming evidence and quite official government insistence that nothing existed anywhere, all of the non-existent employees conceded that their paychecks were real enough to continue boarding the non-existent commuter aircraft on a regular basis.

The JANET terminal and the aircraft were operated by Edgerton, Germeshausen and Grier Inc., or E.G.&G. Technical Services, a huge government contractor with high-tech roots dating back to the atomic weapons programs of the 1940s. The company began airline operations in 1972 at the southwest corner of McCarran, near the intersection of West Russell Road and South Las Vegas Boulevard. The "terminal" consisted of a few trailers supporting a single, well-aged DC-6. As the mission expanded, an additional DC-6 joined the "fleet" in 1977. Three years later, the first jet airliners, three Boeing 737s, went into service, with another three added in 1985. Over the next five years, E.G.&G. added five smaller, turboprop aircraft to the ballooning JANET fleet. During these two decades

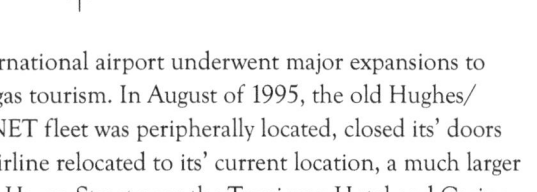

of JANET operations, McCarren International airport underwent major expansions to accommodate the rapid growth of Vegas tourism. In August of 1995, the old Hughes/Signature Air Terminal where the JANET fleet was peripherally located, closed its' doors to commuter traffic. The unmarked airline relocated to its' current location, a much larger terminal facility at East Hacienda and Haven Street near the Tropicana Hotel and Casino. The new location boasted a comfortable terminal building, a huge parking lot surrounded by a barbed wire fence and guarded by large, armed men with serious demeanors. One look from these men, reinforced by the ominous signs on the fence, was enough to ward off the most curious of passers by.

In addition to the non-existent transportation business, E.G.&G. Technical Services also managed security at the Groom Lake Test facility and had its' fingers into just about every nuclear, black project and exotic research pie the government had baking... except Cocheta. Project Director Brogan was the first Project Cocheta director to reject the proposal to have E.G.&G. Technical Services take over security in the early 1980s. Not because he didn't think they could handle the job, but because he was a military man and he liked having nail-hard Marines guarding his facility. The Cold War was still hot and the primary security concern for Brogan was a Soviet raid on Cocheta. In the single, seemingly thoughtful move Project Director Hastings ever made, he too rejected the idea of turning security matters over to E.G.&G. Technical Services when the proposal surfaced again in the mid 1990s. In reality, the real reason Hastings kept the Marines was that E.G.&G. spooked him. He could muscle the military, to a point, but E.G.&G. was notably well-connected in Washington and not likely put up with much of his Napoleanistic bullshit. In essence, it was all about control. Eventually, Hastings was able to dodge the E.G.&G. bullet only because he managed to collect enough political clout to do so.

Special Agent in Charge Simpson, with Kevin Loeffler in tow, approached the long, Egyptian-style front desk and flashed the magic FBI identification card that was a perfect compliment to her equally magic blue, yellow-lettered FBI jacket. Of course, this resulted in a near instant and private audience with the hotel manager. Simpson was accustomed to such official "hospitality" in Vegas. As a whole, Hotel/Casino managers were not thrilled about having high profile cops wandering around their property and universally considered such a spectacle to be bad for business. Jittery guests were less likely to pour the contents of their bank accounts into games of chance when cops were brazenly sniffing about the place. At the same time, hotel/casino management was usually quite eager to cooperate with the LVMPD and FBI, mostly to get them the hell off the property as quickly as possible, and partly because the Nevada Gaming Commission takes hints of impropriety very seriously and could cut the financial throat of a casino in a heartbeat. As a result of such official oversight, a tourist can lose his tookus in a Nevada casino, but sleep well at night knowing it was due to being stupid enough to gamble in the first place and not because the casino made any dishonest efforts to hasten his poverty.

Being relatively new in the Las Vegas area, Loeffler had not been in the majority of the main hotels and was finding it very difficult not to gawk at the architectural and decorative marvels inside the Luxor pyramid. Like the exterior, the interior was an equally odd, but stunning blend of ancient and modern. The lobby was expansive, littered with statues of the Egyptian gods and pharaohs of antiquity intertwined with potted palms on a highly polished marble floor. From the lobby, it was evident that the huge pyramid was, in fact, nearly hollow with what amounted to be a small city located inside. The panorama was inviting, but Loeffler had to content himself with a promise to return to the Luxor when he wasn't tracking down errant scientists.

The manager of the Luxor Hotel, Antonia Boyd, was an attractive, smartly dressed middle-aged woman who didn't waste any time getting down to business. "Welcome to the Luxor, officers. How can I be of service to you?" she said as they entered her almost unearthly clean and organized office.

"We have reason to believe that the man we are looking for is staying here, quite likely registered under an assumed name." Simpson said, matching Ms. Boyds' professional demeanor. "We would like to search your registration records to begin with, then review the registration desk security tapes if it becomes necessary to do so."

"Of course, we will assist your investigation in whatever way we can. May I ask what he is wanted for?"

"A matter concerning national security. Unfortunately, I cannot divulge any other details beyond that." Loeffler answered.

"Oh, my! Is he a terrorist? Is he a danger to my guests?" She asked, a sudden, worried countenance emerging.

"We do not believe him to be armed or dangerous in any way, Ms. Boyd. You need not worry." Simpson reassured. "If he is here, we will be a discreet as possible when we..."

Loeffler's cellular phone interrupted the conversation with its' annoying electronic warble.

"Loeffler here." The security chief answered. Within fifteen seconds, Loeffler's facial expression of irritation changed to that of a man quite obviously shocked.

"Come again... You have got to be kidding me! Stay there and keep your eyes open! We'll be there in 15 minutes!"

"What's going on?" Simpson asked.

"Ms. Boyd, thank you very much for your time and cooperation." Loeffler stood up quickly and turned to his partner. "He's at the Venetian... registered under his own name!"

Chapter 39

The room at the Venetian was, to say the least, splendid. Everything, from the floor to the ceiling, designed to drain the guest of every last shred of stress. Surely engineered by the Sandman himself, the bed possessed the remarkable ability to render one into a near instantaneous coma, as if consciousness could rapidly leave the body by some sort of ethereal osmosis. Dr. Hanson could not think of a single thing in the room he would change, other than perhaps, being there in the first place. Hanson was definitely not accustomed to the kind of luxury found in a top-end room at a premiere Vegas hotel. Not that he couldn't afford such extravagances, he just never saw the point in spending his money that way.

To say Benjamin Hanson was thoughtful when it came to money would be undershooting the truth by a fair amount. He made a handsome six-figure yearly income, yet he lived in a practical house, drove a practical car and wore practical clothes. No doubt, growing up in a household created by very practical parents had much to do with Dr. Hanson's lack of interest in self-indulgence. Paul Sr. was an adequate, dedicated provider for his family. While money didn't exactly "grow on trees," as Paul Sr. and every other father on the planet were fond of saying, there was enough money left over at he end of the month to put a little aside for savings, a yearly vacation and Christmas. Family treats tended to be austere, but nonetheless, these occasional minor luxuries his family shared together were always fun. The young Ben Hanson learned early that "luxury" came in many forms and some of the best were free.

Dr. Hanson hoped his last few days of freedom would be more relaxing, but it was not to be. In total spite of the comforts surrounding him, a combination of guilt over treating himself so lavishly, the ever-increasing pain from a slowly exploding time bomb in his chest, and an unexpected swell of soul searching kept him from enjoying his wind-down from the frenzied weeks before. The guilt was a natural by-product of his ingrained practicality. Rationalizing to himself that it was acceptable for a dying man to pamper himself for a few days did little to attenuate his uneasiness. The pain from his metastasizing cancer was now well beyond the scope of over-the-counter analgesics. In his only trip away from the Venetian, Hanson paid a visit to Dr. Sedgewyk. The good doctor might possess the demeanor of a television Small-Claims Court Judge, but he wasn't afraid to treat pain. He handed Hanson a generous prescription of sustained-release oxycontin, more than enough to last him until well after his arrest. The cancer was also attempting make Hanson weaker by robbing him of his appetite, accomplishing this indirectly by damaging cells, causing white blood cells and dying tissue to release a powerful appetite suppressant known as cachexin, or tumor necrosis factor (alpha). Hanson already new of this eventuality and began forcing himself to eat when he noticed he was losing weight. The soul searching... Well, Hanson should have expected it. He always analyzed his performance in every aspect of his personal and professional life, and during the quiet hours of his second full night at the Venetian, he began to re-examine the wisdom of what he set into motion... and whether or not his motives were as pure as he convinced himself they were.

Staring at the darkened ceiling, Hanson's mind raced. What had he done? Why had he done it? He had easy answers to those questions when he first realized he was dying from cancer, but now that the boulder was tumbling down the mountain, he wasn't as convinced as he was before, but... why? If all went according to plan, the world would finally know the truth and that was a good thing, was it not? Maybe the nations of the planet would begin pointing their weapons at the sky instead of each other. Hanson wanted to see this day come since he started working at Cocheta, and now, on the brink of disclosure, he was troubling over it. "Jitters before the big day... Maybe that's it." Hanson thought to himself, but quickly dismissed the thought outright. In his heart, he knew what the problem was. It was about purity of motive and intellectual honesty. There was a very dark side to his altruism, and in a dimly lit room, lying in the middle of the most comfortable bed he had ever known, Dr. Ben Hanson was becoming keenly aware of it.

Soul searching took him back to 1992, the year his life turned into a nightmare from which he would never wake up. In the preceding 24 years, Hanson understood why Cocheta had to remain a "black operation." The world was teeming with dangerous people, mortal enemies of his country waiting patiently for a clear, tactical advantage to use their nuclear weapons. The extraordinary technology under study was highly destabilizing, both militarily and politically. In the wrong hands, nuclear blackmail was the best outcome out of two dreadful possibilities. In the right hands, the technology posed a threat to an established or potential enemy that might prompt a preemptive strike out of fear or just plain paranoia. Therefore, as long as America had enemies, the official policy of the United States Government was to deny the existence and mission of Project Cocheta. In a broader application of this policy, all sightings of unidentified flying objects would face official denial, debunking and discrediting. Hanson may have understood and agreed with the reasoning behind the official government stance, but the idealistic side of his personality, the one he kept in mothballs, believed humans could and should quickly band together to face the probable extraterrestrial threat. On Christmas Day in 1991, Dr. Hanson unhinged the door to his treasured idealism: the Union of Soviet Socialist Republics had collapsed!

The Soviet political implosion sent shock waves around the world, even to the remote eastern British Columbian hole-in-the-rock that didn't exist. Hanson followed Soviet politics closely since the fall of the Berlin Wall in November of 1989. He sensed that the communist government was stumbling seriously, but he had no idea that there would be nothing left of it by the first day of 1992. The Cold War was over and America's long time nemesis de-clawed. Hanson was jubilant. There was only one, true superpower left and now the world could press on and face the possible challenge from a civilization many light years away.

By January of 1992, Dr. Benjamin Hanson possessed the number three position at Cocheta, Chief Scientific Advisor. Unlike academia, where an inverse relationship existed between the flamboyance of the position's title and the amount of work generated by its' holder, the position of Chief Scientific Advisor was a very busy job. Hanson attended every staff meeting involving research; approved every avenue of investigation; cleared every purchase request for scientific instruments; worked on his own avenues of research; and personally led every "Field Trip." In addition, Hanson recently took over recruiting duties from Hastings, who showed only superficial interest in the critical task. In his seven years of recruiting "talent" for the project, he only managed to acquire two staff members. Unfortunately, they were far better butt-kissers than scientists. As if that were not enough work for one man, when Hanson wasn't whittling away at his own monstrous workload, he was handling an endless series of bullshit tasks that Hastings dumped on him. In spite of the stress and workload, Dr. Hanson never let it show. He had the respect and admiration of nearly everyone at Cocheta. He was affable, extremely intelligent, fair and considered well balanced by all of his peers. Everyone was an equal in his eyes, so nobody ever felt small around him. Even the Marines were fond of him and routinely invited him to high testosterone events like "Poker Night," and summertime, out-of-season moose or elk barbecues by a small lake that was a healthy walk south of the installation. While he more than lived-up to the expectations of the first two "Foremen," the current Foreman was not impressed, but then, nothing really impressed Louis Hastings, except perhaps his own reflection in a mirror.

When the great Bolshevik experiment ended in complete failure and the hide of the Soviet Bear finally adorning the world's living room floor, Dr. Hanson called for a special science staff meeting to discuss the impact of current world events on the Cocheta Project. In particular, Dr. Hanson wanted to discuss the possibility of disclosing the reality of extraterrestrial visitation and the potential negative impact on the human race. Hanson envisioned a gradual release of information to reduce the intensity of the "culture shock" that was bound to occur. Like the frog in a pot of slowly heated water, it was better to gradually ease people into a frightening concept than to toss them into the boiling water of stark reality. Dr. Hanson already knew where most of the scientists stood on the subject, but the meeting was necessary to formulate an official staff position based on a consensus of its' members.

It was no accident that Hanson called for the staff meeting while Hastings was off in D.C. lining up powerful asses to smooch. The demise of the Soviet Union made very nervous people out of those that depended upon the Cold War to make the mortgage payment, and Hastings was one of them. Project Cocheta enjoyed over 40 years of generous and uninterrupted off-budget funding and Hastings was going to make sure it continued. Besides, it was an election year and astute political creatures like Hastings knew to get an early start. If he attended the staff meeting, he would have been disruptive, at best, and Hanson wanted honest opinions voiced without fear of reprisal. As Chief Scientific Advisor, Hanson would deliver the staff position to Hastings for consideration upon his return.

Hanson convened the meeting in the largest of the staff conference rooms, the one used for the Monday situation and planning meeting. All twenty scientists, including Hanson, were given time to air their opinion on the subject of bringing the world up to speed on the fantastic discoveries hidden at Cocheta and the potential dangers ahead. Culture shock was the biggest concern voiced by the staff. A few had mixed feelings about timing, suggesting that the new Russian Government might not survive and that something far worse than the old Soviet Union might emerge in its' place. Both of the Hastings appointments seemed far more concerned about how releasing the truth to the public might affect their job security. Hanson spoke last and put forth his own opinion that the time was right, but releasing the information did entail risk. He felt that since most people already believed in the existence of extraterrestrial life, a thoughtful, measured approach of releasing easily digestible aliquots of information should help attenuate whatever social upheaval that might occur. "But," he added, "there was no way to predict how the world will actually react." The most dangerous part of disclosure would be the assessment that extraterrestrials were likely to be aggressive and may be in the process of mounting an invasion. It would be very difficult to sugar coat that bit of information. There was even a possibility that the aliens might hasten their plans if the people of the world suddenly knew of their intentions. In the end, Dr. Hanson urged his colleagues to consider the opportune timing for uniting the entire world against a common enemy... and pleaded that squandering the planets' vast cerebral and material resources that could be brought to bear on creating a viable defense would almost certainly doom mankind.

The vote was 16 in favor of disclosure, 4 against. The 2 junior scientists, the Hastings appointees, and 2 senior scientists, who felt that more time was needed to watch the progress of the new Russian government, voted against disclosure. Hanson would have preferred a unified front, but an 80% majority was clearly a mandate. Hanson thanked his colleagues for their time and assured them that he would present their opinion to Project Director Hastings and do his best to see full disclosure realized. He also told the dissenting members that he would consider their valid concerns when formulating a disclosure plan and timetable. With that, he dismissed the group and retired to his office. There was a very important briefing to prepare before Hastings returned. Hanson knew that Hastings would resist the idea, but he would insist that Hastings take the proposal to Washington. If Hastings refused, then Hanson would take it to Washington himself.

Caught up in the sudden whirlwind of hope brought on by a world without a "Cold War," Hanson was genuinely passionate about revealing the truth to the public. He wanted to quickly seize the opportunity that a new global peace seemed to present. In his excitement, Hanson failed to take into consideration what disclosure might mean to somebody like Hastings, the man who controlled of every aspect of Project Cocheta and who's sole allegiances were to himself and the bureaucracy that granted him power. Hanson was playing with a loaded gun... aimed squarely at his own head.

Hastings returned to Cocheta in a foul mood. The assholes in Washington were flitting about in glee, talking of "Peace Dividends," and scaling back the military, diverting funds previously earmarked for defense into spending for urgent needs at home. Of course, those were just a catchphrases and code words for "pork barrel" and "vote buying." The collapse of the Soviet Union was a nightmare come true for Louis Hastings. In the coming mad dash to put the military on cinder blocks in order to fund the porkfest, off-budget black projects would surely come under scrutiny. He wanted to believe the words of the "Insiders," advising him that he had no need to worry, but his Washington-honed alarm system was going berserk. Project Cocheta would be scaled-back, perhaps even mothballed. Hastings was sure of it, but what could he do to stop it? He was not a man accustomed to letting others control his fate, but there was little he could do beyond the ass kissing he had already done.

The intercom on his office desk beeped. "Yes, Sonya, what is it?"

"Dr. Hanson is here to see you." His secretary replied.

"Send him in."

Nineteen years later, Ben Hanson arose from the plush, Venetian Hotel bed to stare out the window. Like the city around him, sleep was all but impossible. The memories of that terrible day in January of 1992 were saturating his consciousness. His meeting-turned-confrontation with Louis Hastings was as vivid in his mind as the day it happened, evoking in him the same powerful emotions of astonishment, horror, panic and rage. The years did nothing to attenuate them. He closed his eyes hard, trying to sweep the coming memory from his head, but it came anyway. It was part of who he was and what he set into motion.

"Just who in the fuck do you think you are, Hanson?" Hastings lashed out, eyes full of anger and neck veins bulging. "You, and your scientist buddies do not make national security policy for the United States of America and you sure as hell don't dictate policy around here!"

Hanson reeled from the unexpected viciousness of the attack. "Sir, I... we feel that the..."

Hastings cut him off. "Do you think I give a shit about how you or your staff feels about this or any other matter! You have a job to do and it doesn't involve organizing behind-my-back meetings or demanding policy changes!"

"With all due respect, sir," Hanson replied, composing himself and starting to become angry. "you have some of the brightest minds on this planet working at Cocheta and collectively, they have come to the conclusion that it is time to..."

Hastings cut him off again. "Time to do what? Tell the whole world what we've been doing here? Tell the American people we've been lying to them for almost 50 years? Hanson, you are too fucking old to be so naïve! You think since the commies went tits up that America has no more enemies?" He leaned forward with an ominous stare. "What about the Chinese? What about the Ragheads? Did they just up and disappear?"

"And you think the aliens are less of a threat than they are?" Hanson replied angrily, glaring back at Hastings. "We could be facing an invasion within our lifetimes! That is a lot more concerning to me than the Chinese Communists or petty Arab dictators!"

"You actually believe that Heischler bullshit? You ARE naïve, Hanson!" Hastings laughed in a way that made Hanson want to strangle him. "Heischler conjured up a ghost story that was so bad, he scared the piss out of himself and ran into the woods to hide! Earth is nothing more than a stop on a fucking high school biology field trip for alien teenagers. They study us... so what? They've probably been doing it for a million years! They haven't fired a single shot at us and they never will!"

"You don't know that, and even if it were true, what about the next species, or the one after that?" Hanson snapped back. "Besides, the American people have a right to know what is going on and they need to know about ALL of the possible scenarios!"

"The American people? They can't wipe their own ass without the government's help! You tell them about the big bad aliens and they'll shit all over themselves! They'll demand the government do something to protect them. Their idiot Senators and Representatives will grandstand before every camera they can find and call for investigations. Cocheta will be cracked open like an egg and then what, Hanson? What will the next brilliant idea you and your egghead friends come up with to save the fucking world?"

"Mr. Hastings," Ben said, bristling with anger, "If you are unwilling to bring our recommendations to the appropriate people in Washington, I will do so myself!"

"What?" Hastings jumped from his chair, startling Hanson. "You conniving bastard! You will do nothing of the sort! I'll be damned if you, or anybody else in this project, discloses what we do here!"

Shaken by the outburst, but not deterred, Hanson continued to press. "Then I have no choice but to retire from the project. I cannot continue working under these conditions. You will have my resignation and retirement paperwork on your desk by tomorrow morning."

Hastings began to belly laugh and the laugh turned Ben's blood into ice water. "Dr. Hanson, you aren't going anywhere. Do you think for one moment I am going to let you retire, then have you parade around Washington spilling national security secrets?"

Hanson sensed that he had crossed into forbidden territory through a one-way door. Dark clouds were building, as were the first traces of panic. "I have put nearly 24 years into this project. I have the right to retire if I wish to." Hanson said, shakily.

"I don't think you quite understand the situation you have just put yourself into." Hastings sat back down in his chair and began to smile. "You, my friend, have just become a national security risk. If I cut you loose, you might endanger the project, or compromise the safety of the American people. I take security and maintaining state secrets quite seriously, Dr. Hanson. As I have done in the past, and will continue to do so in the future, whatever is necessary to prevent secrets from leaving this facility. Allow me to sum it up for you, Ben Hanson: I own your ass!"

Hanson's brain was flooded with panic. "What have I done?" He thought to himself. "What in God's name have I done?"

Hastings saw the confusion and went for the jugular. "How are the wife and kids?"

Hanson froze. He knew the situation he found himself in was about to get far worse.

Hasting opened the file drawer on his desk, thumbed through the files and pulled out Hanson's personnel file. He casually flipped through the pages, and then began to speak. "Pretty wife." He began. "Aging nicely... A nurse. Good, good... School Board member. Dabbling a little in politics, I see. Oldest kid... Paul. All American at Texas A&M. First year in minor league baseball... Says here he's a heartbeat away from the majors. Talented kid. Donna... Just as pretty as her mom and as smart or smarter than her Dad! Hmmmm... Graduate School at Michigan... Aerospace Engineering, and sources say a shoe-in at Lockheed! Wasn't that where you were headed before General Marston hijacked you? Well, well... following in Daddy's footsteps! Arthur... high school junior. Some rocky behavior, but settling down... Wants to go to the University of Oklahoma... ROTC... He's going to be a Marine like his grandfather! A very nice family, Ben. Maybe everything will work out for them. Of course, that all depends upon you, doesn't it?"

The message was clear. Hanson's family and their futures had just become hostages. Hanson's rage flared one last time. "You leave my family alone you sonofabitch!"

"Let me restate that last sentence, Ben: Your family's health depends upon you, doesn't it?" His tone changed from flippant to menacing. "I suggest you put a lid on this mutiny of yours, Hanson, and by the way, retirement will never be an option for you. It would be... unhealthy."

Physically and mentally stunned, Hanson knew Hastings wasn't bluffing. In the seven years Hastings had been the Project Director, six Project Cocheta scientists retired. All were dead, plus two more that retired just before Hastings took over. It was not that eight retirees where dead, many people die right after retirement, it was how they died. Three died in single car "accidents," one fell down a flight of stairs in his home, one in a hit-and-run auto-pedestrian "accident," another shot in a burglary of her home, one fell off a cliff while hiking, and one drowned in her bathtub. To have eight retired scientists die violent deaths seemed to stretch probabilities quite improbably. Hanson tried not to subscribe to the notion that Louis Hastings was so obsessed with secrecy that he was making sure that former Project Cocheta scientists never spoke a word about the scientific treasures inside Cocheta. Hanson didn't like Hastings, but surely he wasn't a murderer, was he? His gut instincts, however, told him that he WAS a murderer and a vicious one at that. Hastings was capable of hurting or killing his family. Hanson had no doubts about it.

In the span of less than thirty minutes, Ben Hanson's life lay in ruins. He had unintentionally played a hellish game of chess with one of Satan's business partners, was quickly outmaneuvered and soundly mated. He single-handedly dashed any hope of disclosure and put his entire family in grave danger.

"Do we have an understanding, Dr. Hanson?" Hastings asked.

Ben slowly stood up with his head lowered and turned for the door.

"Dr. Hanson, do we have an understanding?"

"Yes," he said quietly, "I'll do whatever you ask of me, just don't harm my family."

"Agreed." Hastings said smugly. "Oh, Dr. Hanson..."

"Yes?" He replied, not turning around.

"Have a nice day."

Hanson didn't reply, he merely opened the door slowly, exited the office complex, and began his new life in hell.

The vivid light show of the Las Vegas "Strip" began to blur with the onset of tears. The most heartbreaking thing he ever did in his life was telling his beloved wife that she had to leave town with their youngest son and never return. The look of shock, horror and grief in her eyes always haunted him, especially at night, when the stillness of a darkened, lonely bedroom made him long for her. He could not tell Teresa why she had to leave, only that it was for the children's safety as well as hers'. He profusely apologized to her, saying it was all his fault and to please forgive him. She tried to bargain with him, begging for an alliance with him to fight whatever was tearing them apart. He was resolute; he had to be. It was hard enough losing them, but he could not bear the thought of them dead, or their lives ruined because of him. He left with instructions for her and all of his children to never contact him again. She was to file for a divorce and he would send the bulk of his salary to her for alimony and child support. He also told her that she must assume her maiden name and continue on with her life. As Teresa and Arthur began to drive away, tears streaming down their faces, he ran to the window and Teresa stopped the car. He opened the door and gave his lovely wife one last, lingering kiss. He whispered in her ear with a broken voice "I will always love you, Miss Chandler! You are my one and only-est, and every breath still belongs to you!" He told Arthur to be strong and to take care of his mother. After closing the door, they slowly drove away, heading to Picher where a bewildered family awaited them.

Hanson turned his back to the window overlooking the cheerful glitter of Sin City and slid to the floor. The pain of separation never lessened for him and at that moment, it was too unbearable to allow for standing. He was reliving the unrelenting pain in all of its' desolation. He remembered the tear-filled two week "off period" immediately after losing his family's companionship, when he seriously grappled with the idea of suicide every moment he was awake.

In the end, an epiphany of revenge kept him alive. Hanson decided that Hastings would pay dearly for his crimes. He began quietly gathering whatever evidence he could find against Hastings, as well as purloining bits and pieces of alien technology and body parts from right under the nose of Cocheta security. Carl O'Neil, the longtime Chief of Security before Kevin Loeffler, was quite lax with Hanson as they were great friends, frequently sharing many an evening together with the Marines at the poker tables. Dr. Hanson found another purpose in life to replace the one he had with his family, but it wasn't a wholesome one. He became introverted and chronically morose, picking up chain smoking and excessive coffee drinking to help soothe his constant, inner pain.

So, there it was... the answer to his soul searching. Benjamin Harris Hanson, PhD. was a fraud. The circus he created was more about revenge than it was about his lofty goal to inform the world about the alien threat. In his quest for Hasting's blood, he used a good friend's trust to steal extraterrestrial scrap metal and tissue samples, as well as endangering the life and career of a prominent and charismatic scientist. He felt a sudden surge of shame to add to the painful recollections of his past. People were going to get hurt and

Hastings might just get away unscathed in spite of his efforts. What would he have accomplished then? Hanson began to feel that he was no better than the man he was trying to destroy.

He couldn't put a stop to things now and resigned himself to watch it all unfold and pray that his sins would not harm the innocent. The alien threat to the world needed to be revealed and perhaps if that happened, some good might come of his malfeasance. But, as his parents taught him early on in his life, the means used to achieve a goal is every bit as important as achieving the goal itself.

The tears of lost love and family mixed with those of shame. He had no energy or will power to return to bed and sleep born of exhaustion and sorrow overtook him. He slept on the carpet a few steps away from a spectacularly luxurious bed. Dreams were torments and his sleep restless as a result. Even so, sleep he did, until a violent coughing spell awakened him around dawn; the first light of his last day as a free man.

Chapter 40

Ben Hanson was never, ever going to tell his mother that the breakfast he just ate in the remote reaches of the northern Canadian wilderness rivaled her best Sunday morning cooking. He was going to spend 26 weeks out of the year in this improbable culinary heaven and if he didn't want to end up looking like Dionysius of Heraclea, a man so morbidly obese he was said to have choked to death on his own fat, he had better start a rigorous exercise program or watch the calories. After picturing himself needing a piano crate for a coffin, he decided not to return for a third helping.

"Don't they feed you at home?" Marston asked with a smile.

"I'm sorry, sir." Ben replied sheepishly. "I never get a chance to eat food like this anymore, at least not since Christmas. I'm a pathetic cook and the Michigan Student Cafeterias leave a lot to be desired."

"No need to apologize. The food here is responsible for quite a few wardrobe changes." Marston said, pausing to take a sip of his coffee. "If you want to avoid that, we've got a very nice gym you have access to. If you're a glutton for punishment, there are some rabid Marines here who would gladly let you join them for morning PT."

"I'll have to give the latter suggestion some thought, sir. I doubt I could keep up with them."

"So..." Brogan began, leaning back in his chair. "What did you think of the homework we gave you?"

"Pretty scary stuff, Mr. Brogan." Ben replied, "Dr. Heischler made very logical, compelling arguments. Have there been any recent discoveries to strengthen or weaken his hypothesis?"

"Not really, just a continuation of the same scouting tactics they have used for the last 20 years... and not a single diplomatic envoy." Brogan replied.

"Well, what about the completely intact flying machine I saw yesterday? Is that something new for them to do, or have they left them lying around before?" Ben asked.

"The one you saw is the first, and only, fully-intact craft we have recovered." Marston answered, wondering where Ben was going to go with this. "To our knowledge, this is the only one like it in the world. Or, at least we hope it is."

"There is something really odd about it. Why would the aliens do that? I mean, why would they leave a pristine example of their technology behind? If it didn't work, and they couldn't repair it, wouldn't it have made more sense to destroy the craft rather than leave it for us to get our hands on it?"

"We were perplexed by that, too." Marston replied. "We routinely send strike missions to destroy our own downed combat aircraft so that our technology doesn't fall into enemy hands."

"Right! So why didn't they destroy it?" Ben asked.

"Two possibilities: One, we happened upon it before they could repair or destroy it. Two, they wanted us to have it." Brogan said. "We can't be certain which of the two possibilities it is, we only know they tracked their lost property to Cocheta, where we have it impounded."

"You said we recovered the craft in the Quebec wilderness. How did we come across it?"

"The Canadians spotted it on air defense radar engaged in what looked like a controlled re-entry and probable landing." Marston said. "We mounted a joint recovery operation and were on the scene within eight hours. It was just sitting there in a large field, hatch open, with no evidence that any sort of repair work was attempted, and no other craft spotted in the area. We know they repair their damaged or malfunctioning craft. I personally led a 'Field Trip' to Nova Scotia last October where a disabled craft rendezvoused with a second craft and underwent repair underwater!" Marston paused, "I don't know, Ben. Maybe we scared them off, maybe they gave it to us."

"Sounds to me like they handed it to us on a platter!" Ben said in amazement. "But, it doesn't make any sense for them to hand one over to us, unless it's a fake, rigged for surveillance, or it's a bomb." Ben said. "It's a little small to be hiding Trojans."

"God I hope it's not a fake!" Marston said, almost laughing. "If it is, we have been wasting a helluva lot of taxpayer money here! You know we've given the "booby-trap" scenario some thought, but I hadn't considered the surveillance possibility. We assumed that the suspicious timing of the arrival of our alien visitors at Cocheta was due to following our recovery and transportation efforts, or the craft has a homing beacon in it. The thought that they might be watching us from that vehicle is a bit unsettling."

"Art, I have to agree with you about the surveillance possibility." Brogan added. "It is very unnerving! Perhaps we should take precautions when working in and around it."

"Agreed, I'll draft a policy today and have the future 'Doctor' Hanson look it over. Maybe suggest improvements. Might as well get some work out of him while he's here." Marston said with a smile that quickly faded into a more serious countenance. "Ben, regardless of whatever their motives might be for leaving it behind, we simply couldn't pass up the opportunity to acquire and study the technology. We know we're taking chances, but the potential benefits make the risks more than acceptable."

"And with that, maybe we should get on with young Ben's formal in-processing and briefing." Brogan announced.

"Good idea... That is, if we can pry Ben away from the serving line!" Marston laughed.

The trio made their way from the cafeteria to a small meeting room in the office complex adjacent to the main service area. Brogan handed Ben a series of documents outlining Project Cocheta policies concerning security and maintaining highly classified information. He then directed him to sign another "agreement" swearing him to secrecy, and acknowledging that he understood the harsh criminal penalties that would be imposed upon him if he even mentioned to his future wife what kind of coffee pot he had in his Cocheta apartment. Words like "espionage" and "treason" were featured prominently in the security brief, accentuating the seriousness of the position he accepted approximately 24 hours earlier. There were more mundane paperwork tasks to complete as well, mostly financial in nature. Listing insurance beneficiaries, tax forms and such. A solid ninety minutes of his life were lost in the process of crossing each "T" and dotting every "I."

When Ben finished with the security brief, Marston brought in a slide projector and began his "Short Course" in Project Cocheta history. Ben watched the progression of slides visually recounting the story of the most secret project in American history, while Marston added commentary.

Lacking facilities of its' own, the newly reorganized, non-military Project Cocheta, started operations in 1949 at, oddly enough, a military installation, Ohio's Wright-Patterson Air Force Base. Wright Patterson AFB, and Holloman AFB in New Mexico, were the two assigned "repositories" for wreckage debris and alien corpses. Wright-Patterson was home for Headquarters, Foreign Technology Division, United States Air Force (FTD-USAF), and the focal point for the initial investigations into the UFO phenomenon and alien hardware.

With the beginning of the Cold War in the late 1940s, and gaining momentum in the first years of the 1950s, it was determined that FTD-USAF should concentrate on studying terrestrial, Soviet technology and divest itself completely of all responsibilities concerning extraterrestrial technology. As a result, the fledgling Project Cocheta assumed complete control over all materials related to alien visitation. Out of necessity and proximity to the evidence under scrutiny, Project Cocheta shared office space with FTD-USAF until the project relocated to a more remote facility. Holloman AFB was the natural first choice for Project Cocheta because of its' relative isolation and the fact that a portion of the recovered alien wreckage was already warehoused there. Marston, who assumed control the project by that time, insisted that the research facility be located in a much more inaccessible location. Holloman was certainly in the boondocks, but it was a functioning Air Force Base and home of the Holloman Air Development Center, with many important research projects in progress or planned. Marston suggested building the facility in an inhospitable, mountain-ous area, perhaps in the Rocky Mountains or Cascades. The advantages were obvious. An area, a valley perhaps, surrounded by mountains and rugged terrain could effectively shield the facility from casual view. Several sites on American soil garnered consideration, but in the end, the Canadians proposed the most suitable location.

At the start of the Cold War, the Canadian and American governments worked closely together on mutual air defense, establishing the Pinetree Radar and Distant Early Warning Radar lines in the first few years of the 1950s. Designed to spot attacking Soviet aircraft early enough to launch intercept missions, these radar nets, on occasion, also tracked high performance aircraft not of this world. The Canadian government was every bit as con-cerned about extraterrestrial incursions into its' airspace as the Americans and since each played a vital role in the others' strategic defense, Washington and Ottawa readily shared information about UFOs and mounted many dozens of joint intercept missions each year. The Canadians had the perfect location in mind for the American project. It was remote, extremely difficult to access, had a mountain with a sheer face. It was seismically and vol-canically quiet, easy to defend, and had an adjacent, level area large enough to support an 8,000 foot runway. Marston was intrigued by the proposal, and became even more so when an engineering team returned from the site with photographs and expert assessment of the locations' suitability.

In the spring of 1953, Marston personally surveyed the site and was thrilled with it. Not that it was perfect, but close enough to get a hearty thumbs-up. There would be dif-ficulties, to be sure. The winters could be brutal in that part of the world, and operating large transport aircraft in and out of such an area required snow-removal gear and de-icing equipment, as well as staff who knew how to operate them. There were serious power-supply issues, as well. The facility was nowhere near the British Columbia power grid, so it would have to be self-contained. Nuclear reactors held the most promise for supplying the substantial electrical power needed to operate a massive facility in a very remote loca-tion. Marston consulted the Atomic Energy Commission for suggestions, and within six months, Westinghouse Corporation began construction on a land-based (and half-again larger) version of the Naval S1W pressurized water reactor destined for the unfinished hull of the first nuclear submarine, the USS Nautilus. The reactor provided the intense heat needed to turn water into steam in a self-enclosed device called the "steam generator." The steam, piped to the generator turbines, created electricity. Abundant cold water in the area supplied the means to condense the steam back into water and returned it to the steam generator, endlessly recycling the process. The reactor, spinning three large generators, would produce over 36 megawatts of electricity, supplying Cocheta with more than enough energy to meet its' needs. Best of all, the relatively compact, highly enriched uranium reactor would not require refueling for well over 10 years!

April 30th, 1953 marked the first day of construction at Cocheta. The airfield was top priority, as equipment for blasting and boring away solid rock required air transport delivery. In what was nothing short of a massive display of force against the wilderness destined to become the most secretive installation on earth, the paved main runway became operational within two months. Construction workers, materials, equipment, and support services began to flood into the secluded mountain location. The initial objective was to develop enough infrastructure to support construction activities throughout the coming winter season. Hindered by less than ideal logistics, the objective proved to be overly ambitious. Nonetheless, during that first abbreviated year of construction, substantial progress was clearly evident. By the same time in 1954, aided by improved supply lines, Cocheta had easily become self-sufficient enough to sustain year-round construction. On the 3rd day of August 1957, a full month after permanent staff began occupying the facility, Cocheta officially became "fully operational." The nuclear reactor, however, had been generating electricity continuously for more than 13 months.

The engineering feat that created Cochea was impressive, to say the least. A monstrous, high-tech facility, built in the middle of nowhere by literally chiseling it out of a mountain of solid rock... and finished construction in a little over three years. Yet, because of the nature of the facility, the triumph would go completely unnoticed. Lessons learned at Cocheta would prove useful later, when the technology and techniques developed to create the research facility were applied to hollowing out Cheyenne Mountain for the North American Air Defense Command.

The mission of Cocheta, as Marston described it, was evaluating and duplicating alien machinery by any means necessary. This meant that it was not enough to just paw over extraterrestrial wreckage, but to gather all direct and indirect evidence that might shed light on the physics behind how these "objects" managed to fly. Photographs of ground effects caused by the object, as well as shape and color could yield clues as to the method of propulsion, aerodynamics, and even the materials used to construct it. Traces of radioactivity around a landing or crash site, electromagnetic effects on radios and other equipment and even the reaction of animals to the presence of UFOs might add valuable pieces to the complicated puzzle. In the beginning, detailed investigations of important sightings were the responsibility of FTD-USAF. This important job was turned over to the core scientists at Project Cocheta shortly after its' creation. What the concerned public saw, however, was a very serious sounding Air Force investigative project called "Blue Book."

Established in 1947, Project Blue Book was the governments' official investigation into UFO sightings. The project office was located at, not surprisingly, Wright-Patterson AFB, but instead of a staff of scientists picking apart every detail of an incident involving UFOs, a company-grade Air Force officer commanded the small office, assisted only by a lieutenant or junior NCO. Investigations, if any, were rudimentary and the information gathered beyond the report itself, practically worthless. Project Blue Books' mission, however, had nothing to do with investigation. It was merely an illusion to convince the public that the Air Force was taking the UFO phenomenon seriously, while at the same time, using the forum to explain it all away. Serious investigations were indeed taking place and Blue Book was a way to assist in diverting public view from it.

"At one time, serious investigations were underway at the Air Force Foreign Technology Division and Office of Special Investigation, the FBI and the CIA." Marston said at the conclusion of the slide show. "The creation of Project Cocheta changed all that. We handle it all and you will likely see some incredible things during the 'field trips' I'm going to send you on."

"You mentioned 'field trips' before. What exactly are they?"

"When a Cat Two 'Incident of Significance' occurs, we send a scientific crew to the field to investigate it, secure any evidence and return it to Cocheta for further study." Marston replied. "Normally, the crew consists of two senior scientists, cross-trained as field investigators, and myself. I come along to help the scientists and remove the inevitable obstacles that hinder progress. I am going to add you to the team when you arrive in July. That means you will be on call 24 hours a day, seven days a week, even when you are on vacation."

"I'm very honored, but I don't know a thing about that kind of work."

"Don't worry, I'll get you up to speed. Besides, you are going to be a natural at this." Marston said encouragingly. "A Cat Two IOS does not occur very often, maybe once every 6 months to a year. The last one was the incident in Nova Scotia I told you about at breakfast. It was amazing! A malfunctioning craft makes a water entry into a small bay at the southern tip of Nova Scotia, then navigates underwater some 20 or so miles to a location close to a Canadian sub monitoring facility. Of course, the Canadians quickly detect it and surface ships dispatched to the location. The object just sat there while the Canadian warships were floating above it! We started to move assets into place to drag the damn thing out of the water, when a second craft appeared and parked next to it! We weren't sure what to make of it, but it seemed that they were either trying to rescue the crew, or repair the damaged craft. Somehow or another, the Russians caught wind of what we were up to, or maybe they had been tracking the vehicles all along. Well, anyway, before we could get the salvage operation underway, a November-class attack sub showed up, the K-52 we think, forcing the Canadians to redeploy some of the ships that we had sitting on top of the submerged UFOs. When that happened, they both sped away, submerged, into the Gulf of Maine. We went after them, but our ships couldn't possibly keep up. They are incredibly fast underwater."

"That must have been something to see!" Ben exclaimed. "If they are using magneto-hydrodynamic propulsion in the atmosphere, they probably use it underwater, too. Only, instead of creating plasma, they would simply use the seawater around them!"

"It sounds like we really need to look into that." Brogan said. "Maybe we can get our people to contact the scientists currently working on this. We might have something for you to chew on when you set up shop in July."

"I'm looking forward to it!" Ben replied, now certain that his whole career was going to be a series of events no one would ever believe. "Sir," Ben continued, "do you believe it will ever be possible to tell the world about this?"

"I don't see it happening anytime soon, son." Brogan answered. "Not with the Soviets snooping around, looking for ways to get the upper hand. As I see it, the biggest threat to Cocheta is a Soviet incursion or nuclear strike. A raid would be an awfully difficult mission to accomplish, but not impossible. That's why we have the Marines and surface-to-air missiles. If they believe we are on the brink of duplicating the technology, they might take a huge risk and destroy Cocheta with an ICBM. Likewise, we currently have five targets in the Soviet Union where we think they may have reverse engineering projects underway. We would launch a first strike on them if we had hard evidence that they were close to 'operational' with a lightning fast nuclear warhead delivery system. The best way to keep the Soviets from attempting such acts is to make them believe we are not interested in UFOs at all."

"How do we do that?" Ben asked. "I mean, don't they already know about Cocheta?"

"We are not sure what they know about us, so we act as thought they don't know anything." Marston said. "We hide our assets when their satellites fly overhead, keep a tight lid on everything we do and send out a lot of 'white noise.'"

"White noise?"

"To confuse the issues, and 'we' are not exactly the ones sending it out. Other government agencies help muddle the evidence of extraterrestrial visitation by using a combination of official indifference, debunking, ridicule, harassment and good ol' fashioned denial."

"Let me give you some examples." Brogan added. "We have well respected scientists on the payroll who publicly denounce UFOs as pure hogwash, ridicule the people who report them, or debunk every sighting that hits the press. We have operatives who show up at high profile incidents and 'persuade' witnesses into silence." Brogan saw Ben furrow his eyebrows. "Don't worry, Ben, nobody gets hurt, unless you count egos or feelings. We have other professionals who specialize in trashing the credibility of vulnerable people or organizations by planting fake documents in places where they are likely to be found, or producing an 'insider' with a plausible story that falls apart under scrutiny by knowledgeable skeptics. This works well because the 'targets' are usually so eager to believe the information, or the insider, that they toss better judgment aside. When all else fails, we have the 'secret weapons.'"

"What are those?"

"The nut cases." Brogan said with a big grin.

"What?" Ben said, not sure he heard the remark correctly.

"What my erudite colleague meant," Marston began, "was that one of our 'secret weapons' is comprised of the more... well... silly members of our society, the ones who have latched onto the 'UFO' phenomenon and made it their own. You know... the Beatniks, Hippies, Bohemians. Many of them see the aliens as world saviors, or perhaps kindred spirits. This 'association' keeps the snotty academicians entirely away from the subject and everyone else who values their reputation. The other 'secret weapon' is the conspiracists. Those people believe that pretty much everything is a government or secret society conspiracy. In this case, they are actually in the ball park, but their vociferous nature and their wacky chains of evidence make them intellectual lepers."

"Intellectual lepers?" Brogan began laughing. "Where in hell did you come up with that one, Art?"

"Not sure... just popped into my head." Marston said with a smile. "It was probably the onions in my omelet this morning. Made me a little gassy."

"Ben, the beautiful thing about the conspiracists is that, no matter what official explanation you give to them, even if it is the factual truth, the explanation becomes part of the conspiracy!" Brogan said. "For us, it is a win-win situation! The waters become so cloudy, tidbits of truth that bubble to the surface are never seen for what they really are!"

Both men were now laughing, and Ben caught himself with a big smile on his face. He was enjoying the jocularity, and could feel himself becoming more comfortable with the two highest-ranking officials at Project Cocheta. Marston and Brogan shared a common military background that bonded them as brothers, and it showed. It was obvious they were good friends and Ben guessed that each would engage in fierce battle for the other.

"I'm going to let you in on a little secret." Marston said. "You know the 'Blue Book' project I was telling you about?"

"Yes sir."

"Well, the Air Force is shutting it down next year. Do you want to know why?"

"Absolutely."

"Because the nut cases are doing a far better job scaring away legitimate private research into UFOs than our disinformation specialists! Of course, we can't say that, so we'll use the pre-determined outcome of the upcoming University of Colorado Report on UFOs as an excuse to close Blue Books' doors. Seriously, this is a huge deal, Ben. From that point forward, the Air Force can completely rid itself of handling the UFO phenomena, or at least the public part of it. That doesn't mean we completely stop the disinformation campaign. There are some tenacious researchers out there, some of whom have impressive credentials and actually practice the scientific method. We'll periodically supply them with juicy tidbits and see if we can trip them up. Once they've taken the bait, their credibility is shot in the scientific community."

The picture was now complete for Ben. Elaborate measures were being taken to hide or camouflage UFO evidence from all segments of the public, not just to keep the citizens in the dark and ward off serious researchers, but to fool the Soviets into thinking that the American Government was completely uninterested in the subject. Somehow, Ben didn't think the Soviets were buying it, especially if they had a Cocheta of their own. He surmised that in the absence of solid information about what the Russians knew, or did not know, you had to assume the secret was still worth protecting. An unsettling thought occurred to Ben just then. What if they somehow unlocked the secrets of the propulsion system and duplicated it? How long would it be before the top of Cocheta Mountain would turn into subatomic particles? Ben hoped the security of Project Cocheta was as good as its' project managers said it was!

The briefing continued with pictures and comments covering the variety of research projects currently underway. There were also slides of the wreckage of each alien vehicle stored at Cocheta. The most interesting slides, by far, were the "vacation photos" as Marston called them. These were photographs, mostly taken by Marston himself, of investigation scenes and took up an entire 140 slide tray. The photographs were nothing short of astounding. They reminded Ben of crime-scene photographs in their quality and documentation of detail. Some were quite gruesome, capturing the injuries and state of decomposition of the alien corpses. One slide was a close-up of the entry and exit head wounds of the alien shot by the frightened Montana rancher, the undisputed winner in the first and only, albeit quite one-sided, shoot-out between our two worlds. Marston paid particular interest to impact points, damage to trees or other objects that might yield clues to the angle of impact, wide-angle views of debris fields, and items marked with hieroglyphics. There were a few historical slides thrown in, taken at crash sites that preceded the creation of Project Cocheta. Ben viewed some half-dozen slides of a little known 1947 incident that occurred in a sparsely populated area of central New Mexico. Marston made a brief comment that this particular incident was one of the main factors that led to the creation of Project Cocheta, but otherwise paid no further attention to it, moving on to other slides in the presentation. Ben, likewise, attached no significance to it beyond what Marston told him. The incident, however, would surface again in spectacular fashion a little more than a decade later.

They broke for lunch at 11:45 and Ben, again, found himself teetering on the edge of sheer gluttony. He savaged a cheeseburger combo in what must have been record time, swearing that the beef was so good it had to have come from a highly advanced alien cow. Marston and Brogan watched Ben in amazement, wondering how such a skinny kid could put away so much food, but then, Ben really was "just a kid," with the enviable metabolism of a kid.

It was an odd combination to see, one of the planets' most ordered brains in the body of a young man barely in his twenties. Marston was becoming quite fond of young Ben Hanson. Having never had any children of his own, perhaps the feeling was due to Marstons' completely un-utilized fatherly ambitions, or maybe it was because Ben was so damn likable. The kid was polite and respectful, in spite of an intellect that most his age would see as a license to be an insufferable, egomaniacal brat. Maybe that was it. Watching Ben conquer every difficult challenge for so many years sparked the 'proud father' in him. Ben was going to change the world, Marston was certain of it, but his fondness for Ben would need attenuation. "Ben doesn't need another father," Marston thought to himself, "he needs a mentor."

"Where do you put that food?" Brogan asked.

Ben looked around, suddenly realizing he had done it again. "I'm sorry. The food... It's amazing! I'll eat slower, next time."

"I'm not worried about the speed, kid." Marston said. "I'm worried about the amount! If you keep this up, I'll have to request more money from our benefactors to pay for it!"

"Don't sweat it." Brogan said. "We're just jealous because old men like us can't eat like you do. If we did, we'd have the profile of Alfred Hitchcock!"

Ben began to feel the embarrassment ebb from his mind. "Salad for dinner and no desert." He promised to himself.

The afternoon session consisted of more paperwork and a lecture on the organizational structure of Project Cocheta. Ben was surprised to learn that very few people working at Cocheta actually knew the facility's real mission. The technique Marston used to achieve this remarkable feat was what he called "compartmentalizing." Each group of workers had an area of responsibility and given only the information needed to carry out their jobs. Unless authorized, they were restricted from classified areas and forbidden to ask mission-related questions of those who worked within them. Enforcement of this policy was swift and unforgiving, resulting in immediate dismissal and further investigation into the possibility that the behavior may have been an attempt at espionage. Marines caught disobeying this policy, reinforced by an identical standing order from the Garrison Commander, faced punishment under the Uniformed Code of Military Justice. Compartmentalization allowed each group to contribute their essential piece of the puzzle without knowing what the entire puzzle looked like. This technique was also quite effective when mass-producing highly classified aircraft. Each fabricating team, located in a different building, or even from different companies, built a piece of the aircraft to precise specifications, then sent it to another building or company for assembly. Only the crew responsible for completing the aircraft knew what the end-product was and what it could do.

The "official" mission of Project Cocheta was to support classified research into advanced aeronautics and space flight. The mission statement was not exactly a lie, but not exactly the truth, either. The only people who knew what was really going on were the administrative staff, scientists, selected scientific assistants and technicians, the Marine Garrison commander and company commanders, and the few senior enlisted Marines who guarded the buildings within the main hangar that concealed the alien bodies and artifacts. Everyone who had access to the classified areas, including the Marines, wore bright green identification badges. Aviation support crews wore vivid yellow badges, while the remaining staff and VIPs wore plain white. Support and military personnel wandered freely about the facility and the outdoor areas, only restricted by the limitations imposed by the color of their badges and a strictly enforced 8PM to 6AM curfew. The now commonplace visitation by extraterrestrial vehicles posed a potential disruption of Marstons' compartmentalization. There was little he could do about sightings made between 6AM to 8PM, short of keeping everyone inside at all times. Fortunately, daytime sightings were infrequent. After curfew sightings, came to be known as "Code Green" alerts, were limited to viewing only by those possessing green badges and the Marines guarding the facility.

A grand tour of Cocheta, including the power generating facility, followed the lecture on organizational structure. Ben had never seen a nuclear reactor and since the reactor itself was enclosed in a containment shell, there wasn't much to see. The three, large electric generators were far more interesting. The noise in the facility was impressive, making conversation problematic. Ben learned the water needed to cool the steam condenser originated from the larger of the two lakes in front of Cocheta Mountain. A large reservoir within the mountain served as a cooling tank for the steam condenser. A second reservoir cooled water cycled from the first. Hot water from the first reservoir provided heat for the main hanger and the multitude of offices, labs and smaller buildings located in or on Cocheta. Heat exchangers within the hot reservoir water heated the potable water used by everyone.

Eventually the water contained in the internal reservoirs, liberally mixed with fresh, ice-cold water, returned to the lake at the same temperature as it was when removed. If there was any significant temperature difference between the Cocheta lakes and the neighboring bodies of water, infrared cameras on Soviet spy satellites could easily spot it.

The highlight of the office complex tour was Ben's first viewing of his own office. It was utilitarian to say the least. Adorned with gray, government-issue furniture with the requisite number of four-drawer file cabinets and bookcases, it was large enough to contain a plain, black naugahyde couch, presumably for sleeping on if one were too tired to walk to the apartment at the end of a long days' work. A senior executive at a major corporation would have had a heart attack at the sight of this wholly unstylish office. Ben, however, was beyond thrilled. To him, it was perfect because it was HIS office, his very first real office and partly because he probably lacked the gene for higher taste in office accoutrements.

Next came the tour of the evidence processing, display and storage areas located in the far southeast wall and corner of the enormous hangar. Of particular interest to Ben were several rooms of UFO wreckage on display, approximated as much as possible just as the National Transportation Safety Board does when investigating plane crashes. Most rooms had wreckage where only enough pieces fit together to give the roughest estimate of the size and shape of the craft. A few displayed much more detail. The thing that stood out when comparing all of them was the lack of large, heavily shielded pieces that one would expect to find if the craft used a powerful energy source to propel it.

"Why are there no reactor pieces?" Ben asked Marston. "You would think that heavily shielded equipment would survive even the worst of impacts."

"We have wondered about that, too." Marston replied. "There is compelling evidence that the aliens retrieve the powerplants, even before they recover their own dead. We think this because we have noted large areas of gouged earth at debris fields without a corresponding piece of heavy wreckage. Increased levels of radiation, too."

"But if they want to keep their propulsion system secrets away from us, why did they give us that thing?" Ben asked, pointing his finger across the hangar to the large building containing the intact Quebec Saucer.

"I wish I knew." Marston answered with a hint of sad frustration. "Perhaps it doesn't have a poweplant in it, or at least the 'standard issue' powerplant."

"I don't trust it, sir." Ben said, feeling quite sure of himself in front of the Project Cocheta directors.

"Doesn't make a whole helluva lot of sense, does it?" Brogan added. "But, I don't know what we can possibly do about it, other than rigging the hanger to thwart any surveillance it might be doing."

"We'll ponder it further at the next Conclave meeting on Monday." Marston said. "Right now, it's time to shake Ben's hand and congratulate him on his completion of Cocheta in-processing. Of course, he must still partake of the after-dinner cigar on the observation deck to be fully initiated."

"Of course..." Brogan said, "The 'cigar!' Almost forgot about it."

Ben shook hands with the two men as they congratulated him, wondering how he was going to survive a cigar. He had never smoked a cigarette and only taken a puff or two of a cheap cigar. He heard the horror stories about how sick people become when they smoke their first stogie and wondered if they were true. It was obviously a right of passage, so like it or not, Ben Hanson would force himself to indulge, no matter how ill it might make him.

Much to the bewilderment of Marston and Brogan, Ben ordered a Caesar Salad for dinner, and ate it slow... very slow.

After dinner, the three men retired to the observation deck for the promised post-prandial cigar. The deck was located forty feet above the ground on the front face of the main building and hangar. It was made of steel, painted to match the color of the building, and approximately 60 feet in length by 8 feet in width. Attached to the guardrail along the entire length of the structure were mounting points for cameras. The sun had long since set and the air had started to chill significantly. Very little wind was evident and the sky retained its' cloudless, crystal clear appearance from the day before. Ben was certain that he had never seen so many stars in his life. There was something else beginning to happen, something that he had seen to a far lesser degree in Michigan: the Aurora Borealis. It began with faint, incandescent sheets of light dancing across the northern sky. The appearance of these sheets of light reminded Ben of colorful, pleated window curtains being drawn to and fro against a black background. Before long, the show became breathtaking and unlike anything Ben had ever seen in the nighttime sky.

"Quite a sight, tonight." Marston stated.

"Yes sir, it is!" Ben replied, not taking his eyes off the cosmic display before him.

"A fringe benefit of your new job." Marston said. "Shows like this are commonplace here and we have a front row seat. Here's your cigar. Remember to puff it, don't inhale it."

"What kind of cigar is it?"

"Romeo y Julieta, Cuban." Marston replied.

"I thought Cuban cigars were illegal."

"Not in Canada. Another fringe benefit of the job!" Marston said with a big smile. "I make sure the Exchange carries a nice selection. You should see my humidor in Las Vegas!"

"You bring them back into the United States?" Ben asked. "Can't you get into trouble doing that?"

It was obvious that Ben didn't fully comprehend the considerable power of Marston's position. He would learn in time, but for now, rather than tell young Ben he could probably have Castro's hairy ass hauled out of Cuba to personally roll cigars for him, he would enlighten him of the legal non sequitur that it was a crime to import or sell Cuban cigars in the United States, yet perfectly legal to own them.

"You ever smoke a cigar, Ben?" Brogan asked.

"Blackie, the mechanic in Commerce, smoked Swisher Sweets and he let me take a couple of puffs, once." Ben replied. "I accidentally inhaled and coughed for about six hours afterwards."

"Swisher Sweets these are not!" Brogan stated with a grin that suggested to Ben he was hiding something.

Marston finished what Brogan had started. "What my long-time, cigar-smoking buddy here means is that these are hand-made cigars and quite a bit stronger than Swisher Sweets. Best to go slow, take a few moments between puffs and stop when your stomach starts feeling queasy. Of course, wasting more than a quarter of a fine cigar is... well, it borders on criminal."

What started out as a cigar-smoking tutorial by Arthur Marston just turned into the "throwing down" of a gauntlet. Ben knew what was coming but the unwritten rules of manhood prevented him from negotiating a lessening of the blow. Resigned to a 're-acquaintance' with the Caesar Salad he ate at dinner, half a cigar and thirty minutes later, he was. In spite of the unpleasantness that came with the nicotine-induced retching and inwardly swearing that it will be a cold day in Hell before another cigar will find its' way to his lips, Ben felt as if he had accomplished something important. Like a hazed fraternity pledge, the pain and humiliation of the "initiation" process turned quickly into a feeling of acceptance, and that was one of the most powerful needs of the human psyche.

"Mr. Marston?" Ben said, lifting his head from the five-gallon bucket that mysteriously appeared when he began to get ill.

"Yes."

"Could you do me a favor?"

"Within reason, sure."

"Instead of taking me back to Ann Arbor, could you drop me off in Miami. I want to tell Teresa and my family about my new career. I'd also like to buy Teresa her own car so she won't have to borrow her mom's all the time. I'll find my own way back to Michigan."

"Dropping you off in Miami shouldn't be a problem, but I'll have to check with the pilot to see if the runway is long enough to accommodate a Gulfstream. If not, we can get you close. Joplin, Tulsa, maybe Springfield." Marston replied. "What are you going to tell your family about the new job."

"Not much I can tell them, other than my work schedule and salary."

"You can tell them that you work in the defense industry, but you cannot speak of anything that you do within it. I highly recommend that you spend each 2 weeks off with your family and not with a book glued to your nose. You'll have plenty of time for that when you're here. I have found that those who leave work at work face far fewer probing questions at home."

"You don't know Teresa and how inquisitive she can be when somebody keeps a secret from her."

"Let me ask you a question. Do you think we would have offered you this position if we thought your fiancé would pose a security problem?" Marston asked, without explaining that their relationship would have never reached the level that it did if Teresa had been an issue. "I know that Teresa is as level-headed and smart as she is attractive and I have no doubt she will understand your situation. She is also a woman. If you pay plenty of attention to her, she won't care about the details concerning your job in the 'defense industry.'"

Ben considered what Marston said and concluded he was probably right. Maybe the real reason Ben was concerned about Teresa's inquisitive nature was to cover up his own guilt about not talking to her first about accepting this job opportunity and assuming she would be OK with the radical change in locale that came with it. He would profusely apologize for that and beg for forgiveness if need be. He was also hoping that a new car, along with a mountain of cash to finance her wildest dream wedding, one unlike any ever seen in Northeast Oklahoma, might help smooth things out. Deep inside, Ben knew that Teresa would be fine with the changes. They had already talked about moving to Burbank California when Ben had told her that the Skunk Works were offering him a position there. Still, insecurities were tough demons to defeat and Ben would feel a lot better about things after he had a chance to hold Teresa in his arms again.

"Well," Brogan said, "looks like we're going to strike out again."

"What do you mean?"

"Our alien buddies are giving us the cold shoulder." He replied. "It's been a long time since we've had this many consecutive nights without a visit."

"Don't worry, you'll see plenty of them while you're here." Marston said. "We'll take you back home after breakfast tomorrow morning. I'll contact you sometime in the middle of June to arrange for shipment of your household goods to Vegas. I'll also send some pictures of your new home once it is complete. If you and Teresa want to spend your honeymoon in Vegas, let me know. Brogan will pick up the tab for a VIP suite at the Tropicana, food and transportation. Your first duty day is Monday, July 1st. Your first two-week shift at Cocheta will begin on July 8th. The plane leaves from Nellis Air Force Base at 05:00 and returns on the 21st at 18:00. I'll go over this again before you leave."

"Wait a minute!" Brogan protested, going along with the joke. "I'm picking up the tab? I thought we were going to use petty cash to pay for Ben's honeymoon! You didn't use the petty cash on those lumberjack-looking Canadian hookers again, did you?"

All belly laughed at the joke and after a few more minutes of discussing the various off-the-wall ways Brogan could use to come up with the cash to fund Ben's honeymoon, they each retired to their apartments. Ben was not as tired as he had been the night before, and it took him a while to drift off to sleep. A few hours later, Ben awoke to a voice in his room, a female voice. Sleep inertia dulled his senses for a few moments, but eventually he was able to wake up enough to make out where the voice was coming from and what she was saying. It was coming from an overhead paging speaker in the ceiling of his apartment, and she was saying "Code Green, Northwest Sector. Range: one point seven miles."

Chapter 41

Loeffler and Simpson positioned every one of the limited manpower assets available to them in and around the Venetian Hotel and could have used at least two dozen more. The Venetian was a huge property, with towering guest room buildings, expansive Casino and shopping areas that needed to coverage to prevent Hanson from escaping. In spite of the deadly serious mission, it was difficult for Loeffler to ignore the elegance of the hotel. The interior of the Venetian was captivating, with beautiful carpeting, walls tastefully lined with framed paintings and large rooms with ceilings adorned with frescos reminiscent of the Italian Renaissance. Undoubtedly, Michelangelo or Masaccio would have found the Venetian quite to their liking. The external architecture was equally stunning in its' attempt to capture the look and feel of Venice. The sidewalks adorned with Old World lampposts and lined with ornate, green-hued iron fencing. The front of the hotel sported a canal, of sorts, where one could take a gondola "cruise" captained by a brightly dressed pole-man or woman. Unfortunately, the limited space given to the canal, and the shallowness of the water, produced an effect that was laughable, looking more like a swimming pool with large, toy boats floating on its' surface. Even so, the reputation of the hotel for its' amenities, food and service far outweighed the Canal faux pas.

What bothered Loeffler far more than his shortage of agents to cover the Venetian was the fact that he had to wait for Hastings to arrive, and so far, they waited for more than thirty minutes. Hanson was slippery and every moment that passed was an opportunity for him to devise a way out of the trap. It was not so much that Loeffler was actually worried that Hanson would try to prolong the chase any further, the fact that he checked-in under his own name was convincing evidence that this was where he intended to be apprehended, it was the principal of it all. Hastings insisted that he be present for Hanson's capture, even though he was eating dinner at a steak house in North Las Vegas. The evening traffic in Vegas alone would delay him more than thirty minutes, not to mention he would likely take the time to finish his meal before leaving. Of course, if Hanson was not in his room,

Hastings would blame him for it, assaulting him with all manner of public, verbal abuse, made worse by the fact that Loeffler interrupted his meal. If Hastings tore into him again as he did at the Orleans, Kevin Loeffler decided that one of two things would happen: he would resign right then and there, or borrow Special Agent Simpson's pistol and shoot Hastings in the face.

As they did in the Orleans, guests were quietly cleared from their rooms on the floor where Hanson was presumably holed-up, the 21st. A tool the FBI provided, not immediately available at the Orleans, was a flexible fiber-optic scope designed to pass under a door to observe the suspect without his knowledge. Donning Kevlar body armor and helmet, an FBI agent familiar with the use of fiber-optic scopes quietly made his way to Hansons' room. Lying prone in hallway next to the door, the agent gently placed the tip of the long, black, worm-like scope under the door. The agent began looking through the eyepiece, manipulating the upward and downward curvature of the last two inches of the scope using a thumb lever on the eyepiece housing, angling the left and right view accomplished by simply pointing the tip of the scope with the left hand. The agent observed that the lights and television were on, but could not see where Hanson was. Since the scope was looking from the carpet upward, Hanson could be lying on the bed or sitting in a chair behind other furniture that precluded the scope from seeing him. After 10 minutes of observation, the agent terminated his observation and gave his equivocal report to SAC Simpson. Just as it began to look as if the team would not know if their suspect was in the room until they physically entered it, something amazing happened... coughing. Instinctively turning their heads towards each other, all were making sure the coughing was not coming from one of their own team members. Smiles erupted on every face. Hanson was in the room! The chase was over.

If only Hastings would show up...

Chapter 42

Dr. Hanson just finished watching the third replay of the Science and Technology Channel's promo spot for Dr. Alexander's special announcement scheduled to air on Sunday when he heard the light knocking on his door. They were here. It took them a little longer to find him than he figured. Thankfully, they were courteous enough to wait until after he finished dinner and smoked one last cigarette before arresting him, though he really didn't believe that courtesy had anything at all to do with their timing.

Soon it would be over. Within the next minute, he would permanently lose his freedom, but then, how was that any different from the way he had been living for the last 19 years? It was just a matter of semantics and location. His depression deepened considerably due to the revelations from the evening before, wearing heavily on him throughout the day. He risked so much to see this through, but the risks were not borne upon him. He placed them on the innocent, who might very well languish in prison because they foolishly believed in his so-called "vision." The vision, seen now through the pall of deep depression, was a wholesale farce. If the plan failed, Tim Alexander and the executives at the Science and Technology Channel would face the music caused by Hanson's lust for revenge. Even if it worked, they still might end up in prison. Hanson, however, would be conveniently dead and in Hell where he belonged. He spent the entire day weighing the odds over and over in his head, each time coming to the conclusion that aborting the mission, or having it fail, had far worse outcomes for the innocent than if it succeeded. He painted everyone in a corner but himself. So, it would be that the last decision of the free Benjamin Harris Hanson, PhD was to, once again, gamble with the futures of the innocent. He would stay the course and let his plan unfold.

"Mr. Loeffler? Mr. Hastings? Special Agent Simpson?" Hanson spoke as he approached the door. "Is that you? Let me unlock the door so I can invite you in."

Hanson unlocked the dead bolt and chain and began to turn the doorknob. Just as the latch cleared the door swung violently inward, striking Hanson hard in the face and knocking him backward into a desk. His momentum and complete lack of control over his balance sent him hard to the floor. Searing pain from fractured bones in his face and a serious jar to the back of his head, along with the unintelligible screaming from people who were pointing pistols at him, flooded his consciousness. All Hanson could mount for a response to the cacophony was a series of moans and a potentially dangerous nosebleed.

"Dammit, Hastings!" Agent Simpson yelled, obviously quite infuriated by the last second change in the agreed entry technique. "Why did you kick the door in? He was opening it for Christs' sake!"

"You had better keep your mouth shut, little girl." Hastings growled. "You obviously don't know who the fuck you're yelling at. This man is dangerous!"

Simpson looked at the pitiful sight before her. Hanson was a gauntly man, looking much older than his actual age and noticeably thinner than the latest photograph she had seen. His face was covered in blood and his nose quite obviously fractured. It was hard to imagine this frail little man being a danger to anyone. The rage surged inside of her. The agreed plan to enter was one of flexibility based on Hanson's response to the knock. Unlike the previous entry, where Hanson's intentions were clearly not known, the fact that he registered into the hotel in his own name indicated that he intended to be caught. Loeffler was absolutely certain Hanson would surrender without a fight and Simpson trusted the judgment of this highly experienced, former FBI agent. When Hanson began calling each of their names and unlocking the door, Simpson was going to show her badge with her left hand while keeping her pistol ready in her right. Hanson's arrest was likely to be no more exciting than arresting your average priest on a traffic warrant. Before she could get to that point, Hastings quickly stepped up to the door and kicked it hard when it began to open. It was an act of pure cruelty.

"Call for an ambulance!" Simpson barked to one of her agents.

"He is not going to the hospital, Agent Simpson!" Hastings yelled. "He is going to Clark County Detention for booking and interrogation!"

"As I understand it, Mr. Hastings, you do not have the authority to arrest anyone. Since Dr. Hanson is being arrested under my authority, I will not place my department or my people in a position where they may face criminal charges for civil rights violations, or civil lawsuits for withholding medical care!"

Loeffler's jaw was loose enough that unhinging was imminent. He couldn't believe his ears! Simpson was going toe-to-toe with that evil bastard... and winning! It was admittedly a bad time to be distracted by such things, but Loeffler couldn't help it, he found himself becoming even more attracted to her. "Mind on the business at hand!" Loeffler scolded himself on the inside, as he pulled a handful of facial tissue out of a dispenser on the table next to Hanson and placed it under his bleeding nose.

"Dr. Hanson," Loeffler said. "Turn your head to the side and spit the blood out. Don't swallow it because it will just make you vomit."

Hanson looked up at Loeffler and nodded his head. In that instant, Loeffler read the man's eyes for the very first time. "This was no evil man!" Loeffler thought to himself. Over his distinguished career, Loeffler peered into the eyes of hundreds of certifiably evil men and women and each had a look that was beyond description. Empty, soulless eyes that brought a shiver to the spine. Hanson's eyes said something quite different to Loeffler. He had seen it once, many decades before. It was the look in his grandfather's eyes before he took his own life. It was the look of long-standing suffering and despair. His grandfather mourned the loss of one of his sons and wife in an automobile accident he caused. An accident he never forgave himself for and a loss he could never come to terms with. He last saw his grandfather's eyes when he was 14 years old. Loeffler instinctively knew that Dr. Hanson was an enormously tortured soul.

"How dare you speak to me in that tone!" Hastings roared. "I'll have you busted down to bussing cafeteria tables at Quantico, you little bitch!"

Simpson bristled at the statement, but before she could reply to it, Loeffler stood up and stepped between them.

"Mr. Hastings," Loeffler began sternly, "that last comment was uncalled for! Hanson's face and nose is obviously fractured and he is bleeding a lot. Agent Simpson is right, we need to get the prisoner to the emergency room. We'll work out the details of his incarceration and interrogation while he is undergoing treatment."

Hastings was glaring at Loeffler. "You turned out to be quite a disappointment, Loeffler."

"Sorry to hear that, Mr. Hastings, but there is still a lot of work to be done, and Hanson is the key to finding the second suspect. He'll be of no use to us if he bleeds to death."

"When this is over, you'll need to pass your resume around, Loeffler." Hastings said while turning around to exit the door. "But don't bother doing it in Washington. Same goes for you, Simpson."

After Hastings left the room, Loeffler kneeled beside Hanson and began wiping the blood from his face while holding gentle pressure on his nose. Special Agent in Charge Simpson kneeled down beside him.

"I could have handled that prick," Simpson said, "but thanks, anyway."

"I wasn't protecting you." Loeffler said softly. "I saw how tightly you were gripping your pistol and I became concerned for Mr. Hastings' life."

Simpson started to snicker. "And I thought it was some sort chivalrous act to protect me."

"No ma'am. You seem more than capable of protecting yourself." Loeffler said, returning his attention to Hanson. "How are you doing, Dr. Hanson?"

"I'll be OK." Hanson replied with a gurgle to his voice.

"Spit the blood out." Loeffler ordered.

Hanson complied. "Thank you for taking care of me, Mr. Loeffler." Hanson said with a clearer voice.

"Just doing my job, Dr. Hanson."

Chapter 43

Ben rushed to get his clothes on, and in the frenzy, forgot to grab his heavy coat on the way out the apartment door. Seeing several others wearing their heavy coats reminded him of his ill preparedness for the outside temperature and ran back to his apartment to retrieve his own. He felt like he wasted a half hour by doing so, but in reality, he arrived at the front entrance roughly a minute later than he would have. There were roughly two-dozen people standing in front of him in the chilled air, with plenty of animated chatter erupting between them. The last of the Marines were pouring out of their barracks and running to their assigned positions, rifles in hand, at an astonishing pace considering the cold weather gear they were wearing. Ben couldn't see the craft everyone was looking at until he took up a position to the right of the crowd.

It was a scene Ben would never forget.

The object approached to 2000 yards and hovered about 20 feet above the ground. It was discoid in shape, with roughly the same proportions above and below the rim as the captured vehicle in the hangar. It was glowing yellow-orange with what appeared to be white windows around the edge. If Ben was right, these were not windows at all but part of the propulsion system. The edges of the craft were difficult to define, probably blurred by the magnetically controlled shell of ionized gas around it. There appeared to be some sort of ground effect occurring beneath the craft, but it was too far away for Ben to see.

"Try these." A voice from behind him said, startling him.

Ben turned around to see Marston and Brogan standing right behind him.

"You scared the daylights out of me, again!" Ben protested.

"Sorry, son." Marston said, handing a pair of high-grade 10x50 binoculars to Ben.

"Fifty bucks says we get a close approach tonight." Brogan said.

"Inner razor wire or closer?" Marston asked.

"Yep."

"You're on!"

Ben was too busy focusing the binoculars to grasp the meaning of the bet that had just taken place between Marston and Brogan. Once he had the optics adjusted, he studied the craft intensely. It was moving now, slowly, from left to right. Ben watched the ground effects closely, looking for signs of thrust vectoring. If the object were using thrust vectoring to move to the right, an increase in ground disturbance would be visible underneath and to the left of the craft. The problem was that the object was moving entirely too slow to see dramatic changes in the ground disturbance. Suddenly, without warning, the craft disappeared from his view. The loss of view for Ben occurred simultaneously with a collective gasp from the viewers around him.

"I lost it!" Ben exclaimed. "It just disappeared!"

"Put down the binoculars." Marston said.

The moment Ben took the binoculars away from his eyes, he saw what happened to the craft he was looking at. It was hovering a mere 150 yards in front of him! It moved a little more than a mile in under a second! Ben quickly did the math in his head and came up with an estimated speed in excess of 4000 miles per hour and without a sonic boom! He tried to refocus the binoculars of the craft, but it was difficult to find detail on the object in which to focus. Within a few moments, Ben gave up and removed the binoculars from his eyes in frustration. The Marines were in a much higher state of readiness, with every rifle and both batteries of Hawk missiles aimed at the craft. It hovered for a few moments and began slowly approaching the group. A couple of scientists lost their nerve and retreated inside the perceived safety of the building. The rest of the group began to inch backward, including Ben. Marston and Brogan, however, steadied him, stopping his slow egress.

"Don't you think they're getting a little close?" Ben asked with growing tension in his voice, wondering why Marston and Brogan were stopping him.

"Maybe..." Marston said, "but my good friend here, Mr. Brogan, just won a fifty dollar bet with me. He predicted that the UFO would come very close to the facility tonight. You see, Charlie has this theory that every time we bring a new scientist on board, the aliens come close to get a good look at him or her."

Bens' blood began running colder than the freezing air around him.

Marston continued. "It would seem that Mr. Brogans' theory might have some validity to it."

"Three new faces in the last eight months, three close approaches." Brogan bragged. "I'd say that was statistically significant!"

The object stopped less than two hundred feet from the assembled group. This represented the closest approach made by a UFO since they began showing up 10 months earlier.

"Wave to them, Ben! It looks like they're here to see you!" Marston said, patting him on the back.

Ben had never been so frightened in his entire life. This was his worst nightmare turned into vivid reality. The little green men of his childhood were studying him! His instinct was to run like hell and hide where the aliens could never find him. Abject panic was a heartbeat away, fueled by adrenal glands that were working triple-overtime, dumping microgram after microgram of adrenalin into his bloodstream and begging for mercy. Without warning, the object abruptly shot upwards to about 10,000 feet just as Ben was about to bolt from shear terror. Racing at an unbelievable speed to the northeast, it disappeared from view within a few seconds. The small crowd clapped and began to chatter. The Marines, however, were engaged in a collective sigh of relief.

"Congratulations!" Brogan said, shaking Ben's hand. "You just made it into the galactic phone book!"

The young Ben Hanson, heart still pounding wildly in his chest, was not amused.

Chapter 44

Tim Alexander was chatting with Beverly when Darrell Aceveda finally returned from a power lunch with the Science and Technology Channel's programming director.

"Hey Tim! Great to see you!" Aceveda exclaimed with sincerity. "When did you get into town?"

"Yesterday evening. I had to make a stop in inside the beltway this morning to garner a bit of support for the announcement."

"What? You can tell somebody else about this announcement of yours, but you can't tell your very own producer? I'm hurt. Really hurt." Aceveda said while pretending to be stabbing himself in the heart.

"Sorry, you didn't make it onto the short list."

"You're killing me! You know that, don't you? Killing me!"

"Are all producers so melodramatic?"

"Only the good ones!"

"Fair enough. You did manage to get the upper echelon to sign off on this project, so that would make you the best producer in town. Or at least in this room." Tim said with a grin.

"Very funny." Aceveda said with a fake scowl. "Actually, it wasn't hard at all. When I told them you would resign if they didn't let you do this, they all soiled their pants in unison! In fact, they were practically climbing all over themselves to be the first to agree to your demands."

"This story of yours wouldn't be a touch embellished, would it?"

"You know me! Just the facts, Ma'am."

"Hmmm... Beverly told me you started running the promos."

"A couple of days ago. We're already getting a shitload of calls from all kinds of people. The news services want the scoop ahead of time so they can research the topic; your fans want hints; and some guy in Austin wants you to wear the all-black outfit you wore when you did the segment on bats and echolocation. I think he likes you." Aceveda said with a wink.

Tim shook his head. "No hints, whatsoever. Not even to the guy in Austin. Is the studio ready for me to tape the upgraded promos?"

"They are waiting on your call."

"Great, but before we tape, I need to explain to you exactly how this is going to work. You have time to talk now?"

"My time is yours!"

For the next half hour, Dr. Alexander described in technical detail how the announcement was going to work, while Aceveda listened to him in stunned silence.

"So, what do you think?"

Aceveda sat silent for several moments, pondering the plan and his answer to Dr. Alexander. "To my knowledge, nothing like this has ever been attempted."

"I realize that, but it is the only way to insure the announcement will be made."

"Why in God's name would somebody want to stop you from making this announcement?"

"I can't tell you that. You're going to have to trust my judgment on this."

"I do trust your judgment, but this is a helluva tall order! It's a brilliant plan and I'm sure the technical aspects of it will be relatively easy to negotiate, but this is uncharted water for ANY network! Science and Technology Communications is a billion dollar business and I have no earthly idea how the great FCC god, who gives life to our license, will react to this!"

"I know how risky this is, believe me." Alexander said convincingly. "But I am willing to sacrifice my career for this because it is vital to the future of mankind that this announcement be made."

"I'm sorry, you said WHAT?"

"You heard me."

"That's what I thought you said!" Aceveda threw his head back. "Christ Almighty! What have I gotten myself into? Who in the hell is after you? Is it the Feds? Terrorists? A kooky fringe group? Who would have the power to stop you or the Science and Technology Channel from making this..." In his agitated state, Darrell Aceveda had missed the obvious answer, and now it fully dawned on him what it was. "It's the Feds! You're asking ME and Science and Technology Channel Communications to take on the Federal Government?"

"Calm down!" Alexander pleaded.

"Calm down? This IS calmed down! You should see me when I'm facing 40 years in prison instead of 20!"

"It won't go down that way if we follow this plan." Alexander said in the most sooth-ing tone he could muster. "Once the announcement is broadcast, the bad people will be neutralized. You must trust me on this."

"You're certain?"

"As certain as I can possibly be." Alexander said. "And if something does go wrong, I promise you, I will take all the blame."

Aceveda felt a sudden, sharp pang of embarrassment. He was behaving like a spoiled baby. Tim Alexander was a close friend asking for help with a noble cause... and the best his producer could do was piddle on himself?

"No, taking all of the heat won't be necessary." Aceveda said, finally clearing his head of the unruly panic that had gripped him a few moments earlier. "You say this is announce-ment is vital to all mankind... Count me in. How many times during a man's life is he asked to help the human race? It would seem silly to turn the opportunity down, no matter what the risks are."

Chapter 45

Unceremoniously arrested and read his rights by CAS Simpson, Dr. Benjamin Harris Hanson awaited ambulance transportation to the UNLV Medical Center. Amazingly, Hanson waived his Miranda rights, expressing no interest in obtaining a lawyer, though he would likely have one appointed for him anyway. Even though Dr. Hanson was injured, and put forth no resistance whatsoever, Hastings insisted on handcuffing both his wrists and ankles. Loeffler considered it just another act of cruelty from the King of Cruelty. Loeffler rode in the back of the ambulance with Dr. Hanson, partly out of genuine concern and partly because he wanted to talk to Hanson without Hastings and his dislocated nose.

"Dr. Hanson, how is the pain?" Loeffler asked.

"Not so bad right now."

"I apologize for the way you were arrested. That wasn't our plan."

"I know." Hanson said, beginning to gurgle again. Turning his head and spitting out the blood was impossible since the paramedics put a cervical collar around his neck and immobilized his head to a rigid backboard. Loeffler motioned the paramedic to suction blood from Hansons' mouth.

"You certainly put me and my men through the wringer these past several days. Care to tell me why?"

"It was necessary."

"Necessary for what?"

"A safe retirement."

"Aren't there ways to retire without making me chase my own tail all over Las Vegas?"

"Not healthy ones."

"Look, I have the letter you left for me in your car and I promise you, I will look into it as soon as I can. What I need to know right now is what was in that box you were carrying and who did you give it to?"

"The box contained flowers for my girlfriend, but I misplaced it at the hotel. I don't know who has it now."

It was close to the alibi he expected and quite plausible, but Loeffler instinctively knew Hanson was lying.

"C'mon, we both know that's not true."

"I'm afraid that is the only explanation I have." Suddenly, Hansons' face contorted. "Quickly, put a towel or something over my mouth!" He said as if talking and holding his breath at the same time.

Loeffler looked at the paramedic who was already reaching for a towel in one of the storage bins on the wall next to Hanson's stretcher. Just as he laid the towel across the lower half of his face, Hanson began to cough violently, coating the towel with blood that had trickled into the back of his throat. The coughing spell lasted almost two minutes, prompting the Paramedic to attach a monitor that measured the oxygen saturation of the hemoglobin contained in Hanson's blood. A normal reading while breathing air ranges from 94-100%. Hanson's reading was only 81%. The paramedic reached into another bin and retrieved an oxygen mask to replace the towel lying over his patient's face.

"That's a nasty cough!" Loeffler stated with growing concern evident in his voice.

"Bronchitis." Hanson said, out of breath and lying. "I'm a chain smoker."

Loeffler looked at the beat-up old man and felt a surge of pity for him. Benjamin Hanson had been a worthy adversary, challenging him like no other criminal in his entire career. Loeffler, however, was having great difficulty tossing Hanson into the "criminal" bin. Whatever Dr. Hanson was up to, illegal or not, it was probably something he felt he needed to do. Hanson was concentrating the focus on the "retirement" issue that he referred to in his letter and it seemed that he was suggesting that Hastings was involved in the creation of "widows" out of retirees. Hanson said that his only "healthy" retirement option was to play this elaborate hide-and-go-seek game with him, but why the shell game with the box? Was that back-up evidence in case he failed to uncover what Hastings was doing to Project Cocheta retirees? It didn't make sense, unless of course, Hanson had two goals instead of one. Maybe the Hastings angle was a smokescreen to divert attention away from the main objective and the man tasked to carry it out. Loeffler hoped beyond hope that there was substance to Hanson's insinuations that Hastings was involved in murder. He would like nothing more than to have Hastings' cojones bronzed and mounted on a plaque to add to his impressive collection of awards and memorabilia displayed on the wall behind his desk. The Hastings issue, however, would have to wait until Loeffler determined what the man with the box was up to. Hanson would not disclose it. Loeffler was certain of that, but perhaps a more thorough review of the 1992 incident was in order.

"Is there anything I can do for you?" Loeffler asked as the ambulance was backing into a parking slot at the Emergency Room entrance.

"Yes, there is." Hanson said with a muffled voice through the oxygen mask. "Keep Hastings away from me."

"I can't do that. You know I can't do that." Loeffler replied, wishing that he could comply with Hanson's request.

"Please try." Hanson closed his eyes as the Paramedics opened the back door and prepared to unload his stretcher.

A weakness... If this were a cowardly sociopath, Loeffler would exploit the weakness to maximum benefit. That is, if he had a partner who was willing to work it with him. Hastings didn't know the meaning of teamwork. He would hijack the interview process and try to personally muscle the information out of Hanson. Loeffler would talk to agent Simpson to see if they could outmaneuver Hastings, but if they were to have any chance of extracting information from Hanson before Hastings screwed it all up, they would need to be very clever about it.

Special Agent Simpson was walking up to the ambulance just as Hanson entered the sliding glass entrance to the Emergency Department. Hastings would arrive shortly, so the window of opportunity to speak privately would be brief.

"How's Hanson?" Simpson asked.

"He looks like hell, but I don't think he has any kind of life threatening injury. My guess is that they will do x-rays of his face and splint his nose, maybe watch him overnight." Hastings replied. "We need to talk without that asshole Hastings around."

"I agree." Simpson replied. "If they admit him, LVMPD will guard him until he is released for transfer to the city jail. Once they have him settled in, we can catch a late dinner at the Peppermill and talk. You ever eaten there?"

"No, I'm still fairly new to this town."

"It's busy. A little noisy, but we can hold a conversation without worrying if the people at the next table are listening to each word we say." Simpson said. "Oh, and the food isn't bad, either!"

"Sounds good." Loeffler said. "We better get inside before Hastings spots us talking."

Chapter 46

"Teresa, could you get the phone, Dear. I'm a little tied-up right now." Mrs. Chandler asked of her daughter.

"Sure, Mom." Teresa replied, scurrying to the living room telephone. "Hello?"

"Teresa?" Ben Hanson asked. He was always mistaking Teresa and her mom's voice, which led to a few embarrassing moments when he inadvertently whispered 'sweet nuthins' into Mrs. Chandler's ear.

"Ben? Is that you, Ben?" Teresa asked, her voice steadily rising in pitch to match her excitement.

"Hi, sweetheart!" Ben said. "It sure is good to hear your voice!"

"Mom! Mom! It's Ben!" Teresa said, her voice now an excited squeal. "Where have you been, sweetie? I've been trying to call you all weekend."

"Is everything OK?" Ben asked, worried that he might have missed something important.

"Everything is fine, I was just missing you and wanted to hear your voice, that's all."

"I've really missed you, too." Ben said, meaning the words more than he had ever meant them before. "Life is not the same when we're apart!"

"Well aren't you the sweet talker!" She replied with a giggle. "Well, don't stop now!"

"I've got a surprise for you!" Ben said with a whisper.

"Oh Ben, you said something so sweet, now you're going to ruin it by teasing me with a secret." She said, feigning disappointment.

"Nope, no secrets this time. Come on down to the Miami airport and pick me up!"

"Are you at the airport?" She asked, not quite believing her ears. "Mom, Ben's at the airport! Really, Ben? Are you really here?"

"My love, I would never kid you about something like that."

"I'll be there in 20 minutes… maybe a little longer if I get a speeding ticket!"

"You better not speed! I wouldn't want to live if something bad happened to you!" Ben scolded her.

"I won't speed, I promise." She said with somewhat less conviction than Ben would have liked.

"Sweetheart, can you do me a big favor?"

"Anything, my only-est."

"Could you call my parents and let's all meet at your house. I have some important news to tell everyone."

"Did you finally take the Skunk job in Burbank?"

"No sweetheart, I didn't." Ben said, laughing. "I accepted another position, but it's complicated."

"Complicated?" Teresa asked, wondering what could be complicated about accepting a job presumably better than the Skunk job he was always talking about.

"In a good way, sweetheart. I'll explain it all when we get home."

"I'll call your parents, then come pick you up as quick as I can!" Teresa said. "I can't wait to see you!"

"I can't wait to see you, too."

After a reunion full of long hugs and even longer kisses, Teresa drove Ben back to Picher, but not before a stop at their favorite park bench at 5th Ave. NW and A St. NW in Miami, where they spent a half hour holding hands and watching children frolic in the playground under a warm Oklahoma spring sun. By the time they arrived at the Chandler home, Ben's parents were there. They all shared hugs, handshakes and kisses, then Ben wasted no time filling the family in on his new job.

"I'm sorry I couldn't give you any advance warning, but this all happened so quickly!"

Ben began. "Other than every moment I spend with Miss Chandler, I have had the most incredible 48 hours of my life!"

"Good start my only-est!" Teresa interrupted. "I would have hurt you if you changed the order around."

Ben laughed. "Nothing can compare with the time I spend with you, my only-est!"

"You have him trained well, Teresa, and you aren't even married yet!" Mrs. Hanson said with a grin.

"Go on, Son! Don't let the talkative women distract you!" Mr. Hanson said, nudging his wife and getting a playful push in return.

"Well, a man who represents a defense-related research project paid me a visit on Friday and offered me an enormous salary to work for him." Ben started, and then quickly cut off.

"Just how big of salary are we talking about?" Mr. Chandler asked.

"$125,000 a year."

Teresa immediately lost the grip on her glass of iced tea, flooding her lap with the freezing cold liquid. She screeched in surprise at the sudden, steep change in temperature and wetness on her skirt. She ran to the bathroom, crying out of embarrassment and the thought that either Ben might actually make that kind of yearly income... or was completely out of his mind! No one said a thing for what seemed like a very long time to Ben.

"You're joking, right?" Ben's father asked seriously.

"No sir, I'm not." Ben replied, worried about Teresa and not quite understanding the response he was getting from his father, along with the look of incredulity on his future father-in-law's face. The fact was that salaries of that magnitude in rural Northeast Oklahoma were incomprehensible to most of the people who lived there. Ben could have said a "billion dollars a year" and the response would have been the same.

His family could sense Ben's concern about his sobbing fiancé by the troubled and confused look on his face. Reality seemed to strike each the young couple's parents simultaneously.

"Oh my God!" Ben's mother gasped as Ben ran to the bathroom to tend to Teresa. "He's not kidding!"

As electrified conversation broke out in the living room, Ben knocked on the bathroom door. "Teresa, sweetheart, are you OK? Can I come in?"

"Don't you dare! I'm soaking wet, Benjamin Hanson, and it's all your fault!" She said, continuing to sob profusely.

Ben turned the doorknob gently and found it unlocked. He slowly opened the door, half expecting her to push it shut, but she didn't. She turned away from him as he entered, busily trying to dry her blouse and skirt with a towel and intermittently wiping the tears from her face.

"What's the matter, sweetheart?" Ben said softly. "I thought this would make you happy?"

She turned slightly towards him looked up. "Is it true?" She asked. "Please tell me this is not a dream!"

"Yes, sweetie, it's true" Ben replied. "They are even buying a nice house for us."

"That's wonderful, Ben." She said. "You know I don't care about the money, but this means we can afford to start a family right away!"

"How many 'mini-Hansons' did you say you wanted?" Ben asked softly, brushing her tears away with gentle sweeps of his fingers. Her crying subsided to tears and sniffles.

"An even dozen." She said with a broken voice, her eyes glistening with fresh tears.

"A baker's dozen and you've got a deal!" Ben said, bringing her close for an embrace she never wanted to end.

"I love you so much, Benjamin Harris Hanson!" She said, looking up at him from his chest with a radiant, tear-streaked face that God surely sculpted to humble the Angels in Heaven. "We are going to be so happy!"

Ben leaned over and kissed her for what seemed to be hours of warm bliss. Ben was more happy at that moment than he ever thought possible. He felt as if could not ask for any more out of life, yet he knew that so much more was coming. A life of love and passion with Teresa, watching their children grow and achieve wondrous things of their own, then old age with beloved grandchildren and great grandchildren on their laps. When it was all over, there would be an eternity to spend with his only-est. Ben wondered how one man could be so richly blessed.

"Ben? Teresa?" Ben's mother was calling from the living room. "Is everything OK?"

"Yes, mom!"

"You better not be fooling around in there!" She said with hollow firmness. Laughter erupted from the rest of the family.

Teresa began to giggle. Ben shut the bathroom door all the way with a distinct bang and purposefully locked the door as loudly as he could. "We'll be out in a couple of hours, Mom!"

"Benjamin Hanson!" Mrs. Hanson shouted, trying to keep from laughing. "You let that poor girl out of that bathroom this instant!"

"Sure thing, Mom!" Ben said as he began tickling Teresa's sensitive flanks. Predictably, she squealed loudly and within seconds she was begging for mercy between giggles and squeals. The effect was perfect, sounding as if he was ravaging Teresa in the small bathroom. By the time Ben and Teresa emerged, everybody was out of breath from laughing so hard.

"Mom?" Teresa said, clearly out of breath.

"Yes, dear?"

"Ben is evil! Can I still marry him?" She asked, giving Ben a kiss on the cheek.

"Of course you can, Teresa." Mrs. Chandler said with as straight a face as she could muster. "From the way things sounded in there, you were being just as evil as Ben. I would say that you both deserve each other."

"Mother!" She exclaimed in overly dramatic fashion.

"Far from me to interrupt a discussion about which kid is more evil than the other," Mr. Chandler said, "but I'd like to hear more about Ben's job!"

"Yeah, Ben, tell us more!" His dad chimed in.

For the next half hour, Ben described his new job, or what little he could of it, to his family. Some aspects of his new position naturally garnered more attention than other aspects. All considered the salary and house big positives. Not surprisingly, the secrecy, two-week shifts and living in Las Vegas were considered the biggest negatives. Most Christian families in the "Bible Belt" of America had a distinct dislike of the town whose claim to fame was gambling, topless dancers and rampant overindulgence. Vegas would not have been on Ben's top ten list of places to live either, but he felt that Heaven would follow him and Teresa wherever they settled. Teresa could have been happier with the arrangement, but nothing on earth would keep her from making a home and raising children with the man that loved her so much.

"Teresa, my love." Ben said sweetly, almost drippingly so.

"Yes, sweetie?"

"I saved the best three things for last!"

"You have MORE surprises, Ben Hanson?"

"I'm already on the payroll! They deposited an advance on my salary through July 1st!" Ben said with a big grin. "Mom, Mrs. Chandler, how much were you planning to spend on the wedding?"

"We had budgeted about $300, not including Teresa's dress." His mother said. "It's enough for a very sweet ceremony and reception."

"What could you do if you had $5000 to work with?"

"Ben! Your kidding!" His mother replied while Teresa gasped in delight.

"I'm serious, Mom. Would it be enough to give the most beautiful bride in all of recorded history the wedding she deserves?" Teresa began to cry again, afraid to say anything.

"Ben, with that kind of money, your bride will have the nicest wedding Oklahoma has ever seen!"

Ben turned to his father. "Dad?"

"Yes, son?" He replied, wondering what was coming next.

"Teresa needs reliable transportation that doesn't belong to her mother. Could you and Mr. Chandler help Teresa buy a new car tomorrow?"

"Sure, Son! It would be an honor! Bill, can you get tomorrow off?"

"I'm feelin' a virus comin' on already!" Mr. Chandler replied. He turned to his wife, putting his head on her chest and looking up into her eyes. "Sweetheart, could you feel my forehead and see if I have a fever?"

"Bill Chandler! Behave yourself!" Mrs. Chandler replied, playfully scolding him.

Teresa was in full sob by that time. What had she ever done to deserve such a kind, gentle, loving, and generous man? There was no doubt in her mind that she was the luckiest woman on earth!

"One last thing, my love..." Ben started, "My employer has already arranged for you to finish nursing school at the University of Nevada, Las Vegas. All you have to do is send them your transcripts and some paperwork that should be arriving sometime next week."

"Enough, Ben!" Teresa managed to squeak out through the crying. "Please, no more! You are such a sweet, sweet man! I can't possibly tell you how much I love you!"

Ben gently stroked her hair for a few moments then guided her head to his chest where she continued to cry, soaking his shirt with tears of deepest love. "Sweetheart, you don't need to say a word. I know how much you love me."

On May 18th, 1968, Benjamin Harris Hanson was awarded his Doctorate in Aerospace Engineering from the University of Michigan. On the first day in June, 1968, Teresa Rose Chandler became Mrs. Teresa Rose Hanson in what everyone in the community described as the most beautiful wedding ceremony and reception ever witnessed in the tri-state area. The newlyweds honeymooned in Las Vegas, where they found each other as physically in love as they were emotionally. When they were not in bed, they gleefully shopped for furniture and other items needed in their beautiful new home near Nellis Air Force Base. By the time Dr. Ben Hanson reported for duty on July 1st, Teresa Hanson was already pregnant with their first child, only she didn't know it at the time.

Chapter 47

As Loeffler suspected they would, the doctors at the UNLV Medical Center wanted to observe Dr. Hanson overnight. Hastings' door-kicking stunt had fractured Hanson's nose and shattered the fragile bones around his nose in what the Oromaxillofacial surgeons called a "Nasoethmoid Orbital Fracture." They reduced the nasal fracture in the Emergency Department, but said he would need surgery, sooner rather than later, to repair the rest. Hanson allowed them to obtain a Computed Tomogram scan of his face to ascertain the amount of damage done, but somewhat surprisingly, he refused the surgery, electing to allow the comminuted bones in his face to heal in whatever distorted position they were in at the time. Loeffler guessed that Hanson was trying to nail Hastings for the inappropriate level of violence he unleashed on him. Hanson also refused to undergo a chest x-ray, which the Emergency Department physician ordered after learning of the violent coughing spell in the ambulance and listening to Hanson's now distinctly abnormal lung sounds. Hanson brushed the coughing spell aside, saying he had a nasty case of bronchitis and that it would eventually go away on its' own. By midnight, Dr. Hanson was resting in a medical observation unit with an armed police officer stationed outside of his door.

Simpson and Loeffler left the hospital after double-checking the security arrangements for their prisoner. Hastings jumped ship a few hours earlier when he realized that he would not be able to interrogate Hanson that evening. They drove to the Peppermill, ordered a late dinner and began to discuss the upcoming day. The physicians' plan, barring any untoward change in his medical status, was to release Dr. Hanson for transfer to the Clark County Detention Center at 9AM. Once processed, Hanson would undergo interrogation.

"Mr. Loeffler, how are we going to keep Hastings from screwing this up?" Simpson asked.

"Please, call me Kevin." Loeffler replied. "I really don't know how we can stop him from interrogating Hanson. I don't think he'll hit him again, though."

"What is his problem, anyway? Oh, by the way, you can call me Hannah."

"Hannah, Hastings is a ruthless, egotistical bureaucrat, pure and simple."

"You mean he is an asshole."

Loeffler laughed. "Yes ma'am, and a big one at that!"

"Do you think he has the clout to ruin our careers?" Simpson asked with obvious concern in her voice.

"Absolutely! He will can me outright and that's just fine by me. It takes every ounce of willpower in my body to keep from tossing him into a wood chipper. If he doesn't can me, I'll just end up killing him." He said with an evil grin. "You? He'll use more subtle techniques to trash your future in the FBI, but I don't think either one of us has much to worry about."

"Why is that?" She asked, the concern in her voice growing.

"Here, read this." Loeffler said, producing the letter Dr. Hanson left for him in his car.

SAC Simpson read the brief letter, her eyes widening as she reached the postscript that suggested Loeffler should ask her out to dinner.

"This letter is very, very strange!" Simpson said, lowering it to the table. "Reading between the lines, it sounds as if he wants you to look into the deaths of retirees at your organization."

"That was my take on it, too. When I talked to him in the ambulance, he said he created this whole mess so that he might retire 'safely.' I don't buy it. Its' too melodramatic." Loeffler said, resting his chin on clasped hands. "He obviously wants me... us, to look into the retiree deaths as possible homicides, but he is up to something else, too. Something that he does not want us to find."

"The man and the box."

"You got it!"

"Do you know what is in the box?"

"Hanson said it was full of flowers for his girlfriend and he lost it at the Orleans. Given his behavior and everything that has happened, it strikes me as a weak alibi."

"But possible."

"Yeah... Unfortunately." Loeffler said. "Even so, I have to assume the worst."

"What is the worst?" She asked. "What might be in that box that you are so concerned about?"

"State secrets I am sworn to protect."

"That's kind of vague." She said with a touch of ire in her voice. "Can you give me a rough idea of the nature of the state secrets 'we' are sworn to protect?"

"You're right, Hannah, state secrets that 'we' are sworn to protect. Sorry..." Loeffler replied with a smile. "Unfortunately, I'm not allowed to discuss them with anybody outside of Project Cocheta."

"Can you tell me ANYTHING about this organization you work for?" She asked with undeniable exasperation. "It might help me to better understand what I'm up against."

"What 'we' are up against." He corrected her with a smile, returning the earlier favor. "The only thing I can tell you is that it doesn't exist."

"So that means you don't exist and I'm going to have to pick up the tab for dinner!"

Loeffler laughed. "No, I exist enough to pay for dinner!"

Simpson was smiling at him. It was then that Loeffler realized that there was a definite, mutual attraction developing between them. "Was Hanson ever wrong about anything?" Loeffler wondered to himself.

"So, what do you think we should do about Hastings?" She asked.

"Hanson is afraid of him and asked me to keep him away." Loeffler replied. "We could use that, if Hastings will play along with it."

"Do you think he will?"

"Maybe, if we can word it so that Hastings thinks he is the center of attention." Loeffler said. "People like him are best manipulated by playing to their exaggerated sense of self worth."

"Whatever happens," Simpson said, "I don't think Hastings should be left alone with Hanson."

"I agree, but if he wants to steal the show, he's got the horsepower to do it."

"Do you think Hanson is a traitor?" Simpson asked.

"I honestly don't know." Loeffler said. "It's always the ones you never expect. I've read Hanson's detailed personnel file. Except for a single incident in 1992, he has been a valued member of the organization. In fact, he was in line for Hastings' job in 1985, but someone much higher up the food chain thought a prick would do a better job. Hanson holds the number three position, or at least he did until this little circus act he pulled."

"What happened in 1992?"

"Hanson, and a majority of his colleagues, wanted the project to go public. They thought the time was right, but Hastings didn't agree. In fact, Hastings considered the whole idea to be mutinous. When Hanson tried to resign his position and retire in protest, Hastings wrote that he 'persuaded him to do otherwise.' Hanson's wife and 17 year-old son left him in a hurry immediately after that and I suspect Hastings had something to do with it. By all accounts, the Hansons had a rock solid marriage. He never requested retirement again and he has put in over 40 years on the project."

"Maybe Hastings threatened to harm his family. I mean, if he is vicious enough to bump off retirees, he's vicious enough to threaten the lives of family members to keep Hanson's mouth shut." Simpson said. "Hanson may be trying to accomplish what he failed to do in 1992 and extract a healthy dose of revenge on Hastings at the same time."

"That would explain a lot, Hannah." Loeffler replied, impressed with her quick formulation of a motive for Hanson's behavior. "But, I am curious as to his timing. Why now? Why did he wait almost 20 years to try it again?"

"I assume his wife and kids are no longer a factor after that length of time." Simpson said, the wheels spinning rapidly in her highly trained detective's mind. "Maybe his health is failing. People tend to tidy-up loose ends in their life when the health starts to go."

"Other than the chain smoking and caffeine abuse, he had no medical issues of significance on his last complete physical a year ago." Loeffler said.

"Have you noticed how old he looks for his age?" Simpson asked. "Maybe its' just me, but I think he looks sick, really sick. He has that sort of grayish color that chronically ill people get."

"You might be right. Hopefully, we'll be able to extract some useful information from him tomorrow." Loeffler said. "I'd like to get a better handle on who this second suspect is and what Hanson gave him."

"We'll shake something loose." Simpson assured him. She leaned a little forward and began smiling at him again. "So, were you going to take Hanson's advice?"

Loeffler looked puzzled for a moment then realized that she was referring to the letter. "Well, his description of you was right on target and he seems to be a very intuitive man... I mean, who am I to shrug off the advice of a certified super-genius?"

"You like steaks?" She asked.

"Love them, but I haven't been in town long enough to find a good steakhouse yet." He replied, liking where the conversation was going.

"When this is all over, we could have dinner at Gallagher's in the New York, New York. The steaks are pretty good there and the inside of the hotel is constructed to look like streets lined with the kind of shops and eateries you see in New York City. It reminds me a little of the trips I made to the Big Apple to visit my grandparents when I was a kid."

"It sounds wonderful! Loeffler replied with genuine enthusiasm. "I'm already looking forward to it!"

It was well past one in the morning by the time they left the restaurant. Loeffler dropped Simpson off at her car and proceeded to his home on the northwest side of Las Vegas. His thoughts during the drive home were an unusual mixture of an analysis of the facts in the Hanson case and wondering how things would eventually turn out with Hannah Simpson. After he arrived home, the same swirl of thoughts followed him to bed. He only had a four hour window to get some sleep, but swirling thoughts of Hanson and Simpson would trim that to two.

Chapter 48

The interrogation of Dr. Benjamin Hanson was not going well. Hastings refused to let SAC Simpson and Loeffler use him as leverage for information, insisting that he be present for every question and answer, even though he could have watched the entire process on closed circuit television. The presence of Hastings in the interrogation room clearly hardened Dr. Hanson and he refused to answer any questions beyond his name, address, and occupation. To make matters worse, Hastings had a penchant for interrupting questions posed by Simpson and Loeffler and frequently lost his temper with either the content of the questions, or the lack of responses from Hanson. As much as Simpson and Loeffler tried to keep the situation under control, it became obvious that Hastings was going take the interrogation process over the edge. Kevin Loeffler was the one who inadvertently detonated the bomb.

"Dr. Hanson, what can we do to get you to truthfully answer our questions?" Loeffler asked Hanson. "We may be able to get you a much lighter sentence if you cooperate?"

Hanson looked up at Loeffler. "A lighter sentence for what crime, Mr. Loeffler? Playing a prank on my security detail, or losing a box of flowers in a hotel?"

"Dr. Hanson, the FBI is holding you on suspicion of espionage, and if need be, they will hold you indefinitely under provisions provided by the Homeland Security Act."

"So, now I am a terrorist?"

"Are you, Dr. Hanson?"

"You know the answer to that question."

The entire case against Hanson was admittedly weak and without the identity of a mysterious man with Hanson's box, the only way to hold him longer than a few days would be to suggest that Hanson might be involved in plotting an act of domestic terrorism. They might be able to pull it off for a month or so, longer if Hanson continues to refuse counsel or cooperate with the lawyer the court will eventually appoint to him.

Hanson pressed on, his countenance and voice turning dark. "Mr. Loeffler, if you want to have any chance at all of gaining even the slightest bit of cooperation from me, you must remove Mr. Hastings from the room."

The snap in Hastings mind was almost audible. "That's it, you smug little asshole!" Hastings yelled at Hanson. "Clear the room, everybody! And I want the cameras and microphones turned off! NOW!" He yelled at the top of his voice.

Hanson was clearly surprised and frightened at the outburst. Simpson caught the look of terror on his face and stood her ground. "This prisoner is MY responsibility, Mr. Hastings, and I WILL NOT allow you repeat what you did to him last night!"

"Back away, Simpson!" Hastings yelled. "You are in way over your head already! I've had dinner with your director a half-dozen times, and I can, and WILL, have you permanently relieved of duty in less than 2 minutes if you don't shut the fuck up and get out of this room!"

Simpson looked to Loeffler for guidance, but all he could do was shake his head and motion for her to leave.

"You two are pathetic!" Hastings growled with disdain. "I haven't a clue what the FBI ever saw in you! Get the fuck out of my sight!"

As Simpson and Loeffler began to exit the door, Hastings made one last comment. "I'll have the information we need in less than five minutes and I won't need to lay a finger on him."

As the door closed, Hastings used a chair to help him reach the video camera's audio and video cables. Grabbing them both, he jerked them hard enough to break the connectors and disable the camera permanently. He stepped down from the chair and pulled it up next to Hanson, where he sat facing his prisoner with the back of the chair providing a rest for his hands and chin. Hanson was obviously terrified, sensing what was coming next. Something he somehow failed to consider... It was going to be a nightmarish repeat of 1992.

"Ben, Ben, Ben..." Hastings said with the same horrible tone to his voice than Hanson remembered from his last confrontation with him. "You broke the little deal we worked out back in '92. You remember, you were supposed to behave yourself. You were supposed to put away those silly notions of disclosure. Why, Ben? Why did you do such a foolish thing? Did you somehow think that having no contact with your wife and kids for all these years made the deal null and void? Or maybe you thought that your wife and kids were untouchable now. Well, Doctor Hanson, let me assure you that they are not! Bad things can happen to adults, too. Ruined careers, unexpected financial catastrophies... and, of course, 'health problems' can always strike without warning. Oh... in case you didn't know it, you have a handful of grandchildren! Shame how many kids vanish out of their own front yards every year..."

Ben Hanson could barely hear what Hastings was saying. The terrible fear that gripped him was changing into something else, something well beyond Hanson's conscious control. It was untethered, murderous rage. His heart was pounding in his chest and his vision becoming razor sharp through an increasingly narrow angle of view. Stress hormones and adrenalin were pouring into his bloodstream to fuel the imminent attack. He was going to kill Hastings with his bare hands. There was no thought process, no weighing the "pros and cons," just blind homicidal intent. Hanson lunged at Hastings throat with a quickness and viciousness that caught his victim completely by surprise. He had Hastings pinned to the floor, and in spite of his handcuffs, making considerable progress towards crushing the man's trachea with his bare hands.

Then the coughing started... and it was different from all of his previous spells. In his rage, he barely noticed he was coughing at all. Deep within Dr. Hanson's chest, the cancer slowly killing him not only invaded the wall of the largest airway in his left lung, but his left pulmonary artery as well, weakening both substantially. The surge in blood pressure and heart rate that accompanied his attack on Hastings and the additional pressure changes within his chest caused by the coughing spell, created a sudden tear in the tumor-weakened structures. Blood began to spray into his left lung through the new communication between major artery and large airway. Ben Hanson's next cough coated Hastings' face with blood.

In an instant, the surprise appearance of blood on his adversary's face jolted Hanson out of his fury. He relaxed his death grip on Hastings as the second cough sprayed the Project Director's face with a second coat of blood. Hastings recoiled in horror, profusely coughing himself and struggling to crawl away from Hanson. Within a few seconds, the door to the interrogation room burst open and Hanson pinned to the floor. Blood was now everywhere as Hanson's coughing went unabated. Lying in a growing pool of blood, Hanson felt strength ebbing from his body. He was having difficulty catching his breath because he was literally drowning. "Not now!" He pleaded in his mind. "Not this way!" He thought of Teresa and his children and yearned for their presence, but an overwhelming sense of dread began to smother him, along with an intense thirst, the like of which he never experienced before. He was vaguely aware of pandemonium taking place around him, but for some reason it didn't matter to him. The feeling of dread was steadily transforming into a strange, soothing warmth as endorphins, hundreds of times more powerful than morphine, began flowing into his compromised circulation. The chaos he noticed only moments before was becoming increasingly muffled. He was occasionally aware that his body was moving and people were shouting, but it was way off in the distance somewhere. Within a few minutes, his vision gradually faded to darkness and a peaceful quiet was enveloping his remaining consciousness.

"So this is what it is like to die..."

Chapter 49

Paul Harris Hanson, son of Dr. and Mrs. Hanson, was born on March 6th, 1969. He was somewhat small at 5 pounds, 12 ounces, but that would be the only time in his life that he would be "little." Like his namesake, Paul Harris would become the athlete in the family. As a toddler, he was unstoppable and frighteningly adventurous, unafraid of heights, man, nor beast. Even though Ben and Teresa were very attentive parents, Paul Harris managed to break his first bone, his left forearm, by the time he was four. Gravity would become the rambunctious child's arch enemy, thwarting every attempt duplicate the feats of the superheroes he emulated. Much to their dismay, Paul Harris was fond of bringing all manner of desert creatures to his parents, even presenting his mother with a ripe, three-foot long Western Diamond-backed Rattlesnake which, though very dead, sent Teresa fainting to the floor.

To nobody's surprise, Paul had a natural gift for anything athletic. Football and baseball, however, were his passions. He was a standout in both sports through junior high and high school and heavily recruited by colleges seeking his talent in either one sport or the other. Eventually, Paul settled on a full baseball scholarship to Texas A&M. His choice surprised many who speculated he would end up at one of college baseball's perennial powerhouses like Arizona State or the University of Texas at Austin. The simple truth was that, during his visit to College Station Texas, he fell in love with the athletic department, the campus, the Dixie Chicken and a hazel-eyed co-ed from Caldwell named Jessica, who took his breath away and would eventually become Mrs. Paul Hanson.

Paul's little sister, Donna Michelle Hanson was born on May 28th, 1971. Like her father, Donna possessed an enormously gifted mind, with problem-solving capabilities that rivaled his. Unlike her father, however, she was far from quiet and introspective. She had the stunning looks and friendly spunk of her mother and was a force of nature that commanded respect. Her unique combination of sassy self-assuredness and awe-inspiring intellect would constantly keep Ben and Teresa on their toes. Donna was a naturally busy child, requiring a great deal of attention to keep her entertained. Her mind was a giant sponge, begging saturation with answers to the secrets of the world around her. There was no academic task that Donna Michelle couldn't master and would have easily skipped several grades if her parents had allowed it.

Ben and Teresa found themselves constantly walking an academic tightrope with Donna, balancing her need for ever-increasing intellectual challenges with the need to insure proper social development. They allowed her to skip only two grades, 4 years apart, keeping her much closer to peers of her own age than her father had been able to. In order to prevent underachievement due to boredom, they enrolled her in an acclaimed private school and challenged her mind by hiring a personal tutor that would expose her to sub-jects well beyond the scope of her normal studies. In spite of Ben and Teresa's best efforts, Donna was still a bit of a social outcast. She usually had no intellectual equal she could talk to besides her dad and while boys admired her stunning looks, they found her mind and self-assuredness intimidating. Thankfully, Donna was entirely too busy to care about such things. She was definitely a "daddy's girl" in every way, and a classic example of the apple "not falling too far away from the tree." Fascinated by the same things her dad was, she had every intention of following in his footsteps. Only, she could never get Dad to talk about where his footsteps lead to.

The Hanson's youngest child, Arthur Marcus, was born on October 4th, 1975, and named after Ben Hanson's "other" father, who was also his friend and mentor, General Arthur Marston, who passed away earlier that year. Arthur was a wonderful blend of Teresa and Ben. He had above average intelligence and looks, with his mother's sense of humor. Out of the three "mini-Hansons," Arthur was easily the most content. Having a relatively low maintenance baby proved to be a tremendous blessing for Teresa, as she had her hands full will Paul and Donna. Arthur could entertain himself quietly for hours with a set of Lincoln Logs or a coloring book, while his mother was keeping an eye on his more intrepid siblings. As he grew older, Arthur tended to be shy until he knew somebody well, then he allowed his hidden qualities to shine. His combination of good looks and shyness proved irresistible to girls when he reached Junior High School, so there was never a shortage of potential female companions to choose from for school functions.

Living in the shadow of his more dynamic older siblings and having busy parents did contribute to a few behavioral problems for Arthur. Paul had everybody's attention with his athletic achievements and collection of medals and trophies. Donna was bossy, and always commanding their Dad's attention when he was home for two weeks out of every four. When Arthur reached middle school, his mom returned to school to work on her Masters Degree, then ran for, and won election to the local School Board by the time he started high school. While Arthur's "acting out" was never serious, there were a few minor brushes with the law and an occasional heated argument with his parents. Fortunately, Arthur found his stride in his junior year of high school, and began focusing more on his future rather than useless ruminating on how it "sucked" being the "forgotten child," as his teenage mind assessed the situation. His blooming maturity would help his mother immensely when the world crumbled around them in January of 1992.

Ben and Teresa's marriage was not perfect, but it was solid. It took years for Teresa to stop wondering and worrying about what her husband was doing during the two weeks he was gone. He was paid very handsomely for whatever it was he did, and when he was home, he was an attentive husband and father. Early on, when the children were little, Teresa had many frustrating days during Ben's "on" periods. By the time Arthur was born she had become quite adept at juggling children. Eventually, Teresa learned to enjoy Ben's work routine, because the reunions were always passionate and the two-week off period gave the family plenty of time to spend together or travel when school schedules permitted it.

True to his word, Ben never spoke about the details of his job, and Teresa became comfortable with not asking. To Ben, home was home and work was work, with no room to mix the two. There were times, however, when work did encroach on Ben's family life, and a phone call would send him dashing to Nellis AFB to catch a plane to God only knew where.

"Field Trips" were, for Dr. Hanson, the most fascinating aspect of his career. They gave him the opportunity to examine UFO evidence ranging from damaged trees to wreckage fields and on rare occasion, he actually interviewed witnesses. Out of necessity and practicality, field trips were highly screened. To dispatch a Project Cocheta investigative crew, the "Cat Two IOS" had to meet very strict criteria, including the presence of physical evidence. Short of that, credible sightings arrived at Project Cocheta through normal government and military channels for review by the Conclave or a less formal committee if warranted. The purpose behind sending a scientific crew to such occurrences was so that those most familiar with the evidence already in hand could examine the resting state of the new evidence, perhaps yielding clues to the mysteries that continued to plague the reverse engineering of extraterrestrial technology. In particular, the powerplant/reactor and the means of propulsion.

Over the years, Dr. Hanson personally investigated many physical evidence scenes, some in countries other than the United States and Canada. He had been in places ranging from the untamed rainforests of Brazil to the relatively tame forests of eastern England. He saw mangled alien bodies and measured the levels of ionizing radiation standing in the middle of twisted wreckage contained in a shallow crater. On a small handful of occasions, he donned the traditional, non-descript, jet-black black business suit, with white shirt, matching black tie, hat and dark RayBan sunglasses to camouflage his identity while interviewing witnesses. Not once was Hanson or a Project Cocheta crew ever dispatched to the scene of an alien abduction of a human being.

By the 1970s and '80s, alien abduction stories became common fare in the alternative, checkout stand press, and it was gaining in popularity with other media outlets such as radio and television. The first and most famous case, that of Betty and Barney Hill, occurred in rural New Hampshire in 1961; predating the "modern" era of alien abduction cases by several years. The Hill case was fascinating in that it started out as a curious loss of 2 hours after witnessing a close approach by a UFO. Several months passed before hypnosis revealed the full story of the abduction that took place during the couples' induced period of amnesia. Given the inherent problems with hypnosis and the lack of physical evidence, the incident, while compelling, left little to hang a scientific hat on.

Modern alien abduction stories began to surface about ten years after the Hill case and they became more and more numerous as the years passed by. They all seemed to have one thing in common, a complete lack of physical evidence. That was not to say that Project Cocheta completely ignored the reports, but after consultation with highly respected psychiatrists and psychologists, it was determined that the roots of the phenomenon were very terrestrial in origin. Many abduction stories were "retrieved" through suggestion and hypnosis, some were misinterpretations of sleep paralysis, others were pure fabrication. A very significant number of them were due a due to a fascinating psychological quirk called a "well-circumscribed delusion." People who suffer from a well-circumscribed delusion have completely normal thought processes and usually function quite normally from day to day. They have, however, a single belief that is incredibly irrational. Some believe their spouse is sleeping with everybody in town, in spite of a complete lack of evidence that such behavior is actually taking place. Others might believe that aliens have singled them out for routine anal probing. Whatever the delusion, they are perfectly normal otherwise.

One consulted psychiatrist pointed out that any "abductee" reporting to be carrying a message for the human race from the aliens was either lying or suffering from delusions of grandeur. She also suggested that others who claimed they had eggs or sperm removed from them to create "hybrid" babies, or impregnated with alien sperm to accomplish the same, were suffering from similar delusions, but coming from a much deeper and far more disturbing psychosexual source. To the scientists at Cocheta, unless a human woman gave birth to something that looked like the reference specimen in Drawer 32, alien abduction stories were best left to doctors of the mind and those who wished to make frightening movies.

Field trips rarely lasted more than a few days, then average citizen Ben Hanson would return home to his lovely wife and children, speaking absolutely nothing of his unannounced departure, absence and return.

The Hansons were an overall content family, lacking nothing in the way of physical or financial needs and with plenty of love to go around for everybody. Like all families, there were rocky times. Teresa had a tragic stillbirth between Donna and Arthur that devastated the couple, almost to the point of not trying again for a third child. Ben faced the sudden, unexpected death of General Marston in 1975, and the family endured a terrifying heart murmur scare with little Arthur Marcus right after he was born. Brogan's retirement in 1985 was a major, negative turning point in Ben's career, when the top spot he trained for was given to Louis Hastings and the number two spot, that he already ascended to, was given to Oren McMahon, a low-level Hastings sycophant. In spite of these tribulations, Ben Hanson still had his research and more importantly, his family. Each trial strengthened the couple and the bonds that held the family together. As the family aged, so came the inevitable points where parents must let their children make their own way in the world. Ben and Teresa sadly watched two children head off to college in the same year, but because of Ben's schedule, flights to Texas and Michigan became almost routine.

The Hanson family was strong, made so by strong values unerringly passed on from generation to generation. The next generation of Hansons and Chandlers, Ben and Teresa's grandchildren, would also know the secrets of a strong family. In spite of its' seemingly cast iron structure, the Hanson's were sadly vulnerable, as any family would have been, to the unthinkable terrorism of one Louis Hastings.

Chapter 50

August 27th, 1974 – 20 Miles Northwest of Presidio, Texas

"This is nuts!" Dr. Hanson thought to himself while looking at the rugged West Texas desert passing 500 feet below, "Absolutely nuts! I'll be lucky to make it out alive on this one!"

The UH-1 Huey suddenly banked right in unison with two other unmarked Hueys, two AH-1 Cobras and a CH-47C Chinook, giving the young Aerospace Engineer an unobstructed, open-door view of the Rio Grande river below. They were now in Mexican airspace and completely without permission to be there. Ben's fingers were blanching with the death-grip he had on his restraints. His overall state of anxiety caught General Marston's attention.

"You OK?" Marston asked using the intercom function of his headset.

"Is this wise? I mean, we are barging into Mexican airspace like we own it!"

"Son, the Mexican government, for whatever dumbass reason, decided to play games with us on this." Marston replied, "Now there are dead people as a result of contact and they're scared shitless. They haven't uttered a peep or made any move towards the area for well over eight hours. Hell, they're silence is practically an invitation for us to come in and clean up the mess they've made! Besides, we don't have the luxury to wait any longer for official clearance."

"If they want us to come in, why the Cobra gunships?"

Marston smiled at Ben. "Insurance. Local authorities are not always on the same page of music as Distrito Federal."

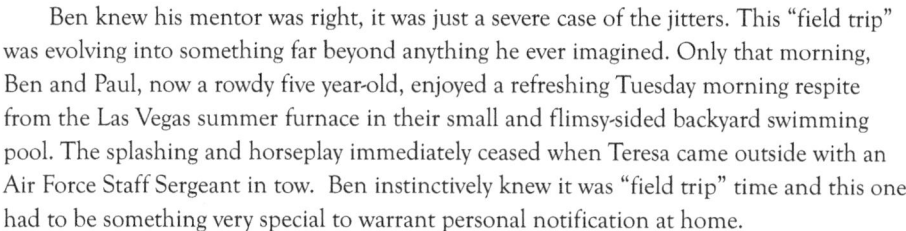

Ben knew his mentor was right, it was just a severe case of the jitters. This "field trip" was evolving into something far beyond anything he ever imagined. Only that morning, Ben and Paul, now a rowdy five year-old, enjoyed a refreshing Tuesday morning respite from the Las Vegas summer furnace in their small and flimsy-sided backyard swimming pool. The splashing and horseplay immediately ceased when Teresa came outside with an Air Force Staff Sergeant in tow. Ben instinctively knew it was "field trip" time and this one had to be something very special to warrant personal notification at home.

Normally, Field Trip notification consisted of a brief telephone call informing him of a "wheels-up" time at Nellis. If away from home, the beeping of his new, bulky and message-less Pageboy One would prompt him to call the Vegas office for instructions. This time, an Air Force NCO would spirit Hanson to Nellis where General Marston was waiting to join him aboard a flight-ready C-130. A surge of adrenalin in his blood weakened his knees a touch at the thought the investigation, or recovery, or whatever the hell awaited him might be serious enough to actually be dangerous. Now that the mission was well underway, the reality of violating Mexican airspace and breaking reams of international law in a quickly "unmarked" helicopter changed his assessment of the field trip to "off-the-scale" hot.

Dr. Hanson was unquestionably rattled. In his six short years at Project Cocheta he met every challenge given him, but this one made him feel as if he were involved in something entirely out of his league. In spite of the tantalizing scientific treasure that lie 20 miles ahead on a desolate dirt road in Mexico, Ben wished he were back in Vegas chasing his boy around the swimming pool.

While en route to Fort Bliss, Marston informed Ben that the Cat Two Incident of Significance, relayed to Project Cocheta by CINCNORAD a few hours earlier, occurred two nights ago and involved a high-altitude craft that suddenly emerged from Cuban airspace 19 miles north-northeast of Caibarièn at nearly Mach 6. The craft quickly violated the U.S. Air Defence Identification Zone and appeared to be heading towards Key West, prompting the FAA to notify NORAD of the potential threat. A snap order was immediately given to scramble ready-alert Phantom IIs from the 31st Fighter Wing at Homestead Air Force Base. Before a single J79 engine could whine its' way to life, the craft abruptly turned west and entered the Gulf of Mexico at an altitude of 71,500 feet, traveling at over 4500 miles per hour. Fifteen minutes later and a thousand miles of open airspace behind it, the ultra-high performance craft slowed to Mach 4 and crossed the coastline of Mexico a few miles north of La Pesca. After six minutes and a decidedly non-ballistic series of maneuvers with stepped decreases in altitude, the "UFO" passed over Monterrey on a level, northwesterly course at 18,000 feet and slowing to subsonic. NORAD closely monitored the path of the unidentified craft until it made a sharp turn west and followed an uncharacteristic ballistic descent in altitude, falling below minimum tracking altitude near Coyame, Mexico. The event was logged as another tracking of a UFO without aggressive intentions against the United States and defensive air assets previously alerted were ordered to stand down.

Also noted in the area at the time of the UFO's last known position was the presence of a southeast bound civilian aircraft en route to Mexico City from El Paso. The twin-engine Cessna C310Q was flying visual flight rules at a relatively low altitude, which made for sporadic radar contact in the mountainous terrain. When Mexican aviation authorities lost radio and radar contact with the plane for over two hours straight, they alerted the Federal Police and Mexican Army units in the State of Chihuahua that the aircraft may have crashed somewhere near Coyame, the town closest to the last known radar contact.

Since the flight originated in the United States but the aircraft registered in Mexico, Mexican authorities notified the FAA as a courtesy. The FAA in turn notified the Air Force of the mishap and its probable location. Within 45 minutes, a NORAD analyst noticed the disturbing coincidence of losing contact with an unidentified flying object at the same time and roughly the same location as a civilian airplane and informed CINCNORAD of the suspicious crash. Major General Vic Ralston, Commander-in-Chief, North American Aerospace Defense Command immediately ordered the earlier UFO tracking file reopened and requested national intelligence assets be assigned to monitor the progress of the search and rescue or recovery operation. Less than an hour later, the United States Army Intelligence Center at Fort Huachuca, Arizona began focusing their attention to the southeast.

The search for the missing Cessna began at daybreak and it took the Mexican authorities only three hours to discover the wreckage. Twenty minutes later, USAIC intercepted another transmission from the recovery operation. They located more wreckage six miles northeast of the Cessna crash, and the Federale who discovered it, was screaming that he found a "platillo volador" or "flying saucer." Animated radio chatter erupted between the search and recovery teams, but abruptly silenced several minutes later when a Mexican Army Officer began screaming at them to keep their mouths shut about what they found. USAIC quickly prepared a translated transcript and flashed it to the Army Intelligence Headquarters for dissemination to the parties wanting to know what was going on in Northern Mexico.

Within a few hours, a U-2 from the 100th Strategic Reconnaissance Wing at Davis-Monthan Air Force Base was loitering over the area at 70,000 feet shooting high-resolution photographs of the sparsely populated area. By nightfall, the CIA had developed and interpreted every frame. The Cessna wreckage, located a few miles north of Coyame, was far more typical of a ground impact than a mid-air collision, confined only to an area a quarter the size of a football field. It was more than obvious that there were no survivors. The second debris field was far more interesting. The reconnaissance photographs clearly showed a metallic disc somewhat less than 20 feet in diameter at the end of a relatively short stretch of gouged earth. The "debris" was limited to the object itself and a number of uprooted desert plants. The craft was remarkably intact, the most glaring damage visible being a gaping hole one third the distance from the center of the disc to its' edge and obvious buckling of the superstructure. There were a number of uniformed and non-uniformed people working around the object, but no heavy equipment and no bodies visible in any of the remarkable photographs.

On the political side, certain State Department officials began offering "assistance" with the search and rescue mission without consent of the two week-old Ford Administration and hours before the first U-2 pictures were developed. The Mexican government politely declined. After the precise nature of the incident became clear, more urgent offers of assistance were relayed to Mexico City and summarily went unanswered. While President Álvarez was ignoring State Department offers, "assets" were gathering at a satellite tarmac on the north side of Biggs Army Airfield in El Paso. Crews were in place waiting for the word to "sanitize" the six helicopters by painting over and grinding off every marking that even remotely identified the machines as belonging to the United States. No one believed for a moment that the ploy would fool a soul if the mission ended in disaster. Bureaucrats would simply label it as a "rogue" operation not sanctioned in any way by the United States Government. As per standard operating procedures in such political embarrassments, a convenient head would find its' way on a platter and that would likely be the end of it.

U-2 flights were flying around the clock to monitor the situation at the crash site. By midnight, Mexican recovery personnel managed to pry the object from the ground and hoist it onto a 2 1/2 ton flatbed truck using a front-end loader and a small crane. They quickly concealed the alien craft with tarps and the small convoy began slowly making their way southeast over rugged desert terrain towards a dusty, infrequently traveled dirt road some 5 miles away. Progress was agonizingly slow in the fading illumination of a first-quarter moon descending in the western sky. The recovery team managed to reach the desert road just before sunrise. By then, each member was beginning to feel the first gastrointestinal symptoms of a lethal exposure to something on or within the alien craft. All of them would be dead within the next hour.

At 7:30AM Coyame time, USAIC at Fort Huachuca intercepted a radio transmission from the previously silent convoy. An agitated male voice was repeatedly calling for medical help, stating that everyone on his team had suddenly taken ill, coughing-up blood and suffering explosive diarrhea. Even through moderate radio static, the terror in his voice was evident, yet his desperate and increasingly weakening pleas for help went unanswered. At 8:05AM, all transmissions ceased. It was clear to all listening to the deafening silence that the Mexican authorities wanted nothing to do with an alien chemical or biologic incident.

At 8:30AM, a U-2 made a three passes over the area and immediately returned to Davis-Monthan for quick analysis of the photographs. The imaging showed the caravan in remarkable detail, including the tarp-covered object on the flatbed truck and several human bodies lying about the vehicles. As good as the imaging was, the analysts wanted more detail. Within minutes, the 67th Tactical Reconnaissance Wing at Bergstrom Air Force Base in Austin was tasked to send a pair of RF-4C Phantom II jets on high speed, low and medium altitude photo runs of the area. By 10:40AM, the intelligence picture was complete. An alien aircraft crashed outside of Coyame, Mexico and it might have been involved in some way with a fatal mishap involving a civilian airplane. Every member of the recovery team sent to retrieve it was likely dead and the Mexican Government, once so eager to own their very own platillo volador, was now silently washing their hands of the matter. United States intervention was now inevitable. At 10:52 AM, CINCNORAD dispatched a flash Cat Two IOS to Project Cocheta. The mission was a "go."

The Air Force C-130 transporting General Marston and Ben Hanson arrived at Biggs Army Airfield at 2:25 PM. Both men were quickly escorted to a small temporary building on the northern edge of the tarmac where they handed over all of their personal belongings and identification, changed into a plain jumpsuit and donned a white contamination outer garment. Within fifteen minutes of landing at Biggs, Marston and Hanson were airborne in the lead UH-1 and headed southeast.

Chapter 51

Ben's reflection of the situation he found himself in were interrupted by the sudden breakaway of one of the Hueys and a Cobra. He turned and looked at Marston.

"They're headed to the two crash sites to do a brief inspection and take photographs. We're headed to the convoy."

Ben shook his head in acknowledgement.

"Son, before we land, you need to know a little something about helicopter etiquette." Marston began. "Last thing I want is my favorite scientist getting scalped by a rotor blade!"

Ben smiled. Marston developed the habit of referring to him as "son," and he didn't mind it at all. In many ways, Marston was just like his own father. Both were intense men with fearsome convictions, yet possessed a down-to-earth humanness that made them very approachable. Ben not only respected Marston, he grew quite fond of him. The man had no family to speak of, so Ben adopted him into his own. Marston visited the Hanson household frequently and seemed to enjoy playing with the little ones. Paul and Donna called him "Pawpaw," which never failed to light up the old man's eyes.

"Old man." Ben sadly thought to himself. "Marston was getting old, and he seemed so much older than the man that recruited him only six years earlier. Still, he insisted on going on these occasional "joy rides" as he referred to them. Ben, at that moment, suddenly realized that at some point in the near future he would be doing these missions on his own or leading a team. The thought gave him a chill. Marston was a born leader of men. Ben considered himself a scientist, nothing more.

"We'll offload hot, so keep your head down as you exit the helicopter." Marston said." Stay away from the rear of the helicopter. Nothing but trouble there. When you approach the helicopter, blades moving or not, make sure you can see the pilot clearly. Direct eye contact is even better. Always come in from the front."

The pilot suddenly interrupted the conversation. "Five minutes out."

"OK, here's how we are going to do this." Marston said, abruptly changing subjects. "We put on the positive pressure breathing system and hood before we land. When we hit the ground, stay put until the other Huey and the Chinook land. The Cobra will orbit the area and make sure we don't have any uninvited guests. One Chinook team will remove the tarp from the object and attach a sling. The other Chinook team will assemble a prefabricated, airtight crate nearby. The Chinook will lift the object from the truck, lower it into crate and land again. The crews will secure the lid on the crate and attach the hoist cable to it. While that's going on, the other Huey crew will be bagging bodies and soaking the vehicles in lighter fluid for the big bonfire we're going to leave behind. Your job is to investigate and document as much as you can in the 20 minutes we plan to be in the area. You know how to use that new Nikon?"

"It's a bit fancier than I'm used to, but I shouldn't have any trouble."

A subtle change in pitch and increase in rotor noise heralded the beginning of the relatively short descent into the landing zone. Both men and three other crewmembers on board quickly donned the remainder of their protective gear. A few moments later, the Huey landed in a cloud of dust and sand 75 yards upwind of the doomed convoy.

The scene that emerged from the settling dust was surreal. There were seven vehicles in the convoy, two jeeps, four pick-up trucks and one flatbed with a poorly concealed flying disc strapped to it. Scattered amongst the vehicles were bodies, at least a dozen of them. Even from a distance, it was easy to see their deaths must have been very unpleasant. All died in a fetal position, suggesting each man suffered unbearable abdominal pain. To a soul, all had soiled themselves with profuse bloody diarrhea and vomit. As he passed by corpses on his way to the flatbed, Ben felt the warm, queasy sensation of building nausea, but was able to fight off the powerful urge to splash the inside of his mask with what little he had in his stomach. Had he not worn a positive-pressure breathing apparatus, the horrific stench that enveloped the convoy would have easily overcome his self-control.

The Chinook crew responsible for handling the disc stripped the tarps free of the alien craft by the time Ben stepped up to the flatbed. Three things immediately caught his eye, the first of which was the size and shape of the disc. It was no more than 18 feet in diameter and noticeably thinner than the specimens under study at Cocheta. Ben quickly concluded the vehicle was unmanned and remotely piloted, or used some form of sophisticated artificial intelligence to carry out its' mission. The next thing he noted was the overall condition of the craft. In spite of its' presumed high-speed impact with the ground, the hull was largely intact except for significant buckling that distorted the disc shape of the craft and the presence of the third item he immediately noted: a gaping hole on the upper surface of the hull. He knew of the holes' existence prior to seeing the craft in person, but he did not expect to see charred edges blown outward! The flying disc crashed due to a systems failure, not a collision! He chided himself for not guessing that sooner. All of the impact and strength testing Cocheta conducted on the baffling alien alloy used in constructing their hulls revealed it to be impenetrable to high velocity projectiles, including a new anti-tank canon round using a depleted uranium and titanium alloy. It would make sense that an aircraft made of such a remarkable metal could slice through a general aviation aircraft made primarily of aluminum without sustaining so much as a scratch. That wasn't to say the alien alloy was indestructible. The ragged wound on top the disc and the thousands of wreckage pieces stored at Cocheta, were ample proof that the metal had limitations to its' strength. The force necessary to blast through an alien hull was quite substantial, leading the young aerospace engineer to conclude that if there was anything alive in the craft prior to the explosion, it was nothing but carbonized goo now.

Ben began taking picture after picture of the craft from every conceivable angle, only stopping when he had to change film. Within minutes, the disc was harnessed and the Chinook hovering overhead ready to lift it off the flatbed and into the crate constructed a hundred yards to the south. After grabbing several shots of the amazing spectacle, Ben began taking pictures of the several corpses not bagged and destined for the coming pyre. As he photographed, crew members from the second Huey were driving or pushing the convoy vehicles close together, then removing gas caps and oil pan bolts. Moments later, they waved Ben away and began tossing the dead into vehicles and dowsing everything with flammable liquid. One of the mission objectives was to char the convoy and the immediate area around it, hopefully sterilizing it in the process. Gasoline was used as the initial accelerant because of its' volatility and ease of ignition with a simple flare launched from a safe distance upwind. Jet "A," essentially a highly refined diesel oil and easily supplied from an internal auxiliary fuel tank on the Huey, was used to provide prolonged burning.

Only 14 minutes elapsed since the first helicopter skid touched earth when Ben heard something that iced his blood.

"Someone's coming! Let's wrap this up!" A muffled voice yelled.

Ben quickly looked around and spotted the source of the consternation. Off in the distance, four or five miles south of their position, was the dust cloud of an approaching vehicle. Just as if the Cobra pilot was reading Ben's mind at that very moment, the orbiting gunship banked violently to the south, assumed a sharp, nose down pitch and raced towards the encroaching threat.

The Chinook landed beside the now crated disc to pick up her two teams. All but two boarded the large twin rotor helicopter as one member of each team remained at the crate to attach a hoist cable to it once the helicopter was hovering well above. Except for a single team member of the second Huey assigned to ignite the convoy with a flare gun, the remainder of the recovery teams were aboard their assigned helicopters and awaiting the order to egress. Ben was the last one to board his Huey, approaching the helicopter from the front as his mentor instructed. He immediately sensed that something was not right.

"Where is General Marston?" Ben asked the other three white clad passengers.

"He was with you." One replied. "The last time I saw him he was with you."

In all the excitement and focus on the tasks assigned to him, Ben lost track of Marston's whereabouts. A sudden dread swept over him.

"We've got to find him!"

"He probably jumped on another bird. I wouldn't worry about it Dr. Hanson."

"No, no, I know the man! He wouldn't do that! He sticks to a plan like glue!" He argued, the dread inside of him growing.

Without hesitation, Ben jumped out of the Huey and began a clumsy run towards the doomed Mexican caravan in his bulky exposure suit. At the very same moment sixty yards away and much closer to the convoy, a team member from the sister Huey was looking away from Ben, awaiting a visual signal from his squad leader to aim and fire his flare gun towards the assembled vehicles, generously prepped with accelerant for incineration.

"Jesus Christ! What the hell is he doing?" Ben's squad leader yelled as he hurriedly unbuckled his restraints and jumped from the bench seat. "He's going to get himself killed!"

Ben was retracing his steps as fast as he could run in the ill-fitting suit. As he approached the convoy, he quickly scanned the area ahead of him for any sign of his mentor. Even through his growing panic and frantic search, Ben couldn't help but notice the sudden appearance of flickering red in the far right fringe of his peripheral vision. Before his mind could process the visual clue, something struck him hard from behind, slamming him to the desert floor. A fraction of a moment later, the air around him erupted in searing heat. Dazed and terrified, he began to claw the ground in a desperate attempt to separate himself from whatever hit him and the inferno raging a dozen yards to his right. Something... no, someone was violently pulling on his exposure suit and airpack!

"Get on your feet, dammit!" A muffled, yet powerful voice bellowed. "Get on your feet NOW!"

First Sergeant "Rabid" Ralph Finnegan, on loan from 2nd Battalion, 5th Special Forces Group at Fort Bragg, was jerking Hanson to his wobbly feet, pulling him away from the conflagration and towards the waiting Huey. Ben resisted with his remaining might, which was no match for the Vietnam-hardened Green Beret.

"Let me go! I've got to find General Marston!" Ben pleaded, "We can't leave him out here!"

Finnegan stopped and turned to face the determined scientist, his eyes boring into Ben's with a fierceness that couldn't be ignored. The young scientist's eyes bore back into Finnegan's with a similar fierceness, not forged by desperate battle, but of intense loyalty to one of his own. In that instant Finnegan found common ground with the civilian. He could respect any man, big or small, that would risk his life for a member of his team.

"Stay upwind of the smoke and as far away from the fire as possible! I'll have the pilot check with the other teams to see if the General is with them. If you locate him, start moving upwind of the fire. I'll find you as long as you are out of the smoke."

Ben shook his head in acknowledgement as the big man let him go. He turned to gather his bearing and saw the convoy now fully engulfed in flames. Unfortunately, Jet "A" burns like many oils do, with a dark smoke. If the wind direction changed unfavorably, finding Marston might quickly become impossible.

Hanson rapidly resumed the retracing of his earlier steps. Intense heat kept him well away from his exact path and with each step came a prayer that God might spare him from finding Marston's cooked body. Tires were beginning to explode by the time he reached what he believed to be the end of the convoy, each report reminding him of how dangerous a situation he was in. Aligned into the southwest breeze, leaping flames and thick smoke obscured the vehicles at the end of the column. If Marston was behind the column, he was dead or almost impossible to find in the smoke.

A mechanical alarm built into Hanson's airpack began sounding, prompting him to look at the pressure gage: only 25% remaining. A quick brief on the airpack provided him with enough information to know that if the alarm went off, he had maybe 10 minutes before his source of uncontaminated air ran out. To make matters worse, it appeared that the wind was turning more southerly in direction. This mild change caused the wall of smoke to move noticeably westward, encroaching into the area Ben believed he had the best chance of finding Marston. He scanned the terrain again, desperately trying to control the increasing panic within him. He couldn't leave Marston behind, and he sure as hell didn't want to run out of air and die from smoke inhalation or whatever killed the Mexican soldiers. His only option was to find his mentor, and find him quick.

Fate would have Ben looking directly at a rock formation 40 yards in front of him and dangerously close to the wall of smoke when the faintest sliver of white fabric flashed briefly into view. Three seconds later, the roiling smoke shifted direction enough to encase the rock formation in its' hazy edge. Ben began running as fast as he could towards rocks, dodging clumps of dry desert brush and smaller outcroppings of rock. The bulky clothing and weighty airpack was taking a toll on Hanson. By the time he reached the rock formation, he was out of breath and sweating profusely. Visibility was less than thirty feet and deteriorating rapidly.

Ben found Marston sitting behind the formation breathing quick and shallow, his airpack alarm sounding in chorus with Hanson's.

"About time... you got here... son!" He said with a grimace, his voice muffled by the facemask and noticeably weaker than usual. "I was beginning... to think I was... going to eat lizards... for dinner."

"You don't look so well Art. Are you OK?"

"You were moving... so fast... Thought I saw a body... over here... Checked it out... Just shadows, nothing to it... Chest pain started... Too hot, too much weight... Damn suit! Bad pain... Won't go away... Havin' trouble breathing."

"I've got to get you out of here! Can you walk?"

"I tried. Too light-headed... almost passed out."

"I'll have to drag you out, then!"

"Too heavy... Too far away! "Marston said with a hard grimace, "Get on back... while you can... still see... where you're going!"

Hanson didn't respond. Rather, he stepped up to Marston's side and worked his arms under the ailing man's shoulders. With a heave fueled by adrenalin, began dragging Marston westward and away from the encroaching smoke. It was backbreaking work over the uneven terrain, every yard of progress seemed like a hundred in distance. After the Herculean effort of pulling Marston 25 yards, Ben stopped to catch his breath. They were clear of the smoke, but only barely. He looked at the pressure gauges on both airpacks: ten percent remaining on his, slightly less on Marstons'. It seemed inevitable that both men would need to remove their self-contained breathing apparatus in a matter of minutes, forced to take their chances with the smoke and whatever chemical or biologic nightmare that might be in the air.

After a few moments, Ben grabbed Marston's shoulders and began dragging him farther west. Sweat was pouring down his face, stinging his eyes and blurring his vision. He could hear the increasing pitch of the jet turbines on the helicopters he couldn't quite see yet. Terror swept over him in an instant. They were going to leave him and Marston behind!

Every muscle in his body aching, Ben found additional physical strength with the realization that he might be spending the night in a Mexican desert with his ailing, perhaps even dying mentor. He dug his heels into the crunching soil and heaved the dead weight of Marston a yard each pull. After 15 or so such pulls, Ben heard muffled voices approaching their position. It was First Sergeant Finnegan and the two other members of his Huey squad coming to their aid, each carrying a replacement bottle for the almost empty ones on their backs.

"Thank God you found us!" Ben yelled to Finnegan, "I thought you were going to leave us! I think General Marston is having a coronary! We've got to get him to a hospital as soon as possible!"

Finnegan gave Hanson a quick glance while beginning to change out the compressed air bottle on Marston's back. "You know the plan, Dr. Hanson." He replied sternly, "We must decon everything and everybody. We cannot deviate from the protocol."

"But..." Ben started to protest. Marston grabbed his right arm firmly.

"He's right... boy." Marston said weakly, but with a look on his face that conveyed his resolve. "Can't... risk the... spread of disease."

"It isn't biological!" Ben protested.

"Do you... know that... for sure?"

Ben's gut told him that the Mexicans died from touching, inhaling or ingesting hazardous material venting from within the damaged craft. Prior to touchdown, a low pass over the craft by one of the Hueys equipped with a radiological monitor ruled out radiation. Disease seemed to be very low on the list because of the rapidity of death, but it could not be eliminated altogether.

Marston studied the changing expression on Ben's face. "I didn't... think so. Let... these men... do their job. I'll be... okay."

Ben knew there was no arguing the point. His mind easily understood the inescapable logic, but emotions were trying to override sensibilities. The old man was dying. He was sure of it. His family was going to be robbed of their precious "Pawpaw." Marston tightened his grip on Ben's arm.

"Thanks for... coming back... to get me."

"My Dad said 'No man left behind.'"

Marston smiled. "You would have... made a... great Marine... Son. For a... skinny little... shit."

Ben returned the smile. He barely noticed that one of the team members had replaced his compressed air bottle, and three more soldiers arrived to assist in the rescue.

"Time to go!" Finnegan barked. With that, the largest member of the team assumed a squatting position while two other soldiers quickly hoisted Marston and positioned him across the big man's very broad shoulders. Together, they began a rapid, seemingly effortless walk towards the Hueys waiting well over a football field away. Even though they were walking, Ben found it difficult to keep up over the uneven terrain. An exhausting five minutes later, they boarded the Hueys. Thirty seconds after that, they were airborne and headed north.

Chapter 52

The assembled task force of unmarked helicopters followed a carefully selected, direct course to a makeshift decontamination station assembled approximately 75 miles north northeast of Coyame. This required the helicopters to remain in Mexican airspace much longer than anyone felt comfortable with, but it insured that no towns in Mexico or Texas were over-flown. Once on the ground, the decontamination crew quickly began the rigorous and time-consuming process of disinfecting every square inch of the helicopters, personnel and the sealed crate containing the alien craft.

General Marston was given top priority because of his deteriorating health. Immediately after decontaminating and discarding his exposure suit, he was stripped naked and thoroughly decontaminated again. After assessing his medical condition, a Navy Corpsman administered oxygen and quickly established an intravenous line. Marston's heart was failing, beating irregularly and his blood pressure much lower than normal. He needed stabilization in an intensive care unit and a Dustoff from the new William Beaumont Army Medical Center at Fort Bliss was already on the way to take him back to theirs.

After his own decontamination, Ben spent as much time with Marston as he could. Having automatically inherited responsibility for the recovered craft and its' safe transportation to Cocheta Mountain, he found himself torn between his deathly ill mentor and an unexpected new role in the mission. A stern rebuke from an ashen-faced Foreman reminded him of his primary responsibility.

"Dammit... Would you get... outta this tent... and get... to work!" Marston said with all the force he could muster, which was frighteningly little.

"I just..." Marston cut him of with a shake of his head and a weak wave of his hand.

"It's not... a request!"

Ben recognized the look of resolve on the old man's face having seen it countless times the previous six years. Even weak and quite likely dying, this was not a man to trifle with and Ben didn't want to make his condition worse by arguing.

Ben shook his head in acknowledgment. "Yes sir. I'll make sure everything is taken care of." He paused for a second, fighting off the threat of tears and a wavering voice. "Just get better, OK? I don't know what Paul and Donna would do without their Pawpaw."

Marston closed his eyes to hide the glistening. "Get busy... boy!"

Ben left the tent wondering if he would see Arthur Marston alive again. Off in the distance, he could hear the unmistakable thumping of the Dustoff Huey from Fort Bliss. The rhythmic sound was a welcome noise, given his concern for Marston's health and the new burdens of responsibility he acquired. Maybe, just maybe, Pawpaw would survive his coronary. The thought lifted his spirits a touch.

Marston survived the debilitating heart attack, but would succumb to a second one almost a year later. Ben successfully shepherded the hermetically sealed alien vehicle to Cocheta via innocuous appearing tractor-trailer convoy to Holloman Air Force Base for additional decontamination and re-crating, then on to northern British Columbia via another convoy and finally Cocheta Mountain by way of Chinook. By the time the craft arrived, word of Ben's exploits in Mexico preceded him. He would never admit to doing anything special or heroic, only stating that Marston would have done the same for him. The incident, however, was a "coming of age" of sorts for Dr. Hanson. It sharpened his resolve and in the eyes of his peers, transformed him from "boy genius" to mature, accomplished scientist and team member worthy of respect and the added responsibilities of leadership. Shortly after Marston's death in 1975, Dr. Hanson was promoted to Deputy Director under Captain Brogan. There was no doubt in anybody's mind that when Brogan retired, Benjamin Harris Hanson, PhD would become "Foreman" of the most deeply buried government project in the history of mankind.

Chapter 53

Loeffler and SAC Simpson sat in the Emergency Department waiting room in shocked silence, barely able to comprehend what happened less than an hour earlier. They rushed into the interrogation room to find Dr. Hanson on top of Hastings with his hands loosely around the Director's neck. Blood was covering Hastings' face and shirt and more was spraying onto him from Hanson's mouth. The scene was horrifying, and getting worse by the second. Loeffler tackled Hanson to the floor, but the hemorrhaging scientist offered no resistance. Loeffler would never forget the look of surprise and terror on Dr. Hanson's face as blood bubbled and spattered from his mouth. He quickly rolled Hanson on his side while screaming for someone to get medical help into the interrogation room. Loeffler was vaguely aware that Hastings was injured, but he really didn't give a damn if he were alive or dead. Loeffler didn't want Hanson to die, not only because he needed him to find the second suspect, but because he actually felt himself liking the man. After what seemed like an eternity, a nurse and physician from the Detention Centers' infirmary arrived with a crash cart and went about the process of resuscitation. Blood was pooling around Hanson's head and torso as he lapsed into unconsciousness.

By the time the Paramedics arrived, the nurse had started an IV and the physician, with great difficulty due to the blood in Hanson's lungs and throat, placed a breathing tube into his windpipe and attempted to deliver oxygen into his lungs. The Paramedics attached him to their monitors and inserted a second, larger IV. His blood pressure had dropped to the point where the paramedics couldn't measure it and his pulse could not be felt. They hurriedly rolled his limp body onto a long wooden backboard and loaded him onto the stretcher where they immediately began CPR. Loeffler felt his heart sink when he watched the paramedics remove Hanson from the building while performing CPR. It was a universally bad sign. A second ambulance was dispatched for Hastings, but Loeffler and Simpson didn't wait around the Detention Center to find out what his fate would be. Hastings could fend for himself as far as Loeffler was concerned. They rushed to the UNLV medical

Center to await what both was certain to be the announcement of Dr. Benjamin Hanson's death.

After 45 minutes of waiting, Dr. Neil Haskett, attending Emergency Department physician, emerged from the double doors that separated the shock-trauma rooms from the rest of the department. His look was grim.

"Special Agent Simpson, Mr. Loeffler?" Haskett asked.

"Yes." Both replied in near unison.

"I was told that you would be waiting out here. Dr. Hanson is in surgery right now. We did an emergency thoracotomy to perform internal cardiac massage and to see if we could find the source of his bleeding. Mr. Hanson has an aggressive lung cancer that eroded into his left pulmonary artery. The weakened vessel apparently ruptured, sending a massive amount of blood into his lungs. We were able to place a clamp on the artery to stop the bleeding and restart his heart by giving him blood transfusions, internal cardiac massage and defibrillation."

SAC Simpson looked at the equally shocked Loeffler, then back to Dr. Haskett. "He's alive?"

"Only in the crudest sense of the word, Agent Simpson." Haskett said. "Dr. Hanson lost the majority of his circulating blood, causing his heart to stop. We have no idea how long his brain and internal organs, including his heart, were deprived of oxygen. He's going into surgery to tie off his left pulmonary artery, if they can, and remove his diseased lung. If, and that is a huge "if," he survives the operation, he likely faces multiple organ failure, brain damage and compromised cardiac function. Frankly, it is a miracle he's made it this far. Realistically, his chance of surviving the next 4 hours are slim to none."

"Thank you, Doctor." Loeffler said, reaching into his wallet and handing him his card. "Please, call me at the cell number listed on the card when you learn of Dr. Hanson's condition and prognosis following surgery."

"Did you want an update on Mr. Hastings condition? Haskett asked.

"Sure, go ahead." Loeffler asked with noticeable indifference.

"We think he'll be fine, but we need to watch him for laryngeal and tracheal edema over the next couple of days."

"Good news!" Loeffler said to Simpson, the words meaning something completely different to her than they did for Dr. Haskett. Hastings and Simpson would have Project Director Hastings out of their hair for a few days. Perhaps now they can make some progress, but how? Hanson was as good as dead.

"Special Agent Simpson?" Loeffler asked.

"Yes?"

"If you would come with me, we have some out-of-town work to do."

As they stepped outside of the Emergency Department, Loeffler dialed a number on his cell phone. Automatically routed to a tower specializing in highly encrypted, two-way cellular conversations, the call took only a moment to connect.

"Triple C. Watch Officer Major Alleyne speaking."

"Major Alleyne, this is Loeffler. I need quick transportation to Cocheta. What's the status of the 35?"

"It's at Groom Lake, sir. Minor servicing. It should be ready in 2 hours. JANET has a King Air available. I recommend you take it to Groom Lake. The Lear should be ready by then."

"Work it up for me, please. I'll be at McCarran in 15." Loeffler said. "And advise JANET I'll have a passenger with me. Oh, Major Alleyne?"

"Yes sir?"

"Have you gotten a raise recently?"

"Now don't get me started, sir!"

"Thanks, again!"

Loeffler closed the cell phone and caught the bewildered look of SAC Simpson.

"Where are we going, and who is 'Janet?'"

"JANET you already know. It is not a woman, it's the hush-hush airport terminal near the Tropicana. Where we are going is that you cannot imagine."

Chapter 54

After a relatively short and somber flight from McCarran International Airport, the plain white King Air Turboprop angled in from the southeast and made a smooth landing on Runway 30 at "Homey Airport," Air Force Flight Test Center - Detachment 3 at Groom Lake. After a short taxi straight ahead towards the collection of hangars, aviation support buildings and dormitories, the King Air made a northerly turn onto the tarmac that lead to Building 400-404, the JANET terminal at Area 51. The Lear was already parked in front of the terminal, awaiting its' passengers. SAC Simpson was sitting on the left side of the small, twin-engine plane, looking out the window.

"So this is what Area 51 looks like!" She said, turning to Loeffler. "Where do they keep the little green men?" She laughed, trying to lighten the mood.

"Not here." He replied. "Never did. This place is just for testing super-secret terrestrial technology. 'They' keep the little green men in Canada. Only they're grayish, not green."

Simpson looked at Loeffler, trying to decipher what exactly he meant by that. He was semi-smiling at her, but the smile betrayed not a hint.

"OK, I give. What did you mean by that?"

"By what?" Loeffler replied without changing expression.

"The 'Canada' and the 'grayish' remark."

"Just what I said." Loeffler replied. "We keep alien bodies and spacecraft wreckage at a facility in the Canadian wilderness that is far more secret than this one. Alien technology was what Dr. Hanson worked on. You and I are taking the Lear 35 there in a few minutes. When we arrive, you and I are going to go over every square inch of Hanson's apartment and office."

Hannah Simpson sat silent in her seat trying to wrap her brain around what she had just heard, but it was all too impossible to absorb. The King Air stopped on the terminal tarmac across from a Beechcraft 1900 and the waiting Lear 35, then began powering down its' engines. Loeffler noticed the consternation on her face.

"I'll fill you in on the details when we get en route."

They exited the plane and immediately boarded the much more luxurious Lear 35 after greeting the pilot and copilot. It took several minutes for the Lear 35A to power up and begin its' taxi to the threshold of Runway 32 left. The sleek white business jet roared to life and took to the air well before reaching the halfway point of the extraordinarily long runway. Hannah Simpson watched the enigmatic facility, nestled at the northeast base of a small ridge of mountains known as the Papoose Range, disappear rapidly behind and to the left of the steeply climbing jet. Within several minutes, the Lear was cruising at 35,000 feet for the four-hour flight to Cocheta.

After the jet leveled off to cruising altitude, Loeffler briefed Simpson on the important details of the Cocheta facility and the need for absolute secrecy. She listened intently to each word, as if she were terrified of missing a single detail. When Loeffler finished, she took what seemed like an eternity to respond.

"Wow..." She said, turning to look out the window at the puffs of cottony clouds under a cobalt sky. "I always thought we were all alone in our corner of the universe. You sure know how to shatter a belief system!"

"I felt the same way." Loeffler said reassuringly. "Hanson was dying and he knew it. Slamming Hastings wasn't all he was up to, I believe he passed evidence to our second suspect and somehow, that evidence is going to bubble to the surface. It's his legacy, Hannah! Hanson wants the world to know what we are facing!"

"What are we facing?" She asked, her countenance turning noticeably darker.

"Hanson and a majority of the scientists he works with believe we are going to be invaded." He replied, looking down at is feet.

"Invaded!" She said, trying to control the fear sweeping over her. "Oh my God! What are we doing to stop it?" She demanded.

"First of all, we don't know for sure that the aliens actually intend to invade us. The conjecture follows an assessment made over 50 years ago. Since then, we have seen no proof that the aliens plan to move militarily against us."

"Because it hasn't happened yet means it never will? Is that what you're telling me? Is that the assessment of a pencil-pusher in Washington, or a man with the insight and intellect of Dr. Hanson?"

"It's more complicated than that!" Loeffler pleaded. "America has enemies that pose a far more tangible threat than aliens do, at least right now. If this technology falls into the wrong hands, or if our enemies feel we are on the brink of a breakthrough with alien technology, we might face a nuclear first strike!"

"If all of this is true, why would Hanson risk the well-being of his country to release this information? ...And don't tell me it's because he wants to be remembered! Hanson just doesn't strike me as someone who would toy with national security for a bit of fleeting notoriety! Besides, if this information led to the terrible consequences you believe it will, wouldn't Hanson go down in history as the biggest traitor of all time? What was his plan, Kevin? Somebody like Hanson wouldn't consider taking a breath without a plan!"

"He wanted a staged release of information to the public and bring all the world's scientists together to assist in duplicating the technology." Loeffler said, wondering if any of his arguments made sense anymore. "But it is naïve to think this is even remotely possible!"

"That doesn't sound very self-serving or naïve to me. In fact, it sounds prudent." She paused, gauging the look on Loeffler's face. "So, you're going to do what you can to keep suspect number two from divulging this information." She said flatly.

"I'm afraid so, Hannah." Loeffler said with a sigh. "I am sworn to keep the secrets of Cocheta from public and enemy view, period."

"Strange that you should use the words 'public' and 'enemy' together like that." She said shaking her head. "I trust your experience and judgment. You have a lot more expertise and insider information in this field than I do. If you feel it is important to keep this a secret, I'm with you 100%."

"Thanks!" Loeffler said, not certain if he was relieved that Hannah agreed to continue helping him, or that the uncomfortable turn of the conversation was coming to a close.

Loeffler was starting to feel as if he were trying to put out a forest fire with a cup of water. He wondered what his chances really were of capturing suspect two. Hanson already proved that he could toy with anybody trying to find him, so what kind of elaborate, foolproof plan did he implement to shield suspect number two? The permutations were staggering. Suspect two might be a courier, or a decoy. Hanson might have passed the evidence to he real suspect weeks or months before. How was he going to release the information? Television seemed the most logical choice. A high profile announcement during prime time would be optimal, but how would he go about doing that? Who would buy off on the subject matter? Loeffler shook his head. Even though the vultures were circling his hospital bed, Dr. Hanson still had the Cocheta Security Chief firmly by the nose. There may or may not be answers at Cocheta, but if Hanson left clues, the only place Loeffler hadn't looked for them was in his apartment and office... and he was taking a huge risk bringing Hannah along to help him find them.

"Kevin?" Simpson asked, the edge in her voice now gone.

"Yes?"

"What really happens if Dr. Hanson wins?"

Loeffler paused for a while, not sure how to answer her question. He had the company "answers" down pat, but knew that Hannah Simpson was looking for more substance.

"I guess that all depends on how Dr. Hanson releases the information. If his spokesperson blurts it all out at once, then chaos ensues. That is not Dr. Hansons' style. He wanted a 'measured' release, probably starting with the basic fact that life exists on other planets then slowly add the rest over several months or years. A lot of the public response depends upon whom he chooses to release the information. The right spokesman with the right amount of content and the 'revelation' might come off smooth as silk. Hanson is careful, so I'm sure he put a lot of thought into who would make the announcement. As far as the political ramifications, the legislative and executive branches will do what they always do, jockey for position. The most self-serving of the windbags will find the nearest camera and posture, taking whatever stand that will likely get them the most votes from their constituents. Some will call for high-profile 'hearings' to assess blame and look for heads to put on top of poles. Others will make ludicrous negative links to their political opponents to smear votes away from them. In other words, the real importance of this disclosure will get lost in the circus-style mayhem. Maybe I'm becoming cynical, but I don't see anything productive coming out of this, insofar as Washington is concerned. The one thing I am absolutely certain of is that Cocheta will probably be forced to open its' doors to the public."

"And our enemies?"

"A properly measured release of information would probably attenuate the anxiety of most countries, but there are 'Wild Cards' out there who might overreact, or elect to overreact aggressively. Russia, China, North Korea, Iran... there will be accusations that America and Israel are planning to use the technology to wage war against Islam, you can count on that. Terrorism will likely increase as a result of the perceived threat, and paradoxically, the 'blasphemous American lie' of extraterrestrial life."

"So, it's really up to how well Hanson put his plan together."

"Or us, if we can stop it from unfolding."

"Mr. Loeffler." The co-pilot called from the cabin door. "We just received word from Agent Wingate at the Medical Center in Las Vegas. Dr. Hanson survived surgery and is now in the Surgical Intensive Care Unit. He is listed in 'grave condition' and not expected to live. Project Director Hastings is resting comfortably, and will likely be discharged on Saturday."

"Thank you." Loeffler replied. He turned to Simpson and shook his head. "If it were only the other way around!"

Simpson smiled. "Someday... He'll get what's coming to him. The really tragic thing is that Hanson won't live long enough to see it."

The light was beginning to fade outside of the aircraft. Loeffler hated night landings at Cocheta, picturing himself as a potential grease spot on the side of one of the numerous mountains in the vicinity. He knew that the Cocheta Command Center-activated instrument landing system was the most sophisticated available and careful GPS approach plots had been developed and safely utilized for years. Still, there was something unnerving about dropping into a runway located in the middle of a mountain range at night. He quickly dismissed his minor phobia and reached into an overhead compartment for a pillow and blanket to give to Hannah Simpson.

"Here, why don't you try and take a nap. We still have a couple of more hours to go." He said quietly while handing the pillow and blanket to her. She took them from him and smiled.

"Thanks." She said, and began nestling against the window next to her seat.

Loeffler retrieved a pillow and blanket for himself and made himself comfortable in a seat across the center aisle from Simpson. He watched her sleep for a while, admiring her uncompromised femininity. Having seen her in action, toe-to-toe with the likes of Louis Hastings, he speculated that many a man had mistaken her soft, beautiful exterior as a sign of a pushover, only to find themselves face down on the hood of a car or eating gravel. It was a tantalizing mix for Loeffler, who had no qualms at all about having a relationship with a woman who could probably kick his ass.

The approach to Cocheta was only mildly turbulent, due in part to the dramatic decrease in updrafts of air caused by sun-generated convection currents. The seasoned pilot made a smooth touchdown on the runway, then exiting to the parallel taxiway. Within a few moments, the Lear 35A rolled to a stop on the large tarmac in front of the Cocheta Research Facility. Simpson and Loeffler egressed the craft into the brisk, night air and immediately greeted by Deputy Project Director McMahon.

"Oren, in case you haven't heard yet, you're acting director until Hastings is discharged from the hospital." Loeffler said as they began walking towards the mountain face entry of Cocheta's largest building. The air was cold, dry and nearly windless, making the perceived temperature much more comfortable than the actual temperature suggested it should be.

"Hastings told me himself about 3 hours ago." McMahon said. "His voice sounded very hoarse from the choking. He wanted to know where the hell you were at."

"He was still being treated and we needed to get here as soon as possible to start pouring over Hanson's office and apartment."

"Who is 'we' by the way?" McMahon said with a deep frown. "This is highly irregular, Loeffler."

"This is Special Agent in Charge Simpson from the FBI Field Office in Las Vegas." Loeffler said with a strong, official tone to his voice. "She has been instrumental in the capture of Dr. Hanson and I need her assistance in searching through his files and personal effects for clues as to the identity of the suspect we have been looking for. She has been appropriately briefed." Loeffler had chosen the words "appropriately briefed" to let the Deputy Director know that Simpson had only a superficial knowledge of the mission and inner workings of Cocheta.

"You couldn't have done it yourself?" McMahon replied, not convinced of the need for Simpson's presence.

"Oren, I have no idea how time-critical this investigation needs to be." Loeffler said. "I am certain Hanson was trying to blow the lid off this place and his plan could be executed at any time. It is critical we find this second suspect as quickly as possible and we have absolutely nothing to go on! This is the only place we haven't looked for clues."

"Hastings is going to be livid." McMahon said, shaking his head.

"I can't concern myself with that now. Have you sealed Hanson's office and apartment?"

"Standard procedure." McMahon replied, sounding a bit as if the question needn't have been asked in the first place.

"We're going to get a bite to eat, then start on Hanson's office."

"Need any help?" McMahon asked.

Cocheta management under Hastings had never been particularly helpful about anything, so Loeffler preferred that McMahon stay out of the way. His response, however, had to be diplomatic. "Maybe..." Loeffler answered. "If we get in over our heads, we'll give you a call."

Simpson, who had been marveling at the sparsely lit exterior of the building they were walking towards while keeping half an ear on the conversation, caught the artful way Loeffler side stepped the Deputy Director. She already sensed that her presence at this altogether fantastic research facility in the middle of nowhere was not welcome and would probably lead to even more negative consequences for Kevin Loeffler than he already faced. She hoped not, but her earlier encounters with Hastings suggested otherwise. It was obvious that duty and principle drove Kevin Loeffler. He would track down suspect two because it was his job and because he knew he was doing the right thing. Hannah Simpson met very few men in her life who were as principled as Loeffler and worried that she might have snuffed the spark that was growing between them by being too judgmental on him as he briefed her about Cocheta. Based on the view before her and the stated mission of the facility she was about to enter, she had a feeling that the shock waves of Loeffler's revelations that stunned her brain were only the first of many. She told herself she needed to do a better job controlling her emotions.

Simpson found the interior of the complex very similar to older Federal office buildings she had been in and had to occasionally remind herself that the structure she was walking in was deep inside a mountain of solid rock. It was approaching 8PM and both Loeffler and Simpson were famished. McMahon had already eaten and decided to retire for the evening. The cafeteria staff prepared a hearty meal of roasted chicken with herbs, sautéed green beans and low country mashed potatoes. After a half-hour of small talk over the best key lime pie either of them had ever tasted, they made their way to Dr. Hanson's Cocheta office in the complex of offices located in the back of the gargantuan hangar. The sheer size of the structure, and the presence of what looked like buildings within buildings left Simpson without words. The Lear 35A they flew to Cocheta in was parked in the front half of the hanger for routine servicing, still attached to the same type of towing vehicle she had seen many times at airports around the world. The outer doors remained open, allowing the night air chill to permeate the expansive hangar. They entered the office complex and made their way to the last office on the right, the one with the Yellow "Do Not Enter!" tape fashioned into a large "X" across the doorway. Signs on the walls warned passers by that the room was "sealed" and only authorized individuals were allowed to enter. Kevin removed the tape and unlocked the door with a master key that could open most any door in the facility. Simpson found Hanson's office very 50s-ish, with functionality completely overwhelming style. The office was extraordinarily tidy and nothing at all looked out of place. Simpson marveled at the orderliness of it all, feeling somewhat embarrassed because her own office was the antithesis of this one. Adjacent to Hanson's office was a large file room, and after a brief and fruitless search of his unlocked desk, that is where Loeffler decided to begin.

It was clear from the beginning that the task before them would be a daunting one. There were 42, four-drawer file cabinets in the room, along with a very large table, on top of which were large stacks of folders of varying thickness. A quick scan of the labels on each filing cabinet revealed three distinct filing classifications: "Case Reports," filed by year; "Research," filed alphabetically; and a utility "A through Z" category. Loeffler decided that the stacks of folders on the table would be the first examined since he guessed they probably represented the last documents viewed by Dr. Hanson several weeks earlier. Loeffler had no earthly idea what he was looking for, but had a feeling that he would recognize it when he saw it. The problem was would Simpson recognize it? He really had no choice but to trust her instincts in spotting something ever so slightly out of place that might represent a significant clue Hanson left behind.

After searching through the folders left on the desk, Loeffler and Simpson began tackling the 168 drawers of files remaining by removing the folders in each drawer and splitting the files between them. Loeffler felt that approach was better than working two different file categories because it gave him closer supervision of Simpson's work without being obvious about it. It also allowed him to answer her questions much faster since they would be nearly face-to-face already. Every so often, Loeffler paused to study the looks on Simpson's face as she searched through the folders. Some of the case files had photographs in them and a significant percentage of those were quite remarkable. In spite of the incredible subject matter she was searching through, Hannah Simpson remained on task, looking through the reams of meticulous, hand-written notes made by Hanson as he was carefully researching each incident of significance. By midnight, when Loeffler decided to call it quits for the evening, they completed a search through seven drawers, finding nothing of value or anything that seemed out of place.

Kevin Loeffler walked Special Agent Simpson to the VIP suite prepared for her. He unlocked the door and handed her the key.

"This is one of the two VIP suites we have here at Cocheta." Loeffler said quietly. "It's rarely used. We don't get many visitors up here in the boondocks."

"The pictures... the reports... It's all real, isn't it?" She asked, hoping by some miracle she was having a bad dream that she would wake up from if Kevin would just say the word.

"It's all real."

She leaned her head against the open doorway and gave Loeffler a look of reluctant resignation. The world was complicated enough without this new and terrifying angle on reality that landed square in her lap.

"You have 'them' here? Their bodies, I mean?" She asked.

"Yes, quite a number of them."

"And their machines?"

"Most are in pieces, but we do have a couple of intact vehicles."

A dark countenance enveloped her face. What she had seen and heard over the last several hours deeply disturbed her and fatigue was magnifying the emotions. "How much time do we have?"

Loeffler reached down and took her hands into his own. "A thousand seconds, a thousand years... maybe we're in no danger at all. I don't know. Nobody knows for sure." He paused for a moment, looking directly into her eyes that were beginning to glisten with tears. "Every time I look up into the night sky here, I wonder if it will be the last time I see it without an armada of alien war machines preparing to melt the top of this mountain. I keep on going because I really don't know when, or if, it will ever happen. I know how you feel, I honestly do, and I wish there were something I could tell you that would make you feel better, but I can't."

She released his hands and immediately embraced him, resting her face on top of his shoulder. He instinctively held her tight as if to shield her from the torments that lay hidden in the bowels of Cocheta Mountain. After what seemed like a small eternity and dozens of silent tears later, she relaxed her embrace and looked up into his face. Both knew instantly that their relationship had moved to a far more meaningful level. In another place and time, their evening would have likely ended the next morning, but both were professionals and both knew that "here and now" was neither the time nor the place.

"Thank you." She said, stepping back from him and wiping the last of the tears from her eyes. "Thank you for being so understanding. I'm usually not this emotional. It's just that... I mean... It's so much to take in at one time!"

"Please, don't be hard on yourself." Loeffler said. "Nobody who steps into this place ever walks away the same. What you're feeling is perfectly normal." He looked at her thoughtfully. "You need to get some sleep. When you wake up, things will look different. Trust me. The second day is always easier than the first!"

She leaned forward and gave him an unexpected kiss on his cheek. "You're a very sweet man."

He smiled warmly at her in return for the kiss and compliment, but their eyes were communicating far more than any word or facial expression could do. The gravitational pull towards each other was becoming intense and Loeffler sensed it was time to part company before the "pull" became irresistible.

"The room should have everything you need. If it doesn't, call me at extension 5077 and I'll have whatever you need brought to you. I'll stop by at eight and take you to breakfast before we hit the file room again."

She nodded her head while lightly brushing the fingers of her right hand down the left side of Loeffler's face. She retreated into her room while they both traded parting "goodnights." Kevin Loeffler was about to have another very restless night.

Chapter 55

Dr. Benjamin Hanson was teetering on the edge of death and each hour that his poorly functioning heart continued to pump blood was an hour of pure defiance against the so-called "odds." The incident that nearly killed him quickly robbed his body of over 4 liters of blood, leading to oxygen starvation in every critical organ system, including his brain, heart and kidneys. The massive blood transfusions helped restore the oxygen carrying capacity of his blood, but were short on the coagulation factors and platelets that allowed his blood to clot. Even after replacement of these critical blood components by specialized transfusions, the tremendous insult to Dr. Hanson's body caused an out-of-control depletion of essential blood-clotting precursors. The doctors called it a "consumptive coagulopathy," and what it meant for Dr. Hanson was that his blood had become so "thin" that he was bleeding spontaneously. Blood was leaking into the space where his left lung used to be, and a tube leading from his chest to a bedside collection container was steadily filling up with it. His face had swollen to the point of being almost unrecognizable and in fact, the rest of his body was beginning to swell with fluid that leaked into the space between blood vessels and cells. His kidneys had all but ceased to function, and were responding poorly to infusions of medications designed to increase kidney output. Dialysis was under consideration to remove fluid and toxins that were building up in his body. Hanson's heart had also been severely damaged by the incident and it's ability to squeeze blood to the rest of the body was being supported by still more intravenous infusions.

As far as the status of Dr. Hanson's brilliant brain, nobody knew for sure how much of it remained. After considering the insult that the rest of his body endured, the consensus was that his mind had suffered irreparable damage and that soon, his brain would begin to swell in response to the death of the cells within it. Oddly, there had been no signs that any degree of swelling was taking place at all. To a person, everyone assisting in the treatment of Dr. Benjamin Hanson predicted he would not survive the weekend. Most predicted he would not survive to the next nursing shift change.

From the very moment Dr. Hanson arrived in the Emergency Department, the medical personnel taking care of him were asked to do everything possible to save his life, even going so far as to tell them that Hanson was a key link in an investigation of importance to the National Security of the United States. The physicians and nurses involved in the resuscitation, surgery and post-operative care of Ben Hanson would certainly do what they could, but no matter how important their patient might be, the cards dealt to him before he reached the hospital would likely determine his fate, making death a formidable and relentless opponent against their most heroic measures.

In an odd, completely missed irony of immense proportions, a television set in an empty nurses lounge within earshot of Dr. Hanson's bed was tuned to the Science and Technology Channel. Dr. Tim Alexander, in the first broadcast of his new, personal promo spot, was reminding viewers to watch the special live telecast of his show on Sunday night.

Chapter 56

Simpson and Loeffler spent the entire day and most of the evening on Friday looking through the remainder of the files marked "Case Reports." Both viewed mountains of evidence detailing how very real the UFO phenomenon was, but failed to stumble across anything that resembled a clue to the identity of the second suspect they were desperately trying to find. Loeffler decided that Simpson proved she could search through the files as well as he could, so he decided to take the "Research" file cabinets and have Hannah take the alphabetized ones. Within an hour, Simpson spotted something unusual.

"Kevin, you need to come look at this." She announced with a hint of urgency in her voice. Loeffler quickly rose and put the file folder he was examining on the chair he was sitting on.

"What have you found?"

"Three file folders in the 'A' section that don't seem to fit with the others." She said with growing excitement in her voice. "Look. All of these folders contain fairly mundane things like accounting information and such. The sorts of things you expect to see in the file cabinets of a complex organization. These four folders are labeled with the names of Internet search engines, AllTheWeb.com, AltaVista, AOL Search and Ask. Look what is inside each of them." She said, handing the folders to him.

The first folder, AllTheWeb.com, contained the first five pages of the nearly 19 million web search results for "Hastings." The results were nonsense, having absolutely nothing to do with Louis Hastings other than the search itself. What was far more interesting was the object taped to the inside back of the folder: a key with a tag attached to it by a short piece of string. Written on the tag was a nine-digit number. The second folder labeled "AltaVista" contained five pages of the 113 million results on the word "Murder." It, too, contained what appeared to be an identical key, but sporting a different nine-digit number. The AOL search was on "Retiree" and the Ask search was on "Monster." Both had identical keys labeled with differing nine-digit numbers. Paydirt!

"You did it!" Loeffler said with genuine excitement in his voice. "These are safety deposit box keys and I'll bet these labels are bank routing numbers! Hanson is not going to give us an inch on suspect two, but I'm sure this safety deposit box contains everything we'll need to bag Hastings! Strong work, Special Agent in Charge!"

Hannah Simpson was beaming. It would have been nice to get a lead on suspect two, but the promise of seeing Louis Hastings in a Federal penitentiary was far more rewarding, at least on a personal level.

"Thanks for the compliment," She said with a smile, "but this was only the 'A's. There are bound to be more."

"Right you are!" He replied, fighting off a touch of unprofessional giddiness.

The pair spent the next two hours scouring for additional folders that followed a similar pattern as the first four. As it turned out, the common factor between the thirty folders recovered was that each was an Internet Search Engine. All thirty keys were identical in appearance and cut, but the routing number attached to each was unique. Both had a strong feeling which key and routing number would prove to be the correct one. An internet site mentioned in Hanson's letter to Loeffler. It had to be in the folder labeled "eBay."

It was 1:30 in the morning, Saturday morning, when Kevin walked Hannah to her VIP suite for the night. Both exchanged long looks that communicated their desire for each other, but parted with an affectionate hug that left them both unfulfilled. He promised to return at 9AM to take her to breakfast, search Dr. Hanson's apartment, then fly back to Vegas to examine the contents of Dr. Hanson's safety deposit box. After she closed the door, Loeffler made his way to his own office and powered-up his desktop computer. He created a list of each file folder they recovered, the routing number attached to each key in the folder and using a convenient on-line resource, the identity of the bank that corresponded to the routing number. As he had suspected, most every bank was located in the Las Vegas area, with one in Barstow California and another in Kingman Arizona. The one associated with the "eBay" routing number was the Bank of America on North Martin Luther King.

It was nearly three in the morning by the time Loeffler finished his list and printed several copies of it for himself and Simpson. He picked up the phone and entered the number for the Command Center to arrange the return flight to Vegas. Afterwards, he found himself much too tired to walk to the living quarters area, so he set an alarm clock he kept in his office and settled into the ancient but comfortable sofa, where several consecutive nights of unsatisfying sleep would finally catch up with him.

Chapter 57

FBI Assistant Special Agent in Charge Nathan Lanning was spending his Saturday at the Las Vegas Field Office catching up on administrative work. The wife and kids were with the visiting in-laws at Lake Mead and Lanning, who possessed precious little affection for his wife's parents, used the excuse that SAC Simpson left him in charge when she disappeared Thursday afternoon. He had to "hold down the fort" while she was away. He was certain the wife saw through it, and knew it would cost him later, but steering clear of two passive-aggressive and vengeful in-laws, who saw faults in everyone but themselves, was worth the "pain" he would surely endure later. After, of course, the in-laws returned to Hell where he was convinced they gleefully tormented Satan himself.

Lanning was watching baseball in his office when the FedEx driver arrived with a package addressed to SAC Simpson from FBI HQ and marked "Urgent." Lanning figured this was probably the video enhancement that she was waiting for. He wasn't officially part of the "Hanson Investigation" but had been fully briefed on it nonetheless and knew that the enhancement was essentially a long shot because of the very poor quality of the original surveillance video. Since the package was marked "Urgent," Lanning opened the box to find the original videotape and two 5.25 inch optical discs, one a DVD-ROM, the other a CD-Video. The note attached to the discs stated that they digitized and enhanced the video using the VISAR workstation at FBI Headquarters, recently installed under the supervision of NASA video enhancement specialists.

Lanning remembered reading a detailed report about NASA assistance in helping the FBI solve several high-profile cases using Video Image Stabilization and Registration (VISAR) software, originally designed for enhancing weather images. The most notable FBI uses were investigations into the 1996 Atlanta Olympic Park Bombing and the more recent Elizabeth Smart Kidnapping in Utah. In addition, the technology greatly enhanced the video imaging of Space Shuttle Columbia's tragic re-entry, aiding in the investigation of its' cause. He first reviewed the CD-Video, a seemingly endless loop of the original clip, followed by the enhanced clip. The image transformation was nothing short of miraculous, prompting a quick call to SAC Simpson's cell phone. Since she was 38,000 feet over Wyoming at the time with her cell phone off, he left a message on her voice mail.

The DVD-ROM contained a QuickTime file of the same loop, only in a much larger format with less data compression. Lanning couldn't make out the face of the suspect, as he was wearing dark glasses and a black cowboy hat, but the man was clearly putting a box matching the description of the one seen in the possession of Dr. Hanson into the trunk of a dark colored Corvette, a generation five Corvette. The Corvette was facing the camera and like so many Corvette owners, this gentleman refused to put a license plate on the front of his. While this was all very fascinating, Lanning couldn't figure out how this image enhancement would aid in the search for suspect two. There were eight model years of fifth generation Corvette and unless it had an unusual paint job or customization, you really couldn't tell the difference between them. Lanning figured the number of dark-colored, fifth generation Corvettes likely exceeded 100,000 plus and the number of those in Nevada, California, Arizona, and Utah? Who knows, but probably a lot!

He knew SAC Simpson would want some kind of official take on the video, so he called a buddy of his, Josh Bonilla, a certified Corvette nut-case, to see if he might be able to identify the model year. If Josh could determine that, then at least he could eliminate owners of Corvettes from the other seven.

Josh Bonilla arrived 45 minutes later, enticed by Corvette talk and the chance to watch the ball game without the kids demanding constant attention. After closely watching the video, Bonilla announced that he couldn't tell him exactly what it was, but he could tell him what it wasn't.

"It's a convertible, so right off you know it isn't a 1997, Z06 or a coupe. No special graphics packages or stripes on it, so that eliminates the Pace Cars. The ragtop is black, so that eliminates the 2003 50th Anniversary convertible. Not really dark enough to be black, but the lighting is crappy. Still, I don't think it's black. Too dark to be Torch Red, Speedway White, Quicksilver, Light Pewter, or Millennium Yellow. Hmm... Blue... dark blue, like Navy, Electron or LeMans Blue, maybe Medium Spiral Gray or Bowling Green. Wait a minute... See the wheels as it's turning sideways to the camera? Definitely a later model! My final guess? 2000 to 2004 'Vette, probably dark blue, but could be dark gray or green."

"How do you remember all that trivia?" Lanning asked.

"I spend a lot of time on the internet Corvette Forums." He said with a chuckle.

"I know you don't own one now, but how many have you owned in the past?"

"Uh... none." He replied sheepishly.

"You are the biggest Corvette enthusiast I have ever known and you NEVER owned one?"

"My wife won't let me have one! She says I'll spend more time with it than I would her!" Both men laughed and the strange irony of a Corvette-less Corvette expert.

Lanning thanked him for his help and ordered a pizza delivered as reward for his help. Both men thoroughly enjoyed burning the early afternoon daylight, escaping from their families, watching baseball and eating pizza in the Las Vegas field office of the Federal Bureau of Investigation.

That was, until the phone rang...

"FBI, Las Vegas Field Office. Assistant Special Agent in Charge Lanning speaking."

"Lanning, Simpson here. I need you to do something for me."

"Sure, boss. What can I do?"

"Get a hold of somebody in charge at the Bank of America on MLK. We need to open a safety deposit box."

"You're going to need a warrant, boss."

"I know. I'm calling Judge Snowden next. I'll have the warrant in my hands within two hours."

"Where are you, anyway?"

"I'm on a private jet that will be landing at McCarran in less than 30 minutes."

"Is this part of the Hanson investigation? The video enhancement you ordered came in earlier today."

"Did you look at it?"

"I did, and it's freakin' amazing what they did to that video! You can clearly see the man in the video putting what looks like Hanson's box into the trunk of a Corvette!"

"Anything distinguishing about the 'Vette? License plate number? Modifications?"

"Not really, but I did have a Corvette enthusiast look at the video. He believes it to be a dark blue, gray, or green convertible between the years 2000 to 2004."

"Thanks for looking into that, Lanning. I think Mr. Loeffler might want to look at the video sometime today."

"I'll have it ready for him."

"I'll call you after I pay Judge Snowden a visit."

"You got it, boss."

The phone went dead. Lanning hung up the phone at looked at Bonilla.

"Do I need to go?" Bonilla asked.

"No," Lanning said, wishing he could finish watching the game before tracking down the bank officer at the Bank of America who could provide access to the safety deposit box that the boss was after. "You can sit tight for a while, but I've got to make some phone calls."

Chapter 58

"I think it's best we split up." Loeffler said, unbuckling his seat belt as the Lear 35A rolled to a stop at the JANET terminal. "We need to keep Hastings clueless. I'll occupy him with the video, while you secure the evidence from the safety deposit box."

"Sounds good." She said. "With any luck, we'll have him in custody before the weekend is out."

"He's a big fish that swims with even bigger fish... This District Court Judge of yours, will he help you obtain a warrant for him?"

"Snowden is a crusty old hard ass who loathes criminals in general and public servants that abuse their power in particular." Simpson said. "If Hastings has been murdering your projects' retirees, Snowden'll burn him alive. We're lucky to have him on the bench in this district. All the defense attorneys hate him because he has zero tolerance for their antics. That's why we love him at the field office! You should hear the way he talks to the defendants and their lawyers!"

"I like him already." Loeffler said with a smile.

"He's actually a very kind and thoughtful man, outside of the courtroom. He sort of took me under his wing when I was transferred here to take command. Showed me the Vegas ropes, from the judicial point of view."

"Sounds like you two are very close." Loeffler said, giving her an almost imperceptible wink.

"We are... professionally." She stopped at the southeastern entrance of the terminal building and turned towards Loeffler, poking him on his left shoulder. "You, Kevin Loeffler, have nothing to worry about!" She said with a convincing tone and an even more convincing smile.

Twenty minutes later, Loeffler's Lexus stopped beside Simpson's unmarked Crown Victoria that was still parked at the Orleans.

"When you find out what's in the safety deposit box, give me a call." Loeffler said.

"I will." She said, her voice turning more serious. "Be careful, Kevin. Hastings scares me. He's capable of anything."

"Hastings is a coward." Loeffler said reassuringly. "He hides behind his powerful position, probably ordering others to do his dirty work and only personally hurts people who are obviously weaker than he is."

"Still..." She started to say.

"I'll be fine. Besides, when you get that arrest warrant from Snowden, Hastings will be much easier to find if he is with me."

Simpson leaned across the seat and hugged Loeffler tightly. Within a few short moments, the hug seemed to effortlessly evolve into a long, warm, and meaningful kiss. Both were surprised at the natural spontaneity of the moment. It was if an expertly composed orchestration was taking place, and they were playing their part in it perfectly.

"Mr. Loeffler," Hannah Simpson said softly, "is there anything you are not good at?"

He smiled affectionately at her. "Numbers... I'm not good with numbers."

A few minutes later, SAC Simpson was on her way to the home of Judge Snowden and Kevin Loeffler was making his way to the FBI Field Office to view the enhanced tape. Just prior to his arrival at the John Lawrence Bailey Building, his cell phone began to chime. It was Louis Hastings.

"Where the Hell have you been, Loeffler?" He yelled, the hoarseness of his voice distorting his normal, ill-tempered growl.

"You know where I've been. McMahon told you. I've been at Cocheta trying to find something... anything that might lead us to suspect two now that Hanson's is no good to us anymore."

"The sonofabitch attacked me! He tried to kill me!" Hastings said angrily and somewhat defensively.

"That's irrelevant now." Loeffler replied flatly. "Hanson is as good as dead. Agent Simpson and I searched Hanson's office and apartment and found nothing remotely relevant to suspect two."

"Taking that arrogant bitch to Cocheta was a big mistake, Loeffler." Hastings said with a tone meant to intimidate. "You should have never taken her there!"

"Fine. Fire me." Loeffler said flippantly. "You take the investigation from here on out. I took her there because she had the most investigative experience and knew what the hell was going on with the case."

There was a long pause on the line. Loeffler hoped it was because Hastings was in the middle of a massive stroke, but knew he would never be lucky enough for that to happen.

"That won't be necessary." Hastings said with a controlled, raspy voice. "At least not right now. What all did she see?"

"Only the case files she helped me look through and we skimmed through those fairly fast." Loeffler replied. "She didn't ask to see anything else and I didn't offer. I'm sure McMahon already told you this, anyway."

"I prefer hearing it from you." Hastings said. "Where do we go from here?"

"The FBI has the only lead on suspect two we have left. The MGM surveillance tape they had enhanced is apparently much better than we ever dreamed it would be." Loeffler said. "I'm almost there now."

"I want to see it too."

Loeffler knew immediately what that meant. Even though he could see the Bailey Building straight ahead, Hastings would make him divert to wherever he was for a ride.

"Where are you at?"

"They discharged me from the hospital two hours ago. I had to catch a fucking cab to my house because they said I couldn't drive while taking narcotics. Now my car is stuck at the goddamn Venetian!"

"I'll be there in 30 minutes." Loeffler said, and then terminated the call. It was going to be a long and frustrating afternoon.

Chapter 59

Judge Snowden listened to Simpson's fantastic story in its' entirety without interruption or a trace of emotion on his face.

"Hannah, if I had heard this from anyone else, I would have turned loose my Rottweilers on 'em!" He said, handing her the signed search warrant he had created and printed in his home office. "Since this involves Sections 535 and 540B, we'll need to contact the Attorney General. Go empty that safety deposit box and if it has the incriminating evidence in it you think it does, bring it back here and we'll contact the Attorney General together."

"Thank you sir!" Simpson said and hurriedly excused herself.

The drive from Judge Snowden's home to the Bank of America took only 20 minutes, but it seemed to Hannah Simpson that it took at least three times that long. When she arrived, Mattie McLeod, a senior bank executive was waiting at the front door to let her in. Simpson showed Ms. McLeod her FBI badge and handed her the search warrant and the safety deposit box key.

"Everything seems to be in order." McLeod said after reading the warrant. "Agent Simpson, we do have a large safety deposit box registered to a B. Hanson; box number 528. I'll take you to the vault area and open it for you."

A few minutes later, Agent Simpson was standing in a private cubical, staring at the contents within the large steel tray. It was neatly packed with stacks of computer discs, audio tapes and numerous file folders. Since Simpson had no immediate access to a computer or audio cassette deck, she began to search through the file folders for clues as to what the cassettes and discs contained. It didn't take much reading to find her answer.

There were transcripts. Word-for-word transcripts of telephone conversations between Hastings and some contact he only referred to as "Mr. Smith." Hanson tapped Hastings' telephone! Simpson shook her head in amazement. This scientist was just full of surprises! There was more. Personnel records detailing the retirement dates of Cocheta scientists, cross-referenced to telephone conversation transcripts between Hastings and "Mr. Smith" discussing the need to arrange for an "accident" to occur and obituary announcements or newspaper clippings describing the circumstances surrounding the scientists' untimely death. If obtained properly, the evidence would have been enough to easily convict Hastings on 15 counts of aggravated first-degree murder. However, with the use of a wiretap and incriminating conversations recorded on foreign soil, the best she could hope for was an arrest warrant on aggravated first-degree murder and a grand jury indictment to buy time for gathering more evidence that would be admissible. She knew she could get an arrest warrant from Snowden, but investigating the deaths of scientists who retired from a facility that is more secret than Area 51 might be very, very difficult. Of course, the sleazy bastard might just panic and roll over on the people who pull his strings...

Simpson requested and received a sturdy box to transport the evidence in. She deposited the box into the back seat of her unmarked car and rushed back to Judge Snowden's house as quickly as the late Saturday afternoon traffic would allow.

"Kevin?" She asked.

"Special Agent Simpson?" Came the reply from Loeffler.

"You're with Hastings, I take it."

"That would be correct. Mr. Hastings and I are reviewing the enhanced video. It is nothing short of fantastic! Unfortunately, it doesn't really tell us much, other than suspect two owns a dark-colored, 2000 to 2004 Corvette. That basically narrows the search down to about 10000 plus cars within reasonable driving distance."

"I have it, Kevin, all of it! Enough to arrest him, but since it's all obtained from a wiretapped phone, convicting him will be a lot more difficult. I'm on my way to Snowden's to discuss charges, talk to the Attorney General and get a warrant."

"Still doing poorly... Thanks for checking on Hanson for me." Loeffler replied to camouflage the real conversation. "Call me if anything changes. I'll be taking Mr. Hastings home after we finish here."

"Perfect! I'll get a team together and we'll bust him there!" She said, then her voice changed from hard-core cop to playful woman. "Steak dinner afterwards, Mr. Loeffler??"

"Absolutely," He said, maintaining the deception while answering her question. "I'll personally check on Hanson in the morning."

"See you soon!" She replied.

"This was shaping up to be the best Saturday night I've had in ages!" Loeffler thought to himself with just the slightest hint of a grin on his face.

Chapter 60

Two hours after speaking with Hannah Simpson, Loeffler was transporting Louis Hastings back to his expansive, suburban Las Vegas home. Hastings looked like warmed-over crap. The frail, cancer-ridden scientist had damn near broken his neck! Even though Hastings was wearing a foam neck brace, the bruising extended to his jaw and cheeks. Whatever he had used to taunt Hanson with, it literally blew up in his own face. Even so, Hanson paid dearly for his rampage. Within a few hours, Louis Hastings was going to start paying dearly for his rampages, but unlike Hanson, Loeffler would feel no pity for him. Hastings had it coming and Loeffler was going to watch the spectacle from the best seat in the house. All he needed was popcorn and a large Diet Dr. Pepper.

There was no conversation between the two men and Loeffler preferred it that way. The silence fostered a drifting of Loeffler's mind to the evening ahead. Hannah Simpson was certainly good company and very easy on the eyes. He was thrilled to know that the evil man beside him would be spending the night in Clark County Detention, but he was looking forward to his promising date with Hannah even more. So immersed in his thoughts, Loeffler almost missed the sound of Hastings' cell phone coming to life.

Hastings painfully retrieved the phone from his belt and flipped it open.

"Hastings here."

"Louis Hastings?" The voice asked, in spite of Hastings' greeting.

"What, are you deaf?" Hastings replied gruffly. "This is Louis Hastings. Who the hell are you?"

"The Attorney General has just authorized a warrant for your arrest. Mr. Smith strongly recommends you keep your mouth shut."

"Who the fuck is this?" He yelled into the phone, but the connection had already terminated. He suddenly felt the blood draining from his head. "An arrest warrant? For what?" He thought to himself, panic exploding throughout his body. Hastings' mind began to race. It could mean only one thing: Loeffler and Simpson had uncovered incriminating evidence against him at Cocheta! That half-dead bastard had somehow turned the table on him! He had to get control of himself. He couldn't allow Loeffler to see him panic, but Loeffler was already looking at him.

"Is everything OK?" Loeffler asked, noting the loud voice and change in Hastings' countenance.

"Stupid sonofabitch! Calls the wrong number and wants to fucking argue with me about it!"

Loeffler nodded and returned to his daydreaming, oblivious to the magnitude of the adrenalin-driven changes taking place in Hastings.

Hastings began weighing his options, what few he had. He could do as the caller suggested, allowing himself to be taken into custody and keeping his mouth shut. "Some option that was." He thought to himself. He trusted the men who controlled the destiny of Cocheta about as much as he trusted anybody else, which was not at all. No... if he ended up in jail, he would leverage information for clemency or a lighter sentence. The only other option he could think of was to run. He had money in Switzerland and Grand Cayman, but with the coming of the Patriot Act, the Cayman money would be tough, if not impossible to access with his debit card without tipping off the authorities to his whereabouts. Even if he used the debit card outside of America, Visa U.S.A. would be required to report the transaction to the IRS. There was, however, the Mexican border and it was only 6 or so hours away down Interstate 15. He could cross at Tijuana and disappear into Latin America. Since he spoke Spanish fluently, he certainly had an edge over other, less fortunate Gringo fugitives. It would be relatively easy to obtain a passport under an assumed name in Mexico. One only needed money. From there, he could fly to Cayman or Zurich and personally obtain portions of the sizable amount of money he had accumulated in his accounts that he neglected to pay taxes on over the years. Perhaps he could discretely pass along information about Project Cocheta to interested parties... for a fee, of course.

The more he thought about it, the more he liked the idea of fleeing the country. The problem was: how to get the ball rolling before the FBI showed up with a warrant? Then a plan materialized in his mind just as Loeffler was pulling into his driveway.

"Thanks for the lift." Hastings said as he was opening the passenger side door of the Lexus. "Wait a minute, I almost forgot... Could you do me another favor? My neck is killing me and I'm not going to get any sleep unless I get my Roxicet prescription filled. There is a 24-hour pharmacy about three miles from here. Could you take me there?"

Kevin Loeffler was not accustomed to hearing Louis Hastings ask nicely for anything and it caught him off guard. "What the hell," he thought, "before the hour is out, your sorry ass is going to be the property of Clark County!"

"Sure, I'll take you there."

"I just need to run inside and get the prescription."

Hastings stiffly made his way into the house and returned to the car a few short minutes later. Loeffler backed out the driveway, asking which direction he needed to go.

"Right... go right, then make your way to Interstate 15."

Before Loeffler could question the ludicrous nature of the directions, Hastings had firmly planted the barrel of a .38 caliber revolver into the right side of his rib cage. Loeffler didn't need to ask what was causing pain under his right arm, he instinctively knew.

"Don't say a word, asshole," Hastings said menacingly, "just make your way towards the California line."

Chapter 61

It was after 8PM when SAC Simpson, ASAC Lanning and three other FBI Agents, along with four Clark County Sheriff's Deputies, assembled at a small park two blocks from Hastings' home to discuss the "take down" of the murder suspect. Since the subject had no prior knowledge of the warrant, the raid would likely be no more difficult than calling him to the door with a ring of his doorbell and throwing a pair of handcuffs on him. Even so, they would cover all potential escape routes in case he decided to bolt out the back door. In spite of the apparent low risk nature of the arrest, SAC Simpson insisted that everyone involved wear body armor. Hastings was a murderer, even if he did contract others to do his dirty work. Apprehending killers demanded extra 'insurance' even when the odds were already stacked convincingly in your favor.

The plan was for SAC Simpson, ASAC Lanning and one of the Clark County Deputies to approach the door and position themselves to the left and right of the doorway. The other FBI Agents and Sheriffs' deputies would take positions around the house to watch for a possible escape from other doors and windows. By 8:30, all assets were in place around the house and squad car barricades positioned across the entry and exit points of the street.

Simpson was beginning to wonder where Loeffler was. She knew he wouldn't miss this show for anything, so his absence was starting to concern her. The other thing concerning her was the deserted look of Hastings' home. Kevin should have dropped him off no later than an hour earlier and should be right here watching the spectacle. There was a growing tension inside of her and it was telling her that something was amiss.

"Let's go now." She spoke into her headset.

All drew their weapons while the arrest team approached the door, weapons also drawn and at the ready. Simpson pressed the doorbell button and knocked on the door.

Nothing... no sound at all was coming from the house. She repeated the doorbell and knock. Again... nothing. She reached for the doorknob and began to turn it. It was unlocked! She quietly spoke into her headset to inform her teammates that she was going to push open the door. She crouched low and began pushing the door open with her left hand. No response. Looking into the partially opened doorway revealed that the home was completely unlit, which escalated the danger to her team by an order of magnitude. Was Hastings armed and waiting in a closet or dark hallway to spring his trap? It was a plausible scenario, but not likely. He would know it was suicide to pull such a stunt and such acts were completely out of character for a coward like Hastings. The home was empty, she was sure of it, but they would work the entry as if there was an armed killer behind every piece of furniture. Simpson called for the pair of AN/PVS-7 Night Vision Goggles she had in her trunk. Within a several minutes of donning her NVGs, Simpson and her team secured the house. It was as she suspected, completely empty. Simpson retrieved a cell phone from her car and dialed Loefflers' number. After several rings, his voice mail prompt activated. A chill shuddered through her body. Something was terribly, terribly wrong...

Chapter 62

Hastings and his hostage were nearing the brightly lit, Nevada side of the state line on Interstate 15 when Loeffler's cell phone began to ring.

"Don't answer it!" Hastings yelled. "If fact, toss it out the window!"

Hastings decided how to handle the situation thirty miles earlier. If he did not act decisively, Hastings was going to force him onto a deserted stretch of road somewhere in the Mojave Desert, then put a bullet in his head. The plan he chose to execute might also leave him dead, but at least he would have a better chance for survival than the alternative.

The timing was perfect. Everything he needed to decrease the odds against him in place, including the added advantage of a ringing cell phone for distraction. He ever so slightly decreased his speed to a relatively tame 55 mph and made a quick sweep of the traffic situation around him. He purposefully drove in such a way to keep a safe distance ahead of the traffic behind him without being obvious to Hastings. It had to be now and he braced himself for the coming violence. As he began rolling down his window to discard the cell phone, he jerked the steering wheel hard to the left and slammed the brake pedal hard to the floor. Hastings was caught completely off-guard as the Lexus began to barrel roll down the highway.

Loeffler felt as if he had entered an odd, slow-motion world alternating between weightlessness and jarring impacts. All of the airbags seemed to deploy at once, giving the momentary impression that he was embraced in a fluffy white cloud. Objects floating past his face would suddenly accelerate out of view. The intense casino lights on both sides of the highway were shining through the white airbag material and reflecting off the sheets of shattered glass suspended in the air, adding shimmering fireworks to the odd beauty of the steel-twisting disintegration occurring around him. The noise was deafening and rhythmic as the car tumbled on the pavement. One brief sound seemed completely out of place in the mayhem. A loud bark that hurt his ears and caused sudden, searing pain and pressure to the right side of his head. Gunfire? Had he just been shot in the head? He was aware of Hastings to his right and the contorted look of terror on his face as his body lifted out of the vehicle like a ragamuffin doll pulled free of a toy highchair. "No seatbelt... dumbass!" He thought with a distant realization that it was a highly strange and calm one to have when the next few seconds inside the increasingly distorted car might be his last on earth. The "roll" he initiated seemed to be going on forever. Hours, maybe. Bad news... Yet, why did he feel so calm? He sensed the roll was slowing about the same time his left forearm snapped. The sudden, severe addition to the multitude of other pains he was vaguely beginning to feel, caused him to black out.

The shredded Lexus finally came to a stop, upright, over 100 yards from where the roll began. Within seconds, cars were arriving from both sides of the highway and the occupants of the vehicles, most armed with cell phones, began flooding the Clark County 911 system. Loeffler began fighting to regain his full senses. He was alive, but for how long? The daze was slowly dissipating and he began responding to the gathering voices around him. One voice, an Australian one, was louder and clearer than the rest.

"Over 'ear!" He yelled to somebody. "No drama, mate. Ambo's on the way! Be 'ear any tic of the clock!"

Loeffler, however, was regaining his faculties quickly. Overwhelming survival instincts were driving him to exit the wreckage as quickly as possible, but as consciousness returned, so came the flood of pain, attenuating his uncoordinated attempt at self-extraction. The right side of his head was throbbing, and as he reached up to put his right hand on the source of pain, he found the area wet and sticky. His left forearm was obviously broken, but with a hundred areas on his body sending pain signals to his brain, the fracture didn't seem to hurt that much. He concentrated on the rest of his body, and quickly determined that he was in one piece. Then he remembered something important... Hastings had a gun! He looked around the almost unrecognizable vehicle and couldn't find him, then recalled his almost dreamlike ejection from the spinning Lexus. He painfully turned towards the Australian man, who was already talking to him through the distorted and much narrower hole where the front windshield had been, but Loeffler had been too distracted to hear what he was saying. "The other man in the car with me. Where is he?"

"Over there a piece." He replied.

"Is he alive?" Loeffler asked, his senses nearly restored.

"D'know, mate. Some are sayin' ees' karked it."

"He's wanted for murder and he had a gun! Make sure he doesn't have it anymore!"

"Bloody 'ell you say! I'll let the others know!"

The Aussie bolted from the car to warn the people who were rendering first aid to Hastings. Other Samaritans were gathering around the once beautiful Lexus and offering aid to Hastings. One older man retrieved a clean shirt from his luggage and gave it to Loeffler to put on the bleeding head wound. The roof of the LS was noticeably lower than it had been and both doors encroached several inches towards the middle. The airbag material lay limp all about him, causing him to briefly ponder how screwed-up he'd be if there hadn't been any airbags in the car. The only way out was through the missing front windshield, that is, if he could negotiate the steering wheel and the center console.

"You need to hold still, mister!" A male voice said to him. "You're pretty banged up!"

"I'll be alright." Loeffler replied. "Can you help pull me through the windshield?"

"I don't think that is such a good idea." The man replied, others agreeing with him.

"Look, my left arm is broken and I've got a gash on the right side of my head. That's it. My neck if sore, but OK." Loeffler pleaded. "Please help me get out. I need to make sure the other man is unarmed!"

Law enforcement had not arrived on the scene yet, so the suggestion that the other victim might be dangerous seemed to lessen their concern over improperly removing Loeffler from the wreckage.

"Are you a cop?" A woman asked.

"Former FBI." Loeffler replied. "If somebody could get a blanket and place it over the dashboard and hood, I think I can crawl out of the windshield without getting cut up."

Within a minute, a blanket arrived, donated to the cause by an elderly couple traveling in an RV. Loeffler freed himself from the carnage with the help of three truck drivers by the time the first Nevada and California Highway Patrol units arrived on the scene. He was limping his way towards the crowd gathered around Hastings some 50 yards away.

"Is he alive?" Loeffler asked.

"Yeah, he's alive, but he refuses to answer any of our questions." A voice answered from the center of the commotion. "Both legs are broken... lots of cuts... He was out of it for a while, but seems to be awake now. Weird thing... he already had a C-collar on!"

"Did you find a gun on him?" Loeffler asked, hobbling towards the center of the crowd, cradling his broken left arm with his right.

"No... no gun."

"Good." Loeffler said, standing over Hastings, looking into his eyes. "Louis Hastings,

I'm going to enjoy watching you fry."

Hastings replied by spitting at him.

Chapter 63

Hannah Simpson watched the Orthopedic Surgery resident splint Kevin Loeffler's forearm fracture. Long gone were the days when casts were only made of white plaster. Loeffler had a choice of vibrant and cheerful colors for his fiberglass cast, yet chose plain off-white, probably reflecting his overly conservative nature. Besides, white "went with everything," he jokingly told her.

Before their relationship even had a chance to start, she almost lost him. The wound to his head was, indeed, a gunshot wound. The bullet entered just in front and above his right ear, but at an angle that caused it to track along the outer surface of his skull, exiting the scalp seven inches behind, and a few inches above the level of the entrance wound. Had the entry angle been more perpendicular to the surface of his skull, the bullet would have easily penetrated his cranium, showering his brain with a fatal mix of bone splinters, bullet fragments and a tissue-destroying transfer of kinetic and hydrostatic energy. Other than a mild concussion, spectacular bruising to his face and neck and a future pair of bald spots, he would likely recover from the head trauma without too much difficulty.

Of his other injuries? The forearm fracture was simple enough to avoid surgery, and the deeper cuts around his body required over 120 sutures to close. Tears welled in her eyes at the realization that she could just as easily be identifying his body at the morgue.

Loeffler saw the shimmer of moisture in her eyes, and decided it was time to lighten the moment. "You can sign my cast if you want to."

Hannah shook her head, wiping from her face the rogue tear that managed to escape her eyelid.

"Hannah, I'm fine. I'm going to be fine. I walked in under my own power, didn't I?" Loeffler said, trying to convince her that he really was going to be fine. The tears Hannah was shedding, however, were not out of concern that he might succumb to his injuries, but of tremendous relief that the man she just might have a future with just survived a completely unanticipated brush with death.

Hannah reached for and began holding his right hand. "This wasn't what I had planned for us this evening." She said, regaining a degree of her composure.

"I was really looking forward to that steak dinner." He replied, managing a smile through the increasing soreness. "I trust I can get a rain check?"

"I have a whole coupon book waiting for you!"

As planned, the doctors admitted Loeffler to an observation unit for neurological checks throughout the night. Hannah stayed at his bedside, holding his uninjured hand and stroking his hair. He drifted in and out of sleep, induced by self-administered intravenous narcotics, interrupted only by breakthrough pain and neurological assessments. She only left him once during the night and that was to relieve her bladder. While she was up, she made her way to the Surgical Intensive Care Unit where Dr. Hanson clung to life with the thinnest of threads. Using her FBI badge, she gained entrance to the patient care area and quietly entered Hansons' room, nodding at the guard stationed at the doorway.

Buried in a sea of tangled intravenous lines and monitoring cables, Hanson surely fit the description of somebody on "life support." She stared at the monitors displaying a myriad of colorful waveforms and numbers, only understanding the meaning of a few of them. It was a sad and pitiful sight. She leaned over the bed and began to whisper in his ear.

"What are you up to, Dr. Hanson? We've done what you asked us to do and now we're at the end of the road." She said to the near lifeless body of Ben Hanson. "We have nothing left to go on."

She stood and turned for the door. "I guess the next move is yours."

Chapter 64

As it so happens, many unsolvable crimes or mysteries become "solved" because of pure luck or happenstance rather than meticulous investigation. Sometimes, it is the seemingly trivial bit of evidence that turns up in a highly unusual place, or a coincidence of staggering proportions that strips an enigma of it's puzzling veil. The mystery surrounding the identity of suspect two melted away in just such a fashion.

It started with a man and his two sons doing nothing more than vegetating in front of a television set on a lazy Sunday afternoon, watching an argumentative family build custom motorcycles. During a commercial break, he watched America's favorite scientist promote a special live broadcast of his show to air on the Science and Technology Channel that evening and he was promising an announcement of great scientific importance. At first, the man second-guessed the connection that popped into his head. Surely, Dr. Tim Alexander was not the one Hanson recruited to blow the lid off Cocheta. The more he thought about it, however, the more it made sense. Alexander was enormously popular, highly respected and he had an immensely visible forum. If anybody could pull it off, it would be Tim Alexander!

The promo said the special presentation would begin at 8PM Eastern Time. The man looked at his watch. It was almost 2 PM in Las Vegas. The broadcast would begin in a little over 3 hours!

"Special Agent Simpson." The female voice answered.

"Ma'am, this is Dawson Wingate. I need to speak to Mr. Loeffler immediately."

"Can it wait?" Simpson said, somewhat annoyed. "He's resting right now. They've decided to keep him in the hospital for another day."

"No Ma'am, it can't wait! I know who suspect number two is and he's going to release the information in three hours!"

"Oh my God!" Simpson exclaimed. "Who is it? How did you find this out?"

"It's Dr. Timothy Alexander! He has a popular show on the Science and Technology Channel called 'Science for the Rest of Us.' He's doing a live broadcast tonight and said he was going to announce an important scientific discovery." He told her excitedly. "It all makes sense. He's the one!"

The information that Wingate was feeding to Simpson rang true to her. He was probably right, and if Dr. Tim Alexander owned a dark-colored Corvette Convertible, Wingate was definitely right. "I'm going to hand the phone over to Mr. Loeffler. Tell him everything. I'm going to call my people and have them find out the make and color of the cars Dr. Alexander owns."

If it were up to her, Hannah Simpson would have let Kevin sleep. The hourly checks and bouts of severe pain robbed him of any quality sleep. If she knew Kevin as well as she thought she did, this new information would get him out of bed and into the hunt in spite of his pain and fatigue. Her gut feeling was to let Alexander release the information. The whole menagerie has caused nothing but pain and suffering!

"Kevin," She said, stroking her hand over his forehead, causing him to slowly open his eyes. "Wingate is on the phone. It sounds like he figured out who suspect two is."

Loefflers' eyes widened as he reached for the phone. He listened intently as Wingate spelled out the details. In the meantime, Hannah Simpson was speaking to ASAC Randy Hammock, tasking him to compile a list of vehicles registered in Timothy Alexander's name.

"Wingate, make sure the Lear is at JANET. Have them prep it immediately and file a flight plan for Washington DC. I'm going to bring Special Agent Simpson with me so she can coordinate the FBI role in stopping this broadcast." Loeffler paused, catching his breath. "I'll need you to report to the office to field calls from me or Agent Simpson. Helluva good catch, Dawson!"

Loeffler closed Simpson's cell phone and handed it back to her. "Can you help me out of bed? Once I get started, I'll be OK."

She shook her head. "You're going to fly across the country in your condition?" She said, helping him move his legs over the side of the bed. "Have you seen yourself in the mirror?"

"I've got to." Loeffler said, easing his feet to the cold hospital floor.

"I suppose you do." She paused, looking at the battered man struggling against pain to make each movement of his body. "There is just no stopping you, is there?"

"I can't let Hanson win this one." He said, attempting to stand up.

"Is that what this is really all about? You versus Hanson?" She said.

"Partly..." He replied honestly. "I hate to lose. I also know that it is my sworn duty to stop him, not to mention that if I fail, I won't be able to get a job protecting the secret prizes at a Cracker Jack factory."

"Then I'll just have to make you a kept man, then." She grinned at him.

He gave her a combination smile and grimace as he took a few wobbly steps. It was amazing how much more he hurt today than last evening. "That is a damn tempting offer. Is it valid if I stop Alexander?"

"We'll see, but if you don't take care of yourself, the deal is off! What good is a kept man if he's all busted up?"

"I see your point, Ms. Simpson." He hobbled his way to the small closet in the room and retrieved a long hospital gown.

"By the way, stud, what are you going to do for clothes?"

"We don't have time to stop by my house..." He pondered. "JANET has a stash of jump suits. I'll change into one on the jet. We had better get going." He said, while moving at the pace of a 100 year-old great grandmother.

Loeffler discharged himself from the hospital "AMA" or "Against Medical Advice" and made his way out to Hannah Simpson's car, his joints and muscles loosening up a bit with the activity. Within 20 minutes, Simpson was parking her car in the near empty lot at the JANET terminal. Little happened there on weekends so the facility operated with a skeleton crew. Even so, the Lear 35A was properly prepared for the journey and waiting for its' passengers. They even put several sizes of jumpsuits in the aircraft, along with toiletry items and bandaging supplies appropriate for someone who recently discharged from the hospital.

Just before the ground crew shut the door on the Lear, Simpson's cell phone rang. It was ASAC Hammock.

"Alexander has two cars registered in his name and one is a 2004 Corvette, VIN 1G1YY32G345103227. According to the 6th character on the VIN number, a '3,' means that it is a convertible. The vehicle registration in California shows that it is blue in color. LeMans blue, according to the Corvette color chips for 2004."

"Thanks, Hammock." Simpson said. "Your reputation for digging up incredible amounts of information on the smallest of subjects remains intact." She closed her phone and turned to Loeffler. "Alexander is definitely our man."

"Good!" He said, feeling the pace quickening. "There is no way we can make it to the DC area in 2 hours, so how do we stop him?"

Chapter 65

"Darrell, is everybody in place?" Alexander asked, his heart pounding in his chest. "Only 30 minutes to showtime."

"Everybody except me." Aceveda said. "I'm going to personally handle the tricky part."

"Thanks, buddy." Alexander said. "There is no way I can ever repay you for this."

"As long as you post my bail, I'll consider us even."

"I hope it doesn't come to that, my friend." Alexander said with a sigh.

It was time for Tim to have his make-up done and as he walked to the make-up room he noted that there were quite a few high profile executive types walking about the facility, each taking a turn staring at him. They were gambling on him, but it was already paying off in big bucks. The reaction to Alexander's promo spots had been precisely what he predicted it would be. The less you announce, the more curiosity it generates. The phone lines were jammed with calls from the curious to the furious, demanding to know what the subject matter was, or whether the announcement was worth missing a portion of their Sunday night baseball game. Sponsors were clamoring for advertising time and that was driving up rates.

Makeup was his least favorite part of preparing for a show. It was far too tedious for a man like Alexander, who always felt the urge to move around. One of the make-up artists asked why he seemed so nervous.

"It's a live show." He replied, conjuring up a quick excuse for his jitters. "I've never done a live show. You can screw-up all you want when you're taping a program, but when it's live, a screw-up is there for the whole world to see."

"You won't screw-up, Dr. Alexander." Cindy said, the one checking his shirt and tie. "You usually don't need a lot of retakes when you tape. I'm sure you'll do just fine."

After his makeup session was complete, Alexander made his way to the set of his show. While the props looked solid enough on television, the design permitted quick assembly and disassembly. His familiar set consisted of two large, oval-shaped platforms, each equipped with a curved medium blue, staggered-plank wall background. The main platform, positioned on the viewer's right, was the one he stood on, or casually sat on a desk. The other platform was for zooming to a screen, or displaying larger props. This platform, positioned several feet farther back, was on the viewers left. Both platforms rested on a highly polished black floor leading to a wall in the far background, brightly lit blue at the floor, fading to deep blue at the top of the viewer's screen. It was a simple arrangement that tended not to draw viewers eyes from the point of interest. As Alexander put it once, "...the star of the show was not him, or having an Emmy-winning background, it was the science. Nothing should ever distract from the wonderful and fascinating science I am presenting to the audience." Tim shunned elaborate, computer-generated graphics unless it added substance to the viewing experience. If it was fluff, it went into the "Recycle Bin."

Tim looked at his watch... ten minutes to go. Only two people in the Science and Technology Production Group building had any idea what was about to take place at 8PM Eastern Daylight Savings Time, and only one of them knew precisely what would happen. The "party crashers" hadn't arrived and with so little time left, it wasn't likely that they would. In less than an hour, the world would be a different place and Dr. Tim Alexander would become the center of a very big controversy. All Tim could do at this point was to pray the world that followed would be wiser than the one before it. The selfish thing that Tim wondered the most about was, when the dust settled, would history paint him good or evil. That, he decided, was completely out of his hands.

Seven minutes to go...

Chapter 66

The previous two hours aboard the Lear had been nerve-wracking. The plan was to either stop the broadcast at it's source, meaning that a court-order had to be obtained to stop the act of televising that specific program, or arrest Tim Alexander before the announcement could be made, forcing the Science and Technology Channel to air alternate programming. Both agreed that with less than two hours left, the first option would be impossible to achieve. It was a Sunday evening and contacting the principal players who could ramrod such a thing would take hours. The most practical approach would be to arrest Alexander, but to do that, the Attorney General and FBI Director would have to be notified, permission obtained and a warrant issued. In cases involving National Security, it was theoretically possible to obtain such warrants in short order, but the behemoth bureaucracies that needed goading were even less responsive on weekends.

Simpson contacted FBI Headquarters and requested a team of FBI agents go to Silver Spring Maryland and arrest Tim Alexander immediately upon issuance of the warrant. With her request granted an almost immediate approval, the team was in place at Dixon and 2nd Street, across the road from the expansive corporate and production headquarters of the Science and Technology Group, by 7:30PM. The only thing holding back the FBI was an arrest warrant, and no judge in the DC area wanted his or her name on a warrant to arrest the beloved Tim Alexander. The story that Dr. Alexander was about to release information that would seriously damage national security was simply not believable to the Judges queried. To make matters worse, the exact details of the kind of information Alexander was supposedly going to release was extremely vague, prompting even further judicial resistance. Finally, at 7:55PM, EDST, a District Judge in the DC area caved in, but only after he demanded that Dr. Alexander not be arrested, but detained for questioning as a "Person of Interest" in an investigation of importance to national security. It was very, very weak, but it would do. If they caught him with evidence stolen from Cocheta, they could escalate the charges and formally arrest him later. Within seconds, the FBI team in Silver

Spring received a mobile fax of the warrant giving them permission to enter the building and "detain" Dr. Tim Alexander for questioning.

"This is as close a to the last second as I have ever seen, Kevin! For a while there, I didn't think we'd pull it off!"

Loeffler smiled at her and nodded. He had Hanson "right where he wanted him" before, only to have him slip from his grasp.

"Is something wrong?" She asked, seeing the look concern on Kevin's face.

"No, not really." He said. "I just wish we had the capability to watch it all go down. With Hanson, I'll believe it's over when I actually see that it's over."

"Call Wingate and keep him on the line while he watches it."

"Great idea!" He replied, reaching for the air phone and dialing the Las Vegas Project Cocheta office. Simpson noticed the near instantaneous improvement in Kevin's demeanor when she suggested a way for him to stay in the loop. He needed to have some sort of connection to the end-game. "What a shame he couldn't be there to see it for himself." She thought to herself.

"Dawson Wingate."

"Wingate! Loeffler here. Turn the Science and Technology Channel on and give me a blow by blow account of what's going on."

"One step ahead of you boss. Already have it on. Right now, they are at the tail-end of the 4PM show."

"Any second now..."

Chapter 67

With 30 seconds to go, Tim Alexander took his spot on the stage-right platform, casually sitting on the front edge of the beautiful office desk on the platform that spoke "academia." On the desk and to his right, was what appeared to be the much sought-after box that Dr. Hanson gave him several days earlier. As the seconds slipped by, he noticed a commotion brewing in the control room. They were here, just as Hanson said they would be; only they were cutting it entirely too close.

"Tim, fifteen seconds." The Director called out.

Dr. Alexander straightened himself and prepared to speak the opening line he knew would never be broadcast.

"Ten seconds... seven, six, five, four..."

Another overhead voice spoke. "Tim, we have a situation here. Could you please come to the control booth.

Bingo!

Tim saw that the network had gone to color calibration bars, but rather than make his way to the control room as he had been asked to, he began to watch another screen that was monitoring the downlink from the geostationary satellite 36,000 kilometers above the equator. It went black. Darrell Aceveda just disabled the network uplink to it's designated satellite transponder and he was personally making sure that there would be no uplink for at least 20 minutes.

"What the hell is going on?" Somebody began yelling. "What happened to our up-link?"

The seconds ticked away.

"C'mon! C'mon!"

"Tim," The overhead speaker blurted. "Please come to the control booth, NOW! And bring the box with you!"

The downlink monitor remained black. Tim's heart rate was soaring, relentlessly beating the inside of his chest wall. "C'mon! C'mon, DAMMIT!"

The monitor began to flicker, then the image of a late middle-aged woman appeared. Attractive, keenly dressed and composed, she appeared to be in a studio, with a background composed of blue drapes behind two flags, one obviously the American flag to her right, the other to her left mostly light blue with a brownish design lost in the furls.

"Somebody has hijacked our uplink!" A voice yelled.

"Shut up! SHUT UP! She's starting to talk!" Someone else yelled.

"Good evening, America and the world," she began, "for those of you who do not know me, I am the Junior Senator from the Great State of Oklahoma, Teresa Rose Chandler. I speak to you tonight about an important scientific discovery, made many decades ago, that must now be revealed to the peoples of the United States and to all our brothers and sisters in every country on our world."

She paused for a brief moment, as if having trouble proceeding with the words that followed.

"Many of you, perhaps most of you watching this broadcast, already believe that life, intelligent life, exists on planets outside our solar system. Many of you do not. The question as to whether or not we are alone in the universe has begged an answer for as long as people have looked into the night sky. The truth is that, indeed, intelligent life does exist elsewhere in the universe and that at least one extraterrestrial species has arrived and is actively engaged in studying our own world. I know this to be true because my husband, Dr. Benjamin Harris Hanson, a brilliant aerospace engineer and scientist, worked for over 40 years on a highly classified project that studies the technology left behind by mishaps involving extraterrestrial vehicles. Like my husband, many dozens of amazingly smart men and women answered the call of their country and spent entire careers analyzing this technology in total obscurity. The sacrifices they willingly accepted to contribute to this monumental effort is a testament to the "can do" spirit of our great nation. All are patriots and all deserve our deepest respect and gratitude."

"Better than sixty years of research has been invested so far, yet we have precious little understanding of their culture or technology. It is critical that the hard work at this facility must continue and the brightest minds, not only from America, but from every corner of the globe, be allowed to contribute to the effort. This was my husband's dream, and for the benefit of all mankind, that dream must become a reality.

"I am asking the President and the Legislative Branch of Government to organize a Commission, composed of scientists, public servants, religious leaders and ordinary private citizens, to analyze the data concerning the likely objectives of the civilization visiting our planet and release pertinent information to the public in a graduated fashion. I urge my colleagues in the Senate, House of Representatives and the President to shelve partisan politics for a change and concentrate their efforts on determining the best course of action for our government and her people. To handle the challenges of the new reality in which we find ourselves, our government must make an effort to reach out to all the nations on earth and join with them to form a unified planet in purpose. Humans can no longer afford to think in terms of nations competing with nations, but of planets competing with planets. My friends, the universe appears to be far smaller than we once thought it to be."

"To the President of the United States: my sincere apologies for announcing something that should have been yours' to announce. There were, however, strong mitigating circumstances. Many years ago, the vicious man running the project my husband worked on, threatened my life and the lives of our children. My husband sacrificed his happiness, his very reason for living, to protect us from this very dangerous and ruthless man. We were forced to separate and never allowed to see each other again. My husband has never met the grandchildren he was so much looking forward to having. He sacrificed immensely and I know he suffered immensely." Tears began streaming down her face and her voice began to waver."

"This past week, when he was finally able to safely contact me, he asked if I could help him release this information to the world. You see, Mr. President, my husband was dying from incurable lung cancer and only had weeks or months to live. He believed strongly that the world should work together to understand the alien culture and technology. How could I deny the dying wish of such a noble man, the only man I ever loved, and the man who sacrificed so much for his family." Her voice was failing her, and the tears were now coming down in torrents."

"My husband lies near death in a Las Vegas Hospital. Through his tireless efforts and the heroic actions of two very special people, one an FBI agent, the other a former FBI agent, the evil man that posed a threat to us for almost 16 years, and responsible for the murders of over a dozen retired scientists, is now in custody. My family and I can safely return home to love and comfort him during the last hours of his life."

Senator Chandler had to turn away from the camera for a moment to compose herself.

"Ben, if by some miracle you can hear me, please hold on! We'll all be there as soon as we can, including the grandchildren... I promise! I never stopped loving you Ben! You have always been my one and only-est!"

"Goodnight... God bless America, and you, her beloved people. Please give us the divine strength to face the challenges ahead."

The screen went black as the hijacked uplink disappeared. A few women in the studio were openly crying, while the men stood around in shock at what they heard. Several men sporting FBI jackets were heading towards Tim with menacing looks on their face.

"Dr. Timothy Alexander?" The agent in front asked.

"Yes." He replied.

"We have a court order to detain you for questioning in a matter concerning National Security."

"I see."

"I need to search the box, as well."

Tim handed over the box and the FBI agent quickly opened it. Inside were twelve, long-stem red roses.

An agent on a cell phone emerged from the rear of the group and whispered into the ear of the agent questioning Dr. Alexander.

"Dr. Alexander." The lead agent said. "I have just been advised that your detention won't be necessary. Please accept our apologies for any inconvenience we have caused."

With that, the agents made their way to the exits.

"So, I'm not going to jail after all." He thought to himself with a subdued sense of relief.

Alexander was not aware of the sudden seriousness of Hanson's condition and it caught him off guard. A deep sadness overcame him. He only met the man once, but was profoundly struck by his depth of character and unbending resolve. Tim didn't know how best to help the Hanson's, he just knew he needed to be there with them and offer what-ever support he could. The mushrooming melancholy in his soul was growing and the only way to soothe it was to get on the next plane to Vegas.

In less than four hours, he was already well on his way.

Chapter 68

Loeffler and Simpson listened in stunned silence to the Senator Chandler's speech on the air phone connection with Wingate. When it was over, Hannah turned away from the phone and began looking out her window, tears streaming down her cheeks.

Loeffler walked up to the cockpit and spoke to the pilot. "Gerry, turn us around, we need to return to Vegas."

"Roger that, Mr. Loeffler."

Returning from the cockpit, Loeffler sat down beside Hannah Simpson, not knowing what to say or do. He was completely taken back by the manner in which Ben Hanson thwarted his final efforts to stop him. It was simply beyond brilliant. He never considered Hanson's estranged wife, a first-term U.S. Senator, in the equation. In retrospect, it made sense. She was the only person on earth he could trust and he knew she would sacrifice for him as he had done for her. Leoffler completely underestimated their devotion to each other even after many years of separation. Most disturbing to him was the fact he never considered that such a love could possibly exist. Kevin closed his eyes and shook his head as sadness enveloped him. Sadness for Ben Hanson and Senator Chandler's family, sadness for a world that would soon enough learn the truth about the threats facing it... and sadness for himself. Not because Hanson probably neutered him in the security industry and his days as an "expert" were likely numbered, but that after five decades of life, he seemed to know nothing of love and sacrifice. The brilliant scientist may go down in history for his pivotal role at Cocheta, but perhaps his most rewarding and lasting accomplishment was creating and nurturing a lifelong love that solidly withstood every attack against it.

He finally put his right arm around Hannah and gently pulled her close. She turned and buried her head in his very sore chest, but he gladly endured the pain for her comfort. He leaned his head over and gently kissed the top of her head.

"Hannah, we need to be there for Dr. Hanson and his family."

She looked up at him, wiping the tears from her face. "Yes... Yes we do."

"Can I ask you a question?"

"Sure."

"I'm not angry that Dr. Hanson outwitted us... well, me. In fact, I guess I'm relieved. I'm also tired. Very tired. Tired of misplaced priorities, cutthroat competition, two divorces... What do I have to show for it?" He paused for a moment, shaking his head. "Dr. Hanson may be on his deathbed, but look what he has accomplished in his life! Not the science, what he had with his wife. Somewhere down the line I must have become a hard core cynic because I never believed anything like what they have together was even remotely possible. I don't want to be like that anymore, Hannah." He stopped and looked her in the eyes. "I look at you and I see a warm, sensitive, beautiful woman who looks at me with a sparkle in her eye that makes me feel good inside! I guess the question I want to ask you is: Do you think it's possible? I mean for us. To have a chance at what the Hanson's had together?"

Hannah looked at him in utter amazement, not entirely certain she could trust her ears.

"Kevin, I really care for you. I like being around you and when I'm not around you, I find myself wishing I were." She paused for a moment to wipe the tears from her eyes. "You make me feel very special! The answer is 'yes,' if we make each other the most important priorities in our lives, I'm sure we could have what they have."

"I think so, too..."

With that, Kevin Loeffler and Hannah Simpson held each other and napped until the jet touched down at McCarran International Airport nearly two hours later.

Chapter 69

It seemed as though only moments passed since the darkness enveloped him that a familiar feeling began to permeate his soul, drawing him somewhere he knew he wanted to go. Something was growing in the darkness. Powerful... irresistible... Whatever it was, it wouldn't be denied. It was saturating him, endowing him strength to push away the darkness. A voice... and a touch... So very long ago, yet it was there, almost within reach. The darkness was, it was... fading! He was beginning to feel things. The stroke of a hand on his forehead, the restraints on his wrists, the tube in his throat... The sensations were cascading in so fast... The light gradually replacing the darkness, and the lightness was beginning to... hurt? Sounds... people talking. The crescendo of energy and emotions compelling him towards consciousness was reaching a peak when he opened his eyes.

"Oh my God!" Senator Hanson exclaimed. "Somebody get the nurse!"

Ben Hanson was blinking his eyes, the first seemingly purposeful movement of his hospital admission. Family members were beginning to gather around the bed.

"Ben, sweetheart, can you hear me? Squeeze my hand once if you can."

Ben responded with a single squeeze to her hand.

Tears began streaming down Teresa Hanson's face. It was nothing short of a miracle!

"Ben, I've missed you so much!"

Ben tried to move his arms, but something prevented him from doing so. Teresa untied his arm restraints and gently unwrapped them from his wrists. He immediately reached for Teresa's hand and held it. Teresa's tears were unstoppable now.

"Everybody is here! I had them put you in a much larger room so everyone could be

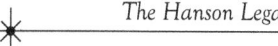

with you at the same time."

Ben squeezed her hand and held it firm.

Starting with his oldest son, Paul Harris, along with his wife Jessica and their two lively, beautiful twin girls, every family member gave Ben hugs, kisses and held his hand. Ben watched the procession with both pride and sadness. Pride in how well his children and grandchildren had turned out and sadness because he would never see them on earth again. Paul matured into fine, solid man. Donna was brilliant and stunning, just like her mom and there seemed to be a mutual attraction developing between her and a very welcomed visitor, Tim Alexander. Arthur was in his Marine Corps "cammos," strong and confident, with his beautiful wife, Myra and their three kids. Ben could feel the darkness tugging at him now and he instinctively knew his return to consciousness was becoming very tenuous.

Ben squeezed her hand again, and then made a writing gesture.

"You want me to get a pen and paper?"

He shook his head up and down weakly.

A very heavily bruised and bandaged Kevin Loeffler stepped up to the bed and handed a pen and note pad to Teresa with his uninjured arm.

Hanson stared at Kevin for a moment, then watched as Hannah Simpson stepped up next to Kevin in a way only a couple does. Ben's eyes seemed to twinkle at the sight.

Teresa put the pen in Ben's right hand and the pad in his left. He began to write slowly and deliberately. Even so, the handwriting looked similar to that of a 2nd grader.

The word was "H A S T I N G S ?"

Teresa leaned close to him. "Sweetie, you did it! Hastings is in jail, nursing two broken legs and charged with 15 counts of murder! The whole world has heard the truth about Cocheta, too. What they do with it... I guess only time will tell.

He began to write again.

"B E A U T I F U L F A M I L Y !"

"You do have a beautiful family and we all love you so much! You also have the sweet grandchildren you always wanted." She leaned closer and whispered into his ear. "I never stopped loving you, Ben Hanson! Every night for years I prayed that we would be reunited and my prayers were finally answered!"

Ben returned a feeble smile. He could feel the darkness gaining strength, pulling at him to return to where he had been. His will to resist was draining from his body. So little time left...

"TIME TO GO"

"Sweetheart, please don't go yet." Teresa begged him. "There is so much I want to say to you!" Teresa was in a panic, sensing that something was going awry. Ben was looking noticeably weaker.

"LUV U"

"I love you too! Please don't leave!" She pleaded.

"MY ONLYEST"

"Oh God, please don't take him from me again! Please!" Everyone in the room had tears streaming down their face. Donna and Hannah gathered at the bedside with Teresa.

"B WAITING 4 U"

Ben slowly lost his grip on the pen and slipped back into unconsciousness. Teresa was sobbing on Ben's chest, pleading with him to return. Five minutes later, Ben's heart slowed and his blood pressure plummeted to undetectable. There would be no medical heroics for Ben Hanson. Nobody wanted to see him suffer any longer. His heart rate continued to slow until it was no more. Benjamin Harris Hanson was dead. He died with his beloved wife, family and friends by his side.

It was the perfect death for a most noble man.

Epilogue

"Mr. Smith" gazed over the complex steel and concrete terrain of New York City from his corner office high above Manhattan. The politicians were already grabbing airtime and spewing self-serving sound bites. The mindless pundits were also talking, mostly to hear their heads rattle again. Some labeled Hanson a traitor, others a patriot. Most, however, predicted that the "Hanson Revelations" were going to change the world.

"Bullshit."

Nothing ever really changed because human nature never changed. That, in and of itself, was the reason every facet of human endeavor followed a predictable pattern. Packaging frequently changed to suggest a "New and Improved" look, but the substance inside never did.

The world was teeming with idiots trying to force their brand of "change" on others. In essence, each so-called "plan" had far more to do with controlling people and enriching their own ruling class than it did about lofty religious or secular belief systems. It was human nature... Nothing more.

Alien invasion? Now THAT represented real change! Human nature was not a factor in the decisions governing the actions of an alien species. Bribery, protection money, blackmail, trading favors, alliances with someone stronger... All tactics designed by humans, shaped by human nature and unlikely to work on highly evolved non-humans. Alien invasion meant enslavement or extinction and that was the type of change "Mr. Smith" could not allow to happen. Cocheta's real mission was to achieve technologic equality, or perhaps even superiority against the aliens. Now it was vulnerable, not from extraterrestrial attack, but from politicians and the monumental, egocentric circuses they create.

The world knew "Mr. Smith" by another name. His public image was that of an extraordinarily low-profile, billionaire philanthropist who owned and ran one of the largest and most successful multinational corporations on earth. If one needed Mount Everest relocated to another continent, "Mr. Smith" and the vast technical and logistical resources at his disposal could easily handle it, right down to the very last snowflake. His overly reclusive nature earned him the nickname "Howard Hughes v2.0" but was generally considered nothing more than a dull curiosity by the press. His quiet philanthropy was, however, legendary. Enormous sums of money were distributed to both noble and trendy causes, not because "Mr. Smith" actually gave a damn about any of them, but to avoid scrutiny and attacks by "socialist pansy" activists and politicians whose goal was to destroy everything that smelled of capitalism.

"The glaring difference between socialism and capitalism," he was fond of saying, "is that socialists only know how to tear things down. They are quite creative at what they do, yet real creation is not in their repertoire."

The private "Mr. Smith" earned his wealth and status by painstakingly clawing his way up to the top of his father's expansive corporation and the inheritance of a sizable fortune upon the old man's death. It was an empire his father built from surprisingly humble beginnings as a minor military contractor with special expertise in logistics and developing test equipment for the Army Air Corps during World War II. His father also prepared him to lead a clandestine organization he founded at the request of President Truman. Though it had no formal name, the six other hand-picked members were amongst the most powerful men in America, if not from sheer wealth, by political might. Collectively, they could make wonderful things happen almost effortlessly, and just as effortlessly, they could topple governments. They were the overseers and guardians of Project Cocheta. They decided who would run daily operations and how to channel federal funds through their well camouflaged sham projects and subsidiaries. In essence, they kept the secret facility running, off the books and completely out of sight.

"Mr. Smith" may have inherited control of his father's little club, but he did not share the Ol' Man's ambivalence towards the Heischler Report. His father was far more concerned about the Russians than the little gray shits violating Earth's airspace. The younger "Smith" was convinced the real threat would come from space and refused to stand idly by watching an extraterrestrial species screw everything up by sticking their damn flag on the planet. When he took over control upon his father's death in 1983, he began reshaping the organization to reflect that belief. He also became obsessed with secrecy, an obsession that found full expression when one of the older members of the group began exhibiting signs of senile dementia. He was overheard talking about "UFOs" in public and a few days later, the poor soul broke his neck while taking a shower. He was "Mr. Smith's" first assassination in what would become a long list of assassinations in the name of security.

By the time Captain Brogan retired in 1985, the membership of "Mr. Smith's" club was very nearly to his liking. He wanted Hanson to focus on research rather than become an administrator so he appointed career bureaucrats, Hastings and McMahon, to the top two positions. Within a few years, it was clear that Hastings was brilliant when it came to getting things done, but lacked finesse. By 1992, a small but growing number of Cocheta retirees were "secured" at Hastings' request. "Mr. Smith" had no trouble with Hasting's security "solution." Death was the one sure way to keep Cocheta's valuable secrets locked inside its' Canadian mountain. He was, however, beginning to doubt The Foreman's judgment, more so when he asked that Dr. Hanson be "retired" after their lopsided confrontation. It was an absolutely ridiculous request. While Hastings flitted back and forth between Washington and Vegas, Deputy Director McMahon wasn't running the Project, Hanson was. That was not what he intended for his most valuable cerebral asset! If a breakthrough was going to be made, Hanson would probably be the one making it and that was not the kind of talent you disposed of because of a single pissing match with management. Hasting's "retirement" request for Hanson was sternly rejected. It was the only such termination request from Hastings that "Mr. Smith" would ever turn down. Afterwards, he toyed with the idea of removing Hastings from the project and moving Hanson to the top, but thought better of it, in spite of a gut feeling telling him otherwise. Given the current, disastrous state of affairs, he wished that he had followed his instincts.

"Sir," came a familiar voice from behind him, "Hastings has a lawyer and is making demands. He's threatening to spill his guts about everything he knows."

"How unfortunate for him." He replied without turning around. "It was a serious mistake to put him in charge of Cocheta. Perhaps Hanson would have been the better man for the job."

"We agreed that he needed to focus on research, not pushing pencils. He was too idealistic, anyway. Proved it in '92. Given our changes in direction, Hanson just wasn't the man for the job."

"I'm not so sure. Marston and Brogan were idealists and they produced tangible results without the mess... We could have shielded Dr. Hanson from the politics."

"Perhaps."

"I want McMahon out of there. He's nothing more than an accomplished oxygen thief. Completely worthless."

"Done. Who do you want to replace him?"

"What about Hanson's daughter?"

"Interesting choice. Same mold as daddy, maybe even more intelligent. Otherwise, same inherent risks and benefits as her old man."

"Look into it."

"I will, sir." The man said. "Any suggestions on Hastings?"

"Accident... Make it a nasty one."

The Hanson Trilogy continues...

Book Two: The Hanson Conundrum

Dr. Benjamin Harris Hanson is laid to rest and the world he left behind shudders from his legacy. Politicians bitterly fight amongst themselves about the significance of Hanson's frightening revelations and what to do about the ultra-secret facility he worked in. Ben Hanson's brilliant and beautiful daughter, Dr. Donna Hanson, is chosen to lead the troubled Project Cocheta. Within weeks of her appointment, America's intensely guarded nuclear weapons stockpile is suddenly compromised and a horrific disaster occurs in Hawaii. Both seem completely unrelated to each other, but are they? Is one an inadvertent trespass by curious "visitors," the other an accident? Or are both opening salvos in an interstellar war?

The answer awaits mankind on a still, high desert night, 75 miles northwest of Las Vegas...

Visit The Hanson Trilogy Website and Store at:

http://www.hansontrilogy.com

Biography

Vince Messbarger was born July 30th, 1958 in Kansas City, Kansas. His family moved to his childhood home of Austin, Texas when he was four. He graduated from Stephen F. Austin High School in 1976 and holds an Associate degree in Paramedic Technology from Austin Community College, a Bachelor of Science degree in Medical Sciences from Texas A&M University and a Doctor of Medicine Degree from Texas A&M University College of Medicine. He completed a residency in Anesthesiology at Scott & White Hospital in Temple, Texas and is Certified by the American Board of Anesthesiology. He served as a Medical Corps Officer in the United States Army from 1998 to 2007.

Married to his wife of eleven years, Stacia Michelle, he has six wonderful children, Christina, Jessica, Lowell, Patrick, Little Jessica and Joseph, along with five beautiful Grandchildren, Celeste, Dawson, Amber, Leslie and Anthony. He also enjoys four Cavalier King Charles Spaniels, Harley, Cassie, Piggy and Murphy, along with a German Spitz named Pixie. He lives with his wife and children in a quiet, south-central Oklahoma community.

Dr. Messbarger began writing *The Hanson Legacy* in October of 2005 and completed the first draft the following February. He is currently working on the second book in the Hanson Trilogy, *The Hanson Conundrum*, which will be available by late 2012. The third book of the trilogy, *The Hanson Prophesy*, is expected to be available by 2013

www.ingramcontent.com/pod-product-compliance
Lightning Source LLC
Chambersburg PA
CBHW060948030726
47503CB00003B/774